D1443398

TROPHY WIDOW

TROPHY
WIDOW

A RACHEL GOLD NOVEL

Michael A. Kahn

A TOM DOHERTY ASSOCIATES BOOK NEW YORK

TROPHY WIDOW: A RACHEL GOLD NOVEL

Copyright © 2002 by Michael A. Kahn

A Forge Book
Published by Tom Doherty Associates, LLC
175 Fifth Avenue
New York, NY 10010

www.tor.com

Forge® is a registered trademark of Tom Doherty Associates, LLC.

Library of Congress Cataloging-in-Publication Data

Kahn, Michael A.
    Trophy window : a Rachel Gold novel / Michael A. Kahn—1st ed.
        p. cm.
    ISBN 0-765-30218-7
    1. Gold, Rachel (Fictitious character)—Fiction. 2. Saint Louis (Mo.)—Fiction. 3. Women prisoners—Fiction. 4. Trials (Murder)—Fiction. 5. Judicial error—Fiction. 6. Women lawyers—Fiction. I. Title.

PS3561.A375 T76 2002
813'.54—dc21

                                                    2001058639

First Edition: July 2002

Printed in the United States of America

0 9 8 7 6 5 4 3 2 1

For my son Josh,
who laughs with me and cries with me

A special acknowledgment to Mike and Martha Hogan and all of the other wonderful men, women, and families of the Small World Adoption Foundation

TROPHY WIDOW

CHAPTER 1

You'd have thought this was my first time.
Not even close.

I don't specialize in celebrities, but I've had my share. The list includes a member of the Chicago Bulls, two major-league baseball players, and the entire morning drive-time crew for one of the highest-rated FM stations in St. Louis. And that only covers contract negotiations and endorsement deals. I've sued Riverport on behalf of an Atlanta rap group in a gate-receipts dispute. When the case ended, the group's manager offered me a walk-on in their next music video. I told him I'd prefer to have my fees paid in full. I've represented a Hollywood star accused of trashing his hotel suite while on location here for a shoot—and we're not talking just any star. He made *Entertainment Weekly*'s "20 Sexiest Men" two years running. Alas, he's also two inches shorter than me and—as I learned while defending him in a four-hour deposition in a small conference room—afflicted with rhino breath.

But the odd thing is that I never felt the tiniest tingle before meeting any of them—not even a hint of that magical frisson that's supposed to radiate from real celebrities like, well, steam from a baked potato. And lest you get the wrong idea, I'm not one of those snooty types who professes to be above all that fawning. Far from it. I once was rendered dumbstruck on an elevator in the Met Square building when I realized that the tall man standing next to me was none other than number 45 himself—Hall of Famer Bob Gibson. For a diehard Cardinals fan, that's the equivalent of coming around the bend on Mount Sinai and finding yourself face to face with a Charlton Heston look-alike in flowing robes and sandals carrying two stone tablets. I rode several floors in flustered silence until I worked up the nerve to ask Mr. Gibson for his autograph, which he graciously signed on a sheet from my legal pad that I have since had laminated.

And that gaga response isn't limited to baseball gods. I would kill to spend an afternoon with Jane Austen. I would swoon like a schoolgirl before Clark Gable—especially the Clark Gable of *It Happened One Night*. And if Marvin Gaye were alive and well, I might just follow him from concert to concert like a Motown version of a Deadhead. With those folks we're talking frisson.

Cosmic frisson.

But not for my celebrity clients. For whatever reason, with them it always seems to be business as usual. Attorney-client. Strictly professional.

Until today.

Today I was driving halfway across the state of Missouri to meet my newest client.

A housewife.

More precisely, a former housewife. Probably the most famous former housewife in America, and surely the only one serving thirty-to-forty in Chillicothe Correctional Center.

Today I was definitely in the grip of that old black magic. That's because today I was going to see Angela Green.

Yes, *the* Angela Green.

The same one whose murder trial came in at number 3 on *People* magazine's "Top Ten Murder Trials of the 1990s," just behind O. J. Simpson (no. 1) and the Menendez brothers (no. 2), but ahead of Timothy McVeigh (no. 4) and Jeffrey

Dahmer (no. 5). The same one whose prime-time jailhouse interview with Oprah Winfrey drew a 41 share and ended with that shot reprinted in newspapers and magazines around the country—the one of Oprah, tears streaming down her cheeks, her head resting on Angela's shoulder as Angela gently patted her on the back. The same Angela Green who had Anita Hill deliver her acceptance speech in absentia at the *Ms.* magazine "Women of the Year" banquet, who caused a rift within the NAACP when she was named one of its "Women of Valor," and who was the subject of Connie Chung's Emmy-nominated profile, which included those extraordinary testimonials from the prisoners who'd earned their high school equivalencies through the special tutoring program Angela helped establish at Chillicothe Correctional Center.

Yes, that Angela Green.

And this coming year—her seventh since entering prison—promised to be her biggest yet. The publication date for her long-awaited autobiography was just six months off. A major Hollywood studio had already snagged the film rights. According to a blurb in *Vanity Fair,* Whoopi Goldberg and Angela Bassett were vying for the lead role while Warren Beatty, Tommy Lee Jones, and Michael Douglas were in the running for the role of Michael Green. *Vanity Fair* picked Bassett and Douglas as the favorites, since "it would be almost too delicious for an Angela and a Michael to play the Angela and the Michael." Meanwhile, Angela's criminal defense attorney, Maria Fallaci, had her own book coming out late in October.

All of which translated into megabucks.

And where there are megabucks, there is usually a lawsuit. That's where I fit in. My name is Rachel Gold—Cardinals fan, daughter of Sarah, big sister of Ann, and, possibly, blushing bride and mother, assuming that a thirty-three-year-old bride isn't too old to blush or too young to become the instant stepmother of two adorable girls. But for the here and now, the only relevant role was lawyer, which is why I was driving through rural Missouri on this lovely Sunday morning in late June. I was somewhere in the northwest quadrant of the state, heading north on Highway 65 through a portion of Missouri I'd never been in before. According to a highway marker on the right, I'd just passed over the Grand River, although it didn't look too grand to me. Of course, when you grow up in St. Louis, it takes a whole lot of grand before any river can claim that label.

Chillicothe was the next exit.

Two hours ago I'd dropped Benny Goldberg off at the University of Missouri in Columbia, where he was delivering a paper on antitrust law at a law school symposium. After my prison meeting with Angela Green, I was going to swing back down to Columbia to pick him up. On our way back to St. Louis we were planning to stop at a farm near Warrenton where Benny would introduce me to two new clients, Maggie Lane and Sara Freed, who were enmeshed in a dispute so outlandish that it had to be true. No one could make up such a story. Not even someone with a mind as warped as Benny's—and Benny's is as warped as it gets.

But Maggie and Sara could wait, I told myself as I pulled off the exit and drove into town. Chillicothe was a typical Midwestern village—chiefly frame houses, most built before World War II, a main street of redbrick buildings, including a bank and a pharmacy and a diner and a dry goods store. I turned down Third Street and slowed halfway down the block, peering out the window. Surprised, I rechecked the address.

I'd been to prisons before—in Missouri, Illinois, and Indiana—but never one for women. Men's prisons are geographically isolated—drab fortresses built on the outskirts of town, far from the women and children, grimly asserting to the world, *Here there be pariahs*. In this architecture of exile, Alcatraz is the quintessential model: a gray fortress on an island, cut off from civilization by frigid water, killer currents, and hungry sharks.

Chillicothe Correctional Center didn't fit that mold. Built in the 1880s as a home for wayward girls, the facility was located in the middle of a pleasant town in the gentle countryside. Its founders envisioned a pastoral haven where lost girls could find Christian salvation far from the wicked temptations of St. Louis and Kansas City. That vision produced a campus reminiscent of a New England women's college with several two-story redbrick buildings arranged like dormitories around a quadrangle.

Times change, though, and the home for wayward girls was now Missouri's main prison for women, housing nearly six hundred inmates. The prisoners ranged from minimum security residents on work-release programs to death row convicts, of which there were presently three. Fortunately, Angela Green wasn't one of them. Nevertheless, when you enter prison at the age of forty-nine, a forty-year sentence might as well be life.

I pulled my car into the administration center parking lot and got out. Stretching, I turned toward the prison buildings across the street. There were several female inmates outside the buildings—some working on gardens, others strolling around the grounds. The only indication that this wasn't the Missouri branch of Mount Holyoke College were the gray work shirts and slacks worn by the women and the security fence topped with coiled razor-wire ringing the campus.

I checked my watch. It was almost eleven o'clock. I turned back to the administrative center, shading my eyes in the late morning sun. Time to check in. Time to meet my newest client. I paused a moment, grinning sheepishly. No question about it. I could feel the tingle.

We were in an attorney-client interview room, facing each other across the table. Unlike the interview rooms in men's prisons, which have all the charm of a concrete bunker at Normandy Beach, this one was softened by a few feminine touches, such as frilly curtains over the barred windows and a vase of irises on the rickety wooden table in the center of the room.

I was explaining the nature of the Son of Sam claim that had brought us together as attorney and client. Angela listened carefully, her chin resting on steepled fingers. Whatever celebrity excitement I'd felt in anticipation of our meeting had vanished the moment we met. Angela Green was someone you warmed to immediately, especially, I think, if you were a woman. It was a special connection, a sisterhood sort of thing that I could feel our first moments together. My reaction was typical, I suppose. This was, after all, the same woman who was adored within the prison not only by the inmates but by the guards as well.

The first thing I noticed about Angela Green was how human she looked. Although celebrities tend to seem diminished in person, here it was hardly Angela's fault. If clothes can make the woman, they can surely unmake her as well. Take the cover girl from a *Sports Illustrated* swimsuit issue, swap her thong bikini for a drab work shirt and an ill-fitting pair of Dickey slacks, deep-six the makeup, can the hairdresser, and we're talking, at best, the Before shot in a back-pages ad in *Cosmo*. While the media's two favorite adjectives for Angela Green were *saintly* and *regal,* try dressing Joan of Arc in the Missouri Department of Corrections' version of *haute couture* and she'd be lucky to pass for a janitor.

As for regal, not even the queen of England could pull that off in prison grays.

Such was the case for Angela. Gone was the stunning African princess from her college days, the elegant suburban mother from her soccer mom days, and the coiffed matron from the final years of her marriage. In their place was a middle-aged woman who seemed older than her fifty-six years and heavier than I remembered from the *Oprah* special.

Nonetheless, Angela Green had presence. There was an aura of dignity about her—a quiet, determined dignity—that was palpable. Although her belle days were long over, she was still a handsome woman. Her skin was a deep mahogany that seemed to glow from within. Her hair—worn in a full Afro during her college days; tamed and straightened during her suburban days—was now braided in dozens of cornrows that reached to her shoulders. It was a striking look, especially for a woman of her age, and it gave her an air of authority. She had strong features—a wide nose; thick, bowed lips; full, high cheeks; broad forehead. But her most remarkable features were her eyes. They were dark and calm and wise. Although she was decades past her African princess days, it was no stretch to imagine Angela Green in the role of the village chief, seated upon her throne and resolving disputes among her subjects.

"I do not understand," Angela said, leaning back and shaking her head. Her voice was soft and husky, the words carefully articulated. "How can that child presume to make a claim against me? I am no relation to him."

"It's not his relation to *you*," I explained. "Under the Son of Sam law, the key is his relation to the victim. Members of the victim's family are the only ones entitled to sue."

"Family?" Angela frowned. "How is that child family to Michael?"

"He claims—well, actually Trent's lawyer claims—that he's the equivalent of Michael's son."

"Equivalent?" Angela repeated, puzzled. "What is that supposed to mean?"

"It's a doctrine called 'equitable adoption.'"

Angela shook her head, angry now. "Michael never adopted that tramp's child. He died before the marriage."

"I know." I gave her a sympathetic smile. "It's a stretch."

I explained the doctrine of equitable adoption, which the courts fashioned for that rare case where justice demands that a child be declared the rightful heir of people who never formally adopted her. In the classic "equitable adoption" situation, a married couple raises a foster child. Although they treat her as their own child, they never get around to making it official. If they die without a will or with one that refers generically to "any child of mine," their unfinished business lands in probate court. That's because the failure to adopt has significant legal consequences: a foster child is not an heir, while an *adopted* child has the same legal status as a biological child. Thus the equitable adoption doctrine typically comes into play in an inheritance battle between the unadopted child and the biological children, or—if no biological children—between the unadopted child and the deceased's blood relatives.

"The law is suspicious of these claims," I explained to Angela, "because the people who file them have a powerful incentive to lie about the dead person's intentions. The courts require the claimant to present direct evidence of a clear intent to adopt. Circumstantial evidence isn't enough. For example, one court ruled that claiming a child as a dependent on a tax return didn't constitute direct evidence."

Angela frowned. "What exactly does that mean here?"

"It means the court will carefully examine Michael's actions. The key issue is whether he expressed a clear intent to

adopt Samantha's son. If so, did he do anything in further-
ance of that intent?"

Angela narrowed her eyes. "And did he?"

"We don't know. We're at the beginning of the lawsuit.
We haven't taken any depositions, especially Samantha's, and
we haven't reviewed the documents. It's too early to say."

"How does it look so far?"

"We have some problems," I conceded, "but nothing fa-
tal. We know that Michael signed a prenuptial agreement
with the child's mother. In paragraph seven of the document
he agreed to adopt her son. We know that he had an attorney
prepare the necessary adoption papers. He also had an attorney prepare new wills for him and for Samantha. Although the wills were never signed, the plaintiff's lawyer
claims that Michael reviewed and approved his draft two
days before his death. The new will adds Trent to the list of
beneficiaries and describes him as an adopted son." I paused.
"Will the court find that to be enough evidence?" I shrugged.
"It's too early to tell."

"He barely knew that child," Angela said quietly, her
voice laced with frustration.

I reached across the table and laid my hand on top of
hers. "We're going to fight it, Angela. We'll have plenty to
say by the time of trial."

She took a deep breath and exhaled slowly. After a moment, she stood up and moved to the window. Pushing the
curtain back, she peered out.

I waited.

She turned to me. "If that tramp wins, I will have Michael
Junior and Sonya file their own Son of Sam claims. They are
Michael's children, too. His only *real* children." She nodded
decisively. "I'll bet that lawyer never considered that."

He didn't need to, I thought to myself. The Missouri
legislature already had. The Son of Sam law barred any claim

by a family member of the victim who also happened to be a family member of the killer. But I said nothing. No need to further demoralize my client this early in the case.

Instead, I explained our various defenses. She was interested to hear about the constitutional challenge to the statute, which would be led by the New York law firm representing her publisher. If we could convince the court to throw out the statute as an abridgment of the freedom of speech, the case would implode and we'd never have to worry about equitable adoption or our other defenses. She listened attentively, asking questions along the way.

When I finished explaining the legal issues, I went over a few more items regarding pretrial matters, including timing issues and the like. Then I had the deputy warden come in so that we could work out a confidential but efficient way for me to communicate with Angela by mail, phone, and fax—essential procedures given that St. Louis was a four-hour drive from Chillicothe.

I checked my watch after the deputy warden departed. We still had a few minutes before I had to drive back to Columbia for Benny. I had one more topic to broach. I wasn't quite sure how to begin, or where to go once we started.

Angela must have sensed it. "What is it, Rachel?"

I gazed at her for a moment. "I reviewed the file."

"Of what?"

"Your case. Everything. Court transcripts, pretrial motions, homicide investigation. Whatever I could get my hands on."

She frowned. "Why?"

"Good question." I leaned back in my chair and crossed my arms over my chest. "I'm not sure, Angela. I started with the trial transcript. Initially, I suppose I was looking for any stray evidence on the equitable adoption issue." I shrugged.

"Maybe to see whether Samantha said anything back then about Michael's relationship with her son—back before her lawyer concocted this adoption theory."

"And did she?"

I shook my head. "Not really. Oh, she said he loved to play with Trent, took him fishing once, gave him a tricycle for Christmas—that sort of thing."

I paused.

"And," Angela said.

"And I saw other things."

"What things?"

"I'm not a criminal lawyer, Angela, but over the years I've had to look through a few homicide files. Yours was unusual."

She leaned forward, curious. "How so?"

I paused, searching for the right words. "There were loose ends."

"Such as?"

"Such as the murder weapon. It's not the sort of weapon you'd expect a housewife to use."

"Why not?"

"The serial number was filed off. The gun was untraceable. It's the kind you'd normally expect to find with a professional hit, the kind you'd buy from an illegal gun dealer."

She rubbed her chin, trying to remember. "I think they asked me where I bought it."

"They did. It's in the arrest report. You told them you'd never owned a gun."

She nodded. "That's true."

"So where'd you get it?" I asked.

She shook her head. "I have no idea."

I studied her for a moment. "Angela, if you wanted to buy that kind of gun, where would you go?"

"I have no idea."

"Neither did the police." I leaned forward. "That's my point. It was a loose end. The police were never asked to come up with an answer because it was never an issue at trial. Maybe there's a simple explanation for the gun, but it's certainly nowhere in the file."

Angela sighed and shook her head. "I supposed I blacked that part out, too."

"Possibly."

After a moment, she asked, "Was that the only loose end?"

I shook my head. "How did you get into his house?"

She frowned, trying to remember. "Did I ring the doorbell?"

"Not likely. He was shot coming out of the shower. He wouldn't have let you in with a gun in your hand and then gone back in the bedroom, gotten undressed, and taken a shower."

"Maybe the gun was in my purse? Maybe the door was open?"

"Maybe. The housekeeper said the door was locked when she arrived. It was the kind that automatically locks when you close it."

"Maybe I had a key."

"Did you?"

She shook her head in frustration. "I don't remember."

"Why would you have a key? The two of you had just finished a bitter divorce. There'd be no reason for him to give you a key."

"Maybe he gave the children a key."

"Did he?"

She shrugged. "I don't know."

"I assume you don't know how to pick a lock."

She smiled. "No."

"So how did you get in?"

"What did the police say?"

"Nothing. It's another loose end."

She stared at the table, frowning. After a moment, she looked up at me. "Are there other loose ends?"

I nodded.

"Such as?"

"Such as John."

John had been her alibi—her embarrassingly weak alibi. She claimed that on the night of the murder she had gone out for a drink with a nice young man named John, last name unknown, and woke up the next morning in Michael Green's bedroom with no idea of how she got there. The police found no trace of the mysterious John.

"In your police interview," I continued, "you said that you'd known John for a couple of weeks, that he used to come visit his mother in the hospital, right?"

She nodded.

"You said that you felt sorry for him. That the two of you became friends. That you used to have lunch together in the hospital cafeteria on the days you volunteered at the gift shop, right?"

"I did."

"So where is he?" I asked. "And *who* is he?"

Angela looked down at the table. "They think I made him up." Her voice was soft, muffled.

"Did you?"

She stared down at the table. When she finally looked up, her eyes were moist. "I wish I knew the answer to that, Rachel. Lord, I do. When I look back on those days, everything seems unreal, like I was living inside a dream." She gave me a sad smile. "More like a nightmare. I can't tell for sure what part was real and what part was imaginary. I believe John was real. I have a memory of the things we used to talk about at the hospital. I can close my eyes and see that young man."

She paused, closing her eyes. I waited. She opened them. In a discouraged voice she said, "I believe John was real."

"The police didn't."

She said nothing.

"But they didn't bother tying up the loose end," I said.

She gave me a puzzled look. "How would they do that?"

"By checking the hospital records. It couldn't have been that difficult to identify every female patient between the ages of, say, forty and seventy who'd been in the hospital for at least the two weeks preceding the killing. Once they had that list, they could quickly check whether any of those women had an adult son named John." I shook my head. "But they didn't bother to."

"Why not?"

Because of your lawyer's theory of the case, I wanted to say. Instead, I said, "Because they thought that they already had enough evidence."

She sighed. "They were right."

CHAPTER 2

I obsessed over those loose ends on the drive back. After I had spent close to two hours alone with Angela Green, her guilt appeared to be even more questionable than before. Of course, eight years had passed since that appalling night, and much had changed in her life since then. But even making allowance for that, the Angela Green I'd met today seemed incapable of gunning down her ex-husband, slicing off his penis with a piece of broken glass, and hurling the severed thing against the wall.

I mulled it over as I drove.

Angela hadn't cleared up any issues, but she wasn't the best person to ask about the loose ends. The decision whether to exploit them at the criminal trial had been a matter of trial strategy, and that decision fell within the bailiwick of Angela's criminal attorney, Maria Fallaci. Maria was an experienced defender—a former assistant U.S. attorney who'd been defending capital murder cases for years. Maria had surely spotted the same loose ends and evaluated their potential. That evaluation had led her to a different trial strategy, namely, to make the focus of her defense the "battered wife" syndrome. That tactical decision landed Maria on the cover of *Newsweek*. Unfortunately, it landed her client in jail.

I thought back again to my own memories of the trial. As the television and newspaper reporters told us over and over during the weeks leading up to the jury selection, the marriage had been one of those Age of Aquarius things. Michael and Angela met in Psychology 101 their freshman year at the University of Missouri in Columbia. It was love at first sight for what seemed a perfect couple for the Woodstock generation. Michael Green was white. Angela White was black. He had shoulder-length brown hair and a Fu Manchu. She had a wild Afro. They both wore tie-dyed T-shirts and faded bell bottoms. As for so many of his generation, the sixties look was not a flattering one for Michael: photographs of him from that era invariably elicited laughter from those who saw them decades later. He looked like a long-haired, mustachioed double for Sonny Bono from the old Sonny and Cher days. By contrast, the photos of Angela from that era depict a stunning African princess: high cheekbones, strong eyes, noble forehead, full lips, ebony skin.

During the summer after their graduation, Angela White turned Green when they exchanged wedding vows. That fall, Michael started law school and Angela took a job as a substitute teacher in the St. Louis public school system. The early years were lean ones for the young couple, made even leaner with the birth of Michael junior during Michael's final year of school. Their tiny apartment became tinier when Sonya arrived two years later. The young family struggled as Michael tried to establish a law practice.

Hard work and perseverance eventually paid off. The Law Offices of Michael Green moved out of the storefront along a seedy stretch of South Grand Avenue and became Green and Associates in an upper floor of the Pierre Laclede Building in Clayton. A few years later, the firm's name became Green and Sanders after Michael's law school classmate Elliot Sanders joined. Elliot's real estate work helped pay the light bills while freeing Michael to focus on his plaintiffs' class action work. The two partners were confident that it was only a matter of time before Michael hit big casino. They were right, although Elliot didn't live to see it happen. A heart attack killed him three months before the court approved the *Vanguard Finance* settlement and awarded Michael Green $1,250,000 in fees. The *St. Louis Business Journal* ran his photo beneath the headline: GREEN—THE COLOR OF MONEY.

Michael and Angela moved their family to an eight-bedroom English Tudor on an acre of prime real estate in the snobby suburb of Frontenac. Michael's law firm moved to elegant new quarters in the Interco Tower overlooking the Ritz-Carlton. Michael traded in his battered Toyota for a silver Porsche with a vanity plate that read FRCP 23, a reference to the federal rule of civil procedure that governs class actions. Gradually, though, his court appearances became less frequent as he devoted his time to the real estate clients he'd inherited from his dead partner. Life was good. He even found himself occasionally voting Republican. After all, he told himself, someone had to get the damn deficit under control.

Like so many other perfect couples of their generation, it was only a matter of time. And as any good lawyer knows, timing is everything. For Michael, the right time came two months after his twenty-sixth wedding anniversary. He chose a brilliant Sunday afternoon in September. Michael junior had graduated from Dartmouth and was now working at an investment banking firm in Chicago. Sonya was in her junior year at Northwestern University.

As Maria Fallaci described the scene in her opening statement to the jury, there were fluffy white clouds against a dazzling blue sky when Michael Green stepped out onto the back patio and paused to take a sip of single-malt scotch from his crystal whisky glass. He strolled down the stairs to the elegant flower garden near the pool, where his wife was on her knees dividing and replanting perennials. Angela looked up with an uncertain smile, a sheen of perspiration on her forehead and upper lip. She shaded her eyes from the sun and listened in disbelief as her husband announced in that matter-of-fact way of his that he was in love with another woman and was moving out in the morning. With the cruel coincidence that novelists and other nasty gossips relish, the object of Michael Green's passion was exactly the same age as his marriage. Samantha Cummings had been born on their wedding day twenty-six years ago.

Her friends called her Sam, and she was as lovely and lissome and honey-blond as any forty-eight-year-old house-wife could fear. Sam operated the 309 Gallery, an art gallery in the trendy Central West End. Best of all, as Michael bragged to his friends, Sam made him feel young again. *Gets me hard as a rock,* he would confide with a wink, *and tastes as good as she looks.* He even got a kick out of her three-year-old son Trent, who was the product of Samantha's brief affair with a man who'd never bothered to see the boy after he was born and hadn't made a child-support payment in two years. *Little kid's a regular pistol,* Michael told his friends. *Give me a chance to try this dad thing again—maybe get the hang of it this time around.*

Angela was devastated. Although at first she seemed to be sleepwalking through the wreckage of her marriage, once the divorce proceedings began to crank up, her outrage did as well. The final predivorce mediation session ended when she grabbed a letter opener off her lawyer's desk and tried to attack Michael.

"It was frightening," Michael's lawyer would later testify at her criminal trial. "I dragged Michael out of there and warned him, 'You better watch out. That woman wants you dead.' "

Two weeks after the letter-opener incident, Angela dumped an entire pitcher of margaritas over Michael Green's head at a glitzy fund-raiser for the St. Louis Zoo. Two security guards hauled her off screeching and sobbing. No charges were pressed.

The divorce decree was entered in due course more than a year later, officially dissolving the marriage of Michael and Angela Green on the fourteenth of March. Wedding invitations went out the following week. The early May ceremony promised to be a spectacular event staged in the Japanese Rock Garden at the Missouri Botanical Gardens. The ornate, gold-foil invitations beckoned the recipients to "join Michael and Samantha as they celebrate a fusion of souls almost too good to be true." Alas, it proved just that. Two weeks before the blessed event, the cleaning woman entered the master bedroom at Michael Green's place and found him facedown on the carpet near the bathroom, very naked and very dead. He'd been shot twice—once in the abdomen, once in the back of the head—the first shot apparently fired as he came out of the bathroom from the shower, the second after he was on the carpet. There was a bath towel crumpled on the carpet near his corpse.

Later that morning, when the medical examiner turned the body over, there was an audible gasp among the investigators in the bedroom, followed immediately by the sounds of one of them vomiting onto the carpet. Michael's penis was missing. A homicide detective discovered it minutes later behind the nightstand and directly beneath the red impact splatter midway up the wall.

In retrospect, as Professor Alan Dershowitz emphasized in his first, sixth, eleventh, and fourteenth appearances on Geraldo's CNBC show during the murder trial, Angela should have refused to say anything when the homicide detectives arrived at her house that evening and recited the *Miranda* warnings. She should have insisted upon her right to speak to an attorney. Instead, a flustered Angela Green told the nice detectives that she'd been home alone the entire night of the killing. When the nice detectives asked her to explain why her cellular phone was at the crime scene, she stammered out a new story—the one about the young man named John and waking up the next morning in her ex-husband's bedroom and panicking and fleeing. Unsure of what to do, she explained to the nice detectives, she'd gone home and done nothing. The nice detectives nodded grimly and snapped on the handcuffs.

By any measure, the evidence had been overwhelming. In addition to her cell phone under the bed, her fingerprints were all over the bedroom. More important, they were on the murder weapon, which was found in a bush at the end of the block. As the final incriminating touch, there was the piece of broken glass that forensics identified as the cutting tool used on Michael's penis. The broken glass had come from the framed portrait of Samantha Cummings, which had been sitting on the victim's nightstand until someone slammed it against the wall in what the prosecutor later told the jury was a fit of rage. Blood tests revealed that Michael's wasn't the only blood on the broken glass. Along two of the sharp edges were smears of Angela's blood. Angela was right-handed, and sure enough, there were cuts precisely where you'd expect to find them along her right palm and thumb and on the inner sides of two fingers. In short, there was enough incriminating evidence to make an attorney consider an alternative defense.

And thus I was perhaps too hard on Maria Fallaci. She no doubt had compelling reasons for her trial strategy—or at least that's what I'd been telling myself for the past week. She was a brilliant and successful criminal defense attorney, albeit a bit too flashy for my taste.

Ironically, she now was a defendant, along with her former client, in the Son of Sam case. The other defendants were her publisher, Angela's publisher, and the motion picture studio that had optioned Angela's book. All defense counsel in the case were meeting in Chicago the day after tomorrow. The meeting would be taking place three blocks from Maria's office. She'd agreed to meet me before that meeting. I needed to find out why she'd elected not to let the jury know about the loose ends.

CHAPTER 3

O h, Benny," I groaned, "how did I *ever* let you talk me
into this case?"

"Talk you into it?" he asked, incredulous. "Talk you into
it? My God, Rachel, you should be sending flowers to my
office, planting trees in my honor in Israel. When are you
ever going to find a case like this again?"

"Hopefully never."

It was late in the afternoon and we were heading east on
Highway 70 toward St. Louis. The Warrenton exit was fifteen miles ahead. Benny had directions from there to the
ranch, where we were going to meet my newest clients, Maggie Lane and Sara Freed. Sara's younger brother Paul was a
first-year law student in Benny's contracts class. One day
after class last week Paul told Benny about a lawsuit involving his sister—a truly preposterous case, and thus one that
immediately appealed to Benny, who'd driven right over to
my office to enlist my help.

Had he been any other law school professor in the
United States, I would have said no. But of course he wasn't
any other law school professor. He was Benny Goldberg,
unique by any standard: vulgar, fat, gluttonous, and obnoxious. But also ferociously loyal, wonderfully funny, and—
most important—my very best friend in the whole world. I
loved him like the brother I never had, although he bore as
much resemblance to my fantasy brother as, appropriately
enough, an ostrich does to an eagle.

Benny Goldberg and I met as junior associates in the Chicago offices of Abbott & Windsor. A few years later, we both escaped that LaSalle Street sweatshop—Benny to teach law at De Paul, me to go solo as Rachel Gold, Attorney-at-Law. Different reasons brought us to St. Louis. For Benny, it was an offer he couldn't refuse from Washington University. For me, it was a yearning to live closer to my mother after my father died.

"Come on, woman," Benny said. "We gotta focus on the big picture here."

"Focus me, Professor."

"Do ostriches have dicks?"

I turned toward him with raised eyebrows. "Pardon?"

"We're talking *schlongs* here, and if the answer is yes, then we're not talking ordinary bird *schlongs*. We're talking big swinging ones. So that's the issue, woman. Do ostriches have them?"

"I have no idea."

"Then we better find out pronto, eh? I mean, what's going on down there between Big Bird's legs? We talking Ken doll or we talking Burger King?"

I gave him a dubious look. "Burger King?"

He winked. "Home of the Whopper."

I sighed and shook my head. "I can't believe this."

"Come on, Rachel, this is a great case. These women pay ten grand for a genetically superior stud and instead they get the Slobodan Milosevic of the ostrich world."

I glanced over and shrugged. "I have no idea."

"Huh?"

"I just assumed that birds had them."

"Not so, O provincial one. Ducks do, but most don't. Canaries and parakeets definitely don't."

"Benny, how in the world do you know this?"

"I worked in a pet store in high school."

"If they don't have penises, how do they—you know?"

"Do it?

"Yeah."

"Ah," he said, segueing into his impression of the narrator in a cheesy documentary. "Join me on a voyage into the strange and wondrous world of ornithological amour, to that magic moment that experts call the 'cloacal kiss.' "

"Which is?"

"Basically," he said, switching back to his standard New Jersey, "they press their butts together."

"Come on."

"I'm serious. The male's sex organs are inside his butt, and the female's are inside hers. When birds get some booty, we're talking booty squared."

"Are you making this up, Benny?"

"Would I make something like that up?"

"Absolutely."

The sign ahead read Warrenton Next Exit.

I mulled over his question, recalling some of the material I'd downloaded from the Internet in preparation for today's meeting.

"Those birds are humongous," I said. "They can weigh three hundred and fifty pounds. Penis or not, that's a lot of ostrich to fight off."

We drove in silence for a while.

I shook my head in disbelief. "Could this case possibly be any stranger?"

"Actually," he said, pausing.

I shot him a look. "What?"

He gave me an awkward grin. "Your clients—the two women."

"What about them?"

"Well, they're—you know."

"They're what?"

"Lezzies."

"Huh?"

"Daughters of Sappho."

"Whose daughters?" I asked, pulling ahead of a truck and into the right lane.

"Sappho. Sappho? Good grief, Rachel," he said in exasperation, "you may have showgirl legs, but don't ever try to win Ben Stein's money."

"What?"

"Your clients are lesbians."

"So? You think I'd have a problem with that?"

"I know *you* don't. I'm not talking about you."

I looked over with a frown. "What do you mean?"

"Charlie Blackwell. He's the breeder who sold them the ostrich. That's his explanation."

"What are you talking about?"

"After the ostrich killed one of their hens, the women demanded their money back. Blackwell refused. Wait until you see his lawsuit. He claims that up until his breeding cock arrived at their ranch it was perfectly normal—presumably a caring, tender, romantic, sensitive lover. He claims the two women messed him up. He accuses them of incompetence and inexperience, and he also blames their lesbianism."

I turned to him, flabbergasted. "Are you serious?"

"There's more. He claims he's suffering mental anguish over the damage to his bird. That's why he's seeking punitive damages."

I could feel my litigator's pulse quicken. "That is absolutely outrageous."

Benny chuckled. "You go, girl."

I took the Warrenton exit and followed Benny's instructions down Highway 47. He had, by now, switched topics to one far dearer to his heart: barbecue.

"I don't care how long they smoke them," I said with a shudder. "I'm not eating noses."

"Not noses, you Philistine. Snouts. Actually, we pig proboscis aficionados call them 'snoots.' Believe me, woman, you ain't done St. Louis barbecue till you scarf down a bucket of hickory-smoked snoots at C and K Restaurant bathed in their sweet . . ." His voice trailed off.

I turned to him with a curious look.

"Rachel," he said, a hint of concern in his voice, "you really shouldn't get so hung up on Angela Green's criminal case."

I leaned back in the driver's seat. "You're probably right."

When I had picked him up from the law school on my return from the prison—long before Benny had changed the subject to ostrich genitalia—I'd filled him in on my meeting with Angela and my growing doubts about the original conviction.

"What's done is done," he said. "She's been convicted, the court of appeals affirmed the conviction. That's the past. The Son of Sam claim is more than enough for you to deal with, especially with those assholes from New York and L.A."

Angela's publisher had retained Braun, Proctor & Silverberg and the motion picture studio had retained Corcoran Fox.

"I've dealt with Braun, Proctor before," Benny continued, "and believe me, those five-hundred-dollar-an-hour yahoos could fuck up a wet dream. Forget about the criminal conviction. You'll have plenty to worry about with those douche bags."

"I know, I know. It's just that all those loose ends bother me, Benny."

"There aren't that many, Rachel, especially compared to

that mountain of evidence against her, starting with the fact that she was physically in his room that night. There's no other explanation."

I mulled that over. He was probably right, I conceded. You couldn't overlook the damning fact that Angela had been in his bedroom the night of the murder.

"Rachel," Benny said, "we've both had cases that are weak and others that are slam dunks. With which ones do you spend more time on pretrial preparations? The weak ones, right? It's the same here. This case was a slam dunk for the prosecution. Their main worry was the battered-wife crap, and that's what they spent their time on, and that's why you've got some of these loose—loose—Sweet Jesus! Check that out."

I slowed the car. "Wow."

It was an astounding sight, made even more so by being here in the middle of the middle of America. We'd been driving past typical farmland vistas: grazing cattle, red barns, fields of soybean, metal silos, green rows of corn stretching to the horizon. And then suddenly we came upon a pasture with a flock of ostriches running parallel to our car. The adults were enormous, all easily over seven feet tall, loping along on long, skinny legs that thickened near the top to massive drumsticks. Their black-feathered torsos were balanced above their pumping legs while their little white wings flapped absurdly, as if they were a garden party of maiden aunts escaping a sudden shower. Their tiny beaked heads were perched on long, reddish necks that undulated in synch with their gait. Scampering behind were about twenty chicks, some the size of adult geese, others the size of third-graders, all looking even more prehistoric than the parents, with their ridged heads and protruding black eyes and juvenile feathers that resembled spiky bristles.

"Whoa," Benny said, peering out the window, "welcome to Jurassic Park."

Maggie Lane and Sara Freed were seated together on the porch swing, each sipping a glass of lemonade, as we pulled up to their snug farmhouse. They came down to greet us.

Simpatico. That's what I felt the moment I met them. Maggie was in her late forties—a tall, slender brunette with the strong, elegant face, wise eyes, and wavy hair of a British stage actress. Her last name could have been Redgrave. Sara was in her late twenties, stood maybe an inch over five feet, and had a sturdy build. She was a perky all-American type: blond hair, blue eyes, lots of freckles, cheerful smile. Both women wore jeans, work shirts, and boots.

We joined them on the porch, where there were chairs for us and a big pitcher of fresh-squeezed lemonade. They filled me in on the background of the lawsuit, starting with the strange world of ostrich ranches. Maggie explained that ostriches had been bred and raised in captivity for more than a century. Originally marketed for their feathers and leather, they were increasingly valued as food. Indeed, the recent boom in ostrich ranching had been fueled by the belief that ostrich steaks—an excellent source of low-fat, low-cholesterol protein—would be the health meat of the twenty-first century. Newborn chicks weighed two pounds and stood ten inches tall. They grew fast and reached processing size in a little over a year.

"Luckily," Maggie said, "we're in the middle of breeding season."

"Luckily?" I asked.

She nodded. "You're likely to see one of our pairs mate. It'll give you something to compare to Rush."

"Rush?" Benny perked up. "That's his name?"

"We changed it," Sara said. "The breeder named him Big Red. We liked Rush better."

Benny chuckled. "As in football?"

"As in Limbaugh," Sara said, wrinkling her nose in disgust.

"What?" Benny said, offended. Unfortunately, Benny's politics were somewhere to the right of Vlad the Impaler.

"Shush," I hissed, grabbing him by the arm. "Behave yourself."

I went over the lawsuit basics with Maggie and Sara, explaining that I'd be able to tell them more once I'd had a chance to review the court papers. Sara had given her only copy of the petition to her younger brother Paul, the one in Benny's law school class. She said she'd call Paul that night and have him send me a copy of the papers.

Time for the tour. We started in the barn, where a portion of the interior had been turned into a hatchery. There were two incubators, each resembling a double-sized white refrigerator, sitting side by side on an immaculate cement floor. Maggie pulled open one of the double doors to reveal dozens of huge eggs in rows in seven stainless steel bins.

"Here," she said, reaching into one of the bins and carefully lifting out an egg with both hands. She placed it into my hands. The egg was smooth and warm and weighed almost five pounds. I could feel a slight movement inside of it.

"Wow," I said, cradling the egg in my hands as I gave it back to Maggie.

From the hatchery we moved to the nursery, which took up part of the barn and extended into a fenced-off pen outside. Milling around were about a dozen brown and black baby chicks and a little white goat. The chicks resembled furry, prehistoric ducks.

"Goats are like nannies," Sara explained as she kneeled down by the fence. "This one's Rita. The chicks learn to eat and drink and avoid the rain by following her around." The little goat trotted over on stiff, pigeon-toed legs. She was adorable—little brown horns, loppy ears, a short, upturned tail, and a streak of black fur running down the middle of her back. Sara put her hand through the fence to nuzzle it against the goat's neck.

We moved on to what Maggie called the "breeding colony," which presently consisted of ten adult hens, two adult cocks, and about two dozen chicks. They lived in a fenced-off area about three times the size of a football field. They were milling around and pecking at the grass as we approached.

Maggie scanned the pasture. "Oh, there's Tracy." She turned to us. "Let's go say hi. She's a doll."

We followed Maggie and Sara across the pasture. As we approached, the bird turned to face us.

"Jesus," Benny said under his breath, "look at the size of that chicken."

Tracy was immense, standing every bit of eight feet tall, her tiny head perched atop a long, rubbery neck. From a distance her long legs had merely looked skinny, but up close I could see the outlines of thick tendons and muscles beneath her rough skin—muscles and tendons powerful enough to propel three hundred and fifty pounds of ostrich at speeds of up to forty miles per hour. I stared down at her feet. They were thin and callused—almost human, but with two toes instead of five. One of the toes was huge, with what looked like a sharpened toenail. It reminded me of another thing I'd read in the material: ostriches used their feet as weapons.

I took a wary step back, but it was quickly apparent that Tracy was no kick boxer. She was delighted to see Maggie, and started rubbing up against her with her wings spread. Maggie gave her a hug around her neck, and Tracy pecked playfully at Maggie's shirt buttons. She took a step toward me, tilting her head to stare.

"Hi," I said to her, smiling.

Tracy lowered her head for a better look. Her huge dark eyes were framed by impossibly long lashes. As she studied me, there was a deep, booming roar off in the distance. Tracy quickly straightened and turned to look.

"What the hell was that?" Benny asked.

"Oh, good," Maggie said, shading her eyes as she stared at a pair of ostriches who were slowly circling each other about fifty yards away. "It's Regis and Kathie Lee."

I burst into laughter. "You're kidding."

Maggie turned to me with a smile. "They're about to mate. You'll be able to see the way it's supposed to be done. We have Rush on video."

"On video?" Benny repeated.

Sara turned to him and nodded triumphantly. "It'll be Rachel's best trial exhibit. The jury will go crazy when they see it."

My God, I thought, trying to imagine how to present this case to a jury.

Another booming roar.

"Come on," Maggie said. "We can get a little closer."

As we approached, one of the ostriches—presumably Regis—seemed to kick his mating dance into high gear. Standing in front of Kathie Lee, he began shimmying his shoulders like some massive go-go dancer on speed. He dropped to his hocks and fanned his wings rapidly. Another bellow, and then he scrambled back to his feet and started rocking forward as if he were *dahvening* in synagogue.

"This is foreplay?" Benny mumbled.

Apparently so. Kathie Lee had been watching Regis impassively—almost disdainfully—through the early phase of his fan dance, but now she was fluttering her own wings and batting her eyelashes. Apparently, she was getting in the mood. Suddenly she spun away from Regis and dropped to the ground, her head extended, her rump slightly raised. Regis moved in quickly.

I felt uncomfortable watching, but Regis was oblivious to his audience, totally caught up in his act. Fifteen seconds, a grunt, and curtains. Regis stood, stretched his neck, and sauntered off without a glance back.

Fifteen seconds, a grunt, and curtains, I thought, feeling a stab of solidarity as I watched Kathie Lee stagger to her feet in the dust.

Y ou see that thing on Regis?"
        "Yes, Benny, I saw it."
"Peculiar-looking, wasn't it?"
We were heading east on Highway 70, the sun setting behind us.
I looked over and shrugged. "No offense, Benny, but they're all kind of peculiar-looking."
"Maybe, but did you see the grooves on that johnson? What the hell's that all about? It looked like a goddamn NASA docking device."
"Probably the same design principle is at work."
"Damn, I'm starving." Benny was peering out the window at the restaurant billboards. "What say we go put on the feedbag, eh?"
I checked my watch and shook my head. "I can't. I have to be at the rabbi's house in a half hour. I've barely got enough time to drop you off."
"The rabbi again? Give me a break."
I looked over at him and sighed. "I made a promise."
"Promise," he snorted. "Jonathan owes you big time."
"It's not about owing, Benny. He's Orthodox. It's a big part of his life."

"So? You're Reform. What's that? Chopped liver?"

"He was angry with me, Benny. I can understand."

"Understand what? Jonathan's a good guy and all, but he's got some chutzpah giving you grief over being Reform. Give me a break. My grandfather was Orthodox. It's a wacko throwback cult from the Dark Ages."

"No it's not. Look, I promised him I'd give this a try."

"Yeah, yeah. What's tonight's topic?"

"I'm not sure," I lied.

"Speaking of which, I got a topic for the rebbe."

"Oh?" I gave him a look. "Not another query about the status of your job application for lifeguard at the *mikvah*?"

"Very funny. I'm talking a topic for the ages."

"Really?"

"I'm talking one of the haunting mysteries of Jewish law."

I rolled my eyes. "Let's hear it."

"Ask that learned scholar tonight to explain the origins of the eleventh commandment."

"The eleventh?"

"The one that applies only to Jewish women."

"Which one is that?"

"Come on, Rachel, don't act coy with me. This is the one they hide from the guys."

"How's it go?"

"Like you don't know."

"Tell me."

"Thou shalt not giveth head."

I laughed.

"I'm serious. You ever read the laws of kashruth? You wouldn't believe the things you can put in your mouth. Pickled herring, fried chicken fat, that grotesque mucus that comes with gefilte fish, chopped liver, boiled tongue, bone marrow, schmaltz—even certain insects, for chrissake! Bugs!

You're telling me this isn't a wacko cult? What kind of religion says yes to cockroaches and no to cocks?"

"It also says no to lobsters."

"The hell with lobsters. I can live without lobsters."

I gave him a look. "Really?"

He paused. "Well, maybe not. Add them to the list. Ask him tonight. Ask him what kind of religion bans lobsters and blow jobs."

"Maybe I'll save it for another night."

"Wait." He jabbed his finger at me. "Bacon, too. Lobsters, bacon, and blow jobs. Listen, I'm not asking for the answer to the riddle of human existence or for the secret to the afterlife, Rachel. All I'm asking for is why the only thing that ever gets blown in a Jewish home is a shofar."

CHAPTER 4

"It's my fault," I said glumly.

"Your fault?" my mother said. "Don't talk ridiculous. What is it with these men? Your father, alev asholem, tried that same number on me before we got married. You know what I told him?"

"What?" I asked, amused.

"I looked him right in the eye," she said, wagging the serving spoon as she reenacted the event, "and I warned him, 'Seymour, if you're looking for a girl who'll do that crazy stuff with you, then you better keep looking because I'm not that kind of girl.'"

I couldn't help but smile as I imagined that scene. My poor father. He never knew what hit him. My mother is the most determined and exasperating woman I know. Life trained her well. She came to America from Lithuania at the age of three, having escaped with her mother and baby sister after the Nazis killed her father, the rest of his family, and whatever semblance of religious faith my mother might ever have had. Fate remained cruel. My mother—a woman who reveres books and learning—was forced to drop out of high school and go to work when her mother (after whom I'm named) was diagnosed with terminal liver cancer. My grandmother Rachel died six months later, leaving her two daughters, Sarah and Becky, orphans at the ages of seventeen and fifteen. Two years later, my mother married a gentle, shy, devoutly Jewish bookkeeper ten years her senior named Seymour Gold. My sweet father was totally smitten by his beautiful, spirited wife and remained so until his death from a heart attack two years ago on the morning after Thanksgiving.

"And you know what?" she continued. "Your father never brought it up again. Never." She nodded with satisfaction, but then noticed an empty centimeter of space on my plate. "How about some more brisket, doll baby?"

"Oh, Mom, I'm stuffed."

"Potatoes?"

"Really, Mom, I'm *plotzing*. It's delicious, but I couldn't eat another bite of anything."

"Wait, I've got strudel."

I leaned back in my chair. "Then let's take a break first. I'll help you clean up the dinner dishes."

I washed, my mom dried.

As I soaped one of the dinner plates, I said, "I still think it's my fault."

"How could it possibly be your fault?"

"I might be able to connect with these traditions if I were a more spiritual person."

"You're plenty spiritual. A saint should have the soul you do. But this Orthodox nonsense isn't spiritual. It's superstition."

"You sound like Benny."

"Benny's no dummy. Orthodox Judaism." She shook her head. "Ridiculous rules and rituals. Worse than ridiculous, and you know why? Because the point of those rules and rituals is to remind us that men are special and we aren't. That's why I told Seymour to forget it."

"Mom, it's not that simple. For every Orthodox Jewish man there's an Orthodox Jewish woman, and those women don't feel oppressed."

"How do you know?"

"I know, Mom. Take the rabbi's wife. Sylvia is brilliant and successful, and she loves every ritual connected with the religion."

"Including this *mishagoss* she told you about tonight? What's it called? *Nadah?*"

"*Niddah.*"

"*Niddah, nadah*—whatever. It's just Jewish men passing rules to make women feel unclean and inferior."

For the past five weeks, I'd been spending an hour one night a week in Rabbi Isaac Kalman's study trying to learn the laws, customs, and traditions of Orthodox Judaism. Although my father had been Orthodox, my sister, Ann, and I were raised as Reform Jews. When my mother told my father that she wasn't going to do that "crazy stuff" with him, she made sure the ban included her children, too. But now, like my mother before me, I'd fallen in love with a devout Jewish man. Unlike my father, however, Jonathan was a widower with two small girls. And unlike my mother, I was willing to at least give Orthodox Judaism a try.

Dating an Orthodox Jew was a new experience. In addition to the strict observance of the Sabbath from sundown on Friday to sundown on Saturday—no cars, no telephones, no electric appliances, no work—there were exacting rules about food, prayer, and sex. Although few organized religions celebrate the joys of marital sex more than Orthodox Judaism, the counterweight is a stern prohibition against premarital sex. I suppose it added a touch of nostalgic charm to our relationship, as if we were a pair of high school sweethearts from a 1950s sitcom. It added plenty of frustration, too.

Tonight, though, had been a real test of faith, because tonight the topic had been the laws of *niddah*. Due to the subject matter, my teacher tonight had been the rabbi's wife, Sylvia Kalman. She'd explained that a woman becomes a *nid-

dah at the onset of menstruation. The *niddah* phase lasts almost two weeks, since the woman must have seven consecutive "clean" days after her period ends. She ends the *niddah* by going to the *mikvah,* or ritual bath, and immersing herself in the waters. She emerges physically and spiritually cleansed.

From the onset of menstruation until the ritual bath twelve to fourteen days later, Jewish law strictly forbids not only all sexual activity but all physical contact between husband and wife. Indeed, sexual intercourse with a *niddah* is punishable by the severest penalty, *kahret,* the Jewish version of excommunication in which the sinner is spiritually cut off from the destiny of the Jewish people.

The rabbi's wife had sensed my resistance. As she no doubt had done for scores of women before me, she explained the various rationales the rabbis offer. The laws of *niddah* give the woman a special time to herself. They protect a couple from the dangers of overindulgence and overfamiliarity, which could lead to monotony and restlessness. The laws of *niddah,* some say, are designed to increase the love between the man and woman by creating a monthly honeymoon. As the Torah promises, when the wife returns to the marital bed after the end of *niddah,* "she will be as beloved to her husband as she was when she entered the *chupah.*"

"It's a beautiful mitzvah," Sylvia told me. "A monthly blessing."

I tried to believe—I really did—but my heart wasn't in it. To me, the various explanations sounded more like rationalizations for a set of rules concocted by a neurotically squeamish guy—the same guy who'd come up with those obsessive washing-of-the-hands rituals at Passover and other holidays. But the rabbi's wife believed in the wisdom and the beauty of the laws of *niddah*—truly believed—and she was no fool. Sylvia Kalman held a Ph.D. from Columbia University and taught modern European history at St. Louis University. She seemed the embodiment of the joy that Orthodox Jewish women shared with their men. I wanted to believe the way she did. Despite my mother's assurances, I knew the failure was my fault.

"*Niddah, smiddah,*" my mother said as she poured us tea. "When you get to be an old lady like me, you don't have to worry about that monthly stuff anymore."

"Old lady? Come on, Mom, you look gorgeous."

With her high cheekbones, trim figure, and curly red hair (colored these days to cover the gray), Sarah Gold was still a good-looking woman at the age of fifty-four. I called her my "Red Hot Mama."

"Ah," she said with a dismissive wave, "enough with this Orthodox craziness. Have another piece of strudel and tell me more about Angela."

I'd already filled her in on my prison meeting. I went through some of my unease about the original conviction.

"Benny's right," she said when I finished. "What's done is done. That's why we have juries. There was just too much evidence against her. Everywhere you looked there was something that said guilty. Even that piece of glass that she used to cut off that poor man's penis."

"That's another gap in the evidence," I said.

"Rachel, it was her blood on the glass. The DNA test confirmed it. Even I remember that."

"Mom, I know it was her blood. That's the point, in fact. Yesterday, I got a copy of the results of the blood tests. There were traces of two drugs in them: a steroid and a muscle relaxer with a long name. Fluni—uh . . ." I paused, trying to remember. "Flunitrazepam."

"Sounds like something from a Groucho Marx movie."

I said, "The cops interviewed her internist as part of the

investigation—mainly for his insights into her mental state. He said he prescribed the steroid for some sort of sinus infection. Over the years he'd prescribed sleeping pills and Valium for her, but never that drug."

"So maybe another doctor did."

"I doubt it. According to a note in the file, the drug is legal elsewhere but not in the U.S."

"Rachel, honey, maybe she had muscle cramps the last time she was on a cruise or overseas on vacation."

"They didn't find any more of those pills in her medicine cabinet."

"So maybe that was the last pill and she pitched the bottle."

"She hadn't been out of the country for a while."

"So it was an old bottle. No big deal. Your father had pill bottles dating back to the Korean War. So does your aunt Becky. There must be plenty of people with expired prescriptions in their medicine cabinet."

She leaned across the table and placed her hand over mine. "Rachel, honey, listen to your mother. What do you have? A blood test showing on the night of the murder she took a muscle relaxer that she must have bought on a trip overseas? And that's going to prove she's innocent? Even our criminal justice system isn't that crazy, and you know what I think of our criminal justice system."

After we finished our tea and my mother had forced me to take four slices of strudel she'd wrapped in aluminum foil, she walked with me to the front door.

"So is Jonathan going to be out of town the whole summer?" she asked.

"Possibly. He told me the government has thirty-eight names on its witness list. Jonathan thinks it may take three days just to pick the jury."

Jonathan Wolf was representing one of the defendants in

a huge securities fraud prosecution in the federal district court in Manhattan. The trial was scheduled to last two months. At least the timing worked well for his daughters, whose school year ended a week ago. His parents still lived in Brooklyn. Although Jonathan would be living in a midtown hotel during the week, his daughters would get to spend the summer in New York with their grandparents.

Jonathan and I met as litigation adversaries a year ago. I'd detested him from the start. My mother, of course, decided that he was the perfect man for me. I told her no way—he was far too arrogant. She told me it was pride, not arrogance. I told her if that was pride, he had too much of it. She told me he sounded like someone else she knew. I told her forget it. She told me mothers know best. I told her not with this guy you don't. She told me to give it a few months. I did.

It's amazing how much smarter mothers grow over time.

"When did you talk to him?"

"Last night. Sounds like the pretrial stuff is going okay." I paused. "I really miss him."

"He's a good man. A little crazy with this Orthodox stuff, but still a good man." She gave me a fierce hug. "I love you, doll baby."

"I love you, Mom."

CHAPTER 5

I waited for Sheila Trumble in the marble rotunda of City Hall. We were scheduled for combat this morning with Nathaniel Turner, aka Nate the Great. Although I hoped we could reason with him, based on my last telephone conversation with him I was afraid that a battle seemed more likely.

I was a few minutes early and happy to spend the time enjoying the interior of my favorite city hall. Unlike the standard Greco-Roman structures that house the mayors of America, the St. Louis City Hall resembles its counterpart in Paris—a resemblance that is hardly coincidental. When the St. Louis city fathers decided to build a new city hall in 1890, they chose to recognize the city's heritage by selecting a French Renaissance Revival design based on the Hôtel de Ville de Paris. The result was striking, with an interior as lovely as its exterior. I was standing in the rotunda, whose walls were illuminated by a graceful set of three-pronged globe lamps. Directly ahead, the grand marble stairway led up to a four-story interior courtyard that was capped by gold-leafed archways and pastel murals of scenes from the early days of the city. High overhead, a ceiling of stained-glass skylights bathed the interior in a soft glow that could almost make you forget the nasty business transacted behind so many of those imposing doors.

"Rachel?"

I turned to see Sheila Trumble approaching, her low heels clicking against the marble floor. She was a handsome woman in her fifties with an aquiline nose, short-cropped black hair streaked with gray, and keen blue eyes. She was dressed, as always, with that understated elegance that whispered "exquisite taste" and "big bucks." She had plenty of both. Sheila was, after all, the wife of Carson Trumble III, who had the good fortune (literally) to be the son of the founder of Trumble Communications.

I smiled, delighted to see her.

"Did you meet with Angela yesterday?" she asked when she reached me.

"I did. She sends her greetings."

"That's sweet." Her smile faded to a concerned frown. "How is she?"

"Hanging in there."

She nodded sympathetically. Sheila Trumble was high on my list of quality people—a genuinely fine woman who'd somehow avoided the perils of wealth. Oh, yes, she and Carson were members of the right clubs, sent their children to the right private schools, and owned vacation homes in the right places (Aspen and Martha's Vineyard). But unlike her social peers—whose definition of a charitable act required a designer gown, a good table, a boldface blurb in the society column, and a flattering photograph in the *Ladue News*—Sheila's commitment to philanthropy was authentic and totally without glitz. She did her good deeds down in the trenches, tutoring third-graders three times a week at an inner-city elementary school and taking part in several rehab projects for Habitat for Humanity each year. Typical of her no-nonsense attitude, a month before her first Habitat project she'd hired a carpenter to train her in the tools of his craft. She wanted to make sure she'd be useful on the job site. She was, too. I'd worked alongside her on a project last winter and watched in amazement at her adeptness with a nail gun.

Although the tutoring and rehab projects would have sufficed for many volunteers, Sheila's overriding allegiance was to the Oasis Shelter, which she founded sixteen years ago and which brought us together today. Back at the beginning, she'd been spurred into action by the plight of her cook, Pearlie Brown, who was trapped in a physically abusive relationship. Sheila found a vacant two-flat in north St. Louis, signed a one-year lease for the entire building, and helped Pearlie and her two children pack up and move in. By the end of the first year, there were six battered women and eleven children living in the building. During the first year, Sheila shopped for all the groceries herself, arranged day care for the children, and hired the security guards posted around the clock to keep out the angry husbands and boyfriends. But by the time of the gala tenth-anniversary celebration at the Hyatt Regency, the Oasis was a self-sufficient shelter—a model, in fact, for other cities—having expanded to include the adjacent apartment building and a full staff of professionals to help the women turn around their lives.

Six months ago, though, the storm clouds known as Renewal 2004 began gathering. That's when Sheila retained me as the attorney for the shelter. Today would be our third meeting with Nate the Great in an effort to avoid a head-on collision between Renewal 2004 and the Oasis Shelter.

Sheila was also my connection to Angela Green. They'd become good friends while serving together on the Oasis board, and their relationship had survived the trial and Angela's incarceration. When Angela needed a civil lawyer to defend her in the Son of Sam case, she turned to Sheila for advice, and Sheila gave her my name.

"By the way," I said as we waited for the elevator, "Angela knows Nate the Great."

"Really?" Sheila said, intrigued. "How?"

"She once baby-sat for him. She told me they grew up

in the same neighborhood. He was a few years behind her younger sister at Soldan High."

"What did her sister think of him?"

"Not much. She said he was one of those slick Casanova types, dressing real fine, checking himself in every mirror, always patting and fiddling with his Afro."

Sheila smiled. "Nate with an Afro. Now there's an image."

"Actually," I said, grinning, "I have a better image. It's a story Angela told me about Nate."

"What?"

"Back when Angela was in college, Nate's mother hired her one summer to baby-sit for Nate and his younger sister while she was out of town. Nate was twelve years old, and his sister was eight. Angela took her to the zoo one day. When she came home that afternoon she caught Nate on his bed with some of her bras and underwear and a pair of her high heels."

"Oh, my God," Sheila said, giggling and covering her mouth. "Was he . . . you know?"

"Probably. He must have heard her coming down the hall because when she walked in on him he had a towel wrapped around his waist."

"What did she do?"

"She slapped him in the face and called him a pervert and told him if he ever misbehaved she'd tell everyone in the neighborhood what he was really like."

"Oh, my."

"I don't think he learned his lesson. From what I hear, he still spends his free time trying to get into other women's pants."

"It's so disgusting. I was at a fund-raiser last year, and he was, too. He acts like he's God's gift to women."

"Maybe we can convince him to be God's gift to the women in our shelter."

H ave a seat," the secretary informed us in a bored tone, barely looking up, the phone cradled in the crook of her neck. She had iridescent fingernails the size of vulture talons. "The commissioner will be with you soon." She swiveled away from us and resumed her telephone conversation. "So, then he goes, 'Girl, don't be talkin' 'bout what . . .' "

I wandered along the back wall of the reception area, studying the framed photographs of the city's flamboyant redevelopment commissioner posed with various visiting dignitaries—Nate the Great shaking hands with Donald Trump; standing next to Sammy Sosa, both of them wearing Chicago Cubs hats; embracing Colin Powell; giving a thumbs-up to the Pope, who looked baffled; grinning alongside President Bill Clinton, the two of them flanked by a pair of St. Louis Rams cheerleaders.

"Ah, welcome, ladies."

I turned to see Nate beaming at us from the doorway of his office.

Sheila stood. "Good morning, Commissioner."

"Sheila, my dear." He stepped to the side and with a sweeping gesture toward his office said, "Please come in, ladies."

He followed us into his office, where a familiar, perennial figure stood by the picture window.

Nate said, "I believe you ladies have already made the acquaintance of my assistant, Herman Borghoff."

Borghoff turned to gaze at us, expressionless, his arms crossed over his chest.

Although both men were in their late forties, Herman Borghoff made such a contrast to his boss that cynics claimed Nate kept him around just to make himself look better.

Borghoff was tall and lumpy and pasty-white. His boss was short and lean and jet-black. Borghoff wore thick horn-rimmed glasses, an old-fashioned black Timex watch with a faded canvas watchband, and his high school class ring. He had a bad haircut that failed to disguise the cowlicks in his brown hair. His boss had a stylish goatee, a shaved head, tinted aviators, and lots of gold jewelry, including a Piaget watch worth more than my car. Borghoff wore an ill-fitting plaid suit and scuffed black shoes. His boss could have stepped out of the pages of GQ in his chalk-striped double-breasted navy suit, starched blue shirt with white collar, elegant silk patterned tie, and shiny black alligator shoes. The contrast remained in their lifestyles as well. Borghoff drove a late-model Chevy, lived with his mother, and rarely was seen outside of City Hall. Nate the Great cruised around town in a gleaming black Jaguar XJ8 and appeared at public functions with an ever-changing procession of gorgeous women of all races and ethnic origins. Never married, Nate made St. Louis Magazine's "Most Eligible Bachelor" list every year.

To me, their eyes were perhaps their biggest contrast. Borghoff's were inert. Staring into them—as I had done on several occasions—was like staring at two gray pebbles. Nate's were dazzling and manic, darting from face to face, sizing you up in an instant, moving on, zooming in, zooming out. Nate's eyes kept me on guard. Borghoff's gave me the creeps.

Borghoff moved off to the side wall, where there was a chair with a legal pad on it. He lifted the pad and settled into the seat as his boss slid into the high-back leather chair behind his imposing desk.

Nate smiled at us. "Sheila, always a pleasure and a privilege to see you, my dear. Rachel Gold, you are looking fine today, girl, yes you are. Gonna make me have to take some of my blood pressure medication."

Typical meaningless jabber from Nate the Great. We'd been tangling over the fate of the Oasis Shelter for more than half a year now, and during that period he'd called me everything from a "stone-cold fox" to a "demon spawn," from "sexy mama" to "goddamn ball-breaking bitch"—and sometimes all four during the same meeting. He had what charitably could be described as a volatile personality.

The walls of his office were festooned with even more framed photographs than the reception area, along with various proclamations, letters of commendations, and the like. The enormous picture window behind his desk displayed the Arch in the distance and the Civil Courts Building up close—two impressive edifices unique to St. Louis, although the Civil Courts Building was easily the more intriguing of the two. Hailed in 1930 as the Skyscraper Temple of Law, it's an otherwise undistinguished fourteen-story limestone structure until you get to the "roof," which consists of an Ionic Greek temple crowned by an Egyptian pyramid crowned by two enormous griffins, those half-eagle, half-lion creatures of myth. This curiosity is actually a replica of the Tomb of Halicarnassus, one of the Seven Wonders of the Ancient World. Why it sits atop the Civil Courts Building is anyone's guess, but the way it dominated the view from the window added an oddly sinister aura to Nate's office.

"So, my lovely ladies," Nate said, "what's on your mind today?"

"Same as last time," I told him.

He chuckled and glanced playfully at Borghoff, who stared back without expression.

Although Nate sometimes assumed the manner of a jester, he was as innocent and harmless as a king cobra—and at least as lethal. After all, his mother was Lucille Turner, which meant that his uncle was the Reverend Orion Sampson, an old-fashioned fire-and-brimstone preacher who'd given up the pulpit thirty years ago to run for Congress. St. Louis had never seen a black politician of his ilk. While others kowtowed to the city's white power elite, Orion Sampson spent thirty years in Congress thumbing his nose at the white boys while his constituents kept reelecting him with increasingly lopsided votes. The Republicans hadn't even bothered putting up a candidate the last four elections. The reverend apparently was as pure and principled as he was self-righteous and arrogant. Three scandal-free decades on Capitol Hill translated into sufficient seniority to chair the types of committees and subcommittees that forced white boys to kowtow to him if they wanted that tax break or federal subsidy or government contract for their Fortune 500 company.

Orion Sampson dearly loved his older sister Lucille, and Lucille dearly loved her precious son Nathaniel. All of which meant that Nate was not only dangerous but untouchable. He was also the city official in charge of Renewal 2004, the ambitious plan to transform a large section of north St. Louis into an urban environment that would attract middle-class whites back to the city. As redevelopment commissioner, he helped administer the special government-guaranteed mortgages that were the city's principal tool for implementing the massive redevelopment plan—tens of millions of dollars in redevelopment funds, much of it from the federal government, thanks to Uncle Orion. The properties intended for redevelopment were principally two- and three-flat apartment buildings acquired by the city over the years through tax delinquency seizures, abandonment, or eminent domain proceedings. Indeed, Nate the Great, through his office as redevelopment commissioner, was now the single largest property owner in north St. Louis.

The target year for completion was 2004, which was the

one hundredth anniversary of the St. Louis World's Fair, which in turn was the one hundredth anniversary of the start of the Lewis and Clark expedition at St. Louis. As part of the redevelopment plan, Nate's office was attempting to condemn various properties within the area that were deemed to be "inharmonious" with the redevelopment plan. The Oasis Shelter was one such allegedly inharmonious property, which made Nate the Great my principal adversary in the Oasis Shelter condemnation dispute. And now that he'd moved to phase two of Renewal 2004, the battle was heating up.

"Ladies," he told us, "I understand your devotion to that shelter, but we're talking about the future." He slid into the singsong manner of a preacher. "As we move further into the new millennium we need to expand our perspectives. We have made a commitment to revive a dying portion of this fine city. The sobering reality is that the march of progress often demands the sacrifice of a few to make life better for the many. I am afraid that is the case here."

"Come on, Nate," I said, "you're not building Disney World out there. You're talking about revitalizing a real city. Any real city has all types—blacks and whites, Asians and Hispanics, rich and poor, good guys and bad guys, and, unfortunately, some innocent women who are victims of abusive husbands and boyfriends."

Nate placed his hands palm-down on the desk and nodded. "I hear you, Rachel. I admire your compassion. But you're refusing to look at the big picture. We got all types living in this city but one. The one type we don't have is the white professional class." He was standing now, turning to gaze out the window at the skyline. "We got to find a way to lure all those white doctors and lawyers and accountants and businessmen back into our fine city." He turned back to face us. "Let me tell you something, ladies, you don't bait that hook with a depressing shelter for abused women. Isn't that the truth, Herman?"

Borghoff slowly looked up from his notes, his expression impassive, his gaze remote.

"That's ridiculous," I said, pressing on. "We're not running a crack house, Commissioner. Those are well-maintained apartment buildings, and the cause is a good one."

"You're missing the point, Rachel. I don't care whether you got the Virgin Mary herself running that operation. My job is to convince Ward and June Cleaver to sell their home out there in the white-bread suburbs, pack up their honky belongings, put Wally and the Beaver in the minivan, and move into the city. I'm never going to close that deal when they find out they're going to be living next door to a bunch of skanky women hiding out from psycho boyfriends. That just ain't gonna fly."

The meeting went downhill quickly from there and broke up ten minutes later with my assurance to Nate that the shelter's supporters would be stocking the war chest to fight any condemnation proceeding.

That just made him chuckle. "You may think you're messing with City Hall," he told me, "but you're forgetting something important, counselor. When it comes to messing, City Hall got a whole lot more ways of messing with your client than you got messing with City Hall. Your client may have enough money to hire a lawyer, but we already got lawyers, girl, and we got a whole arsenal besides, and it's called 'city government.' Before you declare war, counselor, you better first remind yourself that we got lots of different weapons in that arsenal. Isn't that so, Herman?"

I was glad to get out of Nate's office. Everything about him infuriated me—from his indifference to the plight of the women served by the Oasis Shelter to his smarmy male chauvinism to the way he wielded the instruments of power as if he'd actually earned them. Absent Orion Sampson, Nate would be a nobody—a fact that only underscored his own hypocrisy, and vulnerability. The congressman lived by the fundamentalist tenets of his church. According to one joke, he and his wife never had sex standing up because someone might think they were dancing. Swearing, drinking, and fornication were also on Sampson's forbidden list. The consequences of violating that list were wondrous to behold. Seven years ago, Sampson's eldest son, Orion junior, was a state representative, a vice president of a black-owned bank in his father's district, and the heir apparent to his father's congressional seat. Then he got sued by an exotic dancer who claimed that he'd fathered her child. When blood tests confirmed paternity, the congressman responded with Old Testament vengeance. These days, Orion junior sells used cars in north St. Louis.

Fortunately for Nate, his uncle was rarely in town and never frequented Nate's favorite nightspots. According to those in the know, Nate had taken one additional precautionary step—he'd procured a "fiancée" in the form of a churchgoing schoolteacher in her early thirties named Beatrice who accompanied Nate to all family gatherings. Uncle Orion was apparently quite taken with the demure Beatrice and never passed up the opportunity to urge his nephew to finally set the wedding date.

Out in the hallway near the elevators, I conferred briefly with Sheila. She was heading back to the shelter, but I had another meeting in the building to try to straighten out a permit problem for a client.

"Put me on the agenda for the next board meeting," I told her. "I can tell them our options."

"Do we have any?" she asked bleakly.

"Absolutely, Sheila. We have more leverage than you realize. Remember, Nate's goal is to get this situation resolved quickly. He's in there right now telling Borghoff to light a fire under the city's lawyers. He'll want them cranking out condemnation papers. The more we slow it down, the more the balance shifts in our favor."

"But how much can we really slow it down?"

"You might be surprised."

M y other meeting at City Hall lasted just thirty minutes. Afterward, I wandered slowly through the rotunda toward the exit, thinking over Angela's situation. A large plaque on the wall caught my attention. According to the engraved text, it was placed there in memory of "the Distinguished Citizens of Greater St. Louis who perished in the Great Glider Crash at Lambert Field, August 1, 1943." The list of dead included the mayor and nine other Distinguished Citizens.

The Great Glider Crash of 1943?

Here I was, a little over a half century later, with absolutely no idea what the plaque memorialized. I'd never heard of the Great Glider Crash of 1943 and didn't recognize any of the names of the Distinguished Citizens—not even the mayor.

There's a lesson there, I told myself. Fifty years from now, the memories of Angela Green's murder trial would be just as faint. After all, hadn't other "trials of the century" faded long before the century had? Who today could even recognize the names Bruno Hauptmann and Alfred de Marigny, much less recall the details of their respective murder trials, each of which mesmerized the nation while dominating the front pages for months? Were you to suggest to someone of Bruno Hauptmann's era that there would come a time in America when the typical citizen could not recite the age, sex, or first name of the kidnapped Lindbergh baby or the place where the infant's corpse was found, he would laugh in disbelief. Or that Sacco and Vanzetti, the most famous pair of criminal defendants of the first half of the twentieth century, could today be passed off as a perfumery from Florence: "Thrill to the scent of liberation—Anarchy, from Sacco & Vanzetti." Who today even recalled their first names, much less their crime?

And someday, I told myself, Angela's celebrity would fade as well, along with the entourage of lawyers, judges, and witnesses who shared her spotlight. We'll all meet up in the foyer of that celebrity netherworld with Bruno Hauptmann, the Lindbergh baby, O. J. Simpson, and the victims of the Great Glider Crash of 1943. As usual, Shakespeare said it first and said it best:

> *Imperious Caesar, dead and turned to clay,*
> *Might stop a hole to keep the wind away.*
> *O, that that earth which kept the world in awe*
> *Should patch a wall to expel the winter's flaw!*

CHAPTER 6

I was back in my office after lunch trying to focus, trying to prepare for the two meetings tomorrow in Chicago—first with Angela's criminal defense lawyer and then with the lawyers for all defendants in the Son of Sam lawsuit But it was no use. I was distracted—still troubled by the Groucho Marx drug. Was it just another loose end, or an important one? How and why did something called "flunitrazepam" get into Angela Green's bloodstream?

I'd called Brett Abrams that morning. Brett was a lawyer friend in Chicago who specialized in plaintiffs' medical malpractice cases. I knew that Brett, like all medical malpractice lawyers, would have a copy of the *Physicians' Desk Reference* on his desk. He checked the listings for me and reported that there was no entry for flunitrazepam.

Perhaps, I'd mused after hanging up, there was no listing because the drug wasn't lawful to prescribe in the United States. Before leaving for my lunch meeting, I'd asked my secretary, Jacki, to check with the medical school library at St. Louis University to see whether they had a reference book with any information on the drug. When I returned to the office after lunch, Jacki's typed notes of her telephone conversation with one of the librarians were sitting on my desk.

The librarian had found the information in a European equivalent of the *PDR*. According to Jacki's notes, flunitrazepam was in the class of drugs used to treat anxiety, convulsions, muscle tension, and sleep disorders. Developed in the 1970s by Hoffman-La Roche, the drug was more popularly known by its trade name, Rohypnol.

Rohypnol.

I stared at the name.

I said it aloud.

It sounded awfully familiar.

I read through the rest of her notes. The drug was legal in eighty-six countries in Europe, South America, Africa, the Middle East, and Asia. Low doses of Rohypnol could cause "drowsiness, dizziness, motor incoordination, memory loss, gastrointestinal upsets, headache, reduced blood pressure, visual disturbances, dry mouth, and hangover." Higher doses could cause coma, respiratory depression, and even death.

I leaned back in my chair and mulled it over. Flunitrazepam could be prescribed for sleeplessness or anxiety. That was not inconsistent with Angela's history. Over the years, her physician had given her prescriptions for sleeping pills and for tranquilizers.

I studied the notes. Legal in eighty-six countries. According to the investigative file, Angela had visited London, Rome, and Bermuda and had taken a Caribbean cruise during the four years before Michael Green's murder. Maybe Rohypnol was legal in one of those countries.

I turned toward the computer screen. My computer was hooked up to Nexis, a computer data bank of hundreds and hundreds of newspapers, periodicals, and specialized journals. It was worth a shot.

I signed onto Nexis. At the search prompt, I typed in a single word: *flunitrazepam.* I stared at the word for a moment, my lips pursed. This was already a long shot. Better to do the search using its trademark. That might improve my chances of a hit, since newspapers and periodicals were far more likely to use a drug's brand name. Who knew, or could remember, that the dentist numbed you with a shot of procaine hydrochloride, or that the generic name for the twenty-one Ortho-Novums I took each month was norethindrone/mestranol? After all, even Angela's physician had used brand names during his police interview. He told them he had prescribed Nembutal and Valium, not pentobarbital sodium and diazepam.

So I backspaced over *flunitrazepam* and typed in *Rohypnol*. Then I hit the transmit key and leaned back to wait. After fifteen seconds the screen flashed a message:

Search interrupted—your current search request has located more than 1,000 documents. Would you care to modify your search request? Yes/No?:

I frowned in surprise. There were more than a thousand newspaper and magazine articles in which the word *Rohypnol* appeared?

I typed in *yes* and then modified the search to eliminate all articles shorter than one thousand words. It took two more search modifications to get the number under one hundred articles.

By then I was very curious. I pressed the key to view the first document. A moment later, the screen filled with the opening paragraphs of an article that had appeared three years ago in the financial section of the *Washington Post* under the headline:

COUNTERING ILL EFFECTS OF AN ABUSED DRUG; FIRM RAISES AWARENESS IN SEX-RELATED ATTACKS

I leaned forward and started reading.

The pill is small, white and tasteless when dissolved in liquid. It is manufactured by Swiss pharmaceutical giant

Hoffman-La Roche Ltd. for treating severe insomnia.

The prescription sleeping aid is sold and marketed in 80 countries around the world, including many in Europe and Asia, and is a strong revenue producer for the company, though the drug manufacturer has never sought approval to sell it in the United States.

Yet it is in this country where the pharmaceutical, known as Rohypnol, has been branded a "date rape drug" by police and has engendered calls for stricter penalties for those who possess it.

Rohypnol has been called the date rape drug because of a rise in sexual assaults that police suspect have been committed after the illegally imported drug was slipped into a victim's drink. The drug so incapacitates those who ingest it that they cannot resist sexual assault and they often don't remember much of the attack later, police say.

I reread the last paragraph.

Now, of course, I knew why the word *Rohypnol* sounded familiar. The date rape drug.

I leaned forward and read on.

The article focused on the struggle between those fighting to maintain the status quo and those seeking to get the drug reclassified from Schedule 4 to Schedule 1 on the Drug Enforcement Administration's controlled substances list. Schedule 1 drugs include crack cocaine and heroin. According to the article, the legislative compromise had been to stiffen the criminal penalties for the use of any controlled substance in a sexual assault. But the director of the D.C. Rape Crisis Center discounted the value of that approach.

"A drug like Rohypnol can cause amnesia," she explained. "That means that women will not be able to provide the information the police need to prosecute a sexual assault case. You'll never get to the point of using the enhanced penalties."

I paged slowly through the other articles. Rohypnol had started coming into the U.S. about three years before Michael Green's death, much of it smuggled up through Mexico. It had a variety of street names, the most popular being "roofies." Other street names included Roachies, Ropes, La Rocha, Rib Roche, R-2, and Mexican Valium.

Rohypnol's use in sexual assaults had earned it a creepier set of nicknames, including the Forget Pill, Trip-and-Fall, and Mind Erasers. In a case in Broward County, a convicted rapist boasted of using Rohypnol to rape more than twenty women. In Miami, where the drug comes in from Latin America through courier services and passengers on commercial airplanes, the poison control center had logged more than two hundred confirmed "roofie" rapes, with hundreds more suspected. A story in the *Legal Times* described why Rohypnol was the weapon of choice for rapists:

> Rohypnol tablets dissolve easily and quickly. They are odorless, colorless and tasteless. The victim often blacks out, so she cannot piece together enough details to put a rapist away.
>
> "You've got a drug that makes your partner less capable of resisting and unable to remember afterwards," says Mary Hibbard, a drug policy expert at the University of California at Los Angeles. "It really is the perfect crime."

I stared at that last line, feeling a chill run down my spine.

I skimmed the rest of the articles, trying to figure out why, with all this publicity, Angela Green's defense attorney had said nothing about the blood analysis at trial. Nexis had organized the articles in descending chronological order—the most recent first, oldest last. That chronology held at least a partial answer. The media coverage had markedly escalated during the past five years. Indeed, the only articles that mentioned the drug during the three years before Michael Green's death were financial or business profiles on Hoffman-La Roche Ltd. in which the name Rohypnol would pop up on a list of the pharmaceutical company's more successful drugs, along with Valium and a heart-attack medicine called Activase.

All of which might explain why the presence of flunitrazepam had not sent up a red flag in the medical examiner's office when they got the results of the blood tests on the broken glass.

But that was then. This was now.

My mother didn't kill him," Sonya said bluntly. "She was framed."

"Who framed her?"

She took a sip of her wine and shrugged. "Probably that blond bimbo."

We were in the bar at Harry's Restaurant on Market Street—Sonya Green and me. She'd been reluctant to meet, even after I explained that I was representing her mother in the Son of Sam case. After some cajoling, I finally got her to agree to give me thirty minutes after work. I'd suggested Harry's, which was near A. G. Edwards and Sons, where she worked as an analyst in the underwriting department.

Although Sonya was heavier than her mother and had a complexion closer to her father's, she'd inherited her mother's broad facial features. Unlike her mother, though, there was a slightly unkempt quality to Sonya. There were makeup smudges on the collar of her blouse, which was not well pressed. Her straightened hair was a little tousled, her lipstick and eyeliner just a tad off line. I felt a pang in my heart. Although I was probably doing a little projecting, Sonya seemed a big little girl to me, one who still needed a mommy to help her get fixed up, to make sure the blouses were cleaned and ironed and that her the eyeliner was on straight. Unfortunately, the state of Missouri had snatched her mommy and locked her up two hundred miles from home.

How unfair life must have seemed to Sonya. She'd been just a few weeks from graduation at Northwestern when her father was murdered and her mother arrested and charged with the crime. During the same month her classmates celebrated in Evanston with their parents, Sonya was back in St. Louis burying one and visiting the other in jail. For the first two years after graduation, she lived with her grandmother— Angela's mother. She now lived alone in a condominium in Clayton.

"Why Samantha Cummings?" I asked. "Where's the motive?"

"Motive?" Sonya gave me a scornful look. "Money, of course. Look at the lawsuit. If her kid wins, she'll be wealthy."

I shook my head. "The lawsuit is an afterthought— something dreamed up by a lawyer. If she was really after your father's money, the simplest way to get it was to marry him. If she was a gold digger, her best strategy was to keep him alive until the wedding. If he died before that, she'd have no claim to anything—she wouldn't be the wife, she wouldn't be the widow, she wouldn't even be the long-time live-in girlfriend who could try to portray herself as the common-law wife. Look at her situation today. In the eyes of the law, she's a nobody. She can't even be a plaintiff in the Son of Sam case. No, if she were looking for money, the last thing she'd want is for your father to die before the wedding."

"I don't care," Sonya said, her voice laced with anger. "Some things aren't logical. I'm telling you that whore was behind the murder. I may not know why—at least not yet—but I know what I know, and I know there's some connection between her and whoever killed him."

I backed off the topic. We talked more generally about her mother's predicament. Sonya visited her every month and they corresponded frequently. She'd been much closer to her mother than her father while growing up. The opposite had been true for her older brother, Michael junior.

"Mike's been brainwashed," she said, snorting in disgust.

"What do you mean?"

"He turned completely against Mom. He hasn't talked to her since the trial. Can you believe that? His own mother." She shook her head. "But he was turning against her even before my father was killed. Did you know he was planning to go to that awful wedding? I couldn't believe it when I found out. I told him I wouldn't stoop to be in the same room with that whore. He got mad at me, said our father was entitled to happiness, too, said she was a sweet girl. Let me tell you something." She leaned forward and lowered her voice. "I sometimes think Mike might have had the hots for that whore himself back then. He used to visit her whenever he came to St. Louis. Even after the murder. I bet he still talks to her once in a while."

"I'm going to see him tomorrow afternoon."

She looked surprised. "Really? Is he coming down here?"

I shook my head. "I've got meetings in Chicago. On this case, in fact. Your brother agreed to meet me in the afternoon before I fly back to St. Louis."

"Then you're going to see what I'm telling you. When it comes to my father, Mike's a total believer. Like one of those

Moonies." She leaned back in her chair and crossed her arms over her chest. "Funny how things change." She sighed. "When we were growing up, Mike was the rebel and I was Daddy's girl, little Miss Perfect. When Mike was in high school, he and my father used to scream at each other all the time. He actually hit my father out in our backyard one afternoon. Hit his own father. In the face. Have you ever? My father grounded him for a month and took away his car. They didn't speak for more than a year. But now, to hear Mike talk, you'd think he'd been raised by an angel of God." She paused, frowning. "Strange how some things turn out."

CHAPTER 7

M aria Fallaci stared at me, incredulous. "And the punch line is?"

We were in her law office, which was on the fourth floor of an older high-rise along LaSalle Street in Chicago's Loop.

"No punch line." I shrugged. "I'm just saying there were traces of Rohypnol in her blood."

"Which means what? That I should have argued to the jury that he drugged her and fucked her, and when he came out of the shower she rose like some zombie from *The Night of the Living Dead* and cut off his cock? Come on, Rachel. I'm a defense lawyer, not a horror-flick producer." She paused, trying to get herself under control. "Look, I'm sure you're a fine civil lawyer, and I'm sure you'll give Angela a fine defense in this Son of Sam case. But defending a lawsuit over money is totally different from defending a capital murder case."

"I know," I said, trying a conciliatory smile, ignoring her not-so-subtle put-down. I'd only make it worse by acting confrontational. I'd come up here assuming that she would react defensively to anything she could interpret as second-guessing her representation of Angela Green. And I didn't blame her. She'd lost one of the most famous trials of the decade and, in the process, had been subjected to plenty of armchair lawyering from the likes of Geraldo Rivera, Alan Dershowitz, F. Lee Bailey, Gerry Spence, Marcia Clark, and the rest of the cable-TV courtroom mavens. And I'm sure she'd done it to herself as well—during and after the trial.

"Maria, I didn't come up here to critique your trial tactics, and I certainly didn't come here to make you angry. If I did, I'm sorry."

Her nostrils flared and she nodded. "Don't worry," she said, waving her hand dismissively. "I'm a big girl."

She ran her fingers through her long black hair, which was streaked with gray. As she did, she turned toward the window, her profile accenting her strong Italian nose. Now in her early forties, Maria Fallaci was still the "smoldering Sicilian beauty" that *Esquire* had labeled her four years ago in the short profile the magazine ran in its annual "Women We Love" issue. What made her appearance there even more memorable was the Annie Leibovitz portrait that accompanied the copy. Instead of the usual defense-lawyer shot— glaring from the courthouse steps with arms crossed over chest or posed in front of the jury box with a forefinger pointing ominously—Maria was in a silky nightgown reclining on her four-poster bed. In the background, slightly out of focus, was her live-in lover, a young ballerina named Annette.

Like most of the cast in Angela's criminal trial, Maria first became a celebrity and then became an author. Her book, *Battered Justice,* was scheduled for release in November. I'd read somewhere that the book promotion included a twenty-city tour with readings at several women's prisons. Only last week Liz Smith reported that Spike Lee had signed on to film the book-and-prison tour for an HBO documentary. And thus, Maria became a defendant in the Son of Sam case.

The meeting of defense counsel would start at ten o'clock this morning. I'd flown up early to meet with Maria in the hopes that she'd help quell my doubts about Angela's conviction. That seemed less and less likely.

I said, "I'm sure that the Angela Green I met earlier this week is a lot different than the Angela Green you represented back then." I paused. "It's just that..." My voice trailed away.

"That she seems incapable of murder?"

"Exactly."

"That's the way it is in most domestic violence cases." She stood and walked to the window. Staring down at the El train rumbling past, she said, "I've defended husbands and I've defended wives in everything from spousal abuse to murder. Very few of them seem the type." She turned toward me. "It's as if there's a secret chemical reaction going on inside the relationship, something toxic that's hidden from the rest of us. Sometimes it turns one of them into a temporary monster."

"But not always."

She studied me. "Not always. But in Angela's case there was plenty of evidence pointing toward a temporary monster."

In deciding how to defend the murder charge, Maria had had to make a difficult choice between the traditional route of trying to plant reasonable doubt in the jurors' minds and the more unusual route of finding a theme that could turn the case into a trial about something other than the crime charged. Most of the media pundits had assumed long before she rose in court to deliver her opening statement that Maria would choose that second option. After all, the evidence against Angela had seemed overwhelming, with or without the trace of Rohypnol in her blood. But in predicting the second option, the media assumed that the theme would be race. They assumed that Maria would play the "race" card, focusing on the black-white angle. A "reverse O.J.," as Geraldo labeled it—scorned jealous black woman kills the white man she's about to lose to a white woman.

Instead, Maria played the "battered wife" card, calling to the stand a parade of Angela's friends to testify to the emotional abuse Michael had subjected her client to over the years—the withering sarcasm, the nasty put-downs, the racist jabs. After Angela gained twenty-five pounds during the final years of their marriage, one friend testified that Michael took to calling her "Aunt Jemima." In public. Although Michael junior refused to testify, Sonya did, and she recounted to a hushed courtroom the time that her father had reduced her mother to tears at his own birthday party because she'd undercooked the cake.

Angela's psychiatrist spent a full day on the stand testifying about the mental anguish inflicted by her sadistic husband, about how Michael played upon Angela's lifelong fear of abandonment and her deep insecurities, about how Angela's inability to fight back only accelerated the downward spiral of their corrosive relationship. Throughout it all, her psychiatrist explained, Angela struggled to be the good wife, to keep up the façade, to try to placate her demanding husband in the hope that the bad Michael would somehow give way to the good Michael. In the end, when Michael finally walked out on her, she was besieged by feelings of failure. If indeed she'd been driven to kill him, the shrink opined, it would have been in a fit of madness—and the fact that she could remember none of it only proved the magnitude of her remorse.

The national interest in the trial seemed to double each day. Dominick Dunne sniffed around for a week or so and filed an elegant little chatter piece for *The New Yorker*. Even the *New York Post* got into the act, running the headline AVENGING ANGELA on the morning of closing arguments. Geraldo himself appeared on a split screen during the closing arguments. That way, he explained, he could watch Maria Fallaci on the studio monitor as his television audience could watch him watch. Geraldo put on a good show. Overcome by Fallaci's fiery coda, he actually raised his fist toward the camera in a Black Panther salute and shouted, "Right on!"

The analysts from Court TV, CNBC, and CNN agreed that Maria Fallaci's closing was breathtaking. But of course the analysts from Court TV, CNBC, and CNN hadn't been sitting on that white, suburban jury for the past five weeks, and those jurors just plain weren't buying any "battered wife" defense. It took them less than six hours to return a verdict of guilty on one count of murder in the second degree.

"What else bothered you about the file?" Maria asked.

"The gaps."

She shrugged. "There always are gaps. It's the nature of the beast. Which gap bothered you the most?"

"John."

"Her alibi witness?" She shook her head. "A dead end."

"I didn't see anything one way or the other in the file."

"Maybe in the *police* file. I had one of my investigators try to find him."

"And?"

"No such person." She returned to her desk and took a seat. "My investigator started with the hospital's records. He turned up three female patients who'd been in the hospital during the relevant period and had adult sons named John. Two of those Johns lived out of town, and only one of the two had come to St. Louis to visit his mother in the hospital. He'd come only once, and in no way resembled Angela's John. She agreed he wasn't the one."

"What about the third?"

"He lived in St. Louis, but it definitely wasn't him."

"Why not?"

"He's black, he's extremely obese, and he had an airtight alibi for the night of the murder."

I let it sink in. "So no John."

"No John."

"So no alibi."

"No alibi."

I leaned back in my chair and frowned. "I don't get it."

"Neither did I. So I ignored it."

There were twelve of us seated around the enormous conference table. We were on the sixty-third floor of River's Edge Tower, a curved-front steel-and-glass office building along Wacker Drive, high above the Chicago River. Only the caption was missing from our tableau.

Perhaps *Powwow of the Pomposities.*

Or *Assemblage of the Arrogant.*

Or maybe *Synod of the Self-Important.*

Here on behalf of Angela Green's publisher were three lawyers from the 275-lawyer Park Avenue firm of Braun, Proctor & Silverberg, led today by none other than the 275-pound Harvey Silverberg, self-styled First Amendment "freedom fighter"—fighting the good fight today at $600 an hour. But as Hefty Harvey was quick to point out, the price of liberty is not cheap. Nor were Harvey's bespoke London suit and platinum Rolex watch.

A team of four attorneys from the Century City firm of Corcoran Fox was here on behalf of the motion picture studio. At their helm was sixty-eight-year-old Nelson Liberman, tagged "the Silver Fox of Corcoran Fox" by *The American Lawyer.* Reputed to have graduated from Harvard Law School with the fourth highest grade-point average in the school's history, Liberman had represented everyone from Sam Goldwyn and Swifty Lazar to Steven Spielberg and Michael Ovitz. The tinted glasses and raspy voice only added to his Hollywood mystique.

Our hosts today were the Chicago attorneys of Mc-

Cambridge and Faber, retained by Maria Fallaci's publisher. Lead counsel for that crew was Hank Brunanski, who'd earned the moniker "Hammerin' Hank" during his tenure as U.S. attorney. Although Hank loved "dah Bears" and was proud of his "Sout' side" roots, his accent was deceiving. He'd graduated number one in his class at the University of Chicago, clerked for Supreme Court Justice Potter Stewart, and was blessed with a photographic memory. Hammerin' Hank regularly astonished courtroom observers while cross-examining witnesses by quoting verbatim from their depositions, and all without notes—*Do you recall, Mr. Aronson, that I took your deposition two years ago on March third? At page 112 of that deposition, I asked you, and I quote, "When you dictated your letter of April 17, 1997 . . ."*

An even dozen attorneys around the table—three from Braun, Proctor & Silverberg, four from Corcoran Fox, four from McCambridge and Faber, and—ta-da!—one from the Law Offices of Rachel Gold, all of us gathered together today by a clever lawsuit starring Trent Cummings, son of Samantha Cummings. The lawsuit contended that the eleven-year-old Trent was an heir of Michael Green by virtue of the doctrine of "equitable adoption." As Michael Green's alleged de facto stepson, Trent was suing for his inheritance. Ordinarily, this would have been the most pointless of lawsuits, the litigation equivalent of trying to squeeze blood out of a turnip, since the estate of Michael Green was insolvent. Green had gone to his grave at a particularly inopportune time financially, leaving an estate with more debts than assets. But Trent's lawyer was no ordinary plaintiff's shark, and there was nothing in the least bit ordinary about his lawsuit. He'd done something never before attempted in Missouri. He'd filed a Son of Sam claim.

As the name suggests, a Son of Sam claim is based on a law enacted in the aftermath of the serial killer who terrorized New York City during the summer of 1977 under the pseudonym Son of Sam. By the time the police identified David Berkowitz as Son of Sam and apprehended him, the rights to his story were worth millions. The New York legislature—outraged at the prospect of a mass murderer profiting from his notoriety while the families of his victims remained uncompensated—enacted the first Son of Sam law. It provided that all income otherwise payable to a convicted or admitted criminal from any book, motion picture, or other work depicting the crime must instead be paid to the New York crime victims board for use in compensating victims of the crime and their families. Ironically, the law captured millions of dollars from the perpetrators of several highly publicized homicides but not a penny from the original target, since it applied only to people actually convicted of a capital crime. David Berkowitz was found mentally incompetent to stand trial and thus was never convicted of anything.

The U.S. Supreme Court eventually declared New York's Son of Sam law unconstitutional, but other states enacted their own versions, each with its own twist. Missouri's covered not merely royalties payable to the criminal but also half of the revenues payable to anyone else involved in the creation of a book or dramatic work about either the criminal or the trial. Little Trent Cummings, as an alleged heir of the victim, was seeking all royalties payable to Angela and half of the money to be earned by Maria Fallaci, by the respective publishers of her book and Angela's, and by the producers of any movies based on those books. Trent, as the child of Samantha Cummings, was, quite literally, a son of Sam, and thus his lawsuit was truly a first: a real Son of Sam asserting a Son of Sam claim. The media tagged it "Sam Squared."

Although the other firms had each retained a St. Louis attorney to serve as local counsel, that role in this case would be only one small step up the evolutionary ladder from a mail drop. Indeed, none of those St. Louis attorneys was present today. By contrast, I was the local yokel who'd somehow, some way, ended up as the sole attorney for the central defendant in Sam Squared. To say the least, that made me a disconcerting presence at the table. I was a solo practitioner from the boonies who, God forbid, was answerable to no higher authority in a different time zone. While I assumed that one of the flunkeys on each team of lawyers had done a background check on my credentials, they would no doubt assume that the benefits of a Harvard Law School education had long since been squandered during my sojourn in the fly-over land. Their unease made me smile.

We had plenty of important issues to cover that morning—strategy questions ranging from a challenge to the constitutionality of Missouri's Son of Sam law to the various possible defenses to the "equitable adoption" theory. Instead, I spent two hours watching the alpha dogs take turns marking their territory as their entourages looked on approvingly. Harvey Silverberg staked out the First Amendment high ground, subjecting us to an eye-glazing summary of the three "seminal decisions" in the field, all of which, coincidentally enough, featured Hefty Harvey as lead counsel for the victors. Next came Nelson Liberman, who lifted his hind leg and sprayed us with a discourse on the importance of burying the other side in a blizzard of motions and discovery requests. Then it was Hammerin' Hank's turn. He sniffed around the perimeter and spouted a lengthy reenactment of his cross-examination in a bribery case from the 1980s, the relevance of which completely eluded me but apparently galvanized the others into a decision to focus their efforts on a constitutional challenge to the Son of Sam law. I didn't even bother to dissent, having already concluded that this high-priced wrecking crew was as likely to demolish its own clients as the other side. Instead, I would chart my own course and keep a lookout in the courtroom for errant spurts from the big dogs.

As the meeting drew to a close, Hammerin' Hank's first lieutenant, a severe junior partner named Catherine Hart, turned to me with a rigid smile. "Rachel, can you give us some local flavor?"

"Local flavor?" I asked sweetly, ignoring the condescension in her tone.

"A feel for the things down there. For example, have you had any experience before Judge Byrne?"

"Actually, I have."

"Oh, really? And what kind would that be?"

"A trial and two preliminary injunction hearings."

Catherine Hart drew back.

I couldn't resist. "First chair," I added.

As a junior partner in the litigation department of a large Chicago law firm, Catherine Hart probably had yet to first-chair a single trial.

"I see," she said, quickly regaining her patronizing air. "Would you have any helpful suggestions for our constitutional challenge?"

I shrugged. "It doesn't really matter how you pitch it."

"Why do you say that?"

"Because he's going to deny it anyway."

She gave me a perplexed look. "Why would you say that?"

"Judge Byrne ducks tough decisions. That's his style. If there's a way he can pass the buck to the jury, he'll do it. If not, he'll sidestep it and let the court of appeals decide. You should raise the constitutional issue—if for no other reason than to preserve it for appeal. But don't view it as a substitute for trial preparations, because"—I paused to look around the table—"sooner than you realize we're going to be sitting together at counsel's table picking a St. Louis jury."

H ave you met her?"
       I shook my head. "Not yet."
"You're going to be surprised."
"Why do you say that?"
"The press demonized her. They completely missed the mark. She's, well"—his eyes seemed to go out of focus—"she's lovely." He took a sip of his martini and stared down at the green olive. "My father would have been a very lucky man."

Michael Green Jr. and I were in a hotel bar along Michigan Avenue. He'd initially refused to meet, but after three phone calls from St. Louis he agreed to give me a few minutes between the end of my defense counsel meeting and my ride to O'Hare.

Unlike his sister, who'd inherited the worst of each of her parents' features, Michael junior was, in the words of my niece, a "hotty." He had chiseled good looks, light brown skin, clear green eyes, and the lean build of a professional tennis player. As he had strolled through the bar area to my booth in his investment banker pinstripes, I'd noticed several female heads turning to follow him. The waitress giggled and flirted when she took his order, but he hadn't responded.

"How did you get to know her?" I asked.

"I met her when they got engaged. The three of us— Sam, my father, and I—used to go out to dinner whenever I came to town."

"Did you ever see your father around her son?"

"Once or twice. He was good with Trent. Very affectionate. He told me he was looking forward to raising another son."

"What about after your father died?"

His green eyes narrowed. "What about what?"

"Did you still see her?"

He took a sip of his martini and watched the olive shift in the clear liquid. "The rest of her so-called friends abandoned her. The media camped outside her apartment. It was a bad time for her. She was very much in love with my father, and suddenly she was all alone—just her and her son." He paused. "I tried to be helpful."

"What about now? Are you still in touch?"

"What does that have to do with anything?"

"She's suing your father's estate. If she wins, you lose."

He shrugged. "So? She could use the money. I don't need it. Neither does my sister."

"What about your mother?"

He chuckled. "My mother? Are you kidding? She'll have Oprah and the rest of those ridiculous women fawning over her the rest of her life. People used to insult Sam by saying she'd be nothing more than a trophy wife for my father, but look at what's happened to my mother. My God, the woman has become everyone's trophy widow."

"Maybe now," I said, "but that won't last. Nothing changes faster than a celebrity's favorite cause or the media's latest darling. Five years from now her fans will have a new pet."

"So? Forgive me here, Miss Gold, but I'm having trouble working up a lot of sympathy for the person that killed my father."

"Let's get back to Sam."

"What about her?"

"Are you still in touch?"

He frowned. "Haven't you already asked me that?"

"I did. You didn't answer."

"Why do you care?"

"I'm defending your mother, Michael. Sam's on the other side. I'm trying to learn about her."

"That's between you and her, then. I'm neutral."

"Are you?"

He stared at me, a vein pulsing at his temple. "Yes," he finally said. He checked his watch. "I'm also late." He removed a money clip from his pocket, peeled off a twenty-dollar bill, dropped it on the table, and stood up. "Goodbye, Miss Gold."

CHAPTER 8

I didn't expect much help from Beverly Toft, and I didn't get it. Not because she didn't want to help. Far from it. She kept apologizing. It was just that Michael Green had drawn a shroud over his personal life when he started his affair with Samantha Cummings, having correctly assumed that Beverly Toft would side with Angela. Although Beverly had been his secretary for more than a decade, she'd also grown close to Angela. In addition, she had her own reason for empathizing with Angela's situation. Beverly's marriage had ended a few years before Angela's did, and under similar circumstances. Her husband Earl left her for a thirty-three-year-old waitress named Tammy who worked at the Denny's restaurant where Earl and Beverly had been having Sunday dinner for years. Tammy had often been their waitress—a fact that irked and mortified Beverly to this day, especially when she thought back to the huge tips that her tightwad husband used to leave that chippie, who'd wiggled her tight little heinie at him from that very first dinner.

I'd met Beverly for lunch at Café Napoli's in suburban Clayton, where she now worked for a small accounting firm. Although she was about my mother's age, she seemed a full decade older in her 1950s hairdo and bifocals.

"Oh, I knew Mr. Green was up to some hanky-panky," Beverly told me, her penciled eyebrows arching disapprovingly. "A wife might miss it—I certainly did with Earl, that creep. But believe you me, honey, a secretary knows the moment her boss becomes a tomcat. We're talking about long lunches that weren't on his appointment calendar, the bottle of men's cologne that suddenly appeared in his office, those sneaky phone calls, the bills from the florist and the jewelry store and the motels. I kept hoping for poor Angela's sake that it was just a fling, one of those midlife-male-crisis things that fizzle out." She shook her head, her lips pursed with censure.

Although Michael had invited her to the wedding and she had reluctantly planned to attend, her relationship with her boss had long since cooled into a strictly professional one. She'd met Samantha, of course. Once the divorce proceedings started and Michael's affair became public, Samantha used to call the office and occasionally drop by, either at lunch or the end of the day.

"I admit she was a friendly little thing," Beverly sniffed. "You know the type—very perky, very sweet, very young."

"But you never met her son?"

"No."

"Or saw Michael around him?"

She sighed. "I wish I could help you, honey. I really do. But he never even talked to me about the boy. He must have known how disappointed I was in him. I typed the draft of the new will, of course. Mr. Green dictated it himself. But he never said anything about it to me. The will was just one of several documents on a dictation tape in my in box."

"What about Samantha? Did she ever ask you about the will?"

Beverly thought about it and shook her head. "No."

"When she came around, what did you two talk about?"

"Sometimes her son—how he was doing in nursery school, that sort of thing. Sometimes her art gallery. Mr. Green did some legal work for the gallery, you know." She paused. "Come to think of it, you should talk to Stanley Brod."

Stanley Brod was a partner in the small accounting firm where Beverly now worked. I remembered from the police file that he'd been Michael Green's personal accountant.

"Why Stanley Brod?" I asked.

"Mr. Green had him do the accounting for her art gallery. Stanley's people spent a lot of time with her. His firm continued handling her books and records until the gallery closed down. I can talk to Stanley when I get back to the office. He's a very sweet man. I'm sure he'll meet with you."

The waiter brought our meals. We made small talk for a while as I tried to find the best way to broach the other subject I wanted to discuss. I finally decided that the best way was the direct way.

"During the murder investigation," I said, "did the police ask you about other possible suspects?"

Beverly frowned. "What do you mean?"

"When a lawyer gets killed," I explained, "any list of suspects ought to include his disgruntled clients."

Beverly leaned back in the booth, her eyebrows arched. "Interesting. They never even asked."

"What if they had?"

She gave me a knowing look. "Oh, I'd have told them a few things."

"Such as?"

Beverly studied me. "Why do you want to know this? What does it have to do with your case?"

I shrugged. "Maybe nothing. According to the criminal file, Angela became the sole suspect by the end of the second day. No one bothered with other possible suspects, including any enemies Michael Green might have had." I paused and shook my head. "I just can't believe she did it."

She nodded. "Neither can I."

"If they hadn't arrested Angela, would you have suspected any client?"

"Sure."

Beverly told me that from the moment she learned of the murder she'd had her own list of suspects. Number one on that list was Billy Berger, the founder, chairman, and majority shareholder of Gateway Trust Company and a notoriously slick wheeler-dealer. Michael had thousands of trust accounts at Gateway Trust Company, one for each of the children he'd represented in a personal-injury class action against a pharmaceutical company. As such, Michael was not merely an important customer but a force within the trust company through his control of a significant percentage of the assets under management. Three weeks before his death, Michael announced his intention to move the trust accounts to Guaranty Trust. According to Beverly, the two men got into a shouting match in Michael's office three days before the murder.

"I don't think he'd be the one to pull the trigger, of course," Beverly said. "But Mr. Berger would certainly know how to hire one. He was that type."

"What did they argue about?"

"I don't know, and Mr. Green refused to tell me. He said it wasn't any of my business. But they were angry, believe you me. You should have heard the words they called each other." She fanned herself with her hand. "Such language."

Number two on Beverly's list was Millie Robinson, ex-wife of former St. Louis Cardinals outfielder Larry Robinson. Millie was a recovering cocaine addict who'd lost custody of her children in a postdivorce battle in which Michael had represented her ex-husband. When the court awarded full custody to Larry Robinson, he promptly moved to Detroit with the children. That was one month before Michael died.

"Millie called Mr. Green day and night, screaming obscenities and death threats. I was the one who answered the daytime calls." Beverly shuddered. "It was awful."

"Did you report her to the police?"

"Mr. Green said not to. He said she'd get over it."

"Did she?"

"I don't know. The calls tapered off. I didn't receive one from her that last week."

"How about Michael? Was he still getting calls at home?"

"He didn't mention it."

Number three was Jerry Feckler.

"You're kidding. The Dingdong Man?" I was grinning.

Beverly gave me a weary smile. "The very same."

"Good grief, I'd forgotten Michael represented him."

Jerry Feckler, aka the Dingdong Man, became Michael Green's client about a year after undergoing an experimental surgical procedure on his penis. The poor man was hoping that longer and thicker would equal more and better luck with women. Alas, more equaled less and worse. Although he did gain approximately an inch in length, the fat liposuctioned from his love handles and injected into his penis for added girth gradually migrated south, leaving him with a weird appendage about as useful in bed as a bell clapper, which it happened to resemble. Unfortunately for Jerry, a nationally syndicated columnist got wind of the lawsuit, flew down for the medical malpractice trial, and wrote a funny column that got wide distribution during a slow news week. The headline said it all: LONG DONG DREAM BECOMES DINGDONG NIGHTMARE.

When his medical malpractice suit ended in a defense verdict, Jerry's odds of getting laid got a whole lot longer. He blamed it all on his lawyer, whom he then sued for legal malpractice. Two months before Michael Green died, the judge dismissed Feckler's malpractice case against him, inspiring the *Post-Dispatch*'s headline writer once again: JUDGE RINGS FINAL BELL FOR DINGDONG MAN; RULES FECK-LER'S CLAIM FECKLESS.

Feckler's final communication with Michael was a enraged message left the next night on the office phone-mail warning Michael that "misery loves company, especially miserable dicks, you sleazy bastard."

Visions of malformed penises were dancing in my head, though not quite like sugar plums, when I returned to the office and discovered that the afternoon's mail had brought me the petition in *Blackwell Breeders LLC and Charlie Blackwell* v. *Maggie Lane and Sara Freed.*

The crazy ostrich case.

I read the petition with a skeptic's eye. Charlie Blackwell alleged that my clients "acquired sole custody and control of said ostrich at an especially sensitive stage in its development." He claimed that "if said ostrich has any alleged defect, then the proximate cause of said defect is the negligent animal husbandry procedures, general incompetence, and degenerate lifestyles of said defendants."

But he saved the best—or rather, the worst—for last. When I reached the final page, I stared at the signature block: "MacReynold Armour, Attorney for Plaintiffs."

"Oh, great," I groaned aloud.

Mack Armour, aka Mack the Knife, was the kind of litigator who made opponents consider career changes—that is, when they weren't considering ethics complaints and contract hits. Although I'd never faced him before, I knew his reputation. He was belligerent, devious, and brazen—and to top it off, an unabashed male chauvinist pig. He was always looking for the sly angle in his lawsuits, and this case was a perfect example. Blackwell Breeders should have been the defendant in the case, but Armour jumped the starting gun and filed first, seeking a declaratory judgment that his client didn't have to refund a penny. As an added bargaining chip, he tacked on Charlie Blackwell's ludicrous claim for mental anguish. His goal: scare off my clients.

They didn't scare.

"We're not backing down," Maggie told me over the phone after I'd described Mack the Knife.

"He'll drag your personal lives into it, Maggie. He'll try to turn the case into a freak show."

"We understand," she said calmly. "This is a matter of principle, Rachel. Mr. Blackwell cheated us. When he learned of the problem we had with his ostrich, he should have done the right thing on his own, but he refused. So now we'll ask a judge to make him do it. We're not looking for sympathy, Rachel, and we're not looking for favors. We're looking for justice."

"You won't always find it in a courtroom."

"We understand that. If we lose, we lose. We can deal with it, Rachel. We're big girls. Just get us our day in court."

Beverly called around five to tell me that Stanley Brod could meet me tomorrow morning at nine. I'd planned on spending the morning getting ready for a deposition that afternoon in a copyright case, but I thanked Beverly and told her to let Stanley know I'd be at his office at nine. Then I canceled my dinner plans, called Domino's Pizza, and settled down to do tomorrow's deposition preparation tonight. I didn't get home until almost ten o'clock. I was feeling crabby and antsy and tired. I knew the cure.

"Hey, Oz," I said, kneeling next to the greatest golden retriever in the universe. "Wanna go for a jog?"

Ozzie wagged his tail and padded off to the kitchen, returning a moment later with his leash in his mouth.

"Let me change first, cutie." I patted him on the head. "I can't run in these heels."

He followed me to my bedroom, where I slipped off my attorney clothes and put on my jogging outfit. As I tied my Nikes, he sat on the rug at the foot of my bed, the leash on the rug between his front paws. He listened attentively as I filled him in on my day.

"So I'll meet with his accountant tomorrow morning," I told him as I stood up. "We'll see what he can tell me." Ozzie seemed to think that was a good idea, since he wagged his tail, barked once, and picked up the leash.

We took the five-mile route. I spent most of the run trying to figure out what I was doing and where I was going with Angela's case. I supposed that Stanley Brod might be able to shed some light on the equitable adoption issue in the lawsuit, and he'd eventually get to repeat it under oath when the clown patrol representing the other defendants fired up their discovery juggernaut. But I knew that my real interest in Stanley, like my real interest in Beverly Toft, was the possibility of finding a new angle on the crime at the heart of the Son of Sam case. I could rationalize it as part of the defense—after all, the Son of Sam claim would vanish if Angela were exonerated—but that was nothing more than a rationalization. I hadn't been retained to clear her of the murder charge.

Angela had seemed intrigued during our prison meeting when I pointed out the holes in the homicide investigation, but she'd by no means evinced a determination to clear herself of the criminal conviction. Perhaps she'd become reconciled to what she deemed to be immutable. And perhaps there was something more subtle afoot. Seeing what had happened to her since the murder trial, I could understand if she felt a tinge of ambivalence at the prospect of reopening the criminal case. She'd truly become, in the words of her estranged son, a trophy widow. Her role as celebrity martyr for various women's and minority organizations depended upon her image as the abused and spurned first wife who'd finally turned on her tormentor. Her life behind bars had invested her with an esteem and dignity that had eluded her during marriage. Within the controlled and cloistered world of a women's prison, Angela had become a saint—adored by the inmates that she tutored and counseled, honored by the prison administrators who bragged about her at national conventions, and fawned over by visiting members of the press. If it turned out she'd been innocent from the start, that she'd been framed, a mere pawn in someone else's deadly game, how much of her new persona would she lose?

But that was ultimately her decision, not mine. And it was purely conjectural at this point, I reminded myself. Angela had no decision to make—her appeals had run out and it would be years before she was eligible for parole. Talk of freedom was purely academic. But if she hadn't killed Michael Green—if she'd been unjustly convicted—then I owed it to her to try to make an academic choice a real one.

So I'd meet with Stanley Brod in the morning, and I'd give the names of Beverly's three suspects to one of my investigators for a quick background check. If that uncovered anything, I'd follow the leads. And if not, then I'd worry about my other cases and wait for the circus train to arrive with Hefty Harvey, the Silver Fox, Hammerin' Hank, and the rest of the clown patrol.

CHAPTER 9

"None of them," I repeated, shaking my head in outrage. "Not even a telephone interview."

"Can you blame them?" Benny took a long pull on his beer and reached for another handful of Welsh chips. "Would you want to spend time around a guy with a dick that looks like a Tootsie Roll pop on steroids?"

"No, but I'm not a cop investigating a homicide, Benny. These were people with serious grudges against Michael Green. No one talked to them."

It was two days after my night jog with Ozzie. Benny and I were at Llywelyn's Pub in the Central West End, where we'd met for drinks after work. I was headed to a dinner meeting at the Jewish Federation and he was going downtown for a date with a woman lawyer from L.A. named Sheila who was in town for a closing. They'd met at a Practicing Law Institute program last summer, where Benny was supposed to participate in a panel discussion on recent developments in antitrust law. He claimed the two of them remained in his hotel room for all but one of the next thirty-six hours—the lone hour away being for his panel discussion. Of course, Benny claimed a lot of things, especially in the realm of his amatory abilities.

"Hey, Rachel, there are people out there with serious grudges against me, but no cops are talking to them."

"That's because you aren't dead."

"I guess that's a good point. So what's your investigator found on Beverly's three suspects?"

"Not much yet." I watched as he grabbed another enormous handful of Welsh chips and stuffed them in his mouth. "Benny, aren't you supposed to be taking this woman to dinner first?"

"And your point is?"

"This is your second basket. Save a little room, boychik."

He washed the chips down with a drink of beer. "Just stoking the old furnace."

He was dressed to kill, Benny style: red Converse hightops, baggy chinos, and a black T-shirt with the legend I Am an Endomorph—Please Help Me. He gave me a wink. "I'm going to need endurance tonight."

I raised my eyebrows. "Oh?"

"Sheila may hail from L.A.," he said, "but inside a hotel room that woman becomes the Boston Marathon of Love."

"The Boston Marathon of Love?" I rolled my eyes. "Who writes your material? Barry White?"

He grabbed some more chips, pausing to ask, "What about his accountant? Cops talk to him?"

"Nope."

"You met him, right? Stanley something-or-other."

"Brod. Stanley Brod. We met yesterday. I went back to his office this morning to look through some boxes of records he retrieved from the storage warehouse."

"What's the story with him?"

"Seems like a decent guy. Decent enough to get embarrassed and admit ignorance when I asked him about an odd overlap in the records that he'd never spotted before."

"What do you mean?"

"After Michael Green started dating Samantha Cummings, he had Stanley handle the books and records for her art gallery."

"Is that place still around?"

"No, it closed less than a year after Michael died. From

the records, it looks like the gallery's revenues dried up almost immediately after his murder. She ran it at a loss for several months before her creditors finally forced her to close it down and liquidate the assets."

"What's she do these days?"

"She works in that fancy jewelry store at Plaza Frontenac."

"Have you met her?"

"Not yet, but I'm sure we'll be taking her deposition before long. Why? You don't know her, do you?"

He shook his head. "I don't think so, but she looks awfully familiar for some reason."

"Were you ever in her gallery?"

"No."

"She was on TV during the trial."

"She looked familiar back then, too. She's a babe."

I took a sip of my ale and nodded.

Benny said, "So you mentioned an odd overlap in the records. What is it?"

"I spent two hours looking through the files for the art gallery," I explained. "I'm going to spend some more time next week, too. The records I reviewed showed that she paid six thousand dollars to an outfit called Millennium Management Services for every painting sold by an artist named Sebastian Curry. The payments were listed as 'agency commissions.' "

"How many payments we talking about?"

"According to the financial records, over a two-year period the 309 Gallery paid one hundred thirty-eight thousand dollars in commissions to Millennium."

"That's a lot of dough."

"That's also a lot of paintings by one artist. Twenty-three altogether, which is far more than any other artist during that period. They weren't cheap, either. Almost all of the Sebastian Curry paintings sold for fifteen thousand dollars."

"That Millennium outfit got a six grand commission off of that?"

"Looks like it. She'd pay the artist seven thousand, Millennium six, and keep the other two as profit."

"Any other payments to Millennium?"

"No, just the Sebastian Curry paintings."

"Must be his agent."

"That's what I assumed, too."

"But?"

I frowned. "That's where the overlap comes in. Guess who else was paying money to Millennium Management Services?"

"Another gallery?"

I shook my head. "Gateway Trust Company."

"Huh?"

"That's where Michael Green had all those trust accounts for minors when he settled that big class action against the drug company. Gateway was paying Millennium Management Services an annual 'consulting fee' of one-third of a percent on every trust fund he established there."

"How much we talking?"

"According to Stanley Brod, the total settlement amount was about thirty million, which means that the fees had to be running about a hundred thousand dollars a year."

"How did you find out Gateway was paying those fees?"

"Because Stanley maintained a file for Michael on each of those trust funds. The payments to Millennium show up on the annual statements from Gateway."

"So this Millennium outfit represents artists *and* provides consulting services to trust companies. What's the story with that?"

I shrugged. "That's what I'm hoping Billy Berger can tell

me. He's the chairman of Gateway Trust Company. I'm meeting with him tomorrow morning."

"But what does Brod say?"

"He doesn't. He knew about the trust company's fees, but Michael never talked to him about them. He'd never made the connection with the art gallery commissions to Millennium until I pointed it out to him. He seemed kind of embarrassed about it. Felt he should have spotted the overlap himself."

"Why didn't he?"

"It really wasn't his fault. One of his assistants handled the books for the gallery. I don't think Stanley paid much attention to them. He was doing it mainly as a favor to Michael Green. When I was showing him the entries I could tell he wasn't familiar with the records."

"Have you talked to anyone at Millennium?" Benny asked.

"I have to find them first. They're not in the phone book and I don't have an address for them. I've got Jacki working on it."

We paid the bill and stepped out into the late afternoon summer air. Benny walked me to my car, which was parked half a block north on Euclid.

"So when's your next meeting with the rebbe?" Benny asked with a grin.

"We meet tonight," I said. "After the dinner thing at the federation. Actually, I'm meeting with the rabbi's wife again."

"Oh, great. Is this going to be chapter two in the joys of Jewish life on the rag, or is tonight the night she turns you into a *balabusta*?"

Balabusta is the Yiddish expression for "mistress of the house." It's the term of affection and admiration for the classic Orthodox Jewish woman who functions in the role of chairman and CEO of the household.

"Actually, neither. Believe it or not, tonight the topic is sex."

"No shit? Jewish sex?"

I held up my hand. "Don't start."

"Me?" he asked, feigning innocence.

"Yeah, you. Good luck on the marathon, Barry White."

He grinned. "Wait until you see me charge up Heartbreak Hill."

"I think I'll pass."

I miss you, too, sweetie," Jonathan said.

I was lying on the couch in my bathrobe and white socks, the phone cradled between my neck and shoulder. Al Green was on the stereo and Ozzie was curled on the floor below me, his big brown eyes watching my face. I'd been reading *Daniel Deronda* when Jonathan called from the midtown Manhattan law office he was using during the trial. It was close to midnight for him—another late night of preparations in a securities fraud prosecution that was getting daily front-page ink in the *New York Times*. The good news: the defense was going well for Jonathan's client. The bad news: the government was still weeks from resting, which meant the trial would last longer than expected.

We talked about his trial and his daughters and his parents and then he said, "Tell me about Angela Green."

I described what I'd learned so far, including my initial review of the accounting records at Stanley Brod's office. I was relieved to be finally talking to a former prosecutor and thus someone with more experience in this area than me.

He listened quietly. When I was through, he said, "It's still a long shot."

I sighed. "I realize that."

"But you may have stumbled across a money trail. If you have, that could change everything."

"How so?"

"Most murders are about anger or revenge, and this one fits that profile. Whether the killer was Angela Green or one of Michael Green's angry ex-clients, the odds are that the murder was a crime of passion."

"But what if it wasn't?"

"Then there'll be a money trail."

"Why do you say that?"

"Because if it wasn't a crime of passion, then he was killed over money."

"I don't know, Jonathan. He doesn't seem to have had much money."

"Maybe he did and maybe he didn't, but trust me on this. Somebody's money—his or someone else's—will hold the key to his death if it wasn't a crime of passion. He'll be connected to that money somehow. Just follow it."

"I'm trying to."

"Stay on the money trail and you'll up end at the killer's doorsteps."

"Yes, sir."

He paused and then chuckled. "Sorry. I tend to get a little carried away at this time of the night."

"How about at *any* time of the night or the day?"

He laughed.

"Poor thing," I said, glancing at my watch, "it's really late for you. Are you almost ready for bed?"

"Soon. I have maybe an hour of preparation for a cross-examination tomorrow."

I groaned. "I wish that trial would end already."

"I know."

Jonathan Wolf was New York City–born and –bred. He'd been raised an Orthodox Jew, and as a child attended a Jewish day school steeped in bookish traditions. Somehow, though, he fell in love with boxing. From his bar mitzvah on, he fought in every Golden Gloves competition in the area. At the age of seventeen, he won the Brooklyn title and traveled to Madison Square Garden to compete against the title holders from the other four boroughs. Jimmy Breslin tagged him "the Talmudic Tornado."

He started his legal career in the U.S. attorney's office in St. Louis, his wife's hometown. During his prosecutor days he'd been a classic intimidator—stalking criminal defendants in the courtroom as if they were prey, boring in on them with rapid-fire questions. Six years ago his wife died of ovarian cancer, leaving behind two adorable little daughters, Leah and Sarah. He resigned from the U.S. attorney's office and hung out a shingle as a criminal defense attorney. It was an astounding career change, and astoundingly successful. Although one might think that a Brooklyn accent and an embroidered yarmulke would be a drawback in front of a St. Louis jury, he'd become a preeminent defense attorney with a growing national practice. He was in his early forties now, his close-trimmed black beard flecked with gray. He was also drop-dead gorgeous and the sexiest man in the world, although I might have been a little biased on the subject.

"I almost forgot," I said, smiling, "I had another session tonight."

"With the rabbi?"

"No, his wife again."

"And?" His tone was guarded.

"Very interesting."

"That sounds a little more promising. What did you two cover?"

"Sex."

"Ah, yes. The laws of *onah*."

"I'm pleased to report that things are finally starting to look up, big guy."

"That's good to hear."

"You never told me about the sex part."

"You never asked me about the sex part."

"Never asked? How would I have ever guessed? All those pious Jewish men in their beards and yarmulkes and dark suits. How was I supposed to know what was going on behind those bedroom doors."

He was laughing.

"According to Mrs. Kalman," I said, "one of the fundamental commandments of Jewish law is a husband's duty to sexually satisfy his wife. You never told me this."

"You never asked."

"When a wife is ready for some hanky-panky, her husband better be ready, willing, and able to perform—and he better do a good job, too. Otherwise, she has grounds for divorce. The whole thing is right there in the marriage contract."

"I never read the fine print."

"You better, big boy. You would not believe all the official guidelines." I sat up on the couch. "It's like the Jewish *Kama Sutra*. First the husband has to have a nice loving conversation with his wife. Then he has to do lots of hugging and kissing. And he has to be naked. In fact, if the husband refuses to get naked with his wife, it's grounds for divorce."

"What about the wife?" Jonathan asked.

"She has to be naked, too."

"That sounds good."

"I'll say. But wait. There's more. When the husband makes love, he has to be enthusiastic. It's Jewish law. Let me read you this thing." I reached for my briefcase at the foot of the couch and snapped it open. "Mrs. Kalman had me write it down. Listen to this. There was this medieval Jewish sage named Rabenu Yaakov. He wrote the definitive Jewish guide of the Middle Ages, something called the *Tur*. Here's what he said about marital sex: 'When a husband is intimate with his wife, his intent should not be his own pleasure but, rather, he should be as one honoring an obligation to another.' Mrs. Kalman said under Jewish law the husband is commanded to learn exactly what his wife wants in bed. You listening?"

"I'm all ears."

"Good. In fact, the learning part is so important that the Torah says the husband has to spend the entire first year of the marriage free from any outside distraction so that he can devote all of his energies to learning how to satisfy his wife."

"I think I could handle that."

"You better, Jonathan, because as near as I can tell, unbelievably good sex is the only possible explanation."

"For what?"

"For why those poor Orthodox woman are willing to put up with all that obnoxious male chauvinism. Frankly, your rabbi and I are not in synch here. Women can't be rabbis, can't be called up to the Torah, can't be witnesses in a Jewish court of law. Even worse, they have to stand by as their husbands recite that awful morning prayer thanking God for not making them a woman. I don't know about the rest of those women, Jonathan, but let me tell you something about me. It's going to take a steady diet of world-class lovemaking from you to make me put up with that prayer every morning. Now get back to work and win that case."

"Aye, aye, Captain."

"Kiss those adorable girls for me and tell them I miss them."

"I will."

"I love you, Jonathan."

"I love you, Rachel."

CHAPTER 10

Billy Berger's female assistant put me in a conference room and brought me hot coffee in a green mug that had Gateway Trust Company's familiar logo inscribed in gold. The front wall of the room consisted of floor-to-ceiling windows facing east with a dramatic view of the Mississippi River and the Arch. The other three walls picked up the coffee mug's color scheme—green walls hung with gold-framed photographs and historical prints of the St. Louis riverfront dating back to paddle wheelers along the levee. I sipped my coffee and watched a towboat push a double row of barges upriver, its powerful screws churning the brownish water into a cappuccino froth. The barges stretched out in front of the tow by the length of at least two football fields.

The door opened and Berger entered, followed by a younger man. The two resembled one of those before-and-after portraits, although which was which was not quite clear. Billy Berger was large and ruddy, with thick lips, broad features, big teeth, and a thatch of unruly brown hair. He reminded me of the head bear in Disney's Country Bear Jamboree. His sidekick was skinny and pale and fastidious, with severe steel-rimmed glasses resting on a pointy nose. Berger was in his early sixties but seemed far more vigorous than his sidekick, who was at least twenty years his junior.

"Howdy, Rachel," Berger said, reaching across the conference table to shake my hand with a big callused paw. "I'm Billy Berger. It's a real nice pleasure to meet you. This here is Mr. L. George Mizzler, our general counsel."

"Miss Gold," Mizzler said with a curt nod and reached across the table. His handshake was bony and moist and creepy. I resisted the urge to wipe my hand dry with a napkin.

The men took seats side by side across the table facing me. Mizzler placed a set of file folders on the table in front of him and frowned at them.

"I want to thank you both for meeting with me," I said.

Berger nodded and leaned back, lacing his fingers together and resting his massive hands on his paunch. "Our pleasure, Rachel." He gave me a hearty smile. "You have a mighty fine reputation in this town, both for your legal talents and for your loveliness. I'll say this right off the bat: you must be a regular Clarence Darrow if your admirers understated your legal talents to the same degree that they understated your beauty."

"Thank you, Mr. Berger. I think that's the most elaborate compliment I've ever received."

He chuckled and nodded his head as he looked toward his stern assistant. "I can tell this gal's a regular pistol, George." He turned to me. "And let's put a stop to that 'Mr. Berger' nonsense. Makes me feel like an old fart. Call me Billy."

I knew enough about Berger to resist his folksy manner. The trust business was the third snake pit he'd conquered in a remarkable career that had started after he dropped out of high school to sell used cars at his father's Chevy dealership. When a heart attack felled Russ Berger a few years later, his twenty-two-year-old son took over as the president of Berger Chevrolet. Sixteen years later, he sold his thriving dealership to one of his competitors and started a new career selling life insurance. Within three years, he'd become Northwestern Mutual's leading salesman in Missouri. Before the decade ended, he'd realized that there was an even more lucrative way to service the scores of doctors, lawyers, and business executives who were his customers, namely, handle their trusts and estates. Gateway Trust Company, founded nine years ago, now boasted a larger portfolio of assets under management than the trust departments of every local bank. While charm and corny jokes couldn't hurt your business, you don't accomplish in one career what Billy Berger had accomplished without also possessing a keen sense for an opponent's soft spots and a willingness to exploit that knowledge.

"I understand you're representing Angela Green these days," Berger said.

"I am. That's why I'm here."

"I had George here check our accounts." He nodded toward Mizzler. "Couple of living trusts, right?"

Mizzler opened two of the folders and read, " 'The Angela Green Living Trust Number One and the Angela Green Living Trust Number Two.' " He looked up, serious. "She receives monthly statements on both. Current assets in Trust Number One are"—he glanced down—"eighteen thousand three hundred and forty-one dollars and change. As for Trust Number Two, twenty-eight thousand five hundred and twenty dollars and change. If you'd care to review the statements, I have the most recent several months."

"No, thanks. I didn't come down to talk about her trusts. As you may know, I'm representing Ms. Green in a lawsuit filed by the son of Samantha Cummings. Miss Cummings was Michael Green's fiancée. The lawsuit is premised on the contention that Mr. Green had essentially adopted Miss Cummings's son at the time of his death."

"That's about what I heard," Berger said.

"I understand that your trust company did a lot of work with Mr. Green and his clients."

"I don't know that I'd call it a lot," Berger said, "but I'd agree that Michael was a good customer of ours."

"Were you friends?"

"Friends? You could say we were friendly. Not exactly bosom buddies. We grabbed a bite to eat together a few times a year—that sort of thing."

"Did he talk to you about Samantha Cummings?"

Berger pursed his lips in a thoughtful manner—or at least he feigned a thoughtful manner. I'd already realized that Berger—like any good car salesman—was a master of disguise when it came to what was really going on in his head. He could do "sincere" or "innocent" or "thoughtful" or whatever other emotion was to his advantage at the moment, arranging those broad, ruddy features into the appropriate mask. The only clue that something else might be going on behind the mask was the hard glint in his gray eyes.

Finally, he said, "I think he mentioned that gal during one of our last lunches. He was talking about the upcoming wedding—how excited he was and all that."

"Were you invited?"

"I can't recall. Probably."

"Did he talk about her son?"

Berger frowned. "It's not sticking out if he did. I guess it's possible, but I don't recollect."

I hadn't expected to get much out of this line of questioning, and I wasn't. It didn't matter. The questions were mainly fillers up front to cushion the real purpose of my meeting, which was about to start now.

"Your trust company is still handling trusts for a lot of his clients, correct?"

"His *former* clients," Mizzler said, a self-satisfied edge to his voice.

"His former clients," I repeated, giving Mr. Meticulous a pleasant nod. "Specifically, I'm referring to the children in the Merker class action. According to the court records, your trust company still files an annual statement with the clerk of the court on each of those cases."

I knew this because on my way downtown I'd stopped by the clerk's office and looked through several of the individual files in the class action.

"Why do you have an interest in those cases?" Mizzler asked sharply.

I shrugged, acting nonchalant. "Just trying to get a handle on Michael Green's activities during the last few years of his life. It might be relevant for my case. On the subject of those class action files, though, I did notice one difference since Michael Green's death."

"What was that?" Mizzler asked.

"There is no longer an annual service charge by Millennium Management Services."

Mizzler seemed puzzled. "Who?"

"Millennium Management Services," I repeated. "What did they do for you?"

Mizzler turned to Berger, who was gazing at me with his head tilted, as if he were pondering me or my question. Berger gave me a quizzical smile and said, "Now help me here, Rachel. How exactly do those class action files relate to the lawsuit against Mrs. Green?"

"I'm not quite sure."

Mizzler sniffed. "Then I'm not quite sure that we can answer your question. As a regulated financial institution we have certain confidentiality obligations toward our customers—especially those who are minors."

"Actually, Mr. Mizzler," I said, "that's not the case here. Those court files are public, and everything in them, including your annual reports to the court, are public. The reports you filed during the last three years of Michael Green's life show payments to Millennium Management Services. Since

Mr. Green's death, however, the reports show no such service charge."

"How is that relevant?" Mizzler snapped.

"That depends on what that outfit was doing for the trust company back then."

"Apparently," Berger said with an affable chuckle, "they were providing a service. Now I may be just an old car dealer, but I sure as hell don't plan to pay some outfit for nothing." He turned to Mizzler. "Let's check those files, George. See what we can turn up."

"What exactly is Millennium Management Services?" I asked them both.

Mizzler glanced at Berger, who was gazing at me. "I don't seem to recall," Berger said. "Maybe there'll be something in the files on that outfit. If so, we'll be sure to let you know."

"I'd appreciate that," I said, though I doubted whether I'd ever hear anything further from Gateway on the topic of Millennium Management Services. "One last thing. About a week or so before Michael Green's death, he had a big argument with you in his office. What was that all about?"

Mizzler stiffened angrily. "Are you attempting to contend that Mr. Berger's relationship with Mr. Green has any—"

"Hold your fire, George," Berger said, raising his hand like a traffic cop. He gave me a big smile. "I'll be frank, Rachel. I liked Michael, but he had what you could call a volatile temperament. The man could be a real hothead—which I suppose can be a good thing in a trial lawyer. If we had an argument that day, it sure wouldn't have been the first time."

"Did you have an argument?"

"Don't remember yea or nay."

"What did you used to argue about?"

"Oh, everything from sports to business to women."

Mizzler said, "This is entirely outside the scope of your lawsuit, Miss Gold. The trust company and Mr. Berger have been more than cooperative today, and I can assure you that if you need any additional information directly relevant to your client's case, we will be willing to take any such requests under advisement. Until such time, however, I must insist on adjourning this meeting."

Berger smiled and lumbered to his feet. "Guess I better follow my lawyer's orders, eh? It's what we pay 'em for. Been a real pleasure, Rachel. We ought to get together sometime for lunch or a drink. Just give my gal a buzz and see if we can set something up."

Nothing?" I repeated.

"Not a thing." Jacki shook her head. "I checked with the secretaries of state of Missouri, Illinois, and Delaware. I went by the public library and checked phone books from all over the country. Nothing on any company by that name."

We were in my office that afternoon.

"What about an Internet search?" I asked.

"I tried. I got about ten million hits for Millennium, but no Millennium Management Services."

"What about the payments on all those minors' trusts? Where did Gateway Trust send them?"

"According to the court records, to a lockbox in the Canary Islands."

"Terrific," I said glumly.

I reached for my telephone messages. I'd spent the lunch hour at the veterinarian's office getting Ozzie his annual checkup and a shot. Jacki had just returned from lunch with her new boyfriend.

"So how's Bob?" I asked, flipping through the messages.

She blushed. "He's doing fine."

"Things going okay down at UPS?"

"Bob thinks he's in line for a promotion."

"Inside work?"

"Yep."

"That's wonderful."

Bob was a big, burly guy—about as big and burly as Jacki. He had a dark beard and a wonderful smile. He was the UPS delivery guy in our area, which is how he met Jacki. He was an absolute doll, and—given the very existence of his relationship with Jacki—an open-minded individual.

"New dress?" I asked.

"I got it last weekend."

"Very nice."

"Really?" She colored again.

"Really."

I was smiling. After a frustrating morning meeting at Gateway Trust Company and forty minutes in the crowded waiting room at the veterinarian's office, the mere sight of my secretary buoyed my spirits. And what a sight she was. Jacki Brand was a former Granite City steelworker who was putting herself through night law school while working days as my secretary, paralegal, law clerk, and all-around aide. Standing six feet three and weighing close to two hundred and forty pounds, with plenty of steelworker muscles rippling beneath her size 22 shirtwaist dress, she was surely the most intimidating legal secretary in town. And also one of the best. I'd call her my girl Friday, except that anatomically she was still a he—and would so remain until next summer, when she would undergo the surgical procedure that would lop off the last dangling evidence that her name had once been Jack.

"What's on the schedule this afternoon?" I asked, putting down the phone messages and reaching for my calendar.

"Nothing but your meeting with Charlie at four."

Charlie Ross was the investigator I'd hired to do a quick background check on Billy Berger and Beverly Toft's other two suspects, Millie Robinson and the Dingdong Man.

"I called Stanley Brod from the vet's," I told her. "I asked if one of us could go over there this afternoon to look through his records on Samantha's art gallery. Maybe you could do that."

"Sure."

"I've already looked through the art gallery's payables ledger. Samantha was making payments to that Millennium outfit on each painting she sold by an artist named Sebastian Curry. I'm going to try to locate the artist. Meanwhile, we need to review the rest of the gallery's records to find out who bought the paintings."

Jacki frowned. "Why?"

"Because someone was paying Millennium every time one of those paintings sold. That means that Millennium was acting as either the artist's agent or the buyer's agent."

"Or maybe the gallery's agent."

"If so, then the buyer or the artist ought to know that." I paused, mulling over an idea that Jacki's comment had triggered. "Jacki, while you're over at Brod's office, see if he's got a roster of Michael Green's clients. Maybe in the billing files. If so, make a copy for us. Let's see if there are any matches between his clients and the buyers of those paintings."

"Why do you think there might be?"

"Just a hunch. Look at the chronologies. Two things happened shortly after Michael Green died. First, Gateway Trust stopped paying a service fee to Millennium. Second, Samantha's gallery stopped paying commissions to Millennium. Maybe there's no connection to Green's death, but he's the only link we know between Gateway and the gallery.

Jonathan told me to follow the money. So far, this is the only money trail I've found."

B rought us some goodies, counselor."
        I looked up from the appellate opinion I was reading. Charlie Ross stood in the doorway holding aloft a white bakery bag.

I smiled. "From World's Fair Donuts?"

"Where else? Got us some glazed and some cherry filled."

I placed my hand over my heart. "You're my hero, Charlie."

"Just don't tell the wife, huh? She got me on a new diet. Wants me to lose thirty pounds. Got a whole list of things I can eat—rice cakes, raw carrots, chicken bouillon, lettuce without salad dressing. I don't recall glazed doughnuts on that list."

"My lips are sealed."

He came in and sat down in the chair facing my desk. "Some diet. Lots of fiber and a grapefruit before every meal." He grimaced. "The wife's got me eating this cereal—looks like rabbit droppings. Gives me terrible gas. I'm thinking maybe the folks at Maalox are behind this diet."

"No fiber in doughnuts, Charlie."

"Not a trace," he said, with a contented grin.

"I'll get us some coffee. You like black, right?"

"That'd be fine."

Charlie Ross was an ex-FBI special agent who'd worked as a private investigator since his retirement from the government. He was good with records and even better with people, who tended to tell him far more than you'd expect, which was probably because he reminded them, like he reminded me, of the plump neighborhood butcher instead of the square-jawed G-man of crime-fighting lore. Although his jawline had long since softened into jowls, he was a resource-ful investigator who'd proved his mettle during his FBI days in a twelve-hour hostage crisis at Boatmen's Bank downtown and a four-day manhunt through the Ozarks.

As we ate our doughnuts and sipped our coffee, he filled me in.

"Plenty of court files on Billy Berger," he said, checking his notes. "Been divorced two times—looked through those files, talked to one of his ex-wives. Nothing special there. He never told her much about his financial affairs when they were married, and she's happy with the alimony arrange-ment."

"Why'd they get divorced?"

"The usual. Billy's got a zipper problem. Big time." He glanced at his notes. "Let's see. Got sued a few times during his days in the insurance business—disputes with policy holders. Two cases settled, another got dismissed. Been a plaintiff himself three times. Sued the contractor that built his last house, complaining about structural defects. Settled that one for one hundred twenty-three thousand dollars. In another case, he and three other investors sued the general partner of a real estate limited partnership when that deal went south. Some sort of condo development down in Bran-son, Missouri. Case settled last year, but the court file didn't have the settlement agreement in it. At present, he's got a suit pending against the company he bought his private jet from. Breach-of-warranty claim. Case is pending in St. Louis County." He closed his notepad. "Pretty much what you'd expect to find for one of those rich entrepreneur types."

"I had a meeting with him this morning."

"What'd you think?"

"Very smooth. Very slick. Very smart."

"That's why he did so well selling cars and insurance."

"What about the other two people?"

Charlie glanced down at his notes as he sipped his coffee. "Plenty of court files on Millie Robinson—what with the divorce, the cocaine problems, the custody battle with her ex." He looked up. "That's the one where Michael represented her ex-husband—that ballplayer."

"Larry Robinson."

"Right. He's living in Detroit with the kids. Here's an interesting one," he said, reading his notes. "She sued Gateway Trust Company a year ago."

"Really. Over what?"

"Can't tell. File is sealed."

"Which court?"

"City."

"Which division?"

He studied his notes. "Three."

"Three is equity. Could be a dispute over management of a trust. Could you tell from the other files whether she had a trust with Gateway?"

He paged through his notes. "Here we are—good thinking, Rachel. When she had her cocaine problem, the court ordered that her assets and all future alimony payments be deposited into a trust. The order appointed Gateway as the trustee."

"Think it's worth talking to her?"

Charlie scratched his neck. "Might be. I'll look her up."

"How about the Dingdong Man?"

Charlie chuckled. "That's really something, isn't it? Poor bastard." He flipped through his notes. "Feckler moved to Kansas City last year. He's working as a paralegal at the firm that represents all those tobacco companies. No court records on him over there. Must be keeping his nose clean. But here's something interesting from before he moved. Samantha Cummings swore out a complaint against him two years after Michael Green's murder."

"For what?"

"She claimed he was harassing her."

"How so?"

"Nasty phone calls, creepy letters. About her and Michael. Some pretty sick stuff. Like who missed his penis the most—her or Michael."

"Oh, God."

"The guy is one sick puppy. She swore out a complaint and the cops arrested him. Judge gave him six months' probation and ordered him to keep away from her. The arresting officer is a vice squad detective named Vic Riganti. I talked to him this morning. He remembered the case. Said he thought Feckler was your basic harmless wacko."

"Do you agree?"

Charlie frowned as he scratched his neck. "Hard to say. Those types usually are."

"But aren't their phone calls and letters usually anonymous?"

"Usually."

"But not here."

"That's true."

I sighed in frustration. "The police never even talked to him after Michael Green's murder."

Charlie nodded. "That trail's pretty cold by now."

"They all are."

He pursed his lips thoughtfully. "You're better off following the money."

"That's what Jonathan told me, too."

"He's right, Rachel. I worked the Hornig car bombing for Jonathan back when he was at the U.S. attorney. We followed the money trail right to the brother-in-law's door."

I leaned back in my chair. "I wish I could talk to Samantha."

"Why can't you?"

"We're on opposite sides of this lawsuit. I can't talk to her without her lawyer present. I doubt whether he'd let me talk to her anyway—especially with all the other defendants and lawyers involved. He'll tell me to take her deposition. That way he can keep it all on the record and avoid inconsistent statements."

"Maybe," Charlie said, removing a second glazed doughnut from the bag. "But what if you had a topic she didn't want to have on the record?" He took a bite and chewed thoughtfully. He washed it down with a sip of coffee. "What if it was a subject her lawyer didn't want the other lawyers to know about? Maybe he'd let you have a private session."

"Maybe so, but I don't have anything like that here."

"Not yet."

I looked at Charlie. "What's that mean?"

He shrugged. "No promises, Rachel, but let me do a little poking around. You do this kind of work for thirty-five years and you learn to spot patterns. Pretty gal like that, coming out of nowhere, suddenly running her own business, moving in fancy circles, getting romanced by rich lawyers— gal like that often has something in her past she don't want the whole world talking about. You find out what that is, you'll get yourself a private audience with her."

"You really think there's something like that out there?"

"Can't guarantee it, but like I say, you learn to spot patterns."

CHAPTER 11

Fifteen thousand dollars?"

"Not just one time, either," I said.

"How many?"

"I counted twenty-three."

"For Sebastian Curry?" Ellen McNeil shook her head in disbelief. "That's ridiculous."

We were in the back office at Unique Expressions, Ellen's art gallery in the University City Loop. Ellen was tall and thin with intense dark eyes and long curly black hair. She was wearing a black turtleneck, a Navaho silver-and-turquoise necklace with matching dangly earrings, wheat-colored drawstring cotton woven pants, and clogs. Hard to believe that just four years ago, Ellen McNeil had been dressed in conservative business suits and earning tens of thousands of frequent flyer miles as a financial consultant for one of the big accounting firms.

Ellen had graduated from Vassar with a degree in art history twenty-three years ago and moved to Greenwich Village to live the artist's life, which turned out to be three lonely years of waiting tables and scrounging tips to pay the outrageous rent on a roach-infested studio with a panoramic view of a gray airshaft. That experience shocked her into the M.B.A. program at Wharton and a huge starting salary in a Boston merchant banking house. She talked the corporate talk and walked the corporate walk for fifteen years—in Boston and then Chicago and then St. Louis—before quitting to return to her real passion. In just three years she'd become one of the movers and shakers in the St. Louis art community, serving on the boards of the St. Louis Art Museum and the Regional Arts Council while running one of the most successful art galleries in the Midwest.

We'd met when we'd worked together on an Arts Council committee. Since then, I'd represented her on an insurance claim, she'd sold me a piece of sculpture, and we'd been guests at each other's house—she'd come to my house with her Jewish boyfriend Gabe for the second night of Passover this year, and I'd taken Benny to her funky Halloween party last year (we went dressed as Beauty and the Beast, with Benny in drag as Beauty).

"So you know Sebastian Curry's work?" I asked.

"Oh, yes." She shook her head derisively. "Strictly third-rate. I'm embarrassed to say that I actually sold a piece of his work two years ago. He'd been begging me to show his paintings, and I finally gave in. I listed it for twelve hundred dollars. It sat here for almost a year before I unloaded it for eight hundred on a social-climbing bimbo who said it was a perfect match for the wallpaper in her dining room."

"All of these sales," I said, holding up the list Jacki had compiled from the files at Stanley Brod's office, "are from several years back. Was he worth more back then?"

"I doubt it." She paused, gesturing toward the list in disbelief. "You're telling me that Samantha sold almost two dozen of Sebastian's paintings at an average price of fifteen thousand dollars each?"

"According to these records."

"She must be the greatest hustler since P. T. Barnum."

"Do you know her?"

"I don't think so. I may have run into her at a few functions back then—art shows, opening nights, that sort of thing—but her gallery was closed by the time I opened mine. She hasn't been in the business since then."

"What do you know about Millennium Management Services?"

"Millennium?" Ellen frowned. "Never heard of them. What is it?"

"Some sort of agency, I think."

"For who?"

"I don't know. It received a fee on each painting."

"How much?"

"Six thousand dollars."

"Really?" She seemed puzzled. "Six grand on a fifteen-thousand-dollar painting? What's that—forty percent? That's a huge commission. Do you happen to know what Curry got paid?"

"Seven thousand."

She frowned as she mulled it over. "Ordinarily, I'd say the artist got screwed, but the sales prices for those paintings are so outrageous that it's hard to feel sorry for him."

"Maybe Millennium wasn't *his* agent," I said. "Maybe they were somehow responsible for finding buyers for the paintings. Maybe they were the gallery's agent."

"And the payments were finder's fees?" She tilted her head as she thought it over. "I guess that's possible. Some galleries, especially in New York and Chicago, pay finder's fees to interior design firms that get hired to decorate corporate headquarters and big law firms. You don't hear of it down here, though. Still, I suppose it's possible. Are you able to tell from the records who Millennium was working for?"

"The gallery paid the fee."

"That doesn't mean that they were working for the gallery. A lot of agents for artists insist that the galleries pay their fees direct. That way they avoid fee squabbles with their clients." She glanced at the list. "Samantha ought to know who Millennium was working for. Ask her."

"I can't, at least not without her lawyer present."

"Well, Sebastian should know. Ask him."

"I plan to," I said. "What's he like?"

She smiled. "He's big and he's dumb and he's totally gorgeous."

"Gorgeous?"

"Beyond gorgeous, honey. Imagine the African warrior of your hottest sexual fantasy. We're talking total eye candy—tall, great bod, cool dreadlocks, perfect teeth, a smile to die for. He should be the artist's model, not the artist. In fact, I hear that's how he makes some of his money these days. Wait until you see him in tight pants." Ellen gave me a leer as she fanned herself with her hand. "I can understand why Samantha would be willing to carry his work. I can understand why any woman would. That's probably why I agreed to carry one for him. Carrying it's one thing—but selling it is an entirely different proposition."

"Speaking of which," I said, handing her the list that Jacki had put together from the gallery's records. "These are the people that bought his paintings. Do you recognize any of the names?"

She leaned against the edge of her desk, put on her reading glasses, and studied the names, moving down the list one by one. When she reached the bottom she skimmed through the names again and then looked up. "I've sold pieces to six of the buyers. Two of the six are real surprises."

"Why?"

"Because they actually have taste. I can't imagine either one of them hanging anything by Sebastian Curry in their homes, much less paying fifteen thousand dollars for the privilege. The other four—well, I'm not shocked. They couldn't tell quality from crap. If Sebastian Curry happened to be the artist of the hour—and who knows? Maybe he was back then—they wouldn't blink at paying fifteen grand. But as for these two," she said, pointing at the names with her finger, "how Samantha got them to pay those prices is beyond me."

"You interested in talking to them?" I asked.

She nodded. "Actually, yes. I'd like to see their paintings and find out what the fuss was all about."

"You want to visit some of them with me?"

She gave me a curious look. "Rachel, you don't just call these people out of the blue and ask to come over to see their paintings. You'd have to have a good reason."

"I have one."

"Oh?"

"Sure. You and I are putting together a special showing of St. Louis artists. We're thinking of including a few representative works by Sebastian Curry. We'd like to see their paintings for possible inclusion in the exhibition."

"We are, are we?" She was grinning. "And who exactly are we?"

"We're representatives of the Art Guild of Metropolitan St. Louis."

"Which is what?"

I shrugged. "A new group. Brand-new, in fact. This will be our inaugural event. That's why you're helping them put this show together. You've agreed to consult with the group in the selection of artists to include. I handle their legal work, which is why I need to go with you." I winked. "I have to make sure everything is kosher."

She laughed. "You're terrible."

"Come with me for two visits. Once I see how you handle the art part, I can visit a few others on my own and fake it. You choose which two you want to see. I'll buy you dinner afterward."

She considered it for all of two seconds. "It's a deal. But we'll have to meet them today 'cause I'm off to New York tomorrow."

"Then toss me that phone book and let's start calling. I have a court hearing right after lunch, but the rest of the afternoon belongs to you."

CHAPTER 12

I'm here on the motion in *Blackwell Breeders*," I told Judge Parker's clerk.

She paused in filing her nails and glanced down at the calendar. "Are you Gold?"

"I am."

"Knock on the door. The judge is ready."

"Has plaintiffs' counsel arrived?"

"Oh, yeah. He's in there already."

Of course, I said to myself, trying to control my irritation. This was the second time I'd found Mack the Knife already inside the judge's chambers when I arrived for a court appearance in the ostrich case. Not that I was surprised. What Mack lacked in legal talent he more than made up in sheer gall. Over the years, he'd bullied his way through hundreds of lawsuits, building a lucrative practice with clients who believed that the best lawyer was a confrontational lawyer. The book on him was to be patient and hang in there. Although he curried favor with the trial judges—drinking with them after hours, hunting and golfing with them on the weekends—the breaks they gave him in the courtroom rarely survived scrutiny on appeal. But the catch was that few lawyers, and even fewer clients, had the stomach or the wallet to endure Mack the Knife through a trial and an appeal. Most chose to settle.

I rapped on the door and opened it just as Armour was delivering what sounded like the punch line to a dirty joke.

". . . and don't ride your bike for a week."

Judge Parker was seated behind his desk, leaning back in the chair, his arms crossed over his ample gut. He chuckled and leaned forward, noticing my arrival and waving me in. "That's a good one, Mack. Hello, counselor. Come on in."

"Good afternoon, Your Honor."

Armour got up from his chair to face me, his eyes doing a quick body scan. "Miss Gold," he said, nodding curtly.

I returned the nod. "Mr. Armour."

Mack the Knife was a burly, athletic man in his early fifties. He had a golf tan, a smooth shaved scalp, slate-gray eyes, and a neatly trimmed black mustache. In his khaki suit, crisp white shirt, and gleaming brown loafers, he reminded me of a corrupt CIA operative in a Latin American capital.

Judge Lamar Parker, by contrast, was the fleshy, heavy-lidded deer hunter from rural Missouri. Neither saint nor sinner, Judge Parker was a former insurance defense lawyer in his late fifties who'd used Republican Party connections to get appointed to the bench. His demeanor was affable, his rulings unimaginative, and his workday short. He rarely was reversed on appeal because he rarely was bold at trial.

"This is your motion, Miss Gold?" Judge Parker asked.

"It is, Your Honor."

"What's it seek?" he asked, paging through the file. As usual, Judge Parker had read none of the papers and done nothing to prepare for the argument.

"As the court knows," I explained, "my clients seek a full refund on the male ostrich they purchased from Blackwell Breeders. They also seek compensation for injuries inflicted upon several of the hens, including the death of one. I'm here today asking the court to dismiss Mr. Blackwell's claim. He alleges that he suffers emotional distress from the thought of his ostrich residing on my clients' farm. Frankly, Your Honor, the claim is absurd on its face."

The judge turned to Armour. "Mack?"

Armour snorted. "Judge, my client sold those gals a normal, heterosexual stud cock—the kind of animal that's happiest when he's putting the lumber to some hen." He became solemn. "Except now he's stuck out there in Kinkyland with—"

"That's ridiculous," I snapped, immediately regretting my interruption, knowing Armour would take advantage of it.

"Your Honor," he said, pointedly ignoring me, "I'm simply attempting to answer the court's question. May I continue?"

"Please do."

He glanced at me. "Without further interruption?"

"Get on with it," I said through clenched teeth.

"These women," Armour said, shaking his head sternly, "concealed their inexperience and their incompetence and, even worse, their perverted lesbian lifestyle from my client at the time of the sale. Mr. Blackwell is overwhelmed by feelings of guilt and remorse over what he's done to that poor ostrich. When Miss Gold has the opportunity to look him in the eye, she will feel his pain."

"Your Honor, I've already looked Mr. Blackwell in the eye at his deposition. He could barely keep a straight face."

"Smiling through his tears," Armour answered. "The man is devastated. He's entitled to compensation."

"Your Honor," I said, trying to contain my anger, "the only reason Mr. Armour put that ludicrous claim in the lawsuit is to confuse and prejudice the jury. It should be dismissed for that reason alone. More important, the claim has no scientific basis."

Judge Parker turned to him. "What about that, Mack?"

Armour smiled as he unclicked his briefcase. "She wants science, Judge, I'll give it to her in spades." He started pulling scientific journals out of his briefcase and piling them, one by one, onto the judge's desk. I skimmed the titles as they dropped onto the desk—*Journal of Animal Behavior, Field Studies in Evolutionary Biology, Animal Husbandry Quarterly, Zoological Record.*

When he completed his stack, Armour leaned back triumphant and crossed his arms over his chest. "How's that for starters?"

"How's what?" I responded. "What are these?"

"Scientific studies of animal behavior. And there's plenty more where that came from."

I started to answer when the judge held up his hand. "You make some good points, Miss Gold, but I think we'd all agree this is a case of first impression. The safest route here is to let the jury take a crack at it. We can clean up any miscues in the posttrial motions."

L ast chance," Armour told me as we emerged from the courthouse. "Settle now or this trial's gonna put your clients on the cover of the *National Enquirer*."

"What's your proposal?" I responded frostily.

"Well," he said, scratching his mustache thoughtfully, "I might be willing to recommend a dog fall."

I stared at him. "You drop your claims and we drop ours? You call that a good-faith offer?"

"Not an offer yet. I said it's what I'd be willing to *recommend*."

"Forget it, Mack. Your offer is as absurd as your lawsuit."

"Suit yourself, counselor, but you're living in a fantasy world." He chuckled. "The only absurd thing here is someone who thinks a St. Louis jury is going to award one red cent to a pair of muff divers."

I stared at him as a bunch of possible responses flashed through my head—all at the playground level, none a real zinger. Oh, where is Benny Goldberg when you need him?

CHAPTER 13

U nbelievable," Benny said, shaking his head as he sliced off another hunk of sausage. "What did you say to him?"

"Nothing. I just walked away."

"Nothing?" Benny took a big chug of beer and swallowed. "Nothing?"

I shrugged. "What would you have said?"

"Easy," he said, putting down the bottle and stifling a belch, which rumbled ominously in his belly. He jabbed his finger at an imaginary Mack Armour. "I'd say, 'Watch your mouth, bullet-head, 'cause I got chunks of guys like you in my stool.' "

I shook my head. "Works better coming from you."

He gestured toward the cutting board. "You sure you don't want some more?"

I held up my hands. "I'm stuffed."

It was late afternoon. Benny had come by my office for a surprise happy hour. He'd stopped at his favorite Italian deli for a "light snack"—a smoked turkey breast, a thick slab of cheese, a jar of pickled onions, an Italian bread, and a truly repulsive sausage composed of semi-identifiable animal parts suspended in a pink gelatinous goo.

I shook my head in wonder. "An entire turkey breast, Benny?"

"Hey, girl, I bought it because of you."

"Me?"

"You should have seen the smoked ham. Talk about enticing. I got sexually aroused just looking at it."

"Spare me."

"I did. That's the point. Now that you're becoming the Orthodox Jewish Princess, God forbid I should bring *treif* into your office."

"That's sweet. But speaking of *treif*, what in heaven's name is in that sausage?"

"This?" Benny stared at it a moment, rubbing his chin. He finally shrugged. "There are some things man was not meant to know. So when's the ostrich battle scheduled for trial?"

"Not for another month." I leaned back in my chair and sighed. "I just want it to be over, Benny. Armour's been a complete jerk—hid documents from me, lied to the judge, hired an investigator to harass two of Maggie's former lovers. I feel like I'm stuck in an endless backstreet brawl with that guy. Each day brings a new dirty trick. Today, he dumped a pile of scientific journals on the judge's desk, supposedly to support his contention that my clients' actions could have changed that ostrich's behavior."

"And?"

"There was nothing even remotely close in there." I shook my head in exasperation. "Just another sleazy stunt."

"So what'd you expect? Tea and crumpets with Miss Manners? The guy's a fucking scumbag. Hell, I feel like taking a bath after talking to him on the phone. Don't sweat it, Rachel. When that case finally gets to trial, you're going to nail his ass."

"As my father would have said, 'From your lips to God's ears.' "

"You got that right. So how's Angela Green's case coming along?"

"I had an interesting afternoon with Ellen McNeil."

"Oh?"

"We visited two of the people who bought Sebastian Curry paintings from Samantha's gallery."

"And?"

I frowned. "I'm not sure what I was expecting, but it sure wasn't what we found."

"Really?" He looked up expectantly, his fingers jammed in the jar of pickled onions. "Talk to me."

I described our meeting with Martha Galbraith in her stylish home in Chesterfield. Although the list of purchasers included the name Dr. Peter Galbraith, Ellen decided to call Martha instead. Ellen explained to me that Peter, a urologist with a practice in St. Charles, viewed art the way he viewed stocks: purely as an investment. He relied on his broker to pick stocks and on his wife to pick art. Over the years Ellen had sold the Galbraiths two paintings and a blown-glass vase—and all three times Peter had been unable to mask his boredom as he waited for Martha to make her selection. Martha had superb taste and a connoisseur's eye, Ellen told me, and thus she was our best candidate to unveil the mystery of the Sebastian Curry paintings.

But Martha was no help. Indeed, she confessed to being as mystified as Ellen. Peter bought the painting on his own—something he'd never done. Although fifteen thousand dollars was nowhere near as much as they'd paid for other works of art—in fact, as Ellen later told me, the price for one of the paintings she sold them was thirty-five thousand dollars—it was still a lot of money to pay without even consulting his wife. Suffice to say, the good doctor was defensive about the painting from the day he brought it home. He told his wife that Sebastian Curry would be the next big name in the art world, just you wait and see. She waited and she didn't see. The painting hung on a wall in his home office for a year and then he took it to work, where it hung in the waiting room. At some point that year he got it appraised for insurance purposes. The appraiser valued it at four hundred dollars. A few months later, he donated it to some charity—presumably for a tax write-off in the full amount originally paid. Martha Galbraith couldn't remember which charity and had no idea where the painting was now. It wouldn't be worth tracking down anyway, she told them. The painting was—as Martha put it—"decidedly pedestrian and derivative."

"Decidedly pedestrian and derivative, eh?" Benny said in a mock-snooty tone. "Well, la-de-fucking-da."

I watched him slice off a chunk of that revolting sausage and shove it in his mouth. He chased it with two pickled onions, a wedge of cheese, and a big gulp of beer. Even after years of watching him gorge on all manner of things, I was still astounded and grossed out by his eating habits. He must have caught me staring and misinterpreted my nauseous expression for one of longing.

"You want some?" he asked, gesturing toward the food, his mouth full.

"No, thanks," I said.

"Sure?"

"I'm just not feeling hungry right now."

"You're missing a real treat here." He tore off a big piece of bread and took a bite. Chewing, he asked, "So who else did you and Ellen see?"

"Don Goddard."

"The lawyer?"

"Yep."

Don Goddard was one of the name partners in Goddard, Jones & Newberger, a twenty-five-lawyer firm in Clayton that handled corporate, tax, and contract matters for various small businesses. He was a tall, slender, balding man in his fifties with a large nose and an elegant demeanor—a smooth operator, but not quite smooth enough to conceal his social pretensions. Like a lot of corporate lawyers with working-class origins, Don Goddard expended great time and energy on appearance.

"We went to his office," I told Benny. "He had the painting in one of the firm's conference rooms. He was clearly thrilled by the prospect that a painting of his might make it into the show. On the way to the conference room he told Ellen that he'd like the ownership credit for the art show to read, 'From the Donald E. Goddard Collection.' "

"So how was the painting?"

"It was one of those abstract things with lots of bright colors." I shrugged. "I'm no judge of modern art, but it didn't do anything for me."

"What did Ellen think of it?"

"She was polite during the meeting with Goddard, but afterward she told me the painting was mediocre."

"So what did you learn?"

"That something fishy is going on."

"What kind of fishy?"

"While Ellen was busy examining the painting, I started asking him questions—mostly innocuous ones, like you'd need for filling out an information questionnaire. I explained that we'd need some basic facts if we selected his painting for the exhibit. He started getting nervous as soon as I got beyond where and when he bought the painting. Did he own anything else by Sebastian Curry? No. Was he familiar with Curry's work? Not really. What other works of art were in the 'Donald E. Goddard Collection'? That one had him fumbling. Turns out the only other items are a couple of pieces of pottery his wife bought in Cancún, an art print from either Monet or Picasso—he wasn't sure which—and a set of those Lladró ballerina figurines."

"Wow," Benny said, arching his eyebrows. "Sounds like

the Donald E. Goddard Collection is almost ready for its own wing at the Guggenheim."

"By then he was really antsy. I asked him how he ended up at Samantha's gallery. Didn't remember. Had he been there often? Didn't remember. Had he ever heard of Millennium Management? No, he said, who are they? I explained that Millennium received a big commission on the painting. Never heard of them, he snapped."

"You're right," Benny said. "There is something fishy going on here. I think I know what the bait is."

"What?"

"Come on, Rachel. It's obvious. You got a pair of big-money guys who are fairly savvy businessmen but don't know jackshit about art. Both of them plunk down fifteen grand for pieces of crap by some unknown yutz. What's that tell you?"

"I don't know. What's it tell you?"

"That we got two guys choosing art with their dicks."

"What are you talking about?"

"Look who owned that gallery. Samantha Cummings. That girl is a fox. I don't know exactly what she did to those guys, but I'm betting she aimed her sales pitch somewhere lower than their aesthetic sensibility. The thing she was enlarging wasn't their artistic taste."

"Benny, flirting is not going to make a bunch of guys spend fifteen grand."

"Come on, Rachel. We're talking about the male of the species here. And we're probably talking about more than flirting. Fifteen grand is pocket change to a rich guy chasing pussy. You got guys plunking down five times that much on a swanky car with nothing more than the hope that a car like that will make some hot chick overlook the dork behind the wheel. Here, though, you've already interested the hot chick, who happens to own the gallery, which means you have an easy way to prove you're a big spender."

I frowned. "Why waste your money trying to impress Samantha? She was already taken. She was engaged to Michael Green."

"You think guys don't waste time chasing women who're already taken?" Benny paused, frowning as an idea took shape. "Hey, what if one of those guys fell in love with her? And what if he was one of those crazy jealous types?"

I gave him a puzzled look. "So?"

"Wouldn't be the first time a jealous guy killed for love, eh?"

I thought it over. "You think that's possible?"

He shrugged. "It's no more bizarre than what the jury said actually happened, right?"

I tried to imagine Don Goddard, Mr. Smooth, in the role of infatuated, lust-crazed killer. He didn't fit the role, but there were still plenty of other names on the list. In fact, all twenty-three purchasers had been men. After Jacki had compiled the list from the gallery's books and records at Stanley Brod's office, I'd cross-checked the names against Michael Green's Rolodex, which was also at Brod's office. All but two of the buyers had been on his Rolodex. From what I knew of Green's behavior, he apparently bragged about Samantha to nearly everyone he talked to. Who could judge the impact of those boasts?

I checked my watch. "I have one more of these buyers to see before dinner. Ellen is seeing one, too, and then we're meeting for dinner."

"Who are you seeing?"

"Jack Foley. He's a stockbroker. I'm meeting him at his house at six-thirty. His wife will be there, too."

"Ellen's not going with you?"

"No, she's meeting another guy."

"Perfect." Benny was grinning.

"Perfect?"

"Ellen won't be there. You're going to need an art expert, right?"

"Oh?" I said, amused. "Would you perhaps happen to know where I might find such an expert on short notice?"

"If we can swing by my place on the way, I just might be able to rouse one for you."

We were in the Foleys' living room. The Sebastian Curry painting—a large abstract work combining black-and-white splatters and what looked like roller swipes in bright primary colors—was on the floor propped against the fireplace. Benny—or "Benito," as he'd introduced himself in what sounded like an Italian-Hungarian accent—stood in front of the painting, his arms crossed, expression grave, as he pretended to scrutinize it.

Benny had, of course, pushed his art critic routine out near the border between impersonation and farce. He was dressed entirely in black: black turtleneck, black jeans, black boots, black beret, black wraparound sunglasses. He'd done more than just change outfits when we stopped by his house on our way over. For an added bizarre touch, which I hadn't noticed until we stood in the bright light of the Foleys' front hall, he'd slicked back his hair with what appeared to be Vaseline and powdered his face white, which heightened the contrast with his lips. The black stubble of his beard poked through the powder. Perhaps he hoped the overall effect—black outfit, greased hair, powdered face, black stubble—would shout avant-garde art critic. To me, though, it was shouting overweight transvestite geisha from hell.

The Foleys eyed him warily as he frowned and grumbled in front of the painting. I tried to ignore him, tried to keep a straight face, tried to keep the conversation focused on the information I was attempting to elicit. It was not easy.

"So it was in the basement all this time?" I asked.

"Until today," Margo Foley said with a perky smile. "Until you called Jack. Isn't that so, honey?"

"Right," he answered stiffly.

Margo was seated to the left of the fireplace on a white couch with a loose-pillow back. I was facing her across the coffee table on the matching love seat. Jack Foley stood to my left—to Margo's right—behind a wing chair that faced the fireplace from the far side of the coffee table. Both in their late thirties, the Foleys were the type of couple who'd raise the level of tension in any gathering—Margo with her forced cheer and brittle smile, Jack with his edgy stare and slight stammer.

"Isn't that crazy?" she said brightly, looking from me to her husband to Benny, who was still grumbling at the painting. "I mean, I remember that Jack brought it home—what, eight or nine years ago, right, honey?—and put it down in the basement. We had no idea it was so special. Why, we never even unwrapped it until you called today." She looked at the painting. "It's certainly, well, brash."

And, I thought, completely different from the other works of art in their living and dining rooms, all of which were either prints of famous Impressionist paintings or posters advertising museum exhibitions of works by famous Impressionist painters.

"What attracted you to the painting?" I asked Jack.

He shrugged. "I don't know. I supposed I must have liked it."

"Had you bought other art from the 309 Gallery?"

He frowned. "I don't recall."

Benny spun around. "You dona recall?" he said in his strange accent. "But surely you recalla de owner, Meez Cummings, ya?" He gave Jack a lecherous wink and put his hands on his hips and thrust them forward twice. "Magnifica, eh?"

Jack leaned back and frowned. "I don't remember her."

Trying to ignore Benito, I asked Jack, "What exactly appealed to you about this painting?"

"I don't know."

"Did you view other paintings at the gallery?"

"I don't remember. I may have just called over there, asked them if they had a painting by this Curry guy. I remember going by to pick it up. I didn't really spend much time in the gallery."

"What made you interested in Sebastian Curry?" I asked.

He shrugged, clearly uncomfortable with this line of questions. "I think someone told me he was going to be the next big thing. I suppose it seemed like a good investment opportunity."

"Did you have it appraised at the time you bought it?"

"No."

"How about since then?"

"No."

Margo asked me, "Do you think our painting is worth a lot of money?"

"Hard to say," I told her. "Some of his work may have held its value, but I know of at least one of his paintings that was recently appraised for only four hundred dollars."

Margo looked at the painting and then back at me. "That's not so bad, is it?"

"Not if you paid less than a hundred dollars for it," I said, glancing at her husband.

"How much did we pay, hon?" she asked him.

He glanced from his wife to me and back to her. "Uh, something like that—or maybe a little more. I don't remember. It's been a long time."

"Less than four hundred dollars?" I asked, trying to keep my voice neutral.

"Yeah," he answered, averting his eyes, "somewhere around there."

Benny turned around and announced, "Now Benito ees done."

"What do you think of it, Señor Benito?" Margo asked hopefully.

Benny shook his head. "I am sorry to say zat deesa work eesa—how shall I put eet?—decidedly pedestrian and derivative."

The three of us were having dinner at the Lynch Street Bistro in the Soulard area—Benny, Ellen McNeil, and me.

"I don't know about your guy," Ellen told us, "but Allen Sutter definitely did not have a thing for Samantha Cummings."

"How can you be sure?" I asked.

"Because I met his companion Tony."

I looked at Benny. He shrugged. "So maybe Allen swings both ways."

Ellen shook her head. "Not this cowboy. Trust me. Allen and Tony have been a couple for a long time. On a wall in their den are framed photographs of the two of them together that go back more than ten years."

While Benny and I had been meeting with the Foleys, Ellen paid a visit to Allen Sutter, a psychologist who specialized in designing motivational seminars for corporations. His name was one of the twenty-three on the list. Ellen knew Allen, having sold him a painting about a year ago.

"So what was Allen's story?" I asked.

"He was surprised there was that much interest in Sebastian Curry," Ellen said. "He told me he regretted buying his painting and eventually gave it to a gallery on consignment. It sold for about three hundred dollars."

"Did he tell you why he bought it in the first place?" I asked.

"Not really. He was about as vague as your guy—said he thought Curry was an artist on the rise. Claims he viewed the purchase as an investment, but that when Curry's reputation appeared to be going nowhere he decided to cut his losses and sell it."

"What the hell is going on here?" Benny asked. "You've got this Sutter dude claiming he made an investment but then bailing out at a huge loss after only a few years. Why not keep the damn thing in storage in the hopes that one day Sebastian Curry gets recognized as America's answer to Vincent van Gogh? Then you got Jack Foley. That stiff claims that he was making an investment, except he's so secretive about it that he never even unwrapped the painting during all those years, never told his wife that he shelled out fifteen large for that piece of shit, and acts like he remembers almost nothing about it." Benny shook his head, confused. "I was hoping that maybe these guys were *shtupping* Samantha, that maybe that's why they seemed uncomfortable talking about the paintings, but I have to admit that Rachel's got a point there. I mean, we're talking about twenty-three guys in the space of less than two years—and she's engaged to Michael Green for part of that time. Even if she's the greatest lay of the century, fifteen grand is still a lot to pay for some nooky. And where does that leave your gay caballero?"

Ellen nodded. "You've got a lot of smart, successful men making the same dumb decision at the same art gallery. Something's fishy."

"I agree," I said. "It's one thing to overpay for something you love. I did it once. Back when I was in law school and really scraping by, I went to an art fair on the Boston Common one Saturday afternoon and ended up paying two hundred dollars for a painting of a peasant woman." I turned to Benny. "It's the one in my kitchen."

He nodded. "Oh, yeah. Two hundred bucks? Whoa."

"I couldn't help myself. I fell totally in the love with the woman in the painting. I made the artist hold it until I could take the T to my bank in Cambridge and come back with the money. It was a crazy thing to do. Two hundred dollars was my food allowance for two months, but that didn't matter. I had to have that painting. It seemed more important to me than food. It still does. I love it. I keep it in my kitchen so that I can see it every morning at breakfast and every night at dinner and then again when I make some tea before bed. But these guys." I shook my head. "I don't get it. They pay fifteen thousand dollars for paintings that they don't seem to have any emotional bond with. In fact, none of the men that we've talked to even liked their painting. Not even Don Goddard. As for Jack Foley, it sounded like he may not have even seen his before he bought it, and that really makes no sense. Even if he was buying it purely for investment purposes, you'd think he'd at least want to see what he was buying before he wrote the check."

"Or in his case," Benny said, "hand over the cash. Sounded like his wife had no idea what he paid, which tells me he didn't write a check or put it on their credit card."

"So where do you go from here?" Ellen asked me.

I leaned back in my chair and frowned. "I've got to find a way to talk to Samantha Cummings. I have an investigator doing a background check on her. He's coming by tomorrow morning to show me what he's found. Maybe he'll have something worth pursuing. I'm also going out to visit Angela again. Tomorrow afternoon. Bring her up to speed on this stuff. Maybe Millennium will ring a bell for her."

CHAPTER 14

No bells tolled for Angela Green. She knew nothing about Millennium Management Services, had never heard of Sebastian Curry, and had no idea what paintings Samantha Cummings had carried in her gallery.

We were in the interview room at Chillicothe Correctional Center, and I was bringing Angela up to date on my investigation. I'd driven out there that morning through a steady rain that started falling an hour out of St. Louis and stayed with me the whole way. It was still gray and chilly and gloomy outside, the sky occasionally illuminated by a distant flash of lightning, the rain a steady drum roll on the roof. Inside, it was as cozy as I could make it. I'd brought along a large thermos filled with hot green tea blended with honey and ginseng, two pottery mugs, and a big tin of *kamishbroit*, which my mother had baked special for Angela. *Kamishbroit* is a deliciously crunchy Yiddish pastry that's a cousin to the Italian *biscotti*—except that my mother's *kamishbroit* makes the finest *biscotti* taste like stale Wonder bread.

Angela apparently agreed. She was nibbling on her third piece of *kamishbroit* and sipping her tea as I went through the thick investigative file that Charlie Ross had put together on Samantha Cummings. Most of the stuff was fairly unexceptional—creditor claims against her gallery after it closed down; a speeding violation that a traffic lawyer plea-bargained down to excessive vehicular noise; a garnishment action against her son's father, Ray Franco, who worked on the minivan line at the Chrysler plant in Fenton.

The story of Ray and Samantha had briefly occupied the police's attention after Michael Green's murder. The two had never married. They'd been living together when she got pregnant, but Ray moved out a few weeks after Trent was born. He married another woman within a year and had since fathered two children with her. Although Samantha eventually got a child-support order against Ray, his poor compliance record filled the court file with garnishments, show cause orders, and the like.

The police had brought Ray in for questioning during the murder investigation. Oddly enough, he'd briefly been a suspect—odd because Ray seemed to have every financial reason to want Samantha to marry a prosperous man like Green, since maybe she'd finally stop hounding him for child support. In any event, Ray Franco had an airtight alibi. On the night of the murder he'd gone to the Cardinals game with three coworkers from the Chrysler plant. After the game, they'd partied down on Laclede's Landing until the bars closed and then headed over to a strip club on the east side, where they stayed until five-thirty. They watched the sun rise from the parking lot, drove back across the Mississippi, stopped at a Denny's in south St. Louis, had a huge breakfast, and then drove to the plant, where they reported for work at seven sharp. In addition to his three pals, each of whom corroborated his story, there were bartenders or waitresses at each stop along the way who remembered the rowdy foursome.

"Here's an eerie one," I said, handing Angela a photocopy of a three-paragraph news clipping from the *Post-Dispatch*. "This guy committed suicide in front of her town house."

"Really? When was this?"

"About six months after your trial." I pointed to the top of the page, which showed the date of the article. "The guy's name was Billy Woodward. He was thirty-three."

"A pay phone?" she said when she finished the article. "Was he actually talking to someone when he shot himself?"

"That's a really eerie part. Charlie copied the police file. The pay phone across the street was off the hook when the police arrived. The phone company records showed that he was talking to Samantha just before he shot himself."

"Oh, my."

"Samantha confirmed it. Here's a photocopy of his suicide note."

I handed it to her. It read:

dear sam:
no more waiting for woody—sayonara.

"Woody?"

"Nickname, I guess," I said. "His last name was Woodward."

"Who was this guy?" Angela asked. "How did she know him?"

I pulled out the police report and turned it so that both of us could see. "She claimed that Billy was an old boyfriend who'd harassed her on and off for years—both before and after Michael Green's death. He was kind of a creepy, pathetic character. Served four months on a burglary charge when he was twenty. Prison psychiatrist diagnosed him as manic-depressive and put him on medication. Went to a vocational school to become an electrician but dropped out. Held a variety of odd jobs over the years—shoe salesman, bartender, forklift operator. Even acted in a few porno films when he was younger."

Angela made a face. "This was a boyfriend of hers?"

"A long time ago, she claimed. She hadn't seen him in years. According to the police report, he spent most of his time lifting weights at a local gym and visiting talent agencies in town. He worshiped Arnold Schwarzenegger. He used to tell people at the gym that someday he'd be an action-hero movie star, too—just like Arnold." I shook my head. "Not likely. His career was going nowhere. For the last six months of his life he was basically unemployed except for a few short gigs as a fashion model."

"A fashion model? Was he that good-looking?"

"Sort of. The police found a few shots of him at his apartment. The kind you'd use for a portfolio, I guess. Charlie made a copy of one." I flipped through the folder. "Here it is." I studied it a moment. "Not bad, I guess. What do you think?"

Angela took the picture. Her eyes widened and she gasped. "Dear God."

"What?"

"That's—oh, Lord—that's him."

"Who?"

"John. That's my John."

"John?" I repeated with a frown. And then I made the connection. "Oh. My. God."

On the drive back to St. Louis from Chillicothe, I tried to organize my own thoughts, having left my poor client's in a shambles.

That Angela had never until now made the connection between Billy Woodward and her mysterious John was not surprising. She was in prison by the time he'd committed suicide, and the newspaper account had not included his photograph. She hardly seemed a porno fan, and thus wouldn't have been likely to see him in one of his films before prison, and certainly not after. At least that part made sense.

But nothing else about Woodward did. Why had he killed himself on Samantha Cummings's doorstep? Why had he identified himself to Angela as John? Why had he disappeared on the night of the murder and remained incognito until after Angela entered prison? Where had he gone? And why? Why hadn't he come forward during her trial? Maybe there was some connection to Michael Green's murder, but I couldn't even begin to figure out how to connect those dots—or any others, for that matter. From Millennium Management Services to Sebastian Curry's twenty-three paintings to the suicide of Billy Woodward, there seemed no logical relationship to anything, yet all seemed somehow connected. Even more puzzling was the fact that all roads—including the money trail—seemed to lead to Samantha Cummings, who was the least logical connection of all. Even if she despised her fiancé—and where was the evidence of that?—she nevertheless had every conceivable financial incentive to keep Michael Green alive long enough to say "I do." His premarital death was an economic disaster for her.

In the fading light I drove east on Highway 70 and tried to pinpoint my own role in all of this. I'd been retained to defend Angela in Sam Squared. That particular winding road led back to Samantha Cummings, the mother of the plaintiff in Sam Squared. Eventually, I would have the opportunity to take Samantha's deposition and get answers to at least some of these questions. But I had several questions for Samantha that would draw a vigorous objection from her lawyer on the ground that they were entirely irrelevant to the claims in the case. I needed to find a way to overcome that objection. Better yet, I needed to find some golden nugget of information that would convince the lawyer to let me talk to her privately. The best place to pan for that gold now seemed to be in the life and death of one Billy Woodward.

By the time I reached my office, I had the beginnings of

a Billy Woodward game plan. I was surprised to see Jacki still there—it was after six o'clock.

"Rachel, where have you been? I've been trying to reach you on your cell phone."

"The battery's dead. What's wrong?"

"Sheila Trumble has called three times. She's going crazy."

"Why?"

"The health department is closing down the Oasis Shelter. The last time she called she told me they were boarding it up and making all the women and children leave. Sheila is over there now, helping the women pack up their stuff."

"The health department?" I repeated. "I can't believe this. Nate Turner is behind it. I just know it."

Jacki handed me a message slip. "Here's Sheila's cell phone number."

I dialed it, standing at Jacki's desk.

"Sheila?"

"Oh, Rachel, thank heavens it's you. I can't believe this. These poor women. What can we do?"

"I'm coming right over, Sheila."

CHAPTER 15

I slowed as I approached the Oasis Shelter and carefully weaved my car through the obstacle course of TV news vans double-parked at odd angles along the street. The scene in front of the shelter resembled the aftermath of a highly contained natural disaster, as if a tornado had touched down briefly before leaping clear of the county. All was calm on either side of the pair of two-flats, and all was chaos in between. Jumbled belongings—clothes, toiletries, towels, hair dryers—lay in haphazard piles on the lawn. Small children wandered among the piles, barefoot and in diapers; others cried in their mothers' arms. Some of the mothers were crying, too. Other women were gathered in small groups—confused, angry, peering around warily. First-floor windows were boarded up. Yellow hazard tape crisscrossed the door fronts. Stapled to the front doors of both two-flats were white cardboard signs reading Condemned by Order of Health Department. Arc lights from the TV news crew illuminated the scene, casting jumpy shadows as reporters moved among the crowd, trailing minicam crews behind them.

"Rachel!"

I spotted Sheila Trumble off to the side of the front porch of the two-flat on the right. She was huddled with one of the social workers, Rashita Jordan.

"What is going on here?" I asked when I reached her.

"The health department." Sheila shook her head in frustration. "They kicked everyone out and closed us down. They've condemned the buildings."

"Why?"

"Rat infestation."

"Rats? You've got be kidding."

"Rats, my ass," Rashita grumbled. She was a scowling, heavyset black woman. "Bullshit's what that is."

"Were you here when the health department arrived?" I asked her.

"Oh, yeah," Rashita said, nodding her head derisively. "Heard 'em banging around down there, claiming they found nests of rats in the basement, rat droppings all over the place. 'Dangerous infestation,' they say. 'Gots to call in vector control ASAP,' they say." She snorted in disgust. "Vector control, my ass. Only evidence they found down there is what they brought in themselves."

"How do you know that?" I asked.

" 'Cause I know rat droppings, that's why. 'Cause I grew up with rat droppings. 'Cause I been working at this shelter for going on a year now. 'Cause I been in that basement a dozen times, including just last Wednesday. Unless Mayflower moved in a pack of rats yesterday, only rat droppings down there are the ones those deceitful motherfuckers carried in with them."

"When did they start kicking people out?" I asked her.

"About ninety minutes ago."

I checked my watch. "After the courts closed. Of course."

"They called me at home," Sheila said. "I drove down here as quickly as I could, but they'd already boarded the place up. Just look." She gestured helplessly toward the scene on the front lawn. "These poor women."

I shook my head angrily. "Turner."

"What?"

"The great Nate the Great. He's behind this."

She nodded distractedly. "We have to find places for these people tonight. I've got Sara calling around to motels, but she's not having much luck. I can put up a few at my house. Oh, this is terrible."

I fished my keys out of my purse and worked the house key off the chain. "Here," I said, handing the key to Sheila. "This is the key to my house. There are two extra bedrooms, a couch, and a sleeping bag in the basement. I can put up at least six—more if they don't mind sleeping on the floor. My dog's in the backyard. He'll bark, but he's harmless."

I turned to Rashita. She had her arms crossed over her chest and was tapping her foot irately.

"So you know rats?" I asked her.

She snorted. "Honey, I grew up with rats. I knew some of them better than my cousins."

"Then you're coming with me."

"Where we going?"

"To find a judge."

She glanced at her watch and frowned. "Where you going to find a judge at seven-thirty?"

"At home. Come on."

Sheila walked with us to my car. I started the engine and rolled down the window.

"I'll call you on your cell phone when we find a judge," I told her. "Give us about an hour. See if you can delay things here."

The city judges rotated duty call—a different one each night. That meant that the first thing we had to do was find out which judge was on call. I knew from prior experience that the best place to start was the warrant division of the circuit attorney's office at the Muny Courts, which is what most attorneys called the Municipal Courts Building on Market Street. The folks in the warrant division would definitely have the name and phone number of tonight's duty judge, since the principal judicial function after hours was the approval of search warrants and arrest warrants.

As we approached Muny Courts, I recited three names under my breath like a mantra:

Grady, Ritter, or Williams—Grady, Ritter, or Williams—Grady, Ritter, or Williams.

There were twenty-one judges in the Circuit Court of the City of St. Louis, and eighteen of them were men. The other three—Joan Grady, Carolyn Ritter, and LaDonna Williams—were my top picks to hear a motion for emergency relief on behalf of a battered-women's shelter. Judge Williams was number one on the list. Not only was she black but she had handled domestic abuse cases during her years in the circuit attorney's office. We needed a sympathetic judge tonight.

Grady, Ritter, or Williams—Grady, Ritter, or Williams—Grady, Ritter, or Williams.

The assistant circuit attorney was fat guy in his thirties with thinning hair and a messy brown mustache speckled with food crumbs. He gave me a dubious look as he tugged at the edge of his disgusting mustache. "A civil case? I don't know."

"What don't you know?" I asked.

"These judges"—he paused, shaking his head—"they don't want to be bothered by some civil case that can wait until tomorrow."

"That may be true, but this happens to be a civil case that can't wait until tomorrow."

He raised his eyebrows. "That's what you say. How am I supposed to know that's really so?"

"What you know or don't know about my case is irrelevant."

"Oh, yeah?" He thrust his chin forward. "Then how am I supposed to decide whether there's really an emergency?"

"You're not. That decision is mine. I'm the lawyer and it's my client and I've decided that it's an emergency."

He stared at me, his jaws clenched.

Oh, the marvels of testosterone.

Finally, I said, "Are you going to give me the name and number?"

"Are you going to tell me why I should?"

I nodded. "Sure, I'll tell you why. But first tell me your name."

"Dick."

"Dick what?"

"Dick Carple, lady. Now tell me why."

"Sure, Dick. My client is the Oasis Shelter. That's a shelter for battered women. The health department closed them down tonight—kicked all the women and children out. They're out on the front yard right now—children milling about in the dark, clothes and teddy bears and personal belongings piled on the ground. Right now. And guess who else is out there right now, Dick? Reporters and camera crews from every television station in town." I put my hands on the countertop separating us and leaned forward. "You want to know why you should give me the name and the phone number of the duty judge, Dick? Because if you don't, I am going to go right back over to Oasis Shelter and I'm going to stand on the front lawn, and I'm going to hold a press conference. Once I'm sure all those video cameras are running, I am going to announce that the only reason those poor women and children are stranded out there in the darkness is because of a pompous city attorney named Dick Carple who thinks he's too important to give me the name of the duty judge. And then, Dick, I will tell them exactly where they can find you. Ten minutes later, all those TV reporters with their minicams are going to descend on you like a pack of wolves and you're going to get to explain why you think you're so much more important than a bunch of homeless women and children."

I leaned back from the counter. "Tell you what, Dick. I'm going to count to ten. Either you give me that name and number before I finish, or I am going to make sure your name and number are the lead story on every newscast to-night."

Rashita cackled. "You better do like she say, white boy."

"Ready, Dick? One—two—three—four—"

"Here," he said, scribbling out the name and number. "Take it, goddammit."

I took the slightly crumpled sheet of paper and looked down at it. Judge Joan Grady. *Yes.*

I look up and smiled. "Thank you, Dick."

B ut I thought you were the duty judge."
"I am, Miss Gold." There was static on the line. Judge Grady must have been on a cell phone. "But you're seeking a TRO for the shelter. That makes your case a civil equity matter. You need to call Judge Clausen. I have his number here."

"But he's not the duty judge."

"That's okay. The equity judges prefer to control their own dockets. You need to call Judge Clausen. Do you have a pen?"

So much for sisterhood solidarity.

I wrote down the phone number. Rashita and I were at the pay phone down the hall from the circuit attorney's of-fice. I fed more coins into the slot and dialed the number.

Judge Clausen's wife answered the phone with all the

warmth she no doubt displayed for telephone solicitors. "He's not the duty judge tonight, young lady."

"I know that, Mrs. Clausen. I called the duty judge. When she heard that I had an equity matter, she instructed me to call your husband."

"Oh, really? Which one is she?"

"Judge Grady."

"Hmmph," she sniffed. "Well, hold on." And then, in a muffled voice, "It's for you. I don't know—some *lady* lawyer."

I could hear the television in the background. Sounded like the Honorable Martin Clausen was watching a *Seinfeld* rerun.

"Hello?" The voice was raspy with age and cigarettes.

"Judge Clausen?"

"Who is this?"

"Rachel Gold, Your Honor. I have an emergency motion for a temporary restraining order."

"Who's the defendant?"

"The city of St. Louis—or at least the health department."

"What's the emergency?"

I told him who my client was and described the current predicament of the residents. He listened quietly and said nothing when I finished.

"This can't wait until tomorrow," I said. "I've got homeless women and children on the lawn."

I heard a deep inhale. "Okay, but I want the city represented."

"How do I arrange that?"

"Call someone in the city counselor's office. Tell them I'm hearing your motion in my dining room in one hour. Tell them to send someone."

"That office is closed, Your Honor. How do I get a home phone number?"

"Go down to the Muny Courts, young lady. There'll be an assistant circuit attorney in the warrants division. Tell him you want the home phone list for the city counselor's office. If he can't find it, then tell him he's it."

"Pardon?"

"Tell him that I expect him in my dining room when the hearing starts. Got it?"

"Yes, Your Honor."

"See you in one hour, Miss Gold."

Click.

I hung up and turned to Rashita.

"Well?" she said.

I glanced down the hall toward the warrants division. "Guess who we get to talk to again?"

J udge Clausen was seated at the head of the dark walnut table in the dining room of his brick bungalow in south St. Louis. The polished surface of the table gleamed in the spotless room. Like most of his neighbors, the Honorable Martin Clausen was of German descent and no doubt a blood relative to some of the employees of Anheuser-Busch, whose enormous brewery and corporate headquarters anchored this part of town. I was used to seeing Judge Clausen in black robes. Tonight he could have passed for one of those brewery workers in his faded khakis, scuffed brown loafers, and black and gold Missouri Tigers T-shirt stretched tight across his ample belly. His thinning gray hair was slicked straight back. I watched him tug absently on one of his pendulous earlobes as he read through my three-page, hand-written Petition for Temporary Restraining Order, which I'd drafted up on my yellow legal pad between my phone call to him and the drive to his house. His wire-frame reading glasses were perched halfway down his broad nose, which was webbed with tiny red veins.

I'd appeared before the Honorable Martin Clausen twice before—both times on motions in a lawsuit that settled before trial. What had been most striking about him in court was the absence of anything striking about him. He didn't dominate the courtroom with his presence; instead, he seemed just another member of the courthouse staff, albeit one who happened to be seated higher than the others. He entered and left his courtroom without fanfare, leafed through papers or jotted notes as you presented your motion, appeared mildly distracted, rarely asked questions, and generally ruled from the bench without giving any reasons—just "motion denied" or "motion granted." As he called the next motion, the winning lawyer would take an order form and draft up a terse order—*Motion to dismiss called, heard, denied*—and hand it to Clausen's clerk, who'd pass it up to the judge as the lawyers in the next motion droned on. He'd glance at it for unnecessary words, scratch out any he found, scribble his name at the bottom, and pass the order back down to her, never once acknowledging the attorneys. After an hour in Judge Clausen's courtroom, even a trip to the license bureau felt like an opportunity for profound levels of human interaction.

Tonight, though, down from his perch on the bench, stripped of his black robe, and lacking his supporting cast of courtroom bureaucrats, he nevertheless radiated more judicial authority than I'd seen before.

The dining room was silent, waiting.

A scowling Dick Carple sat across the table from Rashita and me. He hadn't been able to reach anyone from the city counselor's office until after he'd arrived at Judge Clausen's house. The judge was unwilling to delay the hearing another hour, which is how long it would take for someone from the city counselor's office to get here. That meant that Carple was the man tonight. He glared at me, his expression suggesting that our relationship was still somewhat short of professional bonhomie.

Judge Clausen studied the last page of my handwritten petition, his lips pursed thoughtfully. He fired up another Marlboro, exhaled twin streams through his nostrils, looked up at us, and rapped his knuckles on the table.

"Court's in session." He turned toward Carple and removed his reading glasses. "Condemned the shelter without any notice, eh? A little extreme, counselor, wouldn't you say?"

"Hardly, Your Honor. Extremism in the defense of health is no vice."

I groaned. "Thank you, Senator Goldwater."

"It's the truth," Carple snarled at me.

I ignored him and focused on Clausen. "Judge, the truth is that the city can't just condemn a property and close it down without any advance notice or an opportunity for the property owner to be heard. The city ignored its own notice requirements. While extremism in defense of my clients' health may not be a vice, a violation of my clients' due process rights is not only a vice but an unconstitutional one."

"This was an emergency situation," Carple said. "The health department has the authority to act without notice and close down a facility that presents a clear and present health hazard to its inhabitants."

"Judge, as Mr. Carple surely knows, the health department's power to suspend due process is triggered only in the extraordinary situation of an imminent threat to life or health. Is the building about to collapse? No. Is there dangerous radiation or the presence of toxic chemicals? No. We're talking, at most, of some rats."

"Some?" Carple said, outraged. "This isn't the suburbs,

Miss Gold. We're talking city rats, not lab rats. You obviously know nothing about city rats."

I nodded. "You're absolutely correct, Mr. Carple. That is why I've brought an expert on rats to this hearing." I turned to the judge. "Your Honor, this is Ms. Rashita Jordan. She is a social worker at the Oasis Shelter. Through her profession and her own background, Ms. Jordan has extensive experience with rat infestations and is quite familiar with the buildings in question. She can assure the court that the health department has grossly exaggerated the rat problem at the Oasis Shelter. To her knowledge there is no rat problem."

Judge Clausen gazed at Rashita, who was glowering across the table at Dick Carple, her arms crossed over her ample chest. Carple eyed her warily.

"Well, Mr. Carple," the judge said, "do you have witnesses to counter that testimony?"

"I'm sure I could find plenty of experts, Judge, but not tonight. Not on such short notice."

"Ah," the judge said with the hint of a smile, "short notice. But at least you had some notice, eh? Unlike the women in that shelter." He turned toward Rashita. "Ma'am, you've been a social worker at this shelter for a year?"

"One year and two weeks, Your Honor."

He nodded. "You have female residents there?"

"Yes, sir. Women and children. Lots of little babies."

"You know these women pretty well?"

"I do, Your Honor."

He stubbed out the cigarette in the crystal ashtray. "You talk to these women?"

"Oh, yeah."

"About intimate things—things that concern them?"

"Oh, yeah."

The judge nodded and lit another cigarette. He exhaled the smoke and asked her, "What about their health concerns?

Do these women ever talk to you about their health concerns?"

"Every day. That's a big topic with them."

"How about their children? Do these women talk about health concerns for their children?"

"Yes, sir. That's one of my jobs—to make sure their little babies get the right medicines and see the doctors and keep healthy."

"Been there a little over a year, right?"

"Yes, sir."

"During that time, ma'am, has any resident of that shelter told you she's been bitten by a rat?"

"No, sir, Your Honor," she answered, smiling.

"During that time has any resident of that shelter told you that her child had been bitten by a rat?"

"No, sir, Your Honor."

"During that time have you heard of any resident of that shelter being bitten by a rat?"

"No, sir, Your Honor." She was beginning to get some rhythm into her answers.

"During that time has any resident of that shelter complained to you about rats?"

"No, sir, Your Honor."

"During that time have you heard of any complaints about rats?"

"No, sir, Your Honor."

Judge Clausen nodded. "Thank you, ma'am." He turned to me. "Anything else you need to ask this lady, Miss Gold?"

"None, Your Honor. You've covered all my questions."

He turned to Carple. "And you have no witness to counter this testimony, correct?"

"Well, not here."

"Is that a *no*, Mr. Carple?"

"It is."

Clausen put on his reading glasses and glanced down at my handwritten petition. After a moment he turned to Carple, peering at him over his reading glasses. "Mr. Carple, maybe the health department found a problem with rats at that shelter. Or maybe someone at City Hall found some other sort of problem with that shelter. But let's assume for tonight that we're talking about a genuine rat problem. Okay?"

Carple nodded uncertainly. "Okay."

"Even so," Clausen continued, "this rat problem hardly sounds to the court like the type of dire emergency that justifies dispensing with the due process clause of our Constitution and throwing a bunch of women and children onto the street after dark. Whatever this so-called rat problem is, Mr. Carple, the residents of that shelter have been putting up with it without any complaint or injury for at least a year and"—he turned to Rashita—"how many weeks, ma'am?"

"Two weeks, Your Honor, sir."

"At least a year and two weeks. Hearing no evidence to the contrary, Mr. Carple, I think we'll let the shelter and its residents struggle with this rat problem on their own for a little while longer while your client gets its act together and gives them a proper notice and a genuine opportunity to be heard." He turned to me. "I'll grant your TRO, Miss Gold. Draft it up for me, but keep it short and to the point." He looked at Carple. "You can use my phone, Mr. Carple."

Carple looked puzzled. "For what, Your Honor?"

"To call whoever you need to call to let them know that I've entered a TRO and that the health department better have that shelter back in operation and those women and children and their belongings moved back inside it in exactly two hours."

I called Sheila Trumble as soon as Judge Clausen signed the order. By the time Rashita and I drove back across town to the Oasis Shelter, the jumble of TV news vans had been joined by several official city of St. Louis cars and vans, some double-parked on the street, others parked along the sidewalks. The yellow hazard tape was gone from the doors, and two minicam crews were filming city workers, their arms loaded with belongings, following the women residents back into the buildings. I didn't see Sheila.

A little toddler in a diaper and T-shirt stood alone in the middle of the lawn crying. I went over and kneeled beside him. "It'll be okay," I said gently as I stroked his hair.

Rashita reached down and picked him up. "Where's your momma, Darius?"

That made him cry harder. As I watched the two of them—Rashita trying to soothe Darius while he cried for his mother—I could feel my fury spike again over the misery that Nate the Great had inflicted through this nasty little gambit.

"Rachel?"

Still angry, I spun toward a familiar face holding a microphone. Sherry McCutchen. I recognized her from Channel Five news. Behind her the minicam nightlights went on, making me squint as my eyes adjusted. I could see the red light on the camera blink on.

"We're standing here live with Rachel Gold, the attorney for the shelter. I understand you just returned from an emergency hearing before Judge Clausen, Miss Gold."

"That's true. The judge heard the facts and ordered the health department to reopen this shelter immediately."

"Is there really a rat problem?"

"My client has seen no evidence of such a problem, which means the real question is location. Is the rat problem here or downtown?"

"What do you mean?"

"It's no secret that certain city officials want this shelter closed. For their sake, these better not turn out to be imaginary rats."

"And if they are imaginary, then what?"

But by now the adult voice in my head was shouting, *Shut up, fool.* It snapped me back to reality.

"It's too early in the case for that kind of speculation," I said. "We're pleased that Judge Clausen has allowed these women and children back in the shelter. Their comfort and safety is our first concern. We'll deal with the other matters in due time."

I walked away from the camera, ignoring the shouted requests from the other reporters.

CHAPTER 16

The hearing before Judge Clausen had been last Thursday night. This was Monday at noon. Last Thursday I'd hinted darkly that someone in City Hall might be behind the phony rat emergency. Four days later I was meeting that same someone for lunch at Faust's, one of the fanciest spots in town.

The tuxedoed maître d' responded with a dignified nod when I told him my name.

"This way, mademoiselle," he said, gesturing toward the dining area. I followed him to a private booth near the back of the restaurant.

"The commissioner called from his car moments ago," the maître d' said, handing me a heavy cloth napkin. "He appears to be running a few minutes late and offers his apologies. Can I bring Mademoiselle something to drink while she waits?"

"Some iced tea, please."

"With pleasure," he said with a slight bow.

I looked around the elegant dining room and recognized a few faces—a pair of corporate lawyers from Bryan Cave at one table, a paunchy alderman huddled in a booth with a redhead young enough to be his niece, sportscasters Bob Costas and Mike Shannon laughing at another booth. Other tables had what clearly were business lunches in progress—executive types talking terms or examining financial pro formas.

Although Faust's had been the scene of many unholy deals over the years, the legend behind its name was strictly local and mostly benign. More than a century ago, a Prussian immigrant named Tony Faust opened a restaurant downtown at Broadway and Elm. By 1890, Faust's had become *the* restaurant of St. Louis—the place to see and be seen, both for local luminaries and visiting celebrities, including the stars who performed at the nationally renowned Olympia Theatre next door. The long bar on the first floor accommodated more than a hundred men (plus spittoons), while the ornate dining room upstairs served meals of such distinction that Faust's was featured in newspapers across the country and throughout the world. By the turn of the century, Faust's was as much the signature restaurant of St. Louis as Lüchow's was of New York. Indeed, Tony Faust and August Lüchow teamed up for the 1904 World's Fair in St. Louis and opened the Lüchow-Faust restaurant in the Tyrolean Alps section of the fairground.

Tony Faust died a few years after the 1904 World's Fair. His children married into the Anheuser and the Busch families, and his restaurant closed for good on the eve of World War I. That last night the waiters passed out extra napkins to wipe the tears shed by the loyal patrons. Sixty years later, the Adam's Mark Hotel—constructed a few blocks from the site of the original Faust's—revived the name for its premier restaurant.

"Hello, counselor."

I looked up to see Nathaniel Turner's beaming face.

I nodded politely. "Commissioner."

He slid into the booth across from me, adjusted his gold cuff links, and gave me an appraising look and a wink. "You lookin' fine today."

I gave him a sardonic wink in return. "You lookin' fine today, too."

"Damn." He chuckled. "I tell you, Rachel, I like a woman with spunk."

A young waitress appeared with a filled highball glass on a tray. She gave him a perky smile. "Hello, Commissioner."

"Belinda. Good to see you, darlin'. My, my, looks like you might have something special on that tray for me."

She blushed. "Boodles and tonic, sir." She set it on the table in front of him. "With a twist of lime."

"You have read my innermost thoughts, young lady." He gestured toward me. "Belinda, this is Rachel Gold, noted attorney and the only graduate of Harvard Law School who could pose for the *Sports Illustrated* swimsuit edition. You want Belinda to bring you something a little more exciting than that watered-down iced tea?"

"Tea is fine for me."

We were still making Nate's version of small talk when Belinda came back to tell us the specials and take our orders. I'd decided to let Nate get to the point of our meeting at his own pace. After all, this was his idea. The call came in Friday afternoon from his secretary. When I learned who the caller was, I had assumed that her boss was waiting to get on the line and blast me for my comment to the TV reporter the night before about a rat downtown—a comment given prominent play in the lead story on the ten o'clock news. Instead, though, his secretary told me that Commissioner Turner would like me to be his guest at lunch on Monday. I was surprised. Was he planning to lecture me over grilled tuna and couscous? As much as I wasn't in the mood for lunch with Nate the Great, I accepted the invitation. Nate and I had only one thing in common: the Oasis Shelter. He posed the single greatest threat to its continued existence. Accordingly, my responsibilities to my client overrode any personal issues I might have with him.

I watched him go through an elaborate selection process

with the waitress as he tried to decide between the catch of the day, the veal chops, and the pasta special. Maybe he still planned to give me an angry lecture, I thought. I'd learned early on that his flirtatious overtures at the beginning of a meeting meant absolutely nothing. But as I watched him banter with the waitress, I realized that my dark hint to the TV reporter probably was as threatening to Nathaniel Turner as an empty water pistol. By the following morning the TV stations had consigned my comment to the news morgue in the scramble to cover that day's stories. Although the print media was not as easily distracted, their resources were so limited that Nate and his henchman, Herman Borghoff, could easily deflect any effort to probe the health department action. Moreover, even if some persistent reporter found Nate's shadow behind the health department smokescreen, there was no guarantee the newspaper would go with the story. Nate the Great was a particularly unappealing target to the local media. Not only were their editors and publishers caught up in the booster hype over Renewal 2004—in which Nate's office occupied a pivotal role—but looming above Commissioner Turner was the ominous silhouette of Congressman Orion Sampson, who'd proven before that he was capable of bringing down a world of hurt on anyone foolish enough to mess with his sister's boy.

Which brought me back to this meeting. I knew that Nate was behind the health department's attempt to condemn the Oasis Shelter, and he knew I knew it, but I couldn't prove it, and he knew that as well. All of which made this meeting ever more mysterious.

After the waitress left with our orders, Nate leaned back and said, "Caught you on TV the other night."

"Oh?"

"Sounded like you had a rough evening."

"Not as rough as the one those women and children had."

"But you got them all back inside. That was mighty fortunate."

"It was."

"A rat problem, right?"

"So they claimed. We had an exterminator inspect the buildings on Saturday."

"And?"

I gazed at him a moment before replying. "He disagrees with the health department."

"Rats can be tricky little devils."

"So I've learned."

He was grinning. "I did some checking around at City Hall. It's not really any of my business, of course, except that my people would like to get your shelter out of there, too. Sooner the better. But unlike the health department, we prefer to do our condemnations the old-fashioned way. I'm referring to the powers of eminent domain, with all the bells and whistles, due process for all concerned."

"How nice, Commissioner. I am tingling with anticipation."

"And while you're tingling, Rachel, you won't have to worry about getting blindsided by the health department." He leaned forward, solemn now. "You have my word on that."

As if his word meant anything to me. But no reason to pick a fight. "That's good to know. Thanks."

"Herman tells me we should have our condemnation papers on file in a week or so."

"Super. I can't tell you how thrilling that sounds."

"We're prepared to go the whole nine yards if we have to, Rachel, but"—he paused, and then continued slowly— "we might still be able to work something out."

Finally, I thought. *Time to get down to business.*

"What does that mean?" I asked.

"For starters," he said, raising his fork and pointing it at me, "you have to understand that any deal we cut must include relocation of that shelter. No way that shelter stays put. No way, no how. But no reason that shelter can't house those women just as well in another part of town. As you know, my office has determined that your client's operation of a shelter in that particular neighborhood constitutes what's known under the statute as an 'inharmonious use' within the redevelopment area. But a use deemed inharmonious there could be just fine and dandy on property outside the redevelopment area." He smiled. "And we got plenty of that kind of property."

"You're suggesting a property swap?"

"I'm suggesting we think about it. The city of St. Louis, through my office and through the collector of revenue, controls lots of property on the north side, including plenty of possible sites outside the redevelopment area, including some buildings bigger than the ones your client is squeezed into now."

The waitress arrived with our meals. Grilled tuna for me, veal chops and a second gin and tonic for Nate. As he flirted with her, I mulled over his settlement concept. The Oasis Shelter was in a marginal area of town, but at least the neighborhood seemed to be rebounding, and property values were on the rise. By contrast, the properties the city controlled outside the redevelopment area were, for the most part, buildings condemned by the health department, seized by the city for nonpayment of taxes, or abandoned by the owners—in short, properties in lousy shape in bad neighborhoods. That meant any swap would be a big step down in quality and surroundings. Nevertheless, a swap would also buy peace with Nate and, just as important, more room. Space

was growing tight in the current facility—there were two
bunk beds in every bedroom, and some of those rooms
housed two mothers and three or four children. Even if we
ultimately prevailed in the condemnation fight and even if
the city approved the addition of another building to the
shelter—an approval that would never happen under Nate
the Great's regime—there was no way we'd have enough
money to expand the current facility. But the value of the
existing facility, if honored in a property swap, would result
in the acquisition of significantly more space. And if I could
convince the city to help fund the renovation of the buildings
as part of the settlement, maybe there was a deal in there
somewhere.

"Well?" Nate said after the waitress left.

"I'll talk to my client and see if there's any interest in a
swap."

"You do that, Rachel, and I'll see if I can hold off those
condemnation papers for a while. See if we can't work this
out to everyone's satisfaction." He gave me a playful smile.
"Like I always say, no need for us to make war if we can
make love."

Nate reverted to meaningless small talk. After the waitress laid the bill at his side and went off to get us more coffee,
he said, "I hear you're putting together an exhibit of paintings by Sebastian Curry."

I looked over, surprised. He was studying the bill.

"How did you hear?" I asked.

"Herman mentioned it to me the other day."

"How did he find out?"

Nate looked up with a frown as he tried to remember.
"Not sure. Someone must have mentioned it to him."

"Does he know Curry?"

"I guess so. He knew I might be interested in the exhibit,
though."

"Why's that?"

"I have one of Curry's paintings."

"Really?"

"Never thought it was worth much before, but maybe I got myself a lost treasure. Where's the exhibit going to be?"

"We're not sure. We're still in the concept stage."

"Who's the *we* you're talking about?"

My mind went blank. I couldn't remember the name of my imaginary organization. "It's a new group of artists," I said, trying to sound matter-of-fact. "I'm helping them on the legal end. Curry is one of the local artists they have under consideration, but nothing's final. How long have you owned yours?"

"Long time. Think it's worth much money?"

"Hard to say. How much did you pay?"

"Somewhere around a grand, I think."

"Did you buy it at a gallery?"

"Think I bought it at one of those art fairs. Does that matter?"

"No, just curious. Do you know Curry?"

"I might have met him. Maybe at that art fair. He's a brother, I believe." He paused and then grinned. "Maybe I ought to put that picture of mine in your show, eh? Might increase its value. Who do I talk to?"

"I'm a good one to start with. I'll pass it along. If they decide to go ahead with the show, I'm sure someone will call."

"Who?"

"Maybe me." I paused as the waitress refilled our coffee cups, grateful for her interruption. When she left, I said, "I'll let you know who."

"Good. You do that."

CHAPTER 17

I was at my desk working on a draft of an appellate brief when Jacki announced that I had a visitor. I looked up in surprise.

"Really? Who?"

"Sebastian Curry." She stepped inside my office and pulled the door closed behind her. "We're talking hot," she whispered.

I smiled. "Really?"

She raised her eyebrows. "Oh, yes."

I touched my hair. "Then show him in."

A moment later, he was standing at my door. "Miss Gold?"

Ellen McNeil had described him as eye candy. That was an understatement. Sebastian Curry was a hot fudge sundae with whipped cream and, well, nuts. He was tall and lean and athletic—broad shoulders, narrow torso, slim hips. He had on a black turtleneck, tan cargo pants, and black army boots. Dreadlocks framed a strong, angular face. His skin was the color of milk chocolate and his eyes were emerald-green.

He was literally breathtaking, as I discovered when I spoke. "Please come in," I said in a hoarse voice.

As he approached my desk, he gave me a pleasant smile that revealed perfect white teeth. "I'm Sebastian Curry."

We shook. My hand disappeared inside his.

He took a chair facing my desk. "I should have called

first. I'm meeting someone for lunch over at Bar Italia and was early so I decided to give it a try. Thanks for seeing me. I've really been wanting to talk to you." He had a friendly, low-key manner.

"What's on your mind?" My voice was back to normal, thank goodness.

"I wanted to find out if it was really true about the show."

"The show?"

"My paintings. I heard there might be a show of my paintings."

His hopeful expression made me feel guilty. It's one thing to mislead a bunch of wealthy purchasers, especially when most of them have no discernible emotional attachment to paintings they apparently bought solely as investments. But it's an entirely different thing to mislead the artist, and especially one in Sebastian Curry's circumstances. From what Ellen McNeil told me, his career had been in the dumps for years.

I said, "We're looking at several local artists. You're one of them. We're not yet sure whether there'll be a show. It's too early to say."

"When will you know for sure?"

I shrugged. "Another month or so."

"Who's the organization?"

"It's a new group of artists and gallery owners."

"Cool. What's their name?"

I still couldn't remember the name Ellen and I had concocted. "They haven't picked an official name, yet. How did you hear about it?"

That question flustered him. He sat back in the chair, eyes blank. "Well, I think someone—I can't remember who—someone must have told me—said you were, you know, looking at my paintings."

"We did look at several of your paintings," I said. "Mostly, we saw ones that were sold several years ago by the 309 Gallery."

"Right. They sold a whole bunch."

"Samantha Cummings ran that gallery, didn't she?"

"She sure did."

"Did you know her well?"

"I guess you could say that she and I—well, what do you mean?"

"Just curious. She sold a lot of your paintings."

He shrugged. "Yeah, I knew her, sure. No big deal."

"How did she end up handling so much of your work?"

"Does that matter?"

I smiled, trying to keep things low-key. "You seem to have been her most successful artist. I thought maybe the two of you had a special relationship."

"What do you mean?"

"Like maybe you were in art school together, or maybe she met you when you were just getting started." I offered a cheerful smile. "Something like that."

"Maybe she just happened to like my work."

"That makes sense," I told him, even though it didn't.

I tried to steer the conversation toward topics that would seem less threatening than his relationship with Samantha Cummings. He told me that he was still painting but hadn't been having much luck with sales or galleries lately. He did occasional modeling work—mostly fashion shoots for the local department stores—and waited tables at a restaurant.

"I work nights. I try to keep my days free to paint." He hesitated, almost sheepish. "Maybe your group would like to look at some of my newer work."

"I'm sure they would."

He took his wallet out of his back pocket. "Here's my card."

"Great." I took the card.

"My studio's in a loft on Washington Avenue. I live there, too. I'm usually up and around by ten in the morning. Just drop by someday and I'll show you my work."

"I'll do that."

"And be sure to let me know what your group decides." He checked his watch and stood up. "I better go. Thanks for seeing me."

"Sure. One last thing, Sebastian. Are you represented by an agency?"

"No. Why?"

"Just so we know who we need to deal with. What about the older paintings? The ones Samantha Cummings handled for you."

"What about them?"

"Wasn't there an agency involved back then?"

He looked puzzled. "An agency?"

"Millennium Management Services?"

His demeanor cooled. "How do you know about that?"

"The name showed up on some of the records."

"What records?"

I pretended that I was trying to remember. "Something with the paintings. I can't recall. I just remember seeing the name. I thought maybe they were your agent."

"No. They never were." He shook his head adamantly. "I had nothing to do with them. Ever."

"Who were they?"

"I don't know. Look, that part was none of my business. I know nothing about them. Nothing. I never did."

"Did they work for the gallery?"

"I just told you I don't know anything about them. They had nothing to do with me. You have to understand that, Miss Gold. Nothing."

"I hear you."

"Nothing."

"Right." I nodded. "Nothing. Got it."

It's obvious, Rachel."

"What's obvious?"

"He was *shtupping* her."

"Oh, come on, Benny. According to you, everyone's *shtupping* everyone."

"I'm serious. Not only that, I'd say that from the way he reacted to your questions he must have been doing her even after she got engaged to Michael Green."

"What? How can you say that?"

He paused with the chopsticks in front of his mouth and shrugged. "Because it makes perfect sense." He popped the shrimp in his mouth and reached for his beer.

Benny and I were eating Chinese take-out at my kitchen table. I'd been working late at the office when Benny called from the law school, where he'd just finished judging several rounds of moot court competition. We agreed to meet at my house for dinner, with Benny to bring the food and me to bring the beer and dessert. I picked up a six-pack of Pete's Wicked Ale and two pints of Ben & Jerry's on my way home. Benny, who should never order take-out on an empty stomach, arrived with four egg rolls, a pint of hot-and-sour soup, and four entrées: twice-cooked pork, Szechwan beef, Hunan shrimp, and kung pao chicken. Not that he'd have trouble finishing his portion—three egg rolls and three entrées fell somewhere between a heavy snack and a light meal for Benny. Indeed, we were down to the Hunan shrimp and my kitchen table was strewn with empty white take-out containers. Ozzie sat at attention in the corner, his eyes on his beloved pal Benny, who'd already tossed him half of the last egg roll, which Ozzie caught on the fly with his mouth. Although Ozzie wasn't picky when it came to Chinese take-out, you could tell he had his hopes pinned on a share of the Hunan shrimp.

Benny took a big chug of beer and set the bottle back on the table. "Look at what we know," he said. "Start with Sebastian Curry. As an artist, the guy is for shit, right? Even I can tell that, and I've got the keen aesthetic taste of a sack of hammers. No gallery would touch his crap until Samantha arrives on the scene. Not only does she touch his stuff. She becomes his goddamn patron saint—stocking her gallery with that schlock, selling it for fifteen, twenty, twenty-five times what it's worth. The woman was clearly promoting the living shit out of that guy. And remember, we're not talking Vincent van Gogh and we're not even talking Jack van Gogh. We're talking Jack Shit, and you know what that tells me? That tells me we got something more going on here than the usual artist/gallery relationship. That tells me that Natty Dreadlocks was pumping more than just her balance sheet. The proof is when you asked him about his relationship with her. What happens? He gets all flustered, right?"

"True," I conceded.

"What's that tell you? If once upon a time they had an affair, what's the big deal? But his reaction tells me we might not just be talking nooky. We might be talking naughty nooky."

I gave him a look. "What in the world is naughty nooky?"

"Look at the time period. She's peddling his schlocky paintings the entire time she's engaged to Michael Green. Maybe the reason Sebastian got defensive was because he was doing her the whole time—right up until Green got killed."

It sounded improbable, but no more improbable than any other scenario. "Maybe."

He shrugged. "You got a better explanation?"

"Not yet."

"Ask him. He gave you his card. Go over to his loft one morning and ask him straight-out."

"He's pretty uptight about it. I'd rather ask Samantha, assuming I can ever figure out a way to talk to her in private."

"Good luck. Her lawyer's not going to let you talk to her."

"He might. You never know. It's worth a try. I've got plenty to ask her besides her relationship with Sebastian Curry."

"Such as?"

"Such as what's the deal with Millennium Management Services? You think Sebastian got uptight when I asked him about Samantha? You should have seen his reaction when I mentioned Millennium Management."

"What makes you think she'll know any more about it?"

"She has to. She was the one who paid Millennium. I also want to find out more about Billy Woodward. He's the number one item on my list."

"The guy who committed suicide in front of her town house?"

"Yep. Angela's mysterious John. I spoke to her about him again this morning. The poor woman calls me every day now. She's obsessed with him."

"Can you blame her?"

"At least I was able give her some new information."

"What?"

"My investigator Charlie confirmed that Woodward's mother wasn't in the hospital when Angela met him. She was living in a trailer park in southern Illinois, somewhere on the outskirts of Metropolis. Still does. Claims she's never been sick a day in her life. Also claims she hadn't heard from her son in more than a decade. Charlie thinks she's telling the truth about that. Apparently, she didn't even know he was dead until Charlie told her."

"Did the guy have any brothers or sisters?"

"One older sister. She died in an auto accident when Woodward was in high school."

"Who else knew him?"

"I've got one name for sure. Harry Silver."

"Who's Harry Silver?"

"He's the head of a little company across the river in Sauget. I've got an appointment to see him tomorrow morning."

"What kind of company?"

"It's called Pinnacle Productions."

Benny frowned. "Pinnacle? What is it?"

I blushed slightly. "I believe they're in what is known as the adult entertainment industry.

"Strip clubs?"

"Movies."

"No shit? Porno? Right here in River City?"

"They operate in an industrial park off Route Three."

"Whoa. So this guy—the dude who killed himself—he was in those films?"

"In the films, around the films, behind the films. He apparently worked for Pinnacle for a few years. Harry Silver knew him fairly well. He's willing to talk to me. He agreed to meet me tomorrow."

"Hey," Benny said with a grin, "make sure you give Harry my phone number. You tell him to give me a buzz if he ever needs the expert services of a fluff boy."

Being Benny's pal means expanding your vocabulary in ways not measured by the verbal portion of the SATs—from the alternative meaning of "pearl necklace" to the job category known as "fluff girl."

I smiled and shook my head. "I hate to break your heart,

boychik, but I don't think they use fluff boys."

He put his hand over his heart in mock dismay. "I am shocked. Women have needs, too. You tell him that when it comes to the fine art of fluffing, Benny Goldberg is a big supporter of women's rights."

"I'll be sure to tell him that."

"I'm serious, woman. You tell him that in ten minutes I'll have his coldest porno queen leaning back with a sigh and saying, 'Thank you, Big Daddy.' "

He peered into the carton of Hunan shrimp and then glanced over at Ozzie, whose tail immediately started flopping. Benny looked back at me. "You want any of this shrimp?"

I shook my head. "I'm *plotzing.*"

He stifled a rumbling belch. "I'm starting to get a little full myself. Better save some room for your ice cream." He turned toward Ozzie. "You in the mood for a little Hunan action, Oz? This stuff'll put lead in your pencil."

Ozzie gave a jubilant bark and dashed over to Benny.

"In his bowl, Professor," I ordered.

Benny patted him on the head. "You hear Miss Manners? Time you and I show a little class, eh? Stay right here, my man."

Ozzie watched as Benny went over to his bowl and used his chopsticks to plop the rest of the Hunan shrimp into it. He turned toward Ozzie, who sat at attention, his eyes fixed on Benny, who glanced at me. I nodded.

He gave Ozzie a wink and a thumbs-up. "Go for it, dude."

Ozzie scrabbled across the kitchen floor to the bowl.

Benny went over to the refrigerator and peered into the freezer section. "Whoa! Chunky Monkey *and* Jerry's Jubilee!" He turned to me with his hand on his heart. "Rachel Gold, you are one awesome babe."

I leaned back with a big sigh. "Thank you, Big Daddy."

CHAPTER 18

Pinnacle Productions was in a nondescript building in a nondescript industrial park along a nondescript section of Route 3 in Illinois. I pulled into a parking space near the front of the building. The top half of the Arch was visible in the distance to the east. The building was one of those windowless warehouse tilt-ups that exist somewhere along the design continuum between airport hangar and Home Depot. There was no name on the building—just the street address stenciled in large numerals above the steel door. To the right of the door was a keypad code device and, for the rest of us, a speaker box and a buzzer. I pressed the buzzer.

"Who is it?" a female voice asked over the static.

"Rachel Gold to see Mr. Silver."

A pause, and then the door buzzed. I pulled it open and stepped into a no-frills reception area. To my left: a metal coat rack. To my right: a wall-mounted fire extinguisher and pay phone. A half-dozen stackable plastic chairs were arranged along each of the side walls. A battered metal magazine rack was at the end of the row of chairs to my left, and a scarred wooden coffee table was in front of the chairs to my right.

Directly ahead was the sole exception to the no-frills décor: a fortysomething receptionist with teased platinum hair and tortoiseshell reading glasses was seated behind a metal desk. She had bright red lipstick, long false eyelashes, a face that had been exposed to far too much sun for far too many years, and a formidable pair of breasts bulging against her royal-blue Tommy Hilfiger T-shirt. She'd apparently been stuffing videotapes, catalogues, and invoices into envelopes when I'd buzzed. Centered on the wall above her head was the company logo in hot-pink script:

PINNACLE PRODUCTIONS
"More Peaks than the Rockies!"

As I approached her desk, she sealed the envelope she was holding and peered at me over her reading glasses.

"Guild, right?" She was chewing gum.

"Gold."

"Gold." She smiled. "Hey, Gold for Silver. That's pretty good."

I smiled politely.

She paused to blow a bubble and pop it. "I'm Jillian Silver, honey. Harry's wife. He had to go to the bank. Oughta be back in a sec. If you don't mind waiting, you can sit out here."

The phone rang. Jillian answered with a cheerful, "Good morning, Pinnacle Productions! . . . Oh, hi, Murray. How are you? . . . Sure, just a sec." With the phone cradled against her neck, she turned toward the computer on her desk and began typing. "Let me get that account up on the screen."

I looked around. On the walls over the chairs were posters advertising various Pinnacle Production videos: *Screwing Private Ryan, Anal Affairs, There's Something Inside Mary, American Hair Pie, Jurassic Pussy, Inside Jenni Chambers.*

I took a seat and sorted through the magazines strewn on the coffee table. To say the least, it was a diverse collection. There were several issues of a glossy periodical called *Adult Video News* along with issues of *The Economist, The New Yorker, Hustler, Glamour, Playboy, American Scholar,*

Soap Opera Weekly, and *Paris Review.* With the exception
of the *Hustler* and the *Playboy,* which had no subscription
labels, and the *Glamour* and *Soap Opera Weekly,* which had
labels for Jillian Silver at the office address, the rest of the
magazines were addressed to Harry Silver at a ritzy suburb
of St. Louis. The fact that Harry Silver subscribed to *American Scholar, The Economist,* and *Paris Review* was intriguing. That he would put old issues in his waiting room—
where aspiring porno starlets and studs awaited their audition calls—was puzzling. Somehow, I couldn't imagine Tyffany Platinum, the featured actress on the *Anal Affairs*
poster, settling down with Harold Bloom's *American Scholar*
essay on nihilism and mockery in Shakespeare's *Troilus and
Cressida.* Nor could I imagine the next Harry Reems scru-
tinizing the piece entitled "Virtual Orphicality in the Romantic Poets," in which the author, an assistant professor at
Wesleyan University, opines that "once proper recognition
is given to the difference-based nature of linguistic meaning
that must necessarily be seen as a 'reaching-beyond' into an
incompletely articulated extra-linguistic presence, one real-
izes that the virtue of gesture is not subsumable under a system of textuality." Then again, if Harry Silver himself was
settling down with these essays, what in God's name was he
doing in this business?

The door to the right of the reception desk opened and
a skinny guy in his twenties came in pushing a cart piled
high with videocassettes, mailers, and various papers. He had
a scraggly beard and was wearing baggy jeans and a Black
Sabbath T-shirt. Still on the phone, Jillian motioned him toward the side of the desk. He set the cart there and gave me
an appraising glance before going back through the inner
door. Self-consciously, I tugged at my skirt, realizing that he
must have assumed I was here for an audition. I glanced up
at the image of Tyffany Platinum, her hands pressed against

the sides of her face, her perky mouth formed into an O of surprise as she looked back over her shoulders at the camera, wearing nothing but a silver thong and spiked heels. Platinum and Silver and Gold—oh, my. Platinum and Silver and Gold—oh, my.

I was leafing through the *Glamour* when Jillian got off the phone. "Oh, brother," she said with a sigh.

I looked up. She was staring at the videocassettes on the cart and shaking her head. She turned to me. "That was a distributor in Maryland. Ever since we put our catalogue on the Internet we've been so busy."

"Are those all your titles?" I asked.

"Pretty much. Harry's partner has another studio in Arizona. That's where we film a lot of our titles. But we still make some here, and we handle the shipping for everything out of here."

The phone rang again.

"Good morning, Pinna— Oh, Harry, the girl's here. What's taking so long at the bank? . . . Well, how much longer? . . . Okay . . . No, he hasn't called yet . . . Okay. See you soon, baby."

She hung up and gave me sympathetic smile. "Harry's running late. Maybe fifteen minutes."

"I can wait."

"You're here about Billy Woodward, right?"

"Did you know him?"

"Naw. Billy was dead before I met Harry."

"When did you and Harry meet?"

"Five years ago. At the *Adult Video News* Awards. I was living in Vegas back then. They hold the awards out there every year." She showed me the diamond engagement ring and matching gold wedding band on her ring finger. "We been married almost three years."

"Billy Woodward was in some of Harry's films, right?"

"I think that's right, but I'm not positive. That was a long time ago."

"Would those films have been made here?"

"Oh, yes. Harry has a whole studio in back." She gestured toward the door to the right of her desk. "Soundstages, editing booths, the whole works. They're filming one today. Why not go back there and look around?"

I glanced at that door. "I don't know."

"You should. Really. We've got other girls back there— besides the actresses, I mean. It'll help give you a sense of what Billy Woodward did on the production side. Let's see where they're shooting this morning." She checked a schedule on her desk. "Okay, here's what you do. Go through the door and turn left. Follow the corridor around to the right and you'll end up in Control Room A. You can watch from there. I'll send Harry back when he gets here."

I followed her directions to Control Room A, which was a small room jammed with electronic equipment—recorders, editing machines, and the like. The room smelled of burned coffee and doughnut grease and cigarette smoke and stale perspiration. There were three guys in the room, all in their late twenties, all dressed in jeans and sweatshirts. Two were seated in front of a video monitor screen. The third was leaning back in his chair against the side wall, his arms crossed over his ample stomach, his head resting on his chest. It took me a moment to realize that what I first mistook for a low electronic buzz was the third guy's snores. On a metal table next to the sleeping man was a coffeemaker, a stack of Styrofoam cups, and a nearly empty box of glazed doughnuts.

The front wall of Control Room A was a large picture window that looked onto a dimly lit film set which consisted of a three-sided façade of a bedroom. A queen-sized bed with a brass-rail headboard was against the back wall. There was a window to the right of the bed that appeared to look out onto a country landscape. The pretty view was actually a poster taped to the other side of the window frame—a bit of set design that reminded me, incongruously, of the Jimmy Stewart movie *It's a Wonderful Life*.

From across the control room I peered through the window, trying to make sense out of the six people on the set, all of whom seemed to be waiting for something to begin. There was a heavyset guy in his forties seated with his back to me in a director's chair. His chair actually had the word *Director* stenciled on the back. He had a headset resting on the back of his neck and was talking on a cell phone. Next to him, seated on a plain director's chair, was a much younger guy with a long nose and thinning brown hair. He was scribbling something on a clipboard balanced on his lap. Leaning against the side wall of the bedroom façade was a fat, bald guy with a big video camera on his shoulder. He was talking to a skinny guy with tattooed arms and a big tool belt. Both were smoking cigarettes and occasionally glancing toward the two people at the far end of the set, who appeared to be the actors in the scene about to be filmed. They were certainly dressed for the roles. The man was naked and the woman was in a black teddy and spiked heels. The naked guy was seated on the edge of the bed and the woman was on his lap. The guy had a blond crew cut and the muscular physique of a bodybuilder. The woman had red hair and the finest pair of breasts money could buy. I glanced at the monitor, which was apparently receiving a live feed from the video camera on the fat guy's shoulder. It displayed a tilted and slightly off-center shot of the man and woman on the bed. She was leaning against him, whispering in his ear as her hand moved slowly up and down between his legs.

One of the guys seated in front of the monitor turned around and looked at me with mild surprise. "Who are you?"

"Rachel Gold. I'm a lawyer. I have a meeting with Mr. Silver."

The second guy glanced back at me and stifled a yawn. Both of them turned toward the monitor, which showed the actors still huddled on the edge of the bed. The naked guy was looking anxiously at something off camera. I shifted my gaze from the monitor toward the window and saw that he was looking at the director, who was still seated but no longer talking on the cell phone.

"Shit," one of the guys at the monitor grumbled. "This looks bad."

The third guy awoke with a start. He looked back at me with a frown and then turned toward the monitor. "What's going on?"

"What else? That's Frankie out there."

"Same as last week," the second guy said, checking his watch. "Fifteen minutes and we're still waiting for wood."

"Who's fluffing him?"

"April."

The third guy squinted toward the monitor and then through the window. "She's getting nowhere, man. It's still a fucking Slinky."

"We got a stunt dick today?"

"I think Bobby's in this afternoon for one scene, but he's usually good for two."

Through a speaker came the director's voice. "Okay, Frankie, how 'bout we try to shoot the scene, huh?" You could hear the impatience in his voice.

Frankie nodded forlornly. The woman in the black teddy stood up and stretched, rubbing her right shoulder as she flexed and unflexed the fingers of her right hand.

The skinny guy with the tool belt went over and flicked on the hot lights. The bedroom set became incandescent.

"Let's back up and start the sequence from the top," the

director was saying as he put his headset on. "Doggie with April. Then we go Cowgirl with April. Lynette comes in. Then Cowgirl with Lynette. Jesus, someone get Lynette on the set already." The young guy with the long nose jumped up and started to leave the set as the director continued. "Then we go Missionary with Lynette and finish with the money shot on Lynette. Hey, Phil?"

The skinny guy stopped at the edge of the set and turned toward the director.

"Does Lynette do face?"

The skinny guy consulted his clipboard a moment and shook his head.

"Okay, money shot on her tits. You got that, Frankie?"

The naked actor nodded glumly.

"How's it coming? Any wood?"

The actor stared down between his legs, his shoulders slumped.

A long pause—everyone but the naked actor watching the director and waiting. Waiting. The director yanked off his headset and stood up, shaking his head with frustration. "Take a break."

Someone doused the hot lights. The set went dark. Everyone but the naked actor left the set. He sat alone on the bed, head down.

"Rachel?"

I turned. Standing in the doorway to the studio was a wiry guy in his fifties with a high bald forehead and reflecting aviator sunglasses.

"Harry Silver," he said. He removed the sunglasses and hooked them into the breast pocket of his shirt.

We shook hands.

I'd been expecting a chewed cigar, lots of bristly ear hair, and beady eyes swimming behind glasses big enough to

squeegee. I'd been expecting a pasty, pudgy sleazeball. Instead, I was facing what appeared to be the senior partner of
a law firm on casual day. Harry Silver stood about my height
and had the slender build of an athlete. He was wearing a
starched white Oxford-cloth shirt, dress khakis, and polished
cordovan loafers. He was tanned and had a neatly trimmed
gray goatee and intelligent blue eyes.

"Let's go back to my office," he said. "We can talk
there."

His office was up a flight of stairs above the reception
area—the only part of the building above floor level. As I
reached the top of the stairs I could look out over the entire
studio. There were three other soundstages in addition to the
bedroom set—a living room set, a bathroom set (with a large
tub and a glass-enclosed shower), and an office set (desk,
couch, etc.). Beyond the sets were storage areas and production areas and equipment areas. I saw a forklift moving
slowly between two rows of boxes on pallets.

Harry Silver's office was as much a surprise as he was.
I'd expected a framed gallery of autographed bimbo shots on
the walls and a few cheesy porno awards on a bookcase.
Instead, the only items on the walls were his diplomas (Williams College, B.A. cum laude; Brown University, M.A.,
Ph.D.), a Las Vegas wedding photograph (he in a black tuxedo, Jillian in a white wedding gown), and a large abstract
painting in a style that looked vaguely familiar. As for the
bookcase, it actually contained books. The bottom two rows
had what appeared to be a complete set of the works of An-
thony Trollope, while the top row had a three-volume set of
the plays of William Shakespeare and a variety of books on
film and film criticism.

"You're a Trollope fan?" I asked.

"I wrote my doctoral thesis on him. Have you read his
works?"

"Just the Barchester novels."

"Superb stuff. The man is grossly underrated. Compared to him, Dickens's novels are comic books. He's every bit the equal of George Eliot. I taught a graduate seminar on him."

"Where?"

"Washington University."

A pause. "You were a professor?"

He grinned. "Hard to believe, eh? Yes, for five years. Assistant professor, actually. Important distinction there." He chuckled. "In this business, the heft of your penis is important. In academia, it's the heft of your title. For the first three years I taught nineteenth-century English literature. The last two years I taught mostly film studies."

"Why'd you leave?" I asked.

He gave me a mischievous look. "Because the chairman of the department asked me to leave. His problems with me began on a personal level. I believe he took exception to the fact that I was fucking his wife on a regular basis. Although he hadn't fucked her in months, he nevertheless had a distinctly nineteenth-century proprietary view of her body. This personal problem between us purportedly escalated to departmental concerns when he learned that I was also fucking one of his students. Not one of my own, mind you. Despite appearances, I do have some scruples. Or at least I did back then. In any event, the object of my desire was one of *his* students, not mine. Indeed, she was a lovely poetry major that he had been attempting in vain to bang for two semesters. I suppose I could have fought him, but after five years in that political cesspool I was ready for a change. You say you've read Trollope." He gave me an approving smile. "You must be a reader."

"I am."

"A passionate one?"

"Actually, yes."

He nodded. "I became an English professor because I loved to read and wanted to convey that love to others." He shook his head ruefully. "How naïve. The love of reading is beside the point in a modern English department. I certainly didn't earn my degree to enlist as a foot soldier in Jacques Derrida's poststructuralist/postmodernist deconstructionist brigade. So I finally said fuck it. I tried film criticism for about a year, but there's no money in that, and most of the films I love date back several decades. Newspaper readers want a review of this year's version of *Pretty Woman*, not an essay on the use of irony in *The Philadelphia Story*. So I decided to quit writing about the latest chick-flick and started making my own versions. I tried the independent film route. That's a one-way ticket to oblivion. Fade out. Cut to interior—Pinnacle Productions." He gestured grandly. "And here I am: the Prince of Porn."

Despite my opinion of his industry, I was charmed.

"Ironically," he said, "I'm far more mainstream than the producers of those artsy independent films that I used to envy."

"How so?"

"Porno is a fourteen-billion-dollar-a-year industry in this country. Let me give you a sense of scale, Rachel. Fourteen billion dollars exceeds the revenues of professional football, basketball, and baseball combined. Combined. We're bigger than baseball, Mom, and apple pie. We have twenty times the revenue of the entire Broadway theater industry. Consumers spend more money on porno movies than they do on regular movies."

"That's remarkable."

"I'll tell you what's even more remarkable. The corporate CEOs and board members who vote straight Republican and grow misty-eyed over family values are the same CEOs and board members whose companies happen to be the biggest players in the porno industry. Who do you think owns the cable and satellite TV franchises and the in-room hotel movie systems that rake in all that money from those X-rated pay-per-view movies and porno networks? Fortune Five Hundred companies, that's who. And guess who owns big chunks of their stock? Pension funds. And that means that Mr. and Mrs. John Q. Public from Peoria are going to retire in comfort someday on the money they've made off movies that would make *Deep Throat* seem like a Walt Disney production." He chuckled. "The greatest source of revenue in this country is old-fashioned hypocrisy. And me? I'm just a bit player in this mad circus—just an independent filmmaker in southern Illinois."

"What in the world brought you to Sauget?" I asked.

"My health." He gave me a wink. "I came to Sauget for the waters."

"The waters?" I replied, playing along. "What waters? We're in the middle of southern Illinois."

"I was misinformed."

I smiled.

He said, "A wonderful film." He grew serious. "So you're here about Billy Woodward?"

"I am."

"Why?"

"Because he has a connection to a case I'm working on."

"A case? Who's your client?"

"Angela Green."

"*The* Angela Green?"

I nodded.

He had a puzzled expression. "What possible connection does Billy Woodward have to Angela Green?"

"He was her alibi."

Silver frowned. "Explain."

I did. He listened carefully.

When I finished, he asked, "What made you think there was a connection to Angela Green?"

"I didn't think there was. I was pursuing the connection to Michael Green's fiancée. That's where Woodward killed himself. In front of Samantha Cummings's town house. He was on the phone to her just before he shot himself."

He leaned back in his chair and stared at the ceiling. "In front of her house," he finally said. He lowered his gaze to meet mine.

"I need to make sense out of that," I said. "Why Samantha? I need to find out more about him. My investigator contacted his mother, but she hadn't heard from Billy in ten years. His sister is dead. He didn't seem to have any close friends or a girlfriend. Just some weight-lifting acquaintances. I'll eventually talk to them, but you're my best hope. He worked for you longer than anyone else."

Silver nodded slowly, rubbing his thumb and forefinger down the sharp edges of his goatee. "I hadn't seen him for a few years," he said, his voice distant.

"Tell me about him."

He pursed his lips as he collected his thoughts. "Billy was one of my first actors. He was in his early twenties back then. Nice-looking kid. Hung like a horse. Fairly reliable, too, at least back in the early days. In this business, reliability is just as valuable as size. Billy was a wanna-be hoping to break into the ranks of the male talent." He paused. "How much do you know about this business?"

"Not much," I conceded.

He scratched his goatee. "The hierarchy in the hard-core world is unlike the hierarchy in any other part of the film business. At the top of the pyramid are contract girls. They're also known as box-cover girls. That's because what sells the film these days is the box cover, not the contents. Video has revolutionized this industry."

He turned toward his credenza, where there were two stacks of videocassettes. He took one off the top and turned it toward me. "Here's a good example." He slid it across his desk.

The video was entitled *On Golden Blonde* and, according to the box-cover blurb, featured April Morning. Ms. Morning was presumably the striking blonde on the cover standing with her legs apart and her fists on her hips. She was dressed in a tiny white teddy, white string bikini, white stockings, white garter belt, and white pumps with six-inch stilettos. In the background, a guy in jeans and a T-shirt sat on the edge of the bed gazing at her from behind.

"The box-cover girls are the superstars," Silver continued. "They get the big bucks—bigger even than the directors. They don't stick around long, either. They all have the same career plan: get in and out of the business fast and become a featured dancer on the strip club circuit, where they can triple or quadruple their income. Below the box-cover girls are the male talent. They're a fairly small group, and each one is cherished. These guys are the Old Faithfuls of the business, the ones who can deliver the two most important male contributions to the genre: the on-screen erection and the on-command ejaculation. Have you ever seen a hard-core movie, Rachel?"

I nodded, blushing slightly.

"Then you are no doubt familiar with the one essential requirement of the genre. As if it is writ on high, all sex scenes must end with a visible ejaculation. Our male clientele demands it, for reasons best left to the disciples of Sigmund Freud. The climax scene goes by many names—*pop shot, cum shot, payoff shot*. My preferred term is *money shot*, since the men are literally paid by the ejaculation."

"Really?"

"No money shot, no money. Moving further down the hierarchy we come to the B-girls. These are the fill-ins—an ever-changing group of women who don't have the star power of a box-cover girl but add variety to the films. We recruit them mostly from the strip clubs here on the east side. Every once in a while you'll find one who can blossom into a box-cover girl, but that's rare. And finally, at the bottom of the pyramid are the wanna-bes—the new male hopefuls, like that yutz you saw in there today. We do a casting call about once a month. Ten to twenty of those guys show up— lots of bodybuilders mixed in with laid-off blue-collar work- ers and an occasional college kid. The guy you saw today was the only one to make it through the last casting call. I thought he had promise, and he did fine his first time. But he had problems last week, and from what I saw in there today this will be his last week in the business."

"What about Billy Woodward? Where was he on the pyramid?"

"Billy started as a wanna-be. I had high hopes for him. He was a good-looking kid with some real acting talent. Had a nice personality, too. At least at the beginning. He did good work his first year, but then he started having problems." Harry leaned back in his chair and stroked his goatee. "There's a nasty irony for the male actors in this business. Most of these guys are macho types—often macho with a nasty twist. Believe it or not, many of them take pride in their ability to ejaculate in a woman's face. They think it's proof of their manhood—and there's the irony. You've got these macho body builders whose entire livelihood depends on the performance of the one muscle in their body they can't voluntarily flex. And each time it fails it only increases the pressure for next time. When guys like Billy Woodward get into an unstable flight pattern, they tend to crash and burn real fast. Especially back before Viagra."

"How long did he last?"

"Maybe eighteen months in front of the camera. But I liked the kid, so I kept him around as a crew hog. He worked as a set designer, an electrician, a general handyman, a shipping clerk. He was a hard worker and a quick study—maybe not the brightest kid, but I'm not running a nuclear physics lab here."

"How long did he work behind the camera?"

"About four years."

"Why did he leave?"

"I fired him."

"Why?"

Harry grimaced. "Billy was a troubled lad—no father, alcoholic mother, a few brushes with the law early on. I suppose I was fond of him. Probably too fond. I overlooked a lot of his personal problems, but then I started hearing things that disturbed me."

"What kinds of things?"

"The performance problems Billy had on the set apparently spilled over to his private life. Eventually, he was incapable of a normal sexual relationship with a woman. Apparently, he had no problem maintaining an erection when he was alone. But when he was with a woman, the same performance anxiety that ruined him as an actor ruined him as a lover. Unfortunately—and unconscionably—he decided that the best way to eliminate the pressure was to drug his date. I heard about it from others on the crew. He used to brag to them about his conquests. They gave him a nickname."

"What?"

"They called him 'Roofer.' "

I let that sink in.

"Why Roofer?" I asked, although I knew the answer.

"It came from one of the street names for the pills he gave his dates. The things were called 'roofies,' I think, or maybe 'roofs.' The drug was in the news a few years back. Rohyper—something like that."

"Rohypnol."

"Yeah, that's it. Anyway, I was furious when I heard what Billy was doing. As far as I'm concerned, drugging a girl for sex is the moral equivalent of rape. I confronted him, he admitted it, and I fired him on the spot. I threatened to call the cops."

"Did you?"

"He begged me not to. Promised he wouldn't do it anymore. I still felt sorry for the kid, I guess. So I didn't report it."

I nodded, trying to fit what I'd learned into the pattern that was emerging.

"This is really troubling," I said.

"What part?"

"All parts." I leaned back in my chair with a frown. "Angela Green met Billy Woodward for a drink on the night of the murder. She doesn't remember what happened after that. They found traces of Rohypnol in the blood samples of hers from the scene of crime."

"Oh, Jesus." He leaned back in his chair. "Do you think Billy was having sex with her?"

"I don't know what Billy was doing with her."

Harry shook his head. "Christ Almighty."

We sat in silence for a few moments.

Finally, I asked, "What do you know about Billy's connection to Samantha Cummings?"

"They worked together. They were lovers for a while. Billy was devastated when they broke up. He kept trying to convince her to come back to him. I lost track of both of them after I fired Billy."

"Here's the suicide note he left," I said, handing it to him.

" 'No more waiting for Woody,' " he read. " 'Sayonara.' " He looked up. "That's definitely him. Woody was his nickname. In fact, one of his screen names was Woodrow Woodpecker. Turned out to be a nightmare name for him, because once he started having performance problems, the crew got a kick out of saying they were 'waiting for Woody.' His nickname became a joke. He hated it. The 'sayonara' part is Billy, too. That's how he always said goodbye." Silver shook his head sadly. "Poor kid."

"You say they once worked together?"

"Right."

"Was that before Billy started working for you?"

"Oh, no. They worked together here."

"Here?"

"Right."

"In front of the camera?"

Silver smiled. "You didn't know that?"

"I don't think anyone does."

"Sam was young then. She worked under a stage name." He paused, searching his memory. "Sammi, no—Staci. Staci Cummer. Staci with an *i* and Cummer with a *u*. Sam was actually a student of mine during my last year at Washington U. She was a freshman. Art history major, I believe. She dropped out of school her junior year. When she found out about my new career, she approached me for work." He smiled wistfully. "Beautiful girl. She was actually quite good, too. Could have been a contract girl if she wanted, but she left the business after just a year or two. Like most who go straight, I'm sure she'd prefer to leave this part of her life behind her. That's certainly her prerogative, and I respect it. One of the local weather girls on TV got her start with me. She did some nasty, kinky scenes, too, including one with a

German shepherd. But she has a new life now—standing in front of the weather map and talking about cold fronts. I have no interest in publicizing her role in those films, or Samantha's role in her films. I make plenty of money as it is." He gave me a wink. "Even we pornographers have our limits."

"Films?" I asked, accentuating the plural. "How many was Samantha in?"

"Maybe half a dozen. She and Billy were in most of them together."

"This is, well—surprising."

"Let me see if I can get you one of their videos to watch," he said, standing up. "We must still have a few in storage."

As I got up, I leaned toward the abstract painting. Sure enough, in the lower right corner was a familiar signature.

I followed Harry Silver downstairs and back toward the storage area. I watched as he opened the drawer in one of the large filing cabinets and started sorting through the videocassettes. "Here we go."

"You have a painting by Sebastian Curry," I said.

He turned to me with a bemused expression, a videocassette in his hand. "Do you actually know his work?"

"I've seen some of his paintings. When did you buy yours?"

"About eight or nine years ago."

"From who?"

"From him."

"Do you like his stuff?"

He pondered the question. "Not at all. I bought it more as a favor."

"What do you mean?"

"Sebastian was your classic struggling artist. Emphasis on the struggling part. I didn't think he'd ever make it, but I liked him and thought it might give him a boost if he could actually sell one of his paintings. How do you know about him?"

"When Samantha Cummings had an art gallery, she sold a lot of his works. In fact, she sold them for way above their market value."

He laughed. "Good for her. Good for both of them. He must have been in heaven over that."

He looked back in the drawer and sorted through the titles. Eventually, he found what he was looking for and exchanged it for the cassette he'd been holding. "Let's try this one instead."

The name of the movie was *All That Jizz*. Despite the title, it had a relatively classy box cover showing two chorus girls shot from behind, their hips canted in a classic Bob Fosse pose. Each was wearing a thong spandex leotard, black stockings, and black spiked heels. Each had on a top hat tilted jauntily to the side. There were two box-cover girls, or at least two actresses identified by name on the box cover. Neither was Staci Cummer.

"Take it home and watch it," Silver told me. "I guarantee that you will find it quite enlightening."

CHAPTER 19

From Pinnacle Productions I drove to the Jewish Federation, where I had a lunch meeting for a committee of Jewish professional women that I served on. The topic was a fund-raiser for one of our scholarship projects. Talk about cultural dissonance—from a money shot on the East Side to a money drive in West County.

I didn't get to my office until almost three o'clock, by which time I had nineteen phone messages, including two urgent ones from Benny.

"He wants a full report on Pinnacle Productions," Jacki said.

"I'll bet he does."

"Did you find out much?"

"Too much. I'm not sure what to make of it all. Especially this." I took the videocassette out of my briefcase.

"*All That Jizz?*" Jacki said, examining the cover. "Are you kidding me?"

"You think that's bad? How 'bout *Jurassic Pussy?*"

Jacki giggled and covered her mouth. "Oh, no."

"Their target audience must have the sense of humor of a seventh-grade boy."

"Is the guy who killed himself on this video?"

"Yep, and so is Samantha Cummings."

Jacki's jaw dropped. "Oh, my God."

"I can't believe it, either. In fact, I won't until I see it." I flipped through the stack of phone messages. "I'm going to return some of these and then we can watch the video. If Benny calls while I'm on the phone, tell him I'm not back yet."

"Really? You know he'd die to see this."

"Sure I do, but you know Benny. He'd turn the whole thing into a comic monologue. I'm not ready for that." I gestured toward the videocassette in her hand. "The stuff I learned today is really troubling. I want to see what's on this tape and figure out my next move without having to deal with his wisecracks."

I returned only those phone calls that sounded like they needed returning—just eight of the nineteen. Even so, by the time I finished with number eight, almost two hours had elapsed and the list of messages had grown by six, including another from Benny saying that he'd be over right after his antitrust seminar. That gave us barely an hour.

I called out, "It's show time, Jacki."

I turned on the TV, put the cassette in the VCR, and fast-forwarded through the previews for a trio of movies that I hadn't recalled seeing on anyone's list of the top ten movies of the year.

"Fasten your seat belts," I told her as the title words appeared on the screen to the accompaniment of generic lounge music.

The "plot"—such as it was—unfolded quickly. The protagonist was supposed to be a legendary director of Broadway musicals named Rob Rosse. His part was played by a middle-aged, potbellied actor who wasted no time in exposing his principal qualification for his role in the film. It was, to say the least, a daunting piece of equipment—an appendage that would have looked more in scale dangling between the hind legs of a Clydesdale. I suppose it made him the envy of the locker room crowd, but I couldn't imagine any woman reacting to its unveiling with anything but alarm.

The scene opened in his office, where he was in the process of casting the female lead for his next musical. Specifically, the scene opened in that segment of the audition where the young actress was kneeling in front of Rob Rosse and demonstrating an oral skill unrelated to singing but apparently pertinent to the casting process. Although she was a blonde, she didn't resemble my photos of Samantha Cummings. I also had the police file photo of Billy Woodward with me to make sure that we could identify him.

The opening sex scene progressed to intercourse and moved through a sequence that, after my morning's education, I could recite like a pro: Cowgirl, Doggie, Missionary, money shot onto her face.

"Oh, gross," Jacki said.

The money shot triggered the main plot twist: moments after ejaculating, Rob Rosse went into cardiac arrest. The paramedics arrived, put him on a stretcher, and loaded him into the back of the ambulance. The remainder of the movie was a series of flashbacks during the ride to the hospital— flashbacks to the leading ladies of Rosse's career, all of whom he'd had sex with and several of whom he'd observed having sex with others. We played the video at regular speed long enough at the beginning of each flashback to confirm that neither Samantha nor Billy was in the scene, and then we fast-forwarded to the next flashback. Sexual intercourse viewed at high speed becomes a weird cross between a human electrocution and a high school driver's ed film on the role of pistons in an internal combustion engine.

"Whoa, that's her," Jacki said.

I hit the pause button and compared my photos to the woman on screen. "You're right."

With her long blond hair parted in the middle and her hiphugger jeans, Samantha Cummings, aka Staci Cummer, seemed barely out of high school. The scene opened with

Rosse spotting her playing a guitar and singing a folk song on a park bench. Struck by her beauty, he was about to approach her when a young man came up and gave her a kiss.

"That's him," I said, hitting the pause button again. I handed Jacki the picture from the police file. Woodward's hair was cut longer in the movie, and he was dressed disco-style, right down to the ankle-high boots.

"You're right," Jacki said.

I hit play.

Billy and Samantha headed off toward his apartment hand in hand, followed in the distance by Rosse. The apartment was on the first floor, which enabled Rosse to spy on them through a window. At the beginning of the scene—the kissing part—there was a tenderness between Samantha and Billy that seemed genuine. But once the sequence began, you could almost sense the cameramen and film crew hovering around the edges of the bed. No place for tenderness there.

The performance problems that would soon afflict Woodward were nowhere evident in the remainder of the scene, which ran Missionary, Cowgirl, Doggie, money shot.

"Oh, not in her hair," Jacki squealed in disgust as one of Billy's spurts arced over her back and onto her hair.

Samantha had a second sex scene, this time with the Rosse character. Moments into the scene they were joined by another young woman. *A pair of B-girls with the male talent,* I thought as I glumly watched the scene play out. Although the sex was explicit and astonishingly vivid, the erotic effect was by now virtually nil. It was more like watching a medical procedure under klieg lights. Jacki and I had giggled through the movie's opening scene on the casting couch, but neither us said a thing now. It was just too depressing. As I watched Samantha finish off Rosse by hand, his semen splattering her neck and breasts, I couldn't even begin to imagine the lure of such a job. Even stripping in a crowded, noisy topless club seemed more appealing than this, although not by much.

The final flashback faded as Rosse's ambulance reached the hospital. Two nurses rolled him quickly down the hall toward the operating room. As they burst through the swinging doors, the scene shifted into fantasy mode and we were in an ethereal white operating room filled with undulating white fog. Rosse, dressed in a white hospital gown, was strapped on a gurney, an oxygen mask over his mouth. One of the box-cover girls appeared out of the fog, dressed in a silky white nightgown that reached to the floor. She had a pair of small white wings on her back. I had to concede that it was a visually powerful scene, totally unexpected in this cheesy video.

The white angel spoke to Rosse, telling him that she'd been the true object of his lifelong desire, but that he'd been too caught up in his ego and ambition to understand that.

"I could have been yours," she told him in a husky whisper as she slowly lifted the hem of the long white gown. "With me you could have known heaven on earth."

He watched, the mask strapped over his mouth, his eyes widening with desire, or maybe anguish.

"But instead," she continued, "you're condemned to that gurney for all time. All you can do is watch."

She slipped off the shoulder straps and let the gown slide down her body, the silk gathering in folds at her feet. She took a step forward, now wearing nothing but white pumps.

"She's gorgeous," Jacki said with a sigh.

Behind her, the swirling fog now had taken on a reddish tint. She turned toward the fog and paused to look back over her shoulder at Rosse. She gave him a wistful smile and turned away. She crooked her finger toward the swirling fog and made a beckoning motion. In a husky voice, she whispered, "Come here, you big devil."

Emerging from the fog was a tall lean black man wearing a red mask over his eyes and a pair of curved red devil's horns sprouting from his forehead. He was naked beneath his floor-length red cape. As he stepped forward, his enormous uncircumcised penis swayed heavily against his muscular thighs.

"Oh, my God," Jacki gasped. "It's him."

I sat there stunned. Despite the mask, the man's identity was unmistakable. I was staring at Sebastian Curry.

In silence, we sat through the final scene and then the credits. Sebastian Curry acted under the name "Ronnie Mandingo." Billy Woodward was "Woodrow Woodpecker."

The answering machine picked up after the third ring.

"Yo, what's up? Sebastian here. Sorry I can't get your call. Just leave me your name and number and I'll be back at you soon as I'm able. If you're calling to come see my work, be sure to leave a few possible dates and times. Bye for now."

I waited for the beep.

"Sebastian, this is Rachel Gold. We met yesterday at my office. I need to come over to ask you a few questions. I'm in court on a motion tomorrow morning. I should be done by ten. If it's okay with you, I'll drop by your place after court. Call me if that's a problem."

I left him my home and work phone numbers.

CHAPTER 20

During the hour that I waited in the packed courtroom for my motion to be called, my emotions fluctuated between anticipation and discouragement—anticipation over my upcoming meeting with Sebastian Curry and discouragement over my inability to embrace the teachings of Jonathan's rabbi.

I'd had another session with Rabbi Kalman last night. Although I was trying—I really was—my resistance to Orthodox Judaism wasn't waning. No matter how I tried to open my heart to the rabbi's teachings, my brain kept interfering, kept parsing through the doctrine, spotting examples of the unequal status of women. And each example only increased my bond to my Reform congregation, where my rabbi was a woman and my cantor played guitar and my liturgy was gender-free.

But, I sternly reminded myself, this wasn't my team versus Jonathan's. The goal of my sessions with the rabbi was to get on Jonathan's team. I loved Jonathan and I loved his daughters and I wanted to be his wife and I wanted to be a mother to his daughters. Their world was the world of Orthodox Judaism. Jonathan and I had already fought about this once, just before he left for New York. In the aftermath, I vowed to start meeting with his rabbi and bridge our gap. I knew that the problem bridging that gap was mine—not the rabbi's or his teachings. Jonathan's religious world was the same world that had nourished and sustained my female ancestors for countless generations.

That's why my resistance was so frustrating. I almost told Jonathan when he called late last night. I'd been obsessing over it, trying to think how to break the news, when the phone rang. It was him. He sounded so exhausted that I didn't have the heart to go into it. So instead we commiserated—I with his marathon trial in New York, which was still weeks from final arguments, and he with my increasingly serpentine investigation of the loose ends in Angela Green's murder prosecution.

His advice on my investigation remained the same: "Stick with the money trail, honey. The other leads are important, of course—that artist, Samantha, the guy who killed himself—but the goal is to use them to move further along the money trail."

*S*ebastian Curry *knew something about the money trail.*
    That's what I told myself as I parked my car across the street from his building in the warehouse district. He'd confirmed as much through his reaction to my mention of Millennium Management Services. As for his obvious unease when I'd tried to probe his relationship with Samantha Cummings, I assume that that was tied, at least in part, to their roles in *All That Jizz.* Perhaps I could use that unease to get him to open up about Millennium.

I found his name on the column of mailboxes in the vestibule: S. CURRY—4B. There appeared to be two tenants per floor and six floors in the building. When it came to security, however, Curry's building was not quite the White House. The buzzer next to his mailbox was missing, as were the buzzers for many of the other tenants. Not that it mattered. The security door between the vestibule and the interior was propped open.

Although the warehouse district had been undergoing a major face-lift in recent years as developers sought to lure suburban couples back to the city with trendy loft apartments and hip décor, Sebastian Curry's building was still in its pre-chic phase. The walls of the small lobby were painted an industrial gray. The plaster ceiling was splotched with yellowish-brown water stains. Directly ahead was a freight elevator dating back to an earlier era—the kind with a scarred wood-plank floor and sliding cage doors you pulled open with a handle.

I closed the elevator cage behind me and pressed the large black button marked 4. With a dull metallic thunk, the elevator started upward, accompanied by the creaks and whines of the cables and pulley. I peered through the crosshatched metal of the cage and watched the elevator rise past each floor. It halted with a shudder at the fourth. Yanking on the handle, I opened the door and stepped out. To my left was Curry's apartment, 4B. The door was slightly ajar. I glanced to my right. The door to 4A was locked.

I knocked on Curry's door and pushed it farther open. "Sebastian," I called, "it's Rachel Gold."

Silence.

I stepped inside. "Sebastian?"

Silence.

I felt a wave of dread.

I checked my watch. Twenty minutes to eleven.

Don't assume the worst, I told myself.

He said he worked nights. *Maybe he's still asleep? Or in the bathroom?*

I was standing in what appeared to be his studio area, which curved around to the right. The living quarters were off to the left. The sun came slanting in from the east, filling the studio with dazzling light. There were several canvases scattered around the room—the smaller ones on easels, the larger ones leaning against the wall, some apparently finished, others still works in progress.

I listened for sounds from the back of the loft—for shower water or a toilet flushing or cabinets closing. Nothing.

"Hello?" I called, my voice tight. "Sebastian?"

I sniffed the air for the morning scents of coffee or bacon. Nothing.

Maybe he ducked out for a moment—maybe to pick up some fresh baked goods for our meeting. That's always possible.

I moved toward the living quarters of the loft, past the couch and assortment of chairs that constituted the living room. The kitchen area was directly ahead. Everything there was neat and tidy—dishes in the drying rack, a crystal vase filled with yellow tulips on the small table, a wicker basket on the counter filled with oranges. On a sisal mat on the oak floor sat nearly empty bowls of cat food and water.

The kitchen was separated from the back area by a freestanding wall of shelving filled with cooking wares, knickknacks, and books. I stared at the books, mostly cookbooks, reading the titles without comprehending a word.

He could be asleep, I repeated, *or maybe he's in the bathroom or maybe he did step out for a moment. Plenty of innocent explanations.*

I hadn't moved.

I couldn't move.

My eyes scanned the knickknacks on the shelves. I was having trouble breathing.

Come on, Rachel. You're a big girl.

I forced myself to the edge of the divider wall, took a deep breath, and peered around the corner. The room was dark, the shades drawn. As my eyes adjusted I could make out a queen-sized bed against the wall to the left and an enormous wooden armoire along the side wall. To my right was the bathroom. The door was open, the light off.

"Meow."

A black cat sat on the edge of the bed. It stared at me with iridescent green eyes. I took a step toward the bed. I could see that the bed was unmade, the comforter pulled back and bunched, the pillows in a jumble.

"Meow."

"Hi," I whispered.

And then I saw the shape on the bed behind the cat.

A leg.

No, two.

A pair of legs—a black man's legs—visible from the feet to knees. Toes up, the pinkish bottoms of the feet facing me.

I stared hard. I could see the bends in the knees where the legs disappeared over the edge of the bed.

I forced myself closer. I moved around the foot of the bed, and as I did the rest of the body came into view.

"Oh, no," I whispered.

I stared down at Sebastian Curry. He was flat on his back, naked, his arms spread out, palms up, his eyes open, a neat black hole in his forehead just above his right eye. The force of the bullet must have knocked him backward off the bed. There was a dark puddle of blood beneath his head.

"Meow."

CHAPTER 21

Brian Morgan came out to greet me in the reception area. He was a short and burly lawyer in his forties with a moon face, flushed complexion, and thick blond hair combed straight back. We stood at eye level.

"She's here," he said after we shook hands.

"Good."

"I have to tell you, Rachel," he said, running his fingers through his hair and frowning, "this is a first for me."

"Me, too."

"I have no idea what's going on here."

"All you need to know is my promise that I won't talk to her about the case."

"Yeah, well, maybe. I'm not comfortable with this, but I'll go along. Let me take you to her."

I followed Brian Morgan down the hall. His four-man firm specialized in plaintiff's personal injury claims—mostly auto accidents and slip-and-falls with an occasional exotic thrown in the mix. This case had to be his most exotic.

Brian was an easy person to underestimate, and many defense lawyers had clients who'd paid the consequences. What he lacked in polish and legal expertise—having graduated near the bottom of his law school class at Mizzou— he more than compensated for with hard work, perseverance, and preparation. He was, after all, the lead lawyer on the first Son of Sam case ever filed in Missouri.

I'd called Brian yesterday, which was the day after I

found Sebastian Curry's corpse. I told him I wanted to talk to his client alone.

"What do you mean 'alone'?" he'd asked.

"Just her and me. But not about the case. I promise."

"Then what about?"

"It's private."

"I'd call that a pretty unusual request, Rachel. Why should I agree to that?"

"Let's let her decide. Do you have a pen?"

"Yeah."

"Take this down. Tell her I want to talk to her about Staci Cummer—that's C-U-M-M-E-R—and Ronnie Mandingo and Woodrow Woodpecker."

"Woodrow Woodpecker? Is that a joke?"

"Just give her those names, Brian. Tell her I need to see her as soon as possible."

He'd called back an hour later, even more mystified. "I have no idea what's going on here, but she'll meet you at my office tomorrow morning at ten."

Earlier today I'd spoken again to the homicide detective on the Sebastian Curry murder—he'd previously interviewed me at length. He told me that the medical examiner determined that Curry had been dead for at least twenty-four hours before I found him, which meant that he was *already* dead when I called and left the message on his machine. Although there were two messages on his answering machine, neither was mine and both had been left *after* I left my message, since the first caller included the time of her call in her message. ("Hi, Sebastian. This is Gail. It's Tuesday night about ten-thirty. I know Jean's still out of town, and I bet you're lonely, you poor baby. Me and Greg Ramsey and Phyllis are going to Galaxy around midnight for Jambalaya's CD release party. Hope to see you there.")

The timing meant that someone had been in the dead

man's loft *after* I'd left my message. Even creepier, it meant that someone had listened to my message—and to any others on the tape—before erasing them. That someone would thus have learned that I was coming by the next morning, which meant that the door to the loft might have been left open intentionally. If so, the person who listened to my telephone message wanted me to find the corpse.

Brian Morgan stopped at the door to a small conference room, rapped twice and opened it.

"Samantha?"

A blond woman was seated on the far side of the conference table. She got to her feet as I followed Morgan into the room.

"This is Rachel Gold," he said. "Rachel, Samantha Cummings."

I was about to reach across the table to shake her hand but stopped when she crossed her arms over her chest. I nodded and said hello.

She nodded back, not saying a thing. She was wearing a burgundy cardigan sweater, the sleeves pushed up, over a gray knit V-neck dress hemmed at her knees.

A moment of silence.

Although I'd seen her on TV back at the time of the trial and more recently in the porno flick, which dated back at least a decade, this was the first time I'd seen Samantha in person. She was in her mid-thirties now. Although she was still stunning from a distance, closer in there were signs of aging—a trace of vertical lines from her nose to the corners of her mouth, a hint of crow's-feet at the corners of her eyes, worry lines in her forehead. Not that she wasn't still beautiful, especially with her high cheekbones and retroussé nose. Just older now, and a little worn. Her most striking features were still her almond-shaped blue eyes. But they too had changed over time. In the adult video, shot back when she was perhaps twenty-one, those eyes had sparkled. That sparkle was gone now, replaced by a muted determination. Samantha Cummings was a survivor.

"Well," Morgan said with a forced smile, rubbing his hands together, "I'll leave you ladies alone. If you need anything, just holler." A pause as he looked from her to me and back to her. "Okay, well, I'll, uh, I'll see you later."

Samantha scowled at me as she sat back down. "I'm not dropping the case," she declared.

"I'm not asking you to."

"Is that so?" There was sarcasm in her voice. "I got your message, Miss Gold. I know exactly what's going on here."

"No you don't, Samantha. I don't care about that part of your life, and I certainly have no plans to tell anyone else about them."

"Then what do you want?"

"I want to talk to you about two of your costars. Billy and Sebastian."

She thrust her chin forward. "Oh? What about them?"

"Look, Samantha, I'm not here today because of your lawsuit and I'm not here because of those films. I'm here because I've learned some very troubling things about Billy Woodward and Sebastian Curry."

"Such as?"

"Such as Billy Woodward was with Angela Green the night Michael Green was killed."

"What are you talking about?"

"She thought his name was John. That's what he told her. She had no idea who he really was—and neither did I—until I showed her a photo of Billy Woodward."

She frowned in disbelief. "What in God's name was she doing with Billy?"

"More important, what was Billy doing with her?"

"What are you talking about?"

"Angela Green has almost no recall of what happened that night."

"So she claims. Guess what? The jury didn't buy it."

"The jury didn't know about Billy Woodward. And the jury didn't know what was in her blood that night."

"What?"

"Rohypnol."

She stared at me. Finally, she said, "How do you know that?"

"The blood tests are in the police file."

"That never came out at trial."

I shrugged. "There wasn't a lot known about illegal uses of that drug back then. And no one in the case had any idea that Angela's John was really Billy Woodward."

She paused, absorbing that information. When she spoke again, her voice was tentative. "You're sure it was Billy?"

"Angela is."

She shook her head. "I don't understand."

"Neither do I. That's why I have to talk to you, Samantha. I have some questions about Billy and about Sebastian. I'm hoping you can answer them."

She studied me for a moment. "Why should I?"

"Did you love Michael Green?"

She stiffened. "Of course I did."

"Then that's why."

"What are you talking about?"

"If you loved Michael Green, then you'll want to make sure that his killer is brought to justice. The jury said Angela Green did it, and maybe they're right. I don't think so. I've looked through the police file and done some poking around on my own. Three names pop up. Yours and Billy's and Sebastian Curry's. At first I had my suspicions about you."

"Me?" she said, stiffening with anger.

"At first, but not now. Even if you didn't love him—

even if you were marrying him only for his money—it wouldn't make any sense to want him dead *before* the wedding. So you're out. But that still leaves Billy and Sebastian. Maybe they had nothing to do with it, either, but I can't say that until I know more. You know things about Billy that no one else does."

"What about Sebastian?" she asked. "He probably knew Billy better than me, at least toward the end."

"Sebastian's dead."

"What? When?"

"I met him for the first time a few days ago. He got really nervous when I asked him about his relationship with you during your art gallery years. When I went back to talk to him two days ago, I found him dead. Someone shot him in the head."

She covered her mouth. "Oh, no."

"I don't know what's going on, Samantha, and I doubt you do, either. But you know things that I don't know about those two men. The more I can find out about them, the better my chances of figuring out what really happened."

She nodded, shaken.

"Tell me about you and Billy," I asked gently.

It took a moment for her to shift focus. "Not much to tell. We met at Pinnacle. Harry Silver always claimed that he was our matchmaker. He made us call him 'Yenta.' Billy and I hit it off. We ended up living together for a year or so." She shrugged. "It didn't work out."

"Harry told me Billy had sexual problems."

"He did, but it was more than that. Billy was a little crazy, a little"—she searched for the word—"scary. It was like he had this split personality. Some days he was just the sweetest guy you'd ever want to know, but other days—" She shook her head.

"Other days what?"

"He was awful. Vicious, nasty, depressed. And when he'd be down like that, he'd start drinking or snorting coke— or both—and that only made him worse. He used to tell me stories about some of the things he did when he was younger—bragging about burglaries, assaults, stuff like that. He claimed he'd broken into lots of homes, stolen jewelry from the master bedrooms while the couples were sleeping. He claimed he killed a man down near the Kentucky border. Said he was never caught. I didn't know whether he was telling the truth or just trying to scare me, but finally it just didn't matter anymore. I couldn't stand the whole thing— the mood swings, the sex problems, the drinking, the fighting. So I ended it."

"Were you still doing films at Pinnacle?"

"I'd left by then. Billy was still there, but he'd become too unreliable in front of the camera to be an actor anymore. Harry kept him on as one of the crew hogs." Samantha smiled at the memory. "Harry had a blind spot for Billy. Treated him like his own kid. Billy got away with stuff that Harry would never have tolerated from others. But eventually Billy crossed the line. Harry's a funny guy, you know. He makes his money in porno, but he's got this strict code of ethics. Like no rape scenes in his movies, private dressing rooms for the women. He pays for medical coverage for his employees, things like that. I heard that when he found out that Billy was drugging women for sex, he fired him on the spot."

"Had you known about Billy's use of Rohypnol?"

"No. He must have found out about it after we split. Shows you how twisted his mind could be. Fucking unconscious girls? Can you imagine?"

"He killed himself in front of your town house."

She nodded.

"Had you been seeing him at the time?"

"Oh, God no. But Billy went through these cycles. I wouldn't hear from him for a year or so, and then he'd start calling every day like some stalker, trying to get me to see him, begging me, telling me how much he loved me, how things would be different this time. I'd always tell him no. He was from a phase of my life that I'd left behind years before. I'd moved on. No way was I ever going back. Never. He'd eventually get the message and stop calling, and then I wouldn't hear from him for a year or so until he hit the next cycle. Well, he started calling again right after I got engaged to Michael. In fact, Michael was over one night when Billy called twice. The second time Michael grabbed the phone from me and really laid into him. He told him that if he ever called me again he'd have him thrown in jail. That stopped Billy for a long time. I didn't hear from him again until the night he killed himself."

"What did he say that night?"

"Mostly the same as before." She hesitated, trying to remember. "He knew about Michael's death, of course."

"Why do you say that?"

"Who wouldn't? I mean, that trial was on TV every day."

"Did he mention it?"

"Not exactly. But I remember him telling me that I was free now, that there was nothing standing between us. That got me so upset. I told him we were history. I told him I wouldn't go back to him if he were the last guy on earth. That made him crazy. He was screaming and pleading with me. Finally, I got fed up and hung up. He called right back. He told me he couldn't live without me. He told me this was my final chance." She shook her head. "How was I supposed to know he was standing at a pay phone across the street with a goddamn gun pointed at his head? I told him to stay out of my life, to never call me again. And then I hung up."

She paused. "I didn't hear the gunshot. I must have been watching TV or going to the bathroom or something." She shrugged. "I didn't know anything was wrong until I saw the flashing red lights outside. It was raining by then. I peered out the window and saw two police cars and an ambulance in the rain. I thought it was car crash or something. I didn't find out what happened until the next day."

Her eyes were red. "I felt so—so guilty." She lowered her head. "I was really down for a long time after that. I started seeing this therapist. She tried to make me understand that it wasn't my fault. That helped a little."

We were silent for a while.

"Do you think he could have killed Michael Green?" I asked.

She raised her face and stared at the wall, frowning in thought. Finally, she turned toward me and shrugged. "That thought never crossed my mind before today. I didn't know that Billy even knew Angela Green until you told me. That stuff about the Rohypnol in her blood—that's scary stuff. But kill Michael? I guess anything's possible with Billy. He could be a really scary guy sometimes."

"Let me ask you about Sebastian Curry."

"Wow," she said, shaking her head in wonder. "I can't believe he's dead."

"Where did you first meet him?"

She colored slightly. "Over at Pinnacle. We did a few scenes together."

"Anything more?"

"More?" She looked puzzled, and then she shook her head. "Oh, you mean a relationship? Like with Billy? No. Sebastian didn't appeal to me that way. Of course, that wasn't really an issue. I wasn't Sebastian's type."

"What do you mean?"

"He's gay."

"Really?" I thought back to the final scene of *All That Jizz*. He'd certainly given a convincingly heterosexual performance there, at least to my inexperienced eyes.

As if reading my mind, Samantha said, "He was the classic reliable performer. Harry put him in gay movies and straight ones. Didn't seem to matter. He could have done a farm animal if they asked." She smiled. "Sebastian was unique. He could get hard on demand, shoot his wad right on cue, and be ready again in a half hour. Talk about stamina. He'd do three or four scenes in one day—each with a money shot, and each time a regular gusher. Seemed like gallons." She giggled at the memory. "Harry used to say Sebastian was just a life-support system for a penis." Her smile faded. "Sebastian and I—we were more coworkers than friends back then. We'd do our scenes and that was that. That may seem weird to you—to have sex with a guy and not even be friends—but that's the way it is in the business. It's nothing like real sex. I mean, can you imagine trying to really make love while you have two cameramen and a lighting guy and sound guy and a director and an assistant director perched around the bed giving you directions?"

"Was Sebastian painting back then?"

"I guess he was, but I didn't learn that until later on."

"You mean when you began selling his stuff at your gallery?"

"Right."

"How did that start?"

She leaned back in her chair. "That's a very weird coincidence."

"What do you mean?"

"Michael brought him to me."

"Michael Green?"

She nodded. "Michael used to visit me at the gallery. He'd come by for lunch or pick me up at closing time. He told me one day that he had a hot new artist for me. Promised I'd make a lot of money off him. Told me his name was Stefani Currant. I remember that part clearly, because I told Michael I'd never heard of any artist by the name. I didn't know every artist in town, of course, but I'd been in the gallery business for a year by then and thought I knew the good ones. Michael told me this Currant guy was represented by a heavyweight outfit from out of town called Millennium Management Services. I'd never heard of them, either. Michael told me he'd handle the business dealings with Millennium, and that my job was to handle the sales of the paintings."

"Did that seem strange to you? Having Michael handle the dealings with the agent?"

She shrugged. "A little, I guess. Usually the gallery would have the direct dealings with the agent, including the commission payments. I guess I didn't think much about it at the time, though. It was just talk when Michael first told me. He was a wonderful guy and all, but he knew next to nothing about art."

"So what happened next?"

"Michael told me the artist was going to drop by the next day with his first paintings. So I'm waiting for some guy named Stefani Currant and in walks Sebastian Curry. I couldn't believe it. In fact, I kind of freaked out. How did Michael know Sebastian? Did Sebastian tell Michael that he knew me? Did he tell him how? But it turned out that the two of them had never even met. Never even spoken on the phone. That's how Michael got his name wrong. Someone else—Millennium, I guess—made all the arrangements." She paused, frowning. "I guess it was Millennium."

"What do you mean?"

"Later on I asked Sebastian about Millennium. I'd been selling so many of his paintings and writing so many checks to that outfit that I was really getting curious. I was kind of hoping that maybe they had another artist or two they could send me. But Sebastian was no help at all. He was real vague, said Millennium did most of their management stuff behind the scenes, whatever that meant."

"Where did you send the commission checks?"

"I didn't. I gave them to Michael. He told me that's how Millennium wanted it handled. I remember asking him once if they were his client."

"What did he say?"

"He got real vague, too. Said he handled some of their business dealings. Said they were obsessed with confidentiality, which is why they liked to have a lawyer act as intermediary." She leaned back in her chair and sighed. "I probably should have asked more questions." She shook her head. "I was so happy about the sales that I ignored the strange stuff."

"What strange stuff?"

"The Millennium arrangement, for one. That was definitely odd. And then Sebastian's sudden popularity. His work really wasn't all that good. When he first told me his list prices, I thought he was insane. I mean, his numbers were totally out of whack. I assumed that we'd never sell a thing until we started slashing the prices. But then these men started coming in—two or three a month—and snapping them up at list price. That part was strange, but what was even stranger were the guys themselves."

"How so?"

"They didn't act like normal art lovers. They didn't browse around or look at other paintings or ask questions about the artists or upcoming shows or things like that. They just showed up—or called in—wanting to know if I had anything by Sebastian Curry. Anything. If I did, they'd buy one." She snapped her fingers. "Just like that. No hassling

over price. Some of them barely glanced at the paintings before they wrote their checks. Two of the guys who called
told me to pick out a good painting, wrap it up, and give it
to their driver, who'd have the check with him. It was as if
they were buying Chinese take-out instead of a fifteen-
thousand-dollar painting."

"That is bizarre," I said.

"I'll tell you something else strange. This Sebastian
Curry craze was happening only at my gallery. I went to
openings at other galleries and occasionally would get together with some of the other owners. I'd ask around, sort
of casually, trying to see who was hot. Sebastian definitely
was not. He was on no one's radar screen. I knew for a fact
that he had paintings at two other galleries. They were similar
to the ones I was selling, except they were listed under a
thousand dollars." She shook her head in wonder. "Under a
thousand, and meanwhile I'm selling them like hotcakes for
fifteen grand. That made no sense." She paused. "It still
doesn't."

"You say Sebastian never met Michael."

"Never face to face. At least that's what Sebastian told
me."

"Did Michael ever talk about him?"

She thought it over. "That's another odd thing. At first
Michael didn't show any interest in Sebastian. He eventually
got his name right, of course, but that was it for a long time.
But the last couple of months or so he got real curious about
Sebastian. Not so much about his paintings, though. He
wanted to know what I thought of Sebastian. In fact, he
wanted to know if I thought Sebastian was gay."

"Really? Why?"

"He never said. I pretended like I didn't know one way
or the other. I'd never told Michael about that part of my
past. I'd debated telling him early on in our relationship, but

I never got up the courage, and after a while there didn't seem any point. So when he started asking personal questions about Sebastian, I got nervous. Michael was a wonderful guy and all, but how was I supposed to tell him the truth? We were engaged by then, for God's sake. What would he do if I told him, 'Yeah, Michael, I know Sebastian. Matter of fact, I gave him two blow jobs and butt-fucked him with a strap-on.'" She shrugged. "So I told him I didn't know much about him. I told him that I'd never seen him with a girl-friend or a boyfriend. And that part was the truth."

"Did Michael tell you why he wanted to know if Sebas-tian was gay?"

"No, and I even remember asking him. I said, 'Why do you care?' 'Just curious,' he told me. I thought maybe he was jealous or something. I told him Sebastian had never come on to me." She leaned back in her chair. "Which brings me to the last strange thing."

"What?"

"Do you realize that I never sold another one of Sebas-tian's paintings after Michael died? Not even one. The irony is that when I reopened the gallery after Michael's death I was worried about what I was supposed to do with the Mil-lennium commissions. Where was I supposed to send them? But there was never another commission check." She frowned. "I really should have asked more questions, but the money kept pouring in. I didn't want to mess anything up. Everything just seemed too good to be true." She gave me a sad smile. "I guess that was the problem."

CHAPTER 22

H ere's the list of buyers," I said. "Twenty-three in all."
This was my third meeting with Stanley Brod.
We'd first met a few weeks ago to discuss his relationship
with Michael Green, for whom he'd served as accountant for
nearly twenty years. The second time we met he let me review the 309 Gallery's financial records, which his firm had
handled the last year or so at Michael Green's request. We'd
determined from those records that over a two-year period
ending around the time of Michael Green's death, the gallery
had made commission payments totaling $138,000 to Millen-
nium Management Services—the same entity that had received tens of thousands of dollars of fees from Gateway
Trust Company for "services" provided to the trust funds
established for the young beneficiaries of one of Green's big
class-action settlements.

Stanley Brod was in his sixties—a bald fastidious little
man with dark gray bushy eyebrows, melancholy eyes, and
delicate hands. He had an Old World courtliness about him,
from the graceful china demitasse service he used for espresso
to the Rembrandt prints framed on the wall to the way he
used a white handkerchief as a barrier between his hand and
the paper as he wrote with a fountain pen. On his desk were
framed photographs of what appeared to be his family—an
elegant gray-haired woman that I assumed was his wife, and
two earnest young women that I assumed were his daughters.

I took a sip of espresso and watched him study the list

of names of the men who'd purchased Sebastian Curry paintings from Samantha's art gallery. All but two of them were also in Michael Green's Rolodex. I'd come here today to find out the reason for that overlap.

He looked up from the list with a pensive expression. "I know some of these gentlemen, Miss Gold, but that knowledge is independent of my work for Mr. Green. Several are passing acquaintances—fellows I see occasionally at my lunch club. One is a client. One is a former client. One lived down the block from me until a year ago."

"Do you recognize any as clients of Michael Green?"

He looked through the list again. "The names are familiar, but I can't be certain of a professional connection to Mr. Green."

"Is there a way to check?"

"Perhaps." He reached for his phone. "Janet, please have Todd see me."

He replaced the receiver and looked at me. "My firm assisted in the administration of Mr. Green's estate. We copied certain accounting and administrative files from his office computers. Because there are still a few open items pending before the probate court, the information we downloaded should still be in our system."

There was a rap on the door and a tall young man with a lumpy nose and thinning blond hair poked his head in. "Mr. Brod? You wanted me?"

"Please come in, Todd."

Todd looked uncomfortable in his ill-fitting blue suit and starched white shirt. Stanley introduced us—Todd had a clammy handshake—and then gave him my list. "Please run these names through the Michael Green data set and bring us any hits."

After Todd left, Stanley asked, "What do you hope to find?"

"Some explanations."

"For what?"

"For starters, why did these twenty-three men—none of whom appears to be an art lover—buy those paintings? Second, why did they buy them at prices that were ten to twenty times above market value? The whole operation smells of money laundering."

He took a sip of his espresso and carefully set the cup back in the saucer. "You believe that Mr. Green was somehow associated with those transactions?"

"I don't know what he was doing, or why, or even how, but I know he was involved."

"What makes you say that?"

"Michael Green brought Sebastian Curry to Samantha's gallery, even though he didn't know Curry's work or even his name. He was somehow responsible for the sales of the paintings. As long as he was alive, Sebastian Curry's paintings sold like crazy at Samantha's gallery and at grossly inflated prices. When Michael Green died, the sales did, too. That has to be more than coincidence. Finally, Michael Green handled all of the financial arrangements between the gallery and what appeared to be Sebastian Curry's agent, which is some mysterious outfit called Millennium Management Services."

"Why do you say mysterious?"

"First, because the company doesn't appear to exist—or at least we can't find any record of its existence. Second, because Samantha gave the checks for the agency commissions directly to Green. She made them payable to Millennium, but she gave them to Green. She had no idea what he did with them." I paused. "You prepared Michael Green's tax returns, right?"

"I did."

"Did he ever report income from an outfit called Millennium Management Services?"

Stanley pursed his lips pensively. "I would need to review the returns to be certain, but I don't believe he ever reported income from that source."

"So where did the money go?"

Stanley sat back in his chair and tugged at his earlobe. "I regret to say that I would not even know where to begin to look."

"I would."

He raised his eyebrows.

"Canceled checks," I explained. "Samantha gave the commission checks to Michael Green. Presumably, he gave them to a representative of Millennium, who presumably deposited them in a bank account. That tells me there ought to be a paper trail that eventually leads back to the bank records of Samantha's gallery."

He nodded with approval. "We should have copies of those bank records in storage. They should be easy to locate."

A rap on the door. It was Todd. He was holding my list of names in his left hand and a sheaf of papers in his right.

"What did you find, Todd?" Stanley asked.

"There were no matches with his client list. But each one of these men showed up as a client contact person for billing purposes." He was shuffling through the papers. "The client billing addresses are the same as the addresses for these men on his Rolodex."

"Who are the clients?" I asked.

"Corporations."

"Can I see?" I asked.

Todd glanced at Stanley, who nodded. "Please give Miss Gold a few samples, Todd, and let me see some as well."

Todd handed me five pages and gave the rest to Stanley.

The first page was the billing information for a Michael Green client known as the Sevens Corporation. The billing address was 7777 Bonhomme Avenue in the St. Louis suburb of Clayton. The suite number sounded familiar. The reason became clear when I saw the client contact: Donald Goddard. Goddard's law firm occupied the same suite as the Sevens Corporation.

The pattern held for the other corporate clients. In each case, the corporate client's bills were being sent to the office address of one of the men on the list.

"What did Michael Green do for these clients?" I asked.

"I have no idea," Stanley said. "Presumably that information would be in the client files. All that one can determine from these sheets is that these were corporate and real estate matters, not litigation."

"How can you tell that?" I asked.

"By the way his office coded each client file. I am familiar with his system. Look at the letters that appear right before the client number at the top of the page. L-I-T stands for litigation. C-slash-R-E stands for corporate and real estate."

I checked the client numbers on my five pages:

C/RE 21563
C/RE 33215
C/RE 35411
C/RE 23287
C/RE 32906

"Where are the files for these matters?" I asked.

"In the warehouse," Stanley answered.

"I'd like to see them. Along with those canceled checks for the agency commissions. Today, if possible."

"We can arrange that." He turned to Todd. "Who handles our dealings with the warehouse?"

"Brian."

"Ask Brian to check with the warehouse, Todd. Tell him which documents we need. Miss Gold will also want to review the final three years of bank statements for the 309 Gallery. Be sure they include all canceled checks."

I asked, "Will those legal files show how much he billed each client?"

Stanley turned toward Todd, who had paused at the door. "Do we have the billing records on the computer?"

"We should."

"After you speak with Brian, please check on the billing records for Miss Gold."

I waited until Todd left.

"Thank you, Stanley."

He frowned at his manicured fingernails. "I am doing this more for me than you, Miss Gold. I knew the two of them for years, Michael and Angela." He paused and gave me a sad smile. "Truth be told, Miss Gold, I preferred Angela. She was a charming woman with a gentle soul. It pained me so to see their marriage fail. The murder was a terrible shock. A dreadful, savage act. But the trial—well, I confess that I never understood the defense. Angela was certainly bitter over the divorce. Who could blame her? But as bitter as she may have been, that woman was incapable of murder." He paused and sighed. "Or so I tell myself. Perhaps I am wrong, Miss Gold. I have been convinced of certain verities in this life that have proven false. Nevertheless, in my heart I believe that Angela is innocent. If there is something in Michael's files that could help exonerate her, I know that I am not alone in believing that you should have access to those materials. I am quite sure that Mr. Green himself would agree."

"Thanks, Stanley."

"As long as you are making the trip to the warehouse

today, Miss Gold, can you think of any other records you
would like to review?"

"The only other area—and it's probably just a wild-
goose hunt—would be any unusual payments or receipts
during the last year of his life."

"Anything in particular?"

"No. But if Angela wasn't the killer, someone went to a
lot of trouble to make her look like the killer. Maybe Michael
Green had some connection to the legal or business affairs
of the killer. I have no idea what kind of connection, but one
place to start looking would be any unusual payments or
receipts."

He nodded. "We shall have all such records available for
you at the warehouse."

"Thank you, Stanley."

A knock on the door. It was Todd again.

"Brian called the warehouse," he said to Stanley.
"They're open today until five. He told them the files we
needed to see." Todd glanced at me. "They'll have all the
boxes ready for your review in one hour."

"Excellent," Stanley said. "I have one more set of files to
add to that list. Tell Brian that Miss Gold would like to see
the payables records for Mr. Green's firm for the year before
his death."

"No problem," Todd said. He held up two sheets of paper. "I checked the billing records on those clients of Mr.
Green. Here's the printout."

He handed them to Stanley Brod, who reviewed them.
"Curious," he said and handed them to me.

I scanned down the information:

Twenty-three clients.

Twenty-three legal bills.

All for exactly the same amount: $25,000.

I'd grabbed a take-out sandwich at the St. Louis Bread Company before heading to the warehouse. Now, as I approached the intersection on Page Avenue out near Westport Plaza, I glanced in my rearview mirror. As I did, I asked myself again whether it could be the same Taurus.

I'd definitely been on edge since discovering Sebastian Curry's body. Was it making me paranoid as well?

When I'd gone to visit Stanley Brod that morning, I'd found a parking space on the street near his office. On the way back to my car I'd walked past a beige Ford Taurus parked three spaces in front of mine. The only reason it even registered in my brain was that its engine was idling, presumably so that the occupant could run the air-conditioning. By the time I'd started my car and pulled away from the curb, the Taurus had dropped from my consciousness.

But twenty minutes later, when I came out of the restaurant and headed toward my car, I walked past a beige Taurus parked with its engine running. *Another beige Taurus—or the same one?* I'd turned my head as I passed. The windows were tinted. By the time I thought to look down at the license plate, my view was blocked by the next parked car. I kept walking.

When I pulled out of my space that time, I drove past the Taurus and began watching for it in my rearview mirror. I purposely took a circuitous route and paced myself to catch a few red lights on the way to the warehouse. No sign of the car at any of the stops. But when I took the exit west off Lindbergh onto Page, I spotted a beige Taurus three cars back.

I had a green light as I approached the intersection. Unsure what to do—they hadn't offered this course in law school—I slowed as I glanced in the rearview mirror and checked the cars in the other lanes. At the last possible moment I made the right turn and pulled over to the shoulder about twenty yards down the road, just in front of the entrance to the small industrial park where the storage facility was located. I looked back to watch the cars pass. The Taurus seemed to hesitate as it entered the intersection, but only momentarily before it continued on its way and passed from view. I couldn't read the receding license plate.

I turned forward, my hands resting on the steering wheel. I sat there for a full five minutes, glancing up at the rearview mirror every few seconds. Finally, I put the car in gear, pulled ahead, and turned into the industrial park.

CHAPTER 23

S unday. Early afternoon.

Angela and I were seated across the table in the interview room at Chillicothe. I'd driven out that morning to bring her up to date on my investigation and to probe her memory of people and events that had been ignored or quickly skimmed over during the original homicide investigation but which now seemed critical—or at least potentially critical.

I started by briefing Angela on the motions in the Son of Sam case, which were scheduled for hearing tomorrow morning. Although she nodded as I spoke, I could tell that her thoughts were elsewhere. She hadn't been all that engrossed in the case at the outset, and now seemed even less so. Not that I blamed her. The only thing at stake in the case was money. From the moment we'd discovered that her mysterious John was actually a former porn star named Billy Woodward who'd killed himself in front of Samantha Cummings's home, the lawsuit took on the air of a sideshow. Although I was sure that the high-powered lawyers for the other defendants would mount a splendid production tomorrow, I was almost as sure that the judge would deny the motions. I'd joined in their court papers more as a show of solidarity than anything else. The best strategy in the case, of course, was to exonerate Angela. Clear Angela of the murder conviction and the Son of Sam case would instantly implode, ending not with a bang but a whimper. But that was still a long shot, which meant that I had to focus on preparing a more traditional defense to the lawsuit.

I paused to refill our coffee mugs. For a treat today, I'd brought along a thermos filled with Shaw Coffee's Sumatra blend and a gooey butter cake from Lake Forest Bakery.

I shifted the conversation to Angela's meeting with "John" on the night of the murder. According to the investigation file, they met for a drink at Culpeppers, a popular restaurant and bar in the Central West End area not far from the hospital where Angela volunteered and Billy Woodward's mother was allegedly a patient.

"So the two of you had a table?"

Angela nodded.

"Did you ever leave the table? For instance, did you get up to go to the rest room?"

"I've been thinking about that night, the whole sequence of events. Yes, I definitely went to the rest room."

"Were you feeling okay when you left the table?"

"I was."

"Not dizzy or drowsy or sluggish?"

"I was fine. I remember reapplying my lipstick in the mirror before coming back to the table where John—uh, where that man was."

"Tell me what happened after you got back to the table. First of all, what were you drinking?"

"Gin and tonic."

"Was your drink full when you left to go to the bathroom?"

"It was empty when I left. I remember that I finished the drink and told John that I was going to the ladies' room."

"And when you got back?"

"There was a fresh gin and tonic."

"Which you drank?"

"Not all at once. I sipped it as we talked."

"What else do you remember?"

"It was crowded. Noisy. We talked." She frowned. "Then it all gets fuzzy." She shook her head. "I've gone over this sequence carefully. I don't actually remember leaving Culpeppers. I don't remember anything else that night."

"So he put it in your drink while you were in the rest room."

She sighed. "I suppose."

"What do you remember before things got fuzzy? About him, I mean. What was he like that night? Calm, tense?"

"Tense."

"More so than usual?"

"Oh, yes. He seemed jumpy. He drank more, too. Usually, we'd both have two drinks—gin and tonics for me, beers for him. But that night he was drinking Scotch on the rocks. Doubles, in fact. He had at least three." She took a bit of the cake and chewed slowly, remembering. "I told him I'd never seen him drink Scotch before. He told me he was feeling lousy because his mother had a bad day of chemotherapy." She stopped and shook her head, horrified. "My God, I still can't believe this. Do you really think he's the killer?"

"If someone wanted Michael Green dead and wanted to have you set up to take the fall for murder, this Woodward was a good choice to carry it out."

"Why do you say that?"

"He was a good enough actor to get close to you. That was critical, since the best way to set you up was to make sure there were plenty of clues pointing toward you and then to make sure to eliminate all possible alibis. Drugging you was the perfect way to eliminate alibis, since he could leave you at the scene of the crime and you wouldn't remember anything that could help you out. Once he got close enough to drug you, the rest wouldn't be that hard for someone like

Billy. He had a history of breaking and entering, so he'd know how to get into Michael's place while you were drugged in the car. If he was as good a burglar as he claimed he was to Samantha, then he'd be able to get in there quietly, which would make it a lot easier to kill Michael. Once he killed him, he could bring you in, make sure he got your fingerprints on plenty of incriminating surfaces, and then leave you there to sleep off the drug."

Angela listened to my explanation with growing distress. "Good Lord."

I took a sip of coffee and frowned. "But even assuming I'm right, even assuming he did all that, we're still missing the key link."

"What?"

"Who wanted Michael Green dead? Was it Billy, or was it someone else? If Billy, why? Jealousy at the prospect of his old girlfriend getting married? Would that be enough of a reason? Possibly. But what if someone else wanted Michael dead? Who? And why? And how in the world did they pick Billy to carry it out? And why all that elaborate effort to frame you? That makes the least sense."

"Why do you say that?"

"If the killer was clever enough to kill Michael *and* to frame you for the crime, then the killer should have been clever enough to kill him without leaving any incriminating evidence. Why not break in, shoot him, and walk away? That's a whole lot easier—and a whole lot safer—than putting together an elaborate ruse to frame you. Why take that risk?"

She shook her head weakly. "I don't know."

"Me, neither." I gave her a smile. "But I'm working on it. Let me ask you this. When you and this John guy talked, did you ever discuss Michael?"

"Sometimes. He knew I'd gone through a difficult divorce."

"What about Samantha? Did you talk about her?"

Angela nodded. "I did. Some days I was so upset about the whole thing I'm sure I just rambled on about them both."

"Did he show any particular interest in Samantha?"

Angela thought that one over. "Not really."

I poured us some more coffee.

"Stanley Brod sends his regards," I told her.

She smiled. "Dear Stanley. I absolutely adore that little man."

"The feeling is mutual."

"His wife Sarah passed last year."

I thought back to the framed photograph on his desk and felt a pang of sorrow. "He still wears his wedding ring."

"I so wanted to be at her funeral, to be of some comfort to Stanley. I felt so helpless locked up in here, Rachel. I wrote him a long letter about how much I loved Sarah, about all the nice things that beautiful woman had done for me over the years. He wrote me back the sweetest letter. I've saved it."

"He believes you're innocent, Angela. That's why he's been so helpful. He arranged for me to look at several boxes of records in a storage warehouse yesterday. I found some interesting things."

She perked up. "Tell me."

I started with the Millennium checks, explaining the unusual system for payment of commissions. "I found all twenty-three canceled checks in the gallery's bank records. All twenty-three were endorsed by Michael Green on behalf of Millennium and deposited in a bank in the Canary Islands."

"He had an account there?"

"Probably not in his name. The checks were payable to

that Millennium outfit, which I assume was his alias. If you recall, Millennium was also receiving management fees for all those minors' trust accounts at Gateway. At the very least, it smells like tax fraud. Stanley confirmed that Michael had never reported any income from Millennium." I frowned. "But there has to be more."

"What do you mean 'more'?"

"If the Millennium account was Michael's account, then why was he collecting an agent's fee on the sale of Sebastian Curry's paintings? Sebastian didn't know him, and Michael apparently didn't know Sebastian. Something else was going on. Which tells me that either Michael Green wasn't the only person on that Canary Islands account or that he was using that money for other purposes."

"What other purposes could there be?"

"I'm trying to find that out. I gave the canceled checks back to Stanley. Normally, there'd be no way to access the records of a bank in the Canary Islands. That's why people put their money there. But Michael's probate estate is still open. Since that bank account could contain assets of the estate, that might give the court enough authority to order disclosure of the bank records on the account. Stanley and the lawyer handling the estate will start that ball rolling first thing Monday."

"That's good."

"I found some other interesting things in those files."

I explained Michael Green's client connection to each of the twenty-three men who'd purchased Sebastian Curry paintings from Samantha. "I checked all twenty-three client files. He didn't seem to do much for his legal fees beyond forming a simple corporation and helping it enter into what appears to be a standard real estate contract for the purchase of a two- or three-flat apartment building in the city of St. Louis."

"Michael handled a lot of real estate deals for his clients."

"I understand that. What surprises me is the fee. Most lawyers will charge less than a thousand dollars to form a simple corporation. The articles of incorporation, the bylaws, the state filings—they're all fill-in-the-blank forms. Same with the real estate contracts. Completely standard. A thousand dollars in fees for the real estate contract like that would be high."

"Okay," Angela said. "And the problem was?"

"Each of those men paid your ex-husband twenty-five thousand dollars in fees for less than two thousand dollars' worth of legal services. Right around the same time, each of those men paid fifteen thousand dollars for a painting worth less than a thousand dollars. Something shady was going on."

I paused to look through the notes I'd taken during my review of Michael Green's documents in the warehouse. "Does the Blitz Agency ring a bell?"

"Blitz?" She frowned. "What is it?"

"A detective agency. Private eye. Doesn't sound familiar?"

"No. Why should it?"

"Michael paid them four thousand dollars about three months before he was killed, which was also a few weeks before the divorce became final. I thought maybe he hired the agency in connection with the divorce."

Angela mulled that over. "I don't know why he'd need a private eye. There was never any issue about my personal life. What did the bill say?"

" 'For services rendered.' Period. No description and no reference to any particular matter."

"I think Michael used investigators in some of his personal injury cases."

"I did a random check through his case files for that period. The only private investigator I found was an outfit called Metro Unlimited. I double-checked by calling Stanley from the warehouse. He ran the Blitz Agency through the accounts payable database for Michael's firm. The payment I found was the only one to Blitz."

The beefy female guard rapped on the door. "Time's up," she announced.

We stood.

"I'll call you after court tomorrow," I told her.

We hugged at the door. She held me tight.

"Thank you, Rachel," she whispered in my ear.

I touched her cheek as we separated.

I watched the guard escort her down the hall and out of sight. Back to her cell, back to her life in prison. I stood there a moment and then returned to the interview room. I gathered my papers, put the coffee mugs, empty thermos, and the leftover cake back in the wicker picnic basket.

I leaned back in the chair. "My head is spinning."

My mother nodded. "So is mine."

Benny and I were having Sunday night dinner at my mother's house. We were on the dessert course—a homemade gooey butter cake even richer than the one I'd bought for Angela. I'd probably drift off to sleep tonight to the gentle hum of my arteries hardening.

I'd spent the last hour filling them in on what I'd found in the storage warehouse yesterday and learned from Angela Green earlier today. I'd skipped the part about the beige Taurus yesterday. And the brown Chrysler minivan today. Turned out I wasn't the only person making the long, multi-highway drive from St. Louis to Chillicothe this morning. Someone driving a brown Chrysler minivan with tinted windows and Missouri plates (090 HHS) made the drive as well—all the way to the Chillicothe exit. It drove past me as I pulled into the prison parking lot, turned at the next corner and disappeared. For good. I didn't see it on the drive back.

Benny was slicing himself another huge piece of cake—his third—while my mother looked on approvingly. He said, "You got twenty-three savvy white boys overpaying for crappy paintings from the same crappy artist and then over-paying Green to set up simple corporations to buy slum properties. What the hell is that all about?"

"I'm having Jacki check the real estate records tomor-row."

"How about the private dick?" Benny asked.

My mother gave him a strange look. "The private what?"

"The detective agency, Mom. Blitz. I thought they might have had something to do with the divorce, but Angela didn't recognize the name."

"Which doesn't necessarily mean a thing," Benny said.

I nodded. "I put them on my list. I'm also going to try to run down the Sebastian Curry connection. I'm hoping he shared whatever he knew about the Millennium connection with someone else. Maybe a lover or a best friend. The prob-lem is, the police searched the loft and couldn't find an ad-dress book, which makes them think that whoever killed him took it."

"How are you going to find someone he was close to?" my mother asked.

"I have the message on his telephone answering machine. From someone named Gail who sounded, at least from the message, like she was a good friend."

"No last name?" my mother asked.

"No last name. But in her message she mentioned some-one named Phyllis and someone named Greg Ramsey. I checked the phone book. There were two listings for Greg-ory Ramsey and one for G. Ramsey. I called all three yes-terday. I struck out with two and left a message on the answering machine of the third. He returned my call today.

He didn't know Sebastian all that well, but he gave me Gail's full name and phone number. I called her before coming over. She wasn't in, but I left a message for her. Hopefully, she'll call back soon. And when she does"—I shook my head wearily—"I'll get to add yet another item to my things-to-do list for this week."

"Sounds like you have a busy week, sweetie," my mother said.

"I could use a clone. I have the Son of Sam motions tomorrow morning and then all of this Angela stuff to run down, which is enough to keep two of me busy." I turned toward Benny with an accusatory look. "But guess what else I have on the docket this week, thanks to a thoughtful referral from a law school professor?"

Benny looked baffled for a moment, but then broke into a grin. "Oh, man, is that ostrich case on the trial docket?"

"It's set for Wednesday."

"Oy," my mother said, shaking her head. "That crazy case."

"You ready for trial?" Benny asked.

I shrugged. "Not really. So far it's Blackwell's word against my clients'. I'm still looking for a third-party witness. Blackwell's operations are down near Crystal City. I hired a local investigator, a guy named Wimmer. He says he found me three possibilities—all ex-employees of Blackwell."

"What do they know?"

"I have no idea. None of them would talk to him, but he's learned that all three left Blackwell Breeders under hushed circumstances."

"That sounds promising," my mother said.

Benny asked, "What happened to them?"

"Don't know." I took a deep breath and exhaled. "That's why I'm driving down there tomorrow. Two still live there."

"What about the third?" my mother asked.

"He lives up in the northwest part of the state—actually not that far from Angela's prison. He won't talk to anyone, but the other two are willing to meet with me."

Benny was chuckling. "Oh, Sarah," he said to my mother, "something tells me that your gorgeous daughter is going to find a way to drill that prick a new asshole."

"Benny," I said, "your delicacy is matched only by your refinement."

CHAPTER 24

Five thousand dollars an hour.

That had to be the minimum aggregate hourly rate of the gaggle of lawyers gathered in Judge Byrne's courtroom that morning for oral argument on the defendants' motions to dismiss the Son of Sam case. Present were all three horsemen of the First Amendment—Hefty Harvey, Hammerin' Hank, and the Silver Fox of Corcoran Fox. Each one clocked in at a tidy $600 an hour. And each one had a supporting squadron of associates and junior partners, each charging anywhere from $200 to $400 an hour.

To say that their clients did not get full value for their fee was akin to saying that the passengers on the *Titanic* did not get full value for their fee. I could confirm it, because I had a good spot on the observation deck to watch us cruise into the iceberg at full steam. More precisely, I'd been at counsel's table seated next to Hefty Harvey. I'd watched as he carefully reviewed the handwritten notes on his yellow legal pad, mouthing words and phrases under this breath.

He'd made twelve pages of notes, no doubt brimming with dazzling analogies, witty ripostes, and elegant lines of reasoning demonstrating the constitutional, legal, and logical flaws of the Son of Sam law.

No doubt brimming.

But that was pure speculation on my part, because Judge Bryne denied all motions to dismiss before Hefty had a chance to state his name for the record. If it was any consolation, none of the other attorneys for the defendants, including me, got to say much more.

The Silver Fox batted leadoff for the defendants. He was maybe two minutes into his presentation when Judge Byrne, who'd been leafing through the court file during the presentation, interrupted.

"Where's your motion?"

"Pardon, Your Honor?"

The judge tilted the bulging court file toward the Century City attorney. "Look at all this paper. How in the world am I supposed to find your motion in here? Who filed this stuff?"

The Silver Fox turned toward his entourage. A Corcoran Fox associate dashed forward with a copy of the motion and the memorandum of law, handing them to his boss and backing away silently, leaning forward in the manner of an Elizabethan manservant. The memorandum numbered forty-seven pages (not including at least a dozen pages of exhibits). The Silver Fox took the papers from the associate and handed them up to the judge.

"Here, Your Honor," he said in his mellifluous voice. "A courtesy copy for the convenience of the court."

Judge Byrne stared at the thick memorandum of law.

I knew how this scene would play out. I'd warned my co-counsel to keep their briefs under ten pages. Judge Patrick Byrne, like most state court trial judges, didn't have a law clerk and didn't have time to read, much less ponder, the dozens of motions he was expected to rule on each week. That meant that the lawyer's motion was likely to be read—or more accurately, scanned—during the actual oral argument. Ten pages was a lot to expect a judge to digest as opposing attorneys argued back and forth in front of him. Here, though, the numbers were ridiculous. On top of the forty-seven-page memorandum filed by Corcoran Fox, the other defendants had filed motion papers totaling more than one hundred pages. That sheer volume of paper—for which the clients had been billed tens of thousands of dollars—guaranteed only one thing: Judge Byrne would not read a single page.

And he clearly hadn't.

As the Silver Fox cleared his throat in a self-important manner and resumed his argument, the judge held up his hand. "Whoa. Hang on there, counsel."

The judge turned toward Brian Morgan, counsel for the plaintiff, who was standing alongside the Silver Fox. "Brian, what's your client say to all this? Is your response in here?"

Brian was ready. "It's in there somewhere, Judge. I'm sure it's feeling kind of lost in that ocean of paper. I did bring along a copy of one of the key cases." He handed it up to the judge.

I had to smile when I saw that Brian had "helpfully" highlighted in yellow the one paragraph he wanted to make sure the judge read. It was a classic state court maneuver, especially in a complex case. Handing an overwhelmed judge a photocopied case with a highlighted passage was the equivalent of throwing a life preserver to a man overboard. Brian waited until the judge finished reading the paragraph from the case and looked up at him.

"Judge," Brian said, "the Missouri legislature made an important policy decision when they passed this Son of Sam law. They decided that crime should not pay. They decided that a victim's rights are greater than the murderer's rights. They decided that if there is money to be made off a heinous crime, that money ought to go to the victims and not to the criminal. Now I've tried to read through all the papers these fancy out-of-town lawyers filed. Near as I can understand, they're claiming that some of the federal judges back where these fine gentlemen live might not agree with the lawmakers of Missouri. Well, Judge, maybe so. Everyone's entitled to their own opinion. It's a free country and all. But I would remind these fine gentlemen that the city of St. Louis happens to be located in the state of Missouri and not in Times Square or out there on the Hollywood Walk of Fame. It sure seems to me that the only lawmakers whose view matters here today are the ones down in Jeff City, Your Honor, and those men and women passed a law that says crime doesn't pay."

"Your Honor," the Silver Fox declared in a irritated tone, "the issue before the court today is not whether—"

"Gentlemen," the judge interrupted, looking around at all of us, "and Miss Gold. I'm not necessarily buying the plaintiff's argument today. And I'd be remiss if I didn't tell Mr. Morgan that I've got some real doubts about that equitable adoption claim. That's going to be a stretch for you, Brian. Of course, I realize that issue isn't before me today, but from the facts I've seen so far, Brian, I'm not sure that dog's going to hunt. Now as for these motions here, well"— he paused to flip through the court file—"I'm counting easily over a hundred pages of arguments." He gazed down on us and shook his head good-naturedly. "The defendants tell me this issue is clear and simple, but one thing I've learned over the years is that if it takes a lawyer this many pages to tell me something's clear and simple, then the one thing it surely ain't is clear and simple. I'm going to deny these motions, gentlemen . . . and Miss Gold, of course, sorry ma'am. One of you all draft me up an order." He turned to his docket clerk and nodded.

"Next case," she announced in a loud voice. "Becker et al. versus Continental Insurance Company."

Two lawyers from the gallery stood and started moving toward the podium as the Son of Sam defense squadrons retreated.

I'd been pleasantly surprised to see Maria Fallaci in the courtroom that morning. As one of the defendants, she was not required to be in court. Hammerin' Hank was her lead lawyer, and he was there to argue the motion on her behalf. Maria sat back in the gallery during the hearing. After the judge denied the motions, I caught up with her in the hallway outside the courtroom, where she was conferring with two of Hank's associates. I waited off to the side until their conversation ended.

I had to concede that Maria had mastered the art of power dressing. The skirt of her gray pin-striped suit was hemmed mid-thigh. Dark stockings and spiked heels displayed long, muscular legs. With her thick mane of black hair streaked with gray, she looked sexy and intimidating.

As she started toward the elevators with her attorneys, I called out to her.

She turned. Her lawyers did, too.

"We need to talk," I told her.

"I have a sentencing in federal court in East St. Louis in less than an hour." Her tone was chilly. "That's why I'm down here today."

"Give me five minutes. I'll buy you a cup of coffee."

She checked her watch and said something to her lawyers. They nodded and headed off toward the elevators.

Maria turned to me. "My car's parked three blocks south of the courthouse. We can talk on the way over."

I talked fast, filling her in on what I'd learned so far. By the time we reached her rental car, a shiny red Mercedes SL 500 convertible, the Ice Queen seemed rattled. She stood facing me on the sidewalk, her hands on her hips.

"Shit," she mumbled, studying the pavement in front of her. "I can't believe this. I cannot believe this." She looked at me, her eyes narrowed. "What else do you have?"

"Nothing solid yet, but I have some leads."

"Shit." She shook her head. "This is unbelievable."

"What else do *you* have?" I asked.

She gave me a puzzled look. "I'm not following you."

"You were her lawyer, Maria. As you've already reminded me, you're the criminal law expert. To free Angela we're going to need more than what I've found. What else do you have?"

She stared at me. I stared right back.

"This isn't about you," I said. "This is about Angela. What else do you have?"

"Not much," she finally said. Another pause. "Our defense was based on the assumption that she killed him."

"Except that she didn't kill him."

"You don't know that. It's just a theory."

"So was your defense. I know what I know, Maria. Are you telling me that you didn't have any investigators on the case?"

"Of course I did," she snapped. Her glance shifted toward the street. "But they were looking into matters related to our defense strategy."

"Which was based on the assumption that she killed him."

She stood there watching the traffic.

I tried to control my exasperation. "Are you telling me that you never bothered looking for evidence that might have exonerated her?"

"The evidence against her was overwhelming." She turned to me. "I made the right call back then."

"That was then," I said, holding her stare. "This is now."

She walked around to the driver's side of the Mercedes convertible and tossed her briefcase in the backseat. She paused with her hand on the door handle. "If you actually find any genuine exonerating evidence, give me a call."

I watched her get in the convertible, race the engine, and pull away with a screech of tires.

"No, thanks," I said.

CHAPTER 25

Crystal City. I'd come down here with a pair of trial subpoenas, hoping I'd find a reason to serve one of them.

First up was Rudy Witherspoon, a gaunt man in his sixties with pendulous ears, a leathery creased face, and watery blue eyes. We met during his afternoon break at the McDonald's near the Home Depot where he worked. Three years ago, he'd been in charge of machinery maintenance for Blackwell Breeders. He was willing to meet with me, he explained, because, in his words, he "hated the bastard."

I quickly decided that Witherspoon was worthless as a witness. His animosity—which stemmed solely from his belief that his former boss had cheated him out of $135 in a poker game one night after work—undercut whatever credibility he might have had if he had actually anything relevant, which he didn't. He'd left Blackwell Breeders before Big Red hatched and hadn't spoken to any of his former colleagues for at least two years. That meant that if there was something recognizably defective about the ostrich's behavior or personality, he neither observed it while there nor heard about it after he left.

"I threw down my cards and stomped out to my pickup and sat there in the dark fuming away," he told me, pausing to rub an age-spotted hand back and forth across his chin. "I waited till his cousin Marvin drove off, and then I grabbed me a length of pipe out of the back of my pickup and busted in every damn window on the son of a bitch's Eldorado. Yes, ma'am, that was my last day working for Mr. Charlie."

And my last hope for him as a witness.

My expectations were only slightly higher for Milly Eversole. The good news was that Milly's three years at Blackwell Breeders included the entire fourteen-month period during which Big Red was reared and delivered to my clients. She'd quit about nine months ago and now worked as a bank teller. The bad news was that she refused to talk about her years with Blackwell or her reasons for leaving. She made that clear to my investigator. Only the threat of a deposition had persuaded her to give me fifteen minutes today.

I'd parked my car with a clear line of sight to her late-model Ford Escort, which was in the lot behind the bank. I'd brought a file of pretrial materials to work on while I waited for the bank to close, but I couldn't concentrate. I wanted to win this case—for my clients, of course, and also because I despised the other side. Although the evidence—at least the relevant evidence—favored my clients, victory can be tricky to define in civil litigation. My clients had paid ten thousand dollars for Big Red. That was a lot of money to them, but chump change to Charlie Blackwell. He was the one with the deep pockets here, and he'd used them to fund Armour's scorched-earth tactics. As a result, my legal fees would exceed Big Red's price tag. A true victory meant finding a way to get my clients much more than just a refund.

But try concentrating on that goal while fighting off ridiculous allegations about homosexual lifestyles and animal husbandry techniques while peering into your rearview mirror for cars that might be tailing you while another client sits in prison for a murder that you're convinced she didn't commit but don't have the evidence to prove it. I hadn't had a good night's sleep in weeks.

Employees began emerging from the building shortly af-

ter five. Although I'd never seen Milly Eversole, I recognized
her the moment she stepped onto the parking lot, shading
her eyes from the late-afternoon sunshine. She was a slender
woman in her twenties with mousy brown hair and horn-
rimmed glasses. Her outfit was bank-teller conservative:
white blouse, navy skirt, navy flats. She moved across the lot
in a hesitant manner. Pausing at her car door, she scanned
the street. I started my car and revved the engine once. Our
eyes briefly met, and then she glanced around, as if afraid
someone were watching.

I followed her through town and onto Highway 55,
checking the rearview mirror to see if we were being followed. As usual, I had no idea.

We headed south, took the second exit, drove along
country roads, and pulled into a small park overlooking the
Mississippi River. Ours were the only two cars in the parking
area. I joined her on a wood bench facing the water. Her
hands were folded on her lap, her head bowed.

"Miss Eversole," I said calmly, "I'm Rachel Gold. Thank
you for agreeing to meet with me."

She nodded, still looking down at her hands.

"I represent two women," I told her. "They own an ostrich ranch. During the time you worked at Blackwell Breeders, they bought a male ostrich. You would have known him
as Big Red."

She looked up at the sound of the name, and then she
turned toward the river with a frown. I tried to gauge her
mental state.

"You remember him?" I asked gently.

She nodded, still looking toward the river.

"Did you see any indication that he might have behav-
ioral problems?"

"What kind of problems?"

"Was he overly aggressive? Violent?"

She hesitated, and then shrugged. "Maybe." She turned to me. "Why?"

"Let me tell you about the lawsuit."

As I did, I could see her interest grow. By the time I finished she was staring at me intently.

"What did Mr. Blackwell say?" she asked.

"He refused to refund their money, and then"—I paused—"he sued them."

She looked confused. "Why?"

"He claimed it was their fault."

"How?"

I glanced at the silver cross dangling from her necklace. "My clients are lesbians."

She squinted at me from behind her glasses. "I don't understand."

"Charlie Blackwell blames their lifestyle, along with their inexperience in raising ostriches. He claims Big Red was perfectly normal when they took him. I know it sounds ridiculous, Milly, but he claims that at least part of the ostrich's problems results from exposure to my clients' sex life."

Her cheeks flushed with anger. "He said that?"

I nodded, heartened by her reaction. "Even worse, he's suing *them* for damages. He claims he's suffering mental anguish over the thought of his ostrich living on their farm."

Milly stared at the ground. She was visibly upset, her breathing irregular. Her hands clenched in her lap. I waited.

She turned to me with a pained look. "He's a bad man."

I nodded. "He is."

"So is his lawyer."

"Mack Armour?"

"I hate that man." There were tears in her eyes. "I hate them both."

"How do you know Mack Armour?" I asked, surprised and concerned.

She looked down at her hands. Her lips were quivering. I waited. A tear trickled down her cheek.

I reached over and placed my arm around her shoulder. "It's okay, Milly," I whispered, pulling her closer to me. "It's okay."

B enny held up his hands in surrender. "Okay, okay, okay, for chrissake. I'll do it."

I grinned and held up my glass. "Welcome aboard the Big Red Express."

Our waitress arrived with a fresh round of drinks—a long-neck Bud for Benny, a pint of Schlafley's pale ale for me.

On the drive back from Crystal City I'd called Benny from the car. "Got a new client for you, stud."

"You got what?"

"Meet me tonight at eight-thirty at Blueberry Hill. I'll fill you in over dinner."

"You got what?"

"Don't be late, big guy."

"Whoa! You got what?"

"You're breaking up. Reception's bad. Talk to you later."

"You got—"

I took a bite of my hamburger and washed it down with a sip of ale.

"Here's her phone number." I slid the piece of paper across the table. Leaning back in the booth, I stretched, trying to work out the stiffness from all the driving. "I told her you'd call her tomorrow morning."

Benny frowned at the slip of paper. "Okay, I'm willing to represent Milly at your trial, Rachel, but she's going to have to understand that I'm supposed to be a professor these days. I can't take on a lawsuit for her."

"I'll do that part. I just want her to have separate representation at the ostrich trial. Mack the Knife is going to come after her with a machete when she takes the stand. She needs you to protect her in court."

Benny popped the rest of his chili dog in his mouth and chewed thoughtfully. "This gal you found probably has more than just a civil claim here."

"I agree."

"We're talking criminal, right?"

"Yep."

"And not just against Blackwell."

I smiled. "My thought exactly, Professor."

"Any idea who'd be best?"

I nodded. "I think there's enough for venue in St. Louis County. I went through the list of possibilities on the drive back."

"And the winner is?"

"Martha Hogan."

Benny laughed. "Rachel, you are a goddamn genius. If Martha is half as tough as her reputation she'll tear off his labanzas and nail them to her trophy wall. Do you know her?"

"I served on a bar committee with her. I'll tell her to expect a visit from you and Milly."

He downed the rest of his beer, flagged the waitress, and ordered another long neck. I asked for a slice of carrot cake and a cup of coffee. After she left, I filled him in on what Jackie had been able to learn about the twenty-three corporations down at the recorder of deeds office.

"Turns out that each corporation purchased one piece of property—a two- or three-flat—directly from the city of St. Louis. The purchase prices ranged from fifteen to twenty-five thousand dollars."

"Sounds like slum property prices," Benny said.

"Probably so. All are on the north side of St. Louis.

From the computer records, Jacki was able to determine that the city had initially obtained the title to each of the properties through some sort of compulsory process. It wasn't clear from the information in the index, but I'm guessing condemnations or foreclosures for failure to pay property taxes."

"So Michael Green helped create twenty-three new slumlords?"

"Yes and no."

"What does that mean?"

"It's not clear from the records why it happened, but the city of St. Louis ended up reacquiring the title to each of these properties."

Benny frowned. "Huh?"

"My reaction, too. Jacki did a quick title history on each property. Somehow or other, the city got back each property around eighteen to twenty-four months after the corporation acquired it."

"What happened?

I shrugged. "I'm going to have to go down to the recorder of deeds office myself and try to figure that out."

"Did this all happen after Michael Green died?"

"No. More than half of the transfers occurred while he was alive."

Benny leaned back in the booth and shook his head. "The economics of these deals are insane. Each man pays Michael Green twenty-five grand in fees to set up a corporation to buy a slum property from the city for another fifteen to twenty-five grand. When the city takes back the property, each man is out the original twenty-five grand to Michael Green plus the purchase price for the property."

"Plus the fifteen thousand for a Sebastian Curry painting," I added, "assuming that there's a connection there."

"And Green got a piece of that action, too, through what

has to be a bogus commission payment to his tax dodge in the Canary Islands."

I took a forkful of carrot cake and chewed it in silence.

Benny frowned. "I'll tell you who knows exactly what's going on."

"Who?"

"Those twenty-three men, that's who."

I nodded. "I'm going to confront one tomorrow. See if I can get him to talk."

"Which one?"

"Don Goddard."

"Why start with a lawyer? I thought you said he was Mr. Smooth."

"That's his reputation, but he really didn't seem all that sharp when I met with him. You know the type, Benny—one of those glib guys who thinks that he's smarter than the rest of us but isn't. I have to be in Clayton for a breakfast meeting anyway. I thought that afterward I might drop in on Don."

"Who are you meeting for breakfast?"

"Remember that message on Sebastian Curry's telephone machine from a girl named Gail? She returned my call today. Sebastian's funeral is tomorrow at ten o'clock. Right after the funeral she leaves town on business. The only time we could meet was for breakfast at eight." I paused. "Actually, as long as I'm in Clayton I might as well stop in to see Martha Hogan as well."

"Hang on, girl. You have a breakfast meeting at eight followed by an encounter with Mr. Smoothie followed by a meeting with Martha Hogan. Aren't you also supposed to be getting ready for your trial?"

I rolled my eyes. "Tell me about it. Maggie and Sara are coming in after lunch tomorrow to go over their testimony. I'll be done with them before dinner. I figure I can have the rest of my case ready by midnight, which ought to leave me just enough time."

"For what?"

"A quick nervous breakdown."

CHAPTER 26

H er name was Gail Harris and she worked in promotions for one of the local FM radio stations—the one with the "classic rock" format. We met for breakfast at the Ritz-Carlton in Clayton. Gail was in her thirties—slightly overweight with high cheekbones, freckles, very curly brown hair, and a cheerful smile. Her first words to me were, "I totally love your hair. Who did your perm?"

"Mother Nature."

"Oh, my God, those big curls. I am *so* jealous."

"You wouldn't have been back in high school. I hated my hair. I used to sleep with it wrapped around an empty orange juice can and then blow-dry it straight in the morning." I smiled and touched my hair. "Times change, and they'll change again."

Gail's outfit had initially struck me as a bit prim for rock radio—dark skirt hemmed at the knee, white blouse, simple gold earrings and matching necklace—but then I remembered that she'd dressed for the funeral.

The waiter arrived. Gail ordered orange juice and an English muffin, toasted and plain. I ordered coffee, fresh strawberries, and oatmeal.

Gail told me that she was heading to an industry convention in Las Vegas, where she'd never been before. To prepare, she'd bought a book on gambling tips and had rented the movie *Vegas Vacation* with Chevy Chase, "which was such a hoot I couldn't stop laughing—I almost peed in my pants." She was extra excited because in the movie Chevy Chase had stayed at the Mirage, which is where she was staying.

The waiter arrived with our breakfasts. After he left, I briefly described my one meeting with Sebastian Curry, mainly to let her know how charming I'd found him.

"Oh, it's so sad," she said, her eyes welling up. "I just adored Sebastian. Everyone did. I can't imagine who would do this to him. That's exactly what I told the police."

"When did they talk to you?"

"On Saturday."

"Do they have any leads?"

"I don't think so."

"How did you and Sebastian become friends?"

Gail sat back in her chair, chewing on the English muffin as she remembered. "The station did this afternoon drive-time event at King Louie's about two years ago. Sebastian was a waiter there. You couldn't miss him—I mean, talk about tall, dark, and handsome. Totally gorgeous. And so sweet—helping us out and all. Afterward, the radio crew was heading over to this bar in Soulard to party and hear some blues. We dragged Sebastian along. I'm telling you, Rachel, by the time the night was over every girl at the bar was ready to take him home. Of course, like every sweet good-looking single guy you meet in this town, he was gay." She glanced at my left hand. "Right?"

"Sure seems that way sometimes. So you knew him for about two years?"

She nodded.

"Did you know he was also a painter?"

"Oh, sure. Poor guy wasn't having much luck. It made you sad because he was so committed to his art."

"Did he ever talk to you about his life before you met him?"

She frowned. "What do you mean?"

"Where he grew up, the things he did before he became a waiter?"

She thought about it. "Not really. He used to say he'd been through some really dark times, but he never talked about them. I remember he once told me his mother was an alcoholic and he never knew who his father was. He said he was raised by his grandmother."

"Is she still alive?"

"No. He said she died of cancer when he was a teenager." She hesitated. "Why are you so interested in this?"

"I represent Angela Green."

Her eyes widened. "Oh, wow. The one in jail?"

I nodded.

"I like totally respect that woman. I taped that show where Oprah interviewed her in jail." She paused and frowned. "But what does Sebastian have to do with that?"

"I think there might be some connection between my client and whoever killed Sebastian Curry."

"Really? Oh, God."

"I had some questions I wanted to ask him. I actually went over to his loft to talk to him. I was the one who found his body."

"Oh, gross. You poor thing. That is so awful."

"So I'm trying to find someone he was really close with—maybe a lover or a best friend, someone he might have confided in. Did he have a boyfriend?"

"He did, but they broke up about three months ago. His name is Gregory. Gregory Johnson. They were together for maybe a month." She mulled it over. "They never really seemed all that close, though."

"Did he have someone before Gregory?"

"Yeah." She paused, trying to remember. "But nothing serious. Nothing that ever lasted more than like a few weeks.

Sebastian was one of those bachelor types. He liked to fool around, if you know what I mean. Who could blame him, huh? I mean he was such a total hunk that gay guys were practically throwing themselves at his feet. He never had a real lover during the time I knew him."

"How about a best friend?"

She gave me a sad shrug. "That was probably me, and we weren't all that close."

"Who else might he have confided in?"

"The best bet would be Reverend Wells."

"Who's that?"

"His pastor. The one surprising thing about Sebastian was how totally religious he became the last year or so. He went to church every Sunday and always had his Bible handy. He really admired Reverend Wells. Those are the only times he'd ever mention his dark times. He'd tell me that Reverend Wells was helping save his soul. I never met the man, but I understand he's doing the funeral today."

I did a quick mental review of my calendar. There was no way I could squeeze in the funeral. "I'll try to talk to him later this week."

"He might know something," Gail said.

I went over some other names with her—Michael Green, Billy Woodward, Samantha Cummings. She'd never met them and had never heard Sebastian mention them.

Before we parted I told her how important it was to keep our meeting confidential. "Gail, I don't know who killed Sebastian or why. All I know is that he was rattled by some of the things I mentioned to him during our meeting. I keep thinking that after our meeting he talked to the wrong person about whatever it was that bothered him, and that person arranged to have him killed."

"Really?"

"I don't know, but I don't want anyone else to make

that mistake. Don't mention our meeting to anyone."

Her eyes widened. "I totally won't."

"And if someone saw us together today and asks you why you were meeting with me, tell them you were trying to arrange a radio station promotion with one of my clients." I mentioned a baseball player I represented.

"Wow, you represent him?"

I nodded. "Understand?"

"Got it. My lips are sealed."

"If you think of anything else, or if someone asks you about our meeting, call me immediately, okay?

"Definitely."

"Thanks, Gail."

"Good luck, Rachel."

M r. Goddard will see you now."
    I looked up from the transcript of the deposition I'd taken of Charlie Blackwell several weeks ago. I'd been so engrossed in making notes for cross-examination that it took me a moment to get my bearings. I was seated in the swanky reception area of Goddard, Jones & Newberger. Don Goddard's secretary, a tall silver-haired woman with a British accent, was standing before me.

"Great." I closed the transcript and legal pad, capped the pen, and put everything back in my briefcase.

"This way, please."

I followed her down the hall to the large corner office of Don Goddard. The great man himself was seated behind an antique Queen Anne library desk in a high-backed leather chair large enough to double as a throne. He stood to greet me.

"Good morning, Rachel." I let him take my hand. "What a delight to see you."

"Thanks for meeting me on short notice."

"It is my pleasure."

There was a gleam in his eyes that I recognized. Goddard assumed that I was bringing him a new piece of legal business. When I'd called on my drive to the Ritz that morning, I told his secretary that I needed to talk to Mr. Goddard about some significant corporate and real estate matters involving a client of mine. That was true, of course, although its meaning was open to varying interpretations.

"I'm just a litigator," I'd told her, explaining that I hoped Mr. Goddard would be able to help me out. She put me on hold a moment and came back on the line to tell me that Mr. Goddard would be delighted to squeeze me in at nine-thirty.

As I took a seat facing him, his phone rang. He hesitated, gazing longingly at it.

"Go ahead," I told him.

During my years at Abbott & Windsor I'd learned that to a rainmaker a ringing phone was more alluring than the song of the Sirens. Indeed, one way to ascertain the pecking order among the partners at any big law firm is to figure who is the inflictor and who is the inflictee in what came to be known among the associates of Abbott & Windsor as "doing a Ma Bell."

Goddard lifted the receiver and was quickly into full smoothie mode. I could almost hear the honey oozing through the phone lines. Not wanting to eavesdrop, I stood and looked around his office. There was the usual trophy wall of framed photographs of a tuxedo Goddard posing with various local and national luminaries, including former president Jimmy Carter, Congressman Richard Gephardt, Senator Ted Kennedy, local radio personality Jack Buck, and Stan Musial. Although Goddard's three years at Washington University's law school had been noteworthy primarily for their lack of anything noteworthy, he'd apparently dedicated the past decade to gilding that connection, as attested by the plaques, certificates, and photographs lining one of his other office walls. It's amazing—or sad—what money can buy at an institution of higher learning.

The telephone call came to end and I returned to my seat.

"I apologize for the interruption, Rachel." He offered what he must have assumed would resemble a sincere smile. "Now let's talk about your client's concerns."

"Great. First off, though, I'd like to get a better sense of the kinds of services your firm can provide in the corporate and real estate area."

"To coin a phrase, you've come to the right place, Rachel. We provide our clients with three interrelated areas of specialization: corporate, real estate, and tax. We dedicate all of our energies and talent to those three areas of the law."

"So if I had a client who needed to form a corporation, that's something you could handle."

"Absolutely. We form new corporations every day of the week."

"And if I had a client who wanted to use that corporation to buy a piece of property—say, a two- or three-flat in the city—is that something your firm could handle as well?"

"Rachel, not only could we handle that type of transaction; we actually do them all the time." He leaned forward, giving me the full bedside manner. "Rachel, I sincerely believe that there's not another law firm in this town with more experience and skill in these two areas. That enables us to give value-added service to our clients and, just as important, cost-effective service as well."

"Tell me a little more about that, Don. I'm just a litigator. I have no idea what those kinds of services even cost."

"Rachel, we are interested in a long-term relationships with our clients. The client who forms a corporation to buy a piece of rental property today may very well blossom tomorrow into a national real estate concern. So while other firms may try to gouge such a client for what they believe is a one-time transaction, we price our services with an eye toward the future."

"Help me there, Don. What do you call gouging, and how does that compare with your firm's billing practices?"

"Certainly. Now fees will vary on a case-by-case basis, of course, but there are firms in this town that would charge six to eight thousand dollars to form a simple corporation and draft the deal documents for the purchase of a small rental property. We'll do those tasks better and we'll do them more efficiently and we'll charge less than three thousand dollars."

Time to see how far out on the limb I could lure him. "When I was an associate in the Chicago office of Abbott and Windsor—"

"An outstanding law firm," Goddard said.

I nodded. "Agreed. Anyway, the partners at Abbott and Windsor used to have the firm's lawyers handle their personal corporate and real estate matters. That always seemed a pretty good testimonial to the quality of the firm's services in those areas."

Goddard chuckled. "Far be it from me to draw parallels between our humble firm here and that great national legal institution, but I can state without hesitation that the partners of this firm consistently rely on the expertise of their fellow partners in personal business matters, especially in the real estate area."

"That's good to know."

"Now," he said, giving me that avuncular smile, "tell me about your client."

"Her name is Angela Green."

He raised his eyebrows. "Really? Fascinating. I take it, then, that she has some business affair to attend to?"

"In a way. It's kind of a sensitive situation."

He lowered his voice. "My firm can be quite discreet, Rachel. We understand the importance of client confidences."

"That's good to know. Actually, the business matter has more to do with her husband than her. You knew Michael Green, correct?"

"Well, I knew of him. Fellow attorneys and all. We may even have served together once on an alumni committee."

I frowned. "Actually, I thought you knew him better than that. You were a client of his, weren't you?"

Goddard leaned back. "A client? I'm not sure I'm following you."

"It is kind of confusing. At least to me. But the records I have clearly show you were one of his clients. According to those records, Michael Green formed the Sevens Corporation for you and did the deal documents for the purchase of a three-flat in the city of St. Louis. Does that ring a bell?"

"Vaguely."

"The services he performed for you are exactly the types of services you just told me your firm does for its partners. Right?"

"Well, yes, in certain cases, right."

"And I think you said that for those types of services your firm would charge a client less than three thousand dollars. Right?"

"Well, so long as there was nothing unusual about the deal, yet."

"But you paid Michael Green twenty-five thousand dollars for those very same services. Why?"

"Why?" he repeated.

"Why did you pay him all that money?"

He pursed his lips, his eyes blank. "I don't recall at this point in time."

"Maybe it'll come to you later. What happened to the

three-flat you bought? We've checked some of the real estate records at City Hall. Your company owned it for only nineteen months."

He was staring at me. "What is this all about?"

"That's what I came here to ask you."

"What are you trying to pull here?" The charm was gone.

"Some answers out of you. I assume that there's also a connection between the real estate deal and that Sebastian Curry painting you bought."

He crossed his arms over his chest, his face suddenly flushed. "We have nothing further to discuss. It's time for you leave."

"Don, you're not the only one. There are at least twenty-two others who did the same thing. You're the first person I've talked to. I'll talk to the others, one by one. One of you is going to talk to me, or, if not me, then to the police. And you know how that works. It's just like that inventory accounting system—FIFO. First in, first out. Same here. First one to talk is the first one out. Why not let it be you?"

"This meeting is over. Out." He was glaring at me. "Get out of my goddamn office, you sneaky little bitch."

I stood up, shaking my head. "Sticks and stones, Don."

"You better leave now, goddammit, or else."

I started toward the door and then turned. "Or else what? You'll call the police? Think about your situation, Don. Think about it carefully. It still makes more sense to talk to me. You have my number. Call me."

I turned and left.

CHAPTER 27

We were in chambers—the final pause before opening statements. Jimmy, the judge's elderly bailiff, was standing by the door, waiting. Judge Parker buttoned his judicial robe.

"Counsel," he said, "Jimmy's about to bring in our jury. Sure there's no chance of getting this thing settled?"

I looked at Armour. "Our demand hasn't changed. Give my clients their money back and we'll drop the other claims."

Armour chuckled. "That's a no-brainer. Let's raise the curtain and bring on the dancing dykes."

Mack Armour's opening statement was every bit as misleading and offensive as I expected. He rambled from New Testament quotes wrenched from context to an animal behavior "study" published in a supermarket tabloid. He ended with a jab at what he labeled the "fem-Nazi cult of political correctness."

"What next?" he said, feigning astonishment. "Does the animal kingdom come flocking to our courts, one by one, seeking redress for their place in God's plan? Will the heirs of the male black widow sue Big Momma for wrongful death because she killed Daddy after they mated? Will the mare sue the stallion for assault for biting her on the neck during sex? And what about that poor praying mantis?" He paused, hand on his heart in mock sympathy. A few of the jurors were smiling. "As soon as he ejaculates the female bites off his head and eats it. Talk about bad sex. Gotta be a claim there, eh?"

He crossed his arms and shook his head. "Of course not. We're all God's creatures. Each of us does what God designed us to do. It's called natural reproduction—a path, ironically, that Miss Gold's clients spurn in their own lives. If these two women are looking around for someone to blame, someone to hold accountable, then I suggest they look in a mirror." With a triumphant about-face, Mack Armour turned from the jury and gave me a satisfied wink as he returned to his seat.

"Miss Gold?" the judge said.

I stood and faced the jury. "Mr. Armour and I will agree on little during this trial," I started, aiming for a low-key tone, "but we do agree that Mother Nature has devised some amazing reproductive strategies. The black widow, the horse, the praying mantis, and, as you will soon learn, even the ostrich—each species performs the sexual act in a way that seems strange or shocking to us. But what Mr. Armour ignores is that the end result of each of these mating rituals— *every single one of them*—is the creation of new life. Here, though, the end result was terror."

I paused, trying to read the jurors' facial expressions— about as helpful as trying to read tea leaves. At least they seemed to be listening.

"Here," I continued, "the end result was serious injury. And in one case, death. Not once did this ostrich engage in the mating dance of his species. Not once did this ostrich complete a sex act with any hen. Not once did this ostrich create new life."

I moved back to counsel's table and stood behind Maggie and Sara, resting a hand on each one's shoulder. "These women," I said, "paid a lot of money for a breeding ostrich. Blackwell Breeders agreed to sell them a stud. Instead, it sold them a dud. And a lethal one at that. They're entitled to compensation."

I came around from behind the table and stopped in front of the jury. "Mr. Armour talks about God's creatures flocking to this courthouse with frivolous claims. As the evidence will demonstrate, only one of God's creatures tried that ploy here." I turned toward counsel's table and gestured at Charlie Blackwell. "And that creature is sitting right there."

I cross-examined Charlie Blackwell late that afternoon. Armour had run him briskly through his paces in what was obviously—to me, at least, and hopefully to the jury—a well-rehearsed two hours of direct. As I got to my feet, I could see Blackwell hunker down for what he assumed would be a marathon cross-examination.

I had other plans.

"Good afternoon, Mr. Blackwell."

"Affer-noon, ma'am," he answered in his high-pitched nasal twang. *MAY-yam.*

Charlie Blackwell had spiffed himself up considerably since I'd taken his deposition a month ago. Today he was wearing a starched white cowboy shirt stretched tight against his belly, black Sansabelt slacks, a bolo tie, and black cowboy boots polished to a high sheen. His gray hair was slicked back, his face clean shaven, and his complexion ruddy. With his long beak of a nose, small dark eyes, and receding chin, he bore some resemblance to a bird himself, although more of a vulture than an ostrich.

"Let me make sure I understand your earlier testimony, sir. You believe that the sexual practices of the humans who handle an ostrich during its formative years will affect its future behavior, correct?"

Eyeing me warily, Blackwell nodded. "Yes, ma'am. At least in part."

"And you believe that the formative years for a male ostrich are the first two years, correct?"

"Yes, ma'am."

"Even though they're basically full-grown after twelve months?"

"On the outside, yep. But they still got some growing to do on the inside. Your males are particularly sensitive, you see. They gotta be brung along careful or they'll go bad on you."

As he spoke, I had moved along the jury box toward the back, resting my arm against the railing. Now he'd be forced to look at the jurors when he answered my questions.

"Nevertheless, your company raised that ostrich for the first fourteen months, right?"

"Yes, ma'am."

"Getting back to the sexual practices of the human handlers. You claim that they'll influence the ostrich's behavior even if he doesn't witness the people having sex?"

"I'm saying it's possible, yep."

"The ostrich just kind of senses it, eh?"

"You could say that, yep."

"But what if the ostrich actually witnessed the sex act?"

He chuckled. "That'd be even worse."

"Oh? And why is that, Mr. Blackwell?"

"To actually see an unnatural act, well, that could mess him up real bad. Matter of fact," he mused, his eyebrows raised, "I bet that happened here. Sure could explain a lot, yep."

Mack Armour snickered behind me.

"You say that could explain a lot?" I repeated.

"Yep." Blackwell was grinning. He glanced over at his attorney and then back at me. "Sure could, ma'am."

"What if there was violence, too?" I asked.

"You mean during the sex act?"

"Yes."

"Oh, boy, now you're talking a whole sack of trouble."

"Really?"

"Mess him up real bad, yep."

"Thank you, Mr. Blackwell." I looked up at the judge. "No further questions."

The judge looked over at Armour. "Any redirect, counsel?"

Armour was grinning. "I should say not, Your Honor."

"You're excused, Mr. Blackwell," the judge said. He turned toward the jury. "Ladies and gentlemen, we'll be in recess until tomorrow at nine A.M."

Jacki, God bless her, had left dinner for me at the office before heading off to night school. I was happily munching on a Mediterranean wrap from Crazy Bowls & Wraps and sipping a diet Dr Pepper as I reviewed my trial notes and outlined tomorrow's testimony and exhibits. It was almost seven o'clock and the light was fading outside. I still had two to three hours of trial preparation ahead of me, which was at least an hour too much for now, since I was meeting Benny and Milly Eversole at Martha Hogan's office at eight-thirty tonight. Martha had picked the time and place. Given my role in getting that particular relationship under way, I really couldn't beg off.

There was a knock at the front door. I looked up, puzzled and mildly irritated. My office was in a converted Victorian mansion in the Central West End, and thus the front door really was a front door. Although the stenciled sign on the door read RACHEL GOLD • ATTORNEY AT LAW, each year a dozen or so strangers would show up after hours by mistake—everyone from deliverymen with packages for someone else to couples arriving at the wrong address for a party to an adorable elderly man last month carrying a dozen long-stem red roses for his dinner date. I wiped my mouth and hands with a napkin, got up, and walked past Jacki's desk and the reception area into the hallway leading to the front door. I peered through the eyehole.

Darkness had fallen. It took a moment to identify the bulky, pallid man in the ill-fitting gray suit standing under the porch light. Herman Borghoff, first assistant to the St. Louis redevelopment commissioner, Nate the Great. Borghoff faced the door, expressionless, his thick horn-rimmed glasses slightly askew. I studied him, torn between my curiosity about his visit and my desire to get back to work. Pretending I wasn't here wouldn't work, since he'd no doubt seen my lights on from outside.

I unlocked the door and opened it.

"Hello, Herman."

"Miss Gold."

"What's up?"

"May I come in?"

"Just for a moment. I'm real busy tonight."

"This will not take a long time."

I hesitated before giving in. "Okay, follow me."

I led him to my office and cleared the pile of trial papers from one of the chairs facing my desk. I went around behind my desk and took a seat facing him. He stared at me with those zombie eyes. Borghoff definitely gave me the creeps.

"Well," I finally said, "what's up?"

"Commissioner Turner is anxious to resolve the Oasis Shelter matter."

"So are we. We're working on it."

"Is your client prepared to do the property swap?"

"We received your proposed swap properties. Someone is looking them over. The board plans to take the issue up at the next meeting."

"When will that be?"

"I'm not sure. I think they have a lunch meeting on the third Thursday of the month." I glanced at my calendar. "That would be two weeks from tomorrow. I'll call you afterward, okay?"

"Will the board approve a property swap at that meeting?"

"Maybe. I don't know." I checked my watch. "Look, I'll call you after the board meeting, okay?"

He stared at me, his expression blank. "The commissioner is concerned that you may not bargain in good faith."

I could feel a spike of anger. "Given your office's actions, Herman, I should think that my client is the only one entitled to be concerned about people bargaining in good faith."

"The proposed swap properties are outside the redevelopment area. That was the key term of the deal."

"I know that. So?"

He gazed at me. "Why are you searching for properties within the redevelopment area?"

"What are you talking about?"

"You have been making inquiries concerning certain properties located within the boundaries of the redevelopment area."

"Oh, I have, have I?" I gave him an incredulous look. "When was this?"

"Your assistant was down at the recorder of deeds earlier this week. I assume that she—or he, or it—was acting under your direction and control."

I opened my mouth and closed it, my mind racing. How did Herman Borghoff know that Jacki had been doing title searches?

"She was," I said evenly.

"Was she searching for alternative swap properties?"

"I don't think that's any of your business, Herman."

"The commissioner is concerned about your client's good faith."

"Tell him not to worry."

"I can only give him that level of assurance after I have received an adequate explanation from you as to why your assistant was making inquiries regarding those properties."

"Then you're going to have to make do without an explanation, Herman. Those properties are none of his business."

"Actually, they are, Miss Gold. All residential properties in which the city holds title are the business of the commissioner."

"Good for him. I'm going to have to ask you to leave now, Herman."

"You still have not given me an explanation."

"And I'm not going to, even if I had the time, which I don't. I have to get to a meeting in Clayton in ten minutes." I gathered my things and stood up, trying to stay calm. Borghoff's creepiness had edged closer to menace. I couldn't wait to get him out of my office. "I'll let you out the front door. I'm parked in back."

He walked silently down the hall in front of me. Stepping out onto the porch, he turned to face me. "The commissioner is going to be disappointed."

"Then the commissioner is going to need to ease up. Tell him my client is considering his proposal and hopes to make a decision by the end of the month."

Borghoff studied me for a moment with those deadpan eyes. Then he shook his head and turned away. I watched him lumber down the front walk, through the gate, and down the street. I watched until he was out of sight.

I kept watching, staring into the night. Finally, I locked the front door and turned off the light.

It was a warm night but I was shivering in the dark.

CHAPTER 28

Second day of trial.

Mack put on only one more witness—an escapee from the junk-science holding pen named Martina Kirkman, a purported animal psychoanalyst that the judge allowed to testify as an expert witness over my objection. The good doctor opined that Big Red appeared to be a manic-depressive suffering from a bipolar disorder likely arising from unresolved hostility toward females caused by a focal confusion over apposite gender roles—or something like that. The jury seemed to be having as much trouble as me following her testimony. Mack's direct examination lasted fifteen minutes, and my cross just five—long enough to establish that she'd been a panelist on a Jerry Springer show where the topic was "Women Who Sleep with Their Dogs."

"Call your first witness, Miss Gold."

I stood and took a deep breath. I'd been up until four in the morning preparing for this next encounter, trying to anticipate every possible scenario. Armour was the wild card, of course. I glanced over at him. He leaned back, his arms folded over his chest, smirking at me.

It's show time, Rachel.

I turned toward the back of the courtroom and nodded to the bailiff, who opened the courtroom door.

I announced, "Defendants call Milly Eversole."

Armour jumped to his feet. "What the— Objection!"

Millie entered the courtroom, escorted by Benny Goldberg. Coming in behind them was Martha Hogan, looking determined as usual. Her black hair was cut in short layers with wispy bangs. Our eyes met as she came up the aisle. She snuck me a wink. I could have kissed her.

"This is outrageous," Armour grumbled. "May I approach, Your Honor?"

I joined him for the sidebar.

"What kind of carnival stunt is this?" Armour demanded. He turned to glare at Milly as she filed past, eyes averted, toward the witness stand.

I said, "Miss Eversole worked in the nursery at Blackwell Breeders from the time this ostrich hatched until my clients bought him. Based on my cross-examination of Mr. Blackwell yesterday, I believe her testimony is highly relevant."

"You're out of luck, lady," Armour said.

"Oh?"

"There's not going to be any testimony. That girl signed a confidentiality agreement. Her lips are sealed."

"Not according to her attorney," I said.

"Her attorney?" Armour turned to me, his eyes ablaze. "Who's that?"

I pointed. "There."

Armour turned toward Benny, who'd taken a seat in the front row. Benny winked at him and gave a thumbs-up. Armour glowered at him for a moment, and then glanced at Martha, who'd taken a seat alongside Benny in the front row, her hands clasped on her lap, her beautiful Irish Claddagh ring showing. Armour knew who she was. We all did. Once upon a time, she'd been little Martha from St. Bernadette grade school in Rockford, Illinois. But for the last twenty years, she'd been a prosecutor in the sex crimes division of St. Louis County. Shrewd and relentless, she had the highest conviction rate in the office.

"What the hell is *she* doing here?" Armour demanded,

gesturing toward Martha. You could almost see the steam coming off his bald head.

Ignoring his question, I turned to the judge. "Your Honor, may I proceed with the witness?"

"Hold it, lady," Armour said. "Can we get the jury out of here and sort this out?"

Judge Parker nodded wanly and looked over at the jury. "Uh, the court will be in recess for ten minutes, ladies and gentlemen."

I turned toward Martha as the jury filed out. She and Benny and I had gone over this very possibility last night in her office. I was ready for him and hoped those two were as well. I gave Milly Eversole a reassuring smile. She was wringing her hands together in her lap, her eyes darting anxiously from lawyer to lawyer.

As the door closed behind the final juror, Armour spun toward the judge. "That girl," he said, pointing at Milly, who flinched in the witness box, "is getting dragged down the primrose path by Miss Gold. Milly had an employment dispute with my client. My client settled with her. A very generous settlement, Judge. He gave her a significant severance payment with one condition: if she *ever* disclosed the terms of the settlement agreement to *anyone*, she'd have to refund the full amount *and* pay my client an additional five grand. Miss Gold's little grandstand play here is going to cost that girl a pretty penny."

"Hey, curly," Benny interrupted, "Rachel isn't her lawyer. I am."

Armour spun toward him. "Really? Do you have any grasp of the financial impact of this on your client?"

Benny nodded thoughtfully. "I have a pretty good idea what it would take to settle it right now."

"Oh, is that so?" Armour said with disdain. "And what is it?"

"About a million from that redneck cretin you represent, another quarter of a mill from you. That ought to do it."

"Have you lost your mind?" Armour asked.

"No," Benny answered, "but you may lose your license."

"Hey," Armour said, taking a threatening step toward Benny, "watch your mouth, buster, 'cause I got chunks of guys like you in my stool."

Benny glanced at me, a twinkle in his eye, and then turned to Armour. "Chunks of what in your stool?" he asked, feigning confusion.

Armour thrust his chin forward. "Guys like you."

Benny gave him a sympathetic look. "Don't lose hope, pal. They may yet find a cure."

"For what?" Armour asked.

"For your eating disorder, you poor bastard."

"Hold on, gentlemen," Judge Parker said, trying to re-capture control of his courtroom. He turned toward Martha. "First things first. Ms. Hogan, are you here on a matter?"

She stood. "I am."

"Let's take care of you first, then. Which matter?"

"This one."

"This case?" Judge Parker looked puzzled. "Why?"

"At Mr. Goldberg's request, I interviewed Miss Eversole yesterday." She nodded toward Milly. "Based on that inter-view, I've determined that there's probable cause for the per-petration of at least four felonies."

"Aw, shit," Charlie Blackwell groaned in the back-ground.

"I don't understand," Judge Parker said.

Martha started ticking them off on her fingers. "One count of forcible rape and one count of forcible sodomy. Both criminal acts perpetrated by Mr. Blackwell during working hours inside the nursery barn at Blackwell Breeders. Miss Eversole was the victim both times."

There was a long pause as Martha stood there with two fingers raised.

"Uh, you mentioned four," Judge Parker finally said.

"Two counts of concealing an offense," Martha answered.

Judge Parker frowned. "Pardon?"

"Section 575.020 of the Missouri criminal code makes it a felony to agree to confer a financial benefit on any person in consideration for that person's agreement to conceal a crime or to refrain from initiating the prosecution of a crime."

"Mr. Blackwell did that?" Judge Parker asked.

"Actually," Martha said, turning toward Armour, "this man did. He not only worked out the financial details, prepared the papers, and had the victim sign them, but he also issued his own threat."

In the hushed courtroom, Martha stared up at Armour like a butcher eyeing a steer.

That's why I ought to be a judge," Benny said. The two of us were at a bar on Laclede's Landing. Through the window you could see the Arch in the distance, its silvery skin gleaming in the late afternoon sun.

As so often happens, the threat of criminal prosecution forced a quick resolution of the civil case. Charlie Blackwell had surrendered by noon in the judge's chambers. With Martha glaring down at Blackwell, the judge wrote out the terms of the agreed settlement order: my clients would receive a full refund of their money (with interest), an additional $25,000 in compensation for injuries to their other ostriches, and payment of all of their legal expenses. Once the agreement was signed, Martha asked—or, rather, instructed—the judge to excuse Mack Armour. After he stepped out, Martha informed Charlie Blackwell that he would have until Monday to find a criminal lawyer prepared to discuss a plea bargain. The terms of the deal would have to include a significant restitution payment to Milly Eversole and an agreement to cooperate in the prosecution of Mack the Knife.

"You should be a judge?" I said to Benny, bemused. "Why?"

"Creative sentencing. Make the punishment fit the crime. That'd be my mantra."

"Enlighten me, O learned adjudicator. Assuming that Martha gets a jury to convict Mack the Knife, what sort of punishment would fit his crime?"

"That's easy. Book the weekend special at the Honeymoon Hotel. Strip him naked, spray him with ostrich musk, and lock him inside with Big Red. Talk about your rehabilitation—by the time you open that door on Monday morning you'll have either a compassionate, New Age attorney ready to champion the rights of women or—"

"Or what?"

Benny winked. "—or Big Red's favorite boy toy."

He took a sip of beer and eyed the remaining two toasted raviolis on the platter. He grabbed one, dunked it in the red sauce, and popped it in his mouth whole. I contemplated the last one as I felt my mind starting to slip its gears. It had been a long, exhausting week, and it was only half gone, and there was so much left to do. I speared the ravioli with my fork, dipped it in the red sauce, and took a bite. I stared through the window at the Arch as I chewed.

"Learning to Fly" by Tom Petty and the Heartbreakers came over the sound system. The song immediately transported me back in time to law school and an October weekend in a New Hampshire farmhouse with my then boyfriend, a Tufts medical student. He'd been a Tom Petty fan and played his greatest hits tape on the drive up from Boston. Near the farmhouse was a small untended apple orchard probably dating back a hundred years, the limbs gnarled but heavy with fruit. We'd picked apples on a cool morning, filling two bushel baskets, the burgundy skins of the apples glowing in the New England sunshine. They'd been crunchy and tart and delicious. Other memories from that weekend floated by—snuggling on the couch in front of the fire, reading Robert Frost poems on the porch swing in the late afternoon sun, slow-dancing under the moonlight to the sound of Tom Petty's "Into the Great Wide Open" on the portable tape player, sipping hot tea from a heavy mug on the back porch while gazing at the mountains shrouded in early morning mist, skipping stones on a still pond at the edge of the forest, eating a picnic lunch of crusty French bread, sharp Vermont cheddar, Greek olives, and icy white wine, walking hand in hand through a pasture late at night beneath a canopy of a million stars, making love under a quilted comforter in a chilly bedroom. Life had seemed so beautiful that weekend. And so simple. And so far from where I was today.

Benny said something.

After a moment, I turned to him. "Pardon?"

He gave me a curious look. "I said I'm glad Milly didn't have to testify."

I nodded. "Poor thing was scared to death. Martha is the perfect guardian angel for her. She'll make sure we get Millie a big restitution payment from Blackwell."

"And something from Mack, too."

I smiled. "I'll make sure of that. He won't get off cheap." I leaned across the table and patted his hand. "Thank you, Benny. You did a good deed today."

He reddened. "Me? Come on. You were the one who found her. You were the one who brought her up here. I was just your stand-in."

"You were a wonderful stand-in."

"Your clients sure seemed pleased."

"Oh, they were. They're going to throw a big victory party out at the ranch."

"Awesome. When?"

"They wanted to do it this weekend but I asked them to hold off one week."

He gave me a sympathetic look. "More Angela stuff?"

I gave him a weary nod. "My dance card is full through Sunday."

"When's Jonathan coming back?"

"Hopefully by the end of the month. Hopefully I'll have my confession ready by then."

"What confession?"

"Well, either a confession or an ultimatum—I'm not sure which." I sighed. "I love him, Benny, and adore his daughters. That's why I've been trying so hard, but this Orthodox Judaism just isn't going to work for me. Maybe someday, but not now. Funny thing is that these sessions with the rabbi have convinced me how much I love Reform Judaism." I leaned back and looked down at the table. "I've got another meeting with the rabbi tonight. It's not his fault. He's been a doll. Tonight we're going over the laws of kasruth. That part's okay. I'm willing to be a trouper. I'm prepared to keep a kosher home and I'm happy to observe *shabbas* every week, but the rest just isn't going to fly."

"Oh, shit. Does this mean no *mikvah* lifeguard spot for me?"

"Sorry."

"Seriously, Rachel, just tell him the truth. You're still Jewish, for chrissake. And a hell of a lot more observant than most Jews, including me. Jonathan ought to understand. He might be religious, but he's not one of those zealots. He'll be cool."

"Maybe."

"If he isn't, you tell him I'll kick his ass. Well, on second thought, given his Golden Gloves background, you tell him I'll hire someone to kick his ass. Deal?"

I smiled. "Deal."

CHAPTER 29

I was in the public reading room of the recorder of deeds office on the first floor of City Hall. Open on the table before me was the grantee index volume for SAI to SUR for the year that the Sevens Corporation purchased its three-flat in north St. Louis. I was staring at the page for that transaction. Surrounding me on the table were piles of other grantor and grantee indexes.

I was dazed and confused.

Fortunately, Betty Watson had taken pity on me. Betty was a file clerk in the recorder of deeds office—a pleasant woman in her late fifties with dyed black hair, a deep cigarette rasp, and a double-knit pants suit outfit that could be described as post-Easter Kmart-markdown. She'd come to my rescue the third time I'd gone back to the main office with a question.

She was now standing at my shoulder and looking at the page with me. Her reading glasses hung from a slender gold chain around her neck.

"What about this?" I asked, pointing to the line that read, "Consideration: $250,000." "That must be a typo."

"Why do you say that?"

"I saw the real estate contract on this property. The sales price was twenty-five thousand, not two hundred and fifty thousand."

"Look here, honey," she said, pointing to the entry above it, which indicated that the trustee was something called Renewal Corporation.

"Okay," I said uncertainly, wishing again that I'd forced myself to pay closer attention in my property law class. Three years at Harvard Law School and I couldn't even remember whether a homeowner was the mortgagee or the mortgagor.

"You see?" Betty said. "The two hundred fifty thousand dollars isn't the purchase price, honey. It's the loan amount."

The loan amount?

I tried to make sense out of that.

I couldn't.

"But that would mean that this Renewal outfit," I said, pointing to the entry, "loaned the buyer two hundred and fifty thousand dollars to buy a three-flat that cost only twenty-five thousand dollars."

"That's what it says."

"But that's crazy. Why would anyone loan a buyer *ten times* the purchase price of the property?"

"That's what Renewal Corp does."

I turned and looked up at her. "What is it?"

"That's the mortgage lender the city runs. They handle all the redevelopment funds. It's part of that Renewal 2004 program for fixing up the north side. You'd have to check with the comptroller's office, or maybe the redevelopment commissioner, for the details. One of those offices administers it."

"Administers what?"

"The loan program."

"What loan program?"

"For properties in the redevelopment area. That's the whole Renewal Corp thing. You can borrow up to ten times the purchase price of one of them rundown properties if you agree to use that money to fix her up real nice. And believe me, honey, there is a ton of funding. We're talking millions— and most of it from the feds."

I stared at the entry in the book, absorbing what Betty Watson had just told me, astounded by its implications, especially multiplied by twenty-three. I reached for the grantor index for the following year. I'd left that volume open to the page with the entries for the same property.

"What does this entry mean?"

She put on her reading glasses and bent over. "Musta been a default."

"Why do you say that?"

"It says here that Mr. Borghoff was appointed successor trustee."

"What's that mean?"

"It's what happens when the borrower defaults on a loan. The mortgage company appoints a successor trustee to start the foreclosure. With a bank, your successor is usually someone at the bank or the bank's law firm. For the city's foreclosures, it's usually a lawyer in the city counselor's office."

"But not here."

"Like I say, *usually* a lawyer. Not always, though. Sometimes Mr. Borghoff gets appointed successor trustee. Sometimes they appoint someone over in the comptroller's office."

"How do they decide?"

Betty shrugged. "They don't tell us."

"Would the results of the foreclosure be shown in these indexes?"

"Eventually. To find the current owner, though, you should check with the assessor's office. If you want to see any executions or other court orders on the property, you could check our land records on microfilm."

"What about the loan agreement with Renewal Corporation? The one where the buyer agrees to spend all that money on renovations?"

"See this number?" she said, pointing to one of the entries on the page from the index. "That's for the microfilm reel and page where you'll find that agreement."

"Where do I find the microfilm?"

"In the microfilm room down in the basement level."

I leaned back and looked around the room, overwhelmed by the sheer volume. "So it's all in here or down there."

She laughed a smoker's hack. "Here and there and elsewhere. Kind of spread out in different places, honey, but you can eventually unscramble one of them deals if you got the time and you got the inclination."

"Well," I said with a weary smile, "I guess I have the latter."

"Then happy hunting. I'm going to go grab me a smoke, honey. I'll check back on you later."

I worked through the lunch hour, slowly unraveling the deals, one by one. By quarter to two I'd deciphered twelve of them—enough to see the pattern, more than enough to call Jacki to ask her to meet me in the City Hall rotunda. She said she'd be there in thirty minutes.

Jacki showed up in a French-blue button-front dress and brown sandals. It was one of my favorite outfits for her—an elegant cotton dress ending at mid-calf with a full collar, dyed-to-match buttons, and a left breast pocket. The look was lean and graceful—no mean achievement with that body. We'd picked the dress out together one afternoon from a Lands End catalogue during the height of our just-say-no-to–Dolly Parton phase in Jacki's fashion evolution.

"What's up?"

"Let's go outside," I said. "I'll tell you there."

We stepped out of the City Hall entrance facing Market Street. Across Tucker Street to our right was the fourteen-story Civil Courts Building—the crazy building topped by the Greek temple, Egyptian pyramid, and silver griffins.

"I need you to go over to the court clerk's office," I said, nodding toward the Civil Courts Building. "Run a defendant search for each of the twenty-three corporations."

"You think they've been sued?"

"I'm guessing twenty-three lawsuits, one against each."

"Who's the plaintiff?"

"Either the city of St. Louis or something called Renewal Corporation. I'm guessing twenty-three lawsuits and twenty-three default judgments."

"What's going on?"

I glanced around at the people milling near the City Hall entrance.

"Come with me," I told her, gesturing toward the back of the building. We found a bench in the shade where we could talk without being overheard. I kept my voice low, just to be safe. I explained the special mortgage program and how it worked.

"Ten times the purchase price?"

I nodded. "Although it's funded mostly by federal grants, the city handles all the paperwork and makes all the lending decisions."

"Okay."

"I've checked twelve of the Michael Green deals so far. In each one, the corporation borrowed the money from Renewal Corporation, bought the property, and promptly defaulted. Never made a single loan payment. The city started a foreclosure proceeding, but the only security it had was the property itself. The city eventually got the property back, but it was still out all the money."

"So you think the city sued each of these corporations for the deficiency on their loans?"

"Exactly, and I bet it only sued the corporation."

Jacki frowned. "Why do you say 'only'?"

"I've only reviewed the paperwork on five of the deals so far. According to the approval guidelines, the lender is supposed to get a personal guarantee from each of the principal shareholders of the corporation, along with a pledge of their assets. That way they have recourse if there is a default, since the loan is ten times the value of the property. But on the paperwork I reviewed, there were no personal guarantees in the loan files."

"Which means what?"

"Which means that somehow those loans went through the approval and funding process without personal guarantees. That's why I'm betting you'll find that the city sued only the corporations. And that's why I'm betting you'll find twenty-three default judgments. Each of those corporations is judgmentproof, since the only asset it had was the property that the city took back in the foreclosure." I leaned back and shook my head in wonder. "The perfect scam."

"I'm not following you."

"Look at Don Goddard's deal. He forms a shell company, the city loans it two hundred fifty grand, he spends twenty-five on a three-flat, pays Michael Green twenty-five in legal fees, and pockets the rest—assuming that the city sues only his company."

I could tell Jacki was doing the math in her head. "So he clears two hundred thousand dollars?"

"Probably closer to one eighty-five. Don't forget the fifteen thousand he paid for the Sebastian Curry painting."

Jacki frowned. "How's that fit in?"

"Michael Green couldn't run a scam like this solo. He had to have someone on the inside—someone who'd make sure that the loans got approved without personal guarantees, who'd make sure that no Boy Scout in City Hall would try to find a pattern with these defaults." I paused. "Come to think of it, when you search the court files, look for other suits involving Renewal Corporation. There must be legitimate deals out there with real defaults. Let's see whether there were personal guarantees on those loans."

She was making notes on a yellow legal pad. She looked
up when she finished. "How do the Sebastian Curry paintings fit in to this?"

"I'm not sure, but look at what we know so far. Each
sale of a painting generated a commission for that Millennium outfit, which appears to be an offshore entity somehow
connected to Michael Green. Green's scam requires a City
Hall insider, right? I'm guessing a big chunk of those Millennium commissions got funneled back to someone at City
Hall."

"Wow."

"It's a clever scheme because the real estate deals look
legit. The client puts up no money but ends up walking away
with close to two hundred grand, tax-free. Michael Green
gets his cut of the action in the form of a twenty-five-
thousand-dollar payment called a legal fee. Multiply that by
twenty-three deals—not bad. The client supplies the bribe
money by laundering fifteen thousand dollars of the loan
through the purchase of a piece of art—hardly a suspicious
transaction for a person of means. When the loan goes into
default, the whole clanking foreclosure machinery kicks into
action—but it's just one of dozens and dozens of foreclosures grinding through the courts. At least that's my theory."

"How do we test it?" she said.

"We start by checking the court files."

"What else?"

"I'll review the rest of the loan deals—especially the paperwork on microfilm."

"And then?"

"Depending upon what you find in court and what I find
back in City Hall, maybe we see what happens when we
confront one of our twenty-three upright citizens."

Jacki's eyes widened. "Really?"

"I want to get this over with. And the sooner the better.

Whatever Sebastian Curry knew about this scam was dangerous enough to get him killed. Maybe it was also dangerous enough to get Michael Green killed and to get Angela framed. Jonathan told me to follow the money, and that's what I've been doing." I took a deep breath and exhaled slowly. "I think we're starting to get warm."

"I think I'm starting to get nervous."

I stood and glanced toward the entrance to City Hall. "It's back to the coal mine for me. Good luck over there."

I watched Jacki head down Market Street toward the Civil Courts Building and then turned back toward City Hall. The weather was warm and the sky was clear. I had a sudden urge to play hooky—to hop in my car and drive over to the Missouri Botanical Gardens and wander among the flowers and buy pellets to feed the carp in the Japanese Gardens—or maybe hop a plane to New York and surprise Jonathan and whisk him off to a jazz bar on the West Side and then back to a suite in the Parker Meridien where I'd convince him to pretend for one evening that he was a Reform Jew. But as I looked up at the sky and took a deep breath and closed my eyes, I had a vision of Angela Green in her prison grays. My smile faded, my eyes opened, my shoulders sagged, and I headed toward City Hall.

Returning to that dank microfilm room felt like returning to a dungeon. One of the four fluorescent lights was out and another one sputtered overhead, which cast annoying, flickering shadows. The clunky microfilm readers dated back to the Sputnik era, the dull green paint on the walls was chipped and peeling, and the odor of mildew permeated the air.

Two hours later, I clicked off the reader, leaned back in my chair and reached my arms toward the ceiling. I'd now reviewed the loan documents for more than half of the deals, and the pattern still held: no personal guarantees. I rubbed my neck and moved my head from side to side, trying to get out the kinks. I needed a break.

I stood and stretched and took in a deep breath. There were vending machines down a back corridor on the first floor. I gathered my notes, put them in my briefcase, reached for my purse, and walked down the hall toward the elevator.

I bought a can of diet Coke and a package of pretzels. After checking my voice mail, I stepped outside to enjoy my little feast in the late afternoon sun. It was a quarter after four. If I hurried, I could finish the rest of the deals before five. Tossing the empty soda can and package in the trash, I went back inside, headed down the hallway, and took the elevator back to the basement level.

I slowed as I reached the door. The microfilm reader I'd been using was against the wall on the far side. Although I'd turned the power off when I left, I hadn't bothered to rewind the tape. Now the power was back on and the loan documents I'd been studying were displayed on the screen. Leaning forward to study them was Herman Borghoff. I took a step back to duck out of sight if he turned. He stared at the screen, his back to me, his palms resting on the table, his face close to the illuminated text. He straightened in the chair and looked down at the microfilm boxes containing the other reels I'd reviewed. He picked up one of the boxes and squinted at the label on the side. Frowning, he looked back toward the screen.

I turned and moved quickly down the hall on my tiptoes toward the elevator, my heart racing.

When I got back to my office I found a memo from Jacki on my desk:

Rachel—
  You were right 23 lawsuits, 23 default judgments.

Copies of the docket sheets are attached. Note that none of the corporations bothered to hire an attorney.

Found 32 other lawsuits over properties in the redevelopment area. Your theory seems to hold up. Copies of those docket sheets are attached.

I studied the bundle of docket sheets she'd attached to her memorandum. The ones for the suits against the Michael Green clients were exactly as I predicted—default judgments solely against the corporations. Any doubt about the existence of a scam vanished when I scanned the docket sheets for twenty-eight of the other cases. In each lawsuit, the defendants included the borrower *and* the personal guarantors. Thus, the city knew how to make a redevelopment loan with proper documentation.

I picked up the final four docket sheets and slowly paged through them. These were the loans that had no relation to Michael Green—all, in fact, were made after his death. Nevertheless, these four loans, like the twenty-three involving Green, were also missing personal guarantees.

I looked at my watch. Three minutes before five o'clock. Opening my legal directory, I flipped to the phone number for the corporate records division of the Missouri secretary of state. I dialed, praying that the state employees didn't leave early.

A woman answered on the third ring. "Secretary of state's office."

"This is Rachel Gold calling. Can you run a quick check for me on four corporations?"

A weary sigh. "Let me have the names, honey."

It took her less than five minutes to run the names through the computer and pull up the results. Although by then it was after closing time, she was nice enough to read me the information slowly so that I could copy it down. I thanked her and hung up.

Leaning back in my chair, I stared at the page of notes. The first of the four corporations was formed about a year after Michael Green's murder. The other three followed at roughly four-month intervals. Each corporation had one shareholder. Two of those shareholders I recognized from puff pieces that had appeared in the *St. Louis Business Journal.*

But all four corporations had one thing in common: Percy Trotter. He was the lawyer on all four sets of incorporation papers.

Percy Trotter?

"Son of Scam," I mumbled, reaching for the phone.

Benny answered on the second ring. "Talk to me."

"Hey."

"Hey."

"You busy?"

"Hell, yes, woman. I'm busy waiting for goddamn ESPN to give me the goddamn Mets score. My boys had an afternoon game against the Giants and I'm sitting here listening to these two douche bags talking about a fucking golf tournament. What's up?"

"I need a man."

"Then this is your lucky day."

CHAPTER 30

At six-thirty that evening, Percy Trotter and I were in a booth near the back of the Summit, a downtown restaurant that was a shrine to Frank Sinatra—from the menus made out of his record albums to the framed glossies of him on the wall to the sound system that had him crooning "I Get a Kick Out of You." I could safely assume that the lyrics did not echo Percy Trotter's sentiments toward me. It was also accurate to say that a more appropriate Sinatra tune for my state of mind was "How Little We Know."

Percy Trotter was an African-American attorney in his early forties—a plump, light-skinned man with a round bald head, thick eyebrows, and a pencil-thin mustache. Although he started off as the son of a city factory worker, he was now a prominent member of the Missouri Republican Party who lived in a gated community in the suburbs, drove a Range Rover, sent his two children to an exclusive private school, owned a summer home on Nantucket, and had a wardrobe of elegant double-breasted suits from his London tailor. Today's was navy blue with maroon chalk stripes.

Trotter and his wife Lucinda were avid social climbers who'd started on ground level and managed so far to reach the lower rungs of the St. Louis corporate elite. His legal practice, however, had not kept pace. Although he had a big enough book of business to become a partner at one of the larger firms in town, his clients were hardly silk stocking, consisting instead of minor-league banks and second-tier entrepreneurs at whose glitzy country clubs he played golf and in whose private jets he traveled to Super Bowls and Las Vegas trade shows.

Percy Trotter had all the traits of a successful phony— the hearty laugh, the warm handshake, the soulful gaze, the photographic memory for names, the affable grin. He was what we used to call a "show partner" in my days at Abbott & Windsor—long on form, short on substance, a superb salesman who could lure the clients into his lair while concealing the fact that he wouldn't actually be doing any of their legal work. It wasn't that Trotter was a poor lawyer; he simply had no interest in reviewing a twenty-five page stock purchase agreement or drafting a set of corporate resolutions, especially if he could be out hustling a prospective client on the links or schmoozing one of his client contacts at the Rams game.

In short, I didn't like him.

I'd been astounded to see him listed as the attorney for the four corporations that appeared, at least from the docket sheets, to be engaged in the same type of real estate scam Michael Green ran. Not because Trotter was a saint—or even close. The scent of sin trailed from him like cheap cologne. No, I was astonished when I realized that this flamboyant Republican must have had a key connection within that ultimate bastion of Democratic politics, St. Louis City Hall.

That realization made me call Benny. We'd originally planned to confront one of the other twenty-three tonight— perhaps Jack Foley, before whom Benny had already given his demented performance as the art critic Benito. But Foley was a long shot, since he probably knew nothing of the City Hall side of the details. Michael Green had been savvy enough to understand that whatever his clients didn't know couldn't come back to hurt him.

From the loan records, Percy Trotter appeared to have

occupied the same role as Michael Green in a subsequent but smaller version of the same scam—four deals versus twenty-three. If so, then he would know what Jack Foley and Don Goddard and the other twenty-one Green clients might not, namely, the identity and the role of each of the coconspirators.

Although Benny had wanted to join me in the booth, I figured that my chances were better if I met Trotter alone. I'd run into him at enough professional and charitable functions over the past two years to know that he'd recognize my name and probably recall that I was single. Marital status was an important piece of information for Percy Trotter. According to what I'd heard from a female partner at his firm, he had a special room arrangement at the Marriott for his noontime trysts. All of which meant that he might be more susceptible without Benny there.

Not that Benny wasn't near. The good professor was, in fact, seated on a stool in the bar area, ostensibly keeping an eye on me while directing the rest of his attention and all of his charm and energy toward the flashy blonde in the black cocktail dress and pearls seated on the stool to his left.

Percy Trotter and I zipped through the small talk. By the time the waitress brought us our drinks, he'd realized that this was not a conversation likely to end with the uncorking of a room service bottle of champagne.

"Michael Green?" Percy Trotter frowned. "I am not in the least bit following you, Rachel."

"Here's how he worked it," I said, and took him through a quick version of the scam.

He listened, his expression neutral.

"Assuming that Green pocketed the full legal fee," I said, "he was paying up to eight thousand dollars per painting as a bribe to someone connected to City Hall. I assume your numbers are similar."

"Numbers?" Trotter tugged on his earlobe, looking bewildered. "Rachel, you must be confused if you believe that I have any idea what you are talking about or attempting to suggest."

"Look, Percy, I'm here to give you an opportunity. I have twenty-three names connected to Michael Green, including some big fish in this town. That's more than enough to convince an ambitious U.S. attorney to launch a criminal investigation. I don't need to give her your name, and I don't need to give her the names of your clients. That's why I asked you to meet me here. You give me the City Hall connection and I forget we ever had this conversation."

Percy leaned forward. "Rachel, I can assure you that I have no idea what Michael Green may have been doing, if anything. Although I never met the gentleman, I have no reason to believe that he was involved in any illicit activity. Now that he has passed, and tragically at that, I cannot imagine why anyone would want to besmirch his reputation." He took a sip of his Glenfiddich. Lowering his voice, he fixed me with a severe look. "As for my clients, Rachel, despite the fact that I am offended by your insinuation that any of them could have been involved in such questionable activity, I will nevertheless look into the four transactions you have identified. Although I am not generally involved in the preparation of the legal documents for my clients' deals, I shall try to determine whether there was anything even colorably amiss in those transactions. I must emphasize, though, that I seriously doubt that I will find anything wrong." He paused, his face somber. "I can sense that you are under great strain, Rachel. I only hope that in your zeal to uncover some irregularity involving your client's former husband you will not stain the reputations of innocent men and women with no connection to those matters."

I had to concede that it was a superb performance—the

concern for my mental health coupled with the lawyer's professional obligation to protect his clients, the voice perfectly modulated to mingle confusion over my accusation and innocence on his part. I'd underestimated Percy Trotter. He was not going to give up a thing.

Unless he had nothing to give up.

Maybe his façade of bewildered innocence wasn't a façade. I'd made several key assumptions in building my case against Michael Green. Although every piece seemed to fit logically, I had to concede that each one was circumstantial. Were there alternative hypotheses out there, especially for Percy Trotter? While twenty-three defective loans might be enough to incriminate Green, were just four such loans enough to incriminate Trotter?

He finished his glass of Scotch and signaled the waitress. She came over all smiles and giggles. "Yes, Mr. Trotter?"

Percy glanced at me. "Another, Rachel?"

"No, thanks."

"Well, Suzie," he said to her with a chuckle, "guess it's time for this ol' cowboy to saddle up and hit the trail." Before I could reach for my purse he'd slipped a pair of twenties off his gold money clip and placed them on the table.

After she left, he turned to me. "Rachel, I assure you that I will personally review those files—if not tomorrow, then early next week. Should I detect anything of a questionable nature, I will find a way to notify you, within the bounds, of course, of my professional obligations under the attorney-client privilege. All I ask from you is time enough to complete my investigation. Is that fair?"

I stood, gathering my purse and briefcase. "I don't know what's fair here, Percy. You do what you need to do, and I'll do what I need to do."

"Come on, Rachel," he said, a trace of annoyance in his voice now. "A few days is surely not much to ask, especially if it turns out that my clients have done nothing wrong." He leaned in close. "Why put their reputations at risk, and in the process put yourself at serious risk of liability for defamation, when the prudent course is to first determine the facts? Mr. Green has been dead for several years now. A few more days won't matter one way or the other."

"I'll think about it."

"You do that."

"No promises."

W hat a load of crap," Benny said in disgust.

"But effectively delivered," I said. "I'll give Percy that much."

We were standing by my car, which was parked just down the block from the Summit. I'd gone into the rest room to avoid leaving with Trotter. I stayed in there for ten minutes, and then waited outside of the restaurant for Benny to join me. He did—but only for a few minutes. Benny had high hopes for the flashy blonde, whose name was Sabrina.

After her second martini, Sabrina had told him that she liked a big man. "I like 'em built for comfort, not for speed," she'd said, borrowing a line from Howlin' Wolf.

After her third martini, she confided that her husband had divorced her because he claimed she was "too kinky."

Benny was, to put it mildly, anxious to return to his perch alongside Sabrina. But God bless him, raging lust hadn't shut down the cognitive region of his brain.

"He's going to examine his clients' files to see whether anything's wrong?" Benny snorted. "That's like a husband telling his wife that he's going to examine his appointment calendar to see whether he was *shtupping* his secretary over the lunch hour last Friday. That slick bastard either is or isn't up to his asshole in this cesspool, and he surely doesn't need to look at any goddamn files to figure that out. Right?"

"I guess so."

"All of which means that Mr. Clean is dirty. Examine his files?" Benny snorted. "Guy is jerking you around, Rachel—just trying to buy time."

"But for what?"

"To cover his fat ass."

We stood there in silence.

"So what's your next move?" he asked.

"I'm going to see Sebastian Curry's minister, and I'm going to talk to Ron Blitz. He's the Blitz of the Blitz detective agency."

"Tomorrow?"

"No, the day after. I've got a hearing down in Crawford County tomorrow."

"What case is that?"

I groaned. "That's the creepy family that's been battling over their grandmother's estate for four years. I represent the younger sister. I'll be there the whole day."

"Good luck."

"Thanks."

Benny glanced toward the restaurant. "Well, my dear, ordinarily I'd love to shoot the shit out here with you, but we must not forget that I have an extremely attractive lady waiting back there who claims she likes a full-figured man and says her husband divorced her because he thought she was too kinky. Think of that." He shook his head in wonder. "A good-looking chick who's kinky *and* has the hots for me." He placed his hand over his heart and gazed heavenward. "Forgive me, Lord. You have finally sent this humble servant irrefutable proof of Your existence."

CHAPTER 31

The sun was setting the following evening as I pulled into my garage after the drive back from the Crawford County courthouse, where the Bensinger family had fought Round 8 of their version of Dysfunctional Family Feud. We'd spent several hours proving beyond a reasonable doubt that a courtroom is no place to look for moral closure, especially in a trust-and-estate battle among adult siblings who hated one another. On the upside, my client and her husband walked out of the courthouse with $175,000 more than they had when she walked in—and $100,000 more than the other side's final settlement offer. On the downside, she walked out of the courthouse with just half of what she'd sought in the case. Even more galling for her was that the court had awarded her detested older brother the same amount it awarded her. All of which meant that we were headed for Round 9 in the Missouri Court of Appeals.

But that was behind me, at least for now. I'd driven back with the top down and my Rolling Stones greatest hits tape on full blast—a good combo to get the ya-yas out. Though I don't normally turn to Mick Jagger for spiritual guidance, he could have reminded my Crawford County client that you can't always get what you want, but if you try sometime, you just might find you get what you need.

It was a beautiful late summer evening—warm breeze, the scent of honeysuckle in the air, a clear sky, a quarter moon already visible low on the horizon. I got out of my car and stretched. I was feeling antsy after the drive.

Ozzie was waiting at the door inside, his tail wagging.

"How 'bout some exercise, Oz?" I patted him on the head. "We can eat afterward."

He barked twice. I took that as a yes.

He followed me upstairs to my bedroom and sat at attention on the rug as I changed into my jogging outfit: a red Cardinals T-shirt, gray running shorts, white socks, and my Nike running shoes. I checked myself in the bathroom mirror. My hair was on the verge of unruly—way overdue for a cut. I shook my head side to side and the curls brushed against my eyes. Forty minutes of that would drive me crazy. I found my St. Louis Browns baseball cap in the closet downstairs and put it on to help control my hair. I opened the door and looked back at Ozzie, who had the leash in his mouth.

"Ready?"

He dashed through the door and turned at the edge of the porch to wait. I locked the front door, put the key in my pocket, and bent down to fasten the leash to his collar. "Let's go."

We took the long route, which included the pathway through the Ruth Park golf course. The fairways were empty as dusk edged into darkness. During the early part of the run, I replayed my conversation with Percy Trotter from the night before, but gradually my thoughts turned to tomorrow. After morning services at my synagogue, I had an early afternoon meeting with Sebastian Curry's minister followed by a late afternoon meeting with Ron Blitz. I'd called him from the courthouse today during a break, hoping that he'd turn out to be one of those gallant knights errant from one of my favorite mystery novels—a Spenser or a Lew Harper. Our five-minute phone conversation was sufficient to remind me that this was no mystery novel. Blitz grudgingly relented only after I agreed to pay him for his time.

"Seventy-five bucks an hour, lady. We're talking cash, and we're talking cash in advance."

Oh, Travis McGee, we hardly knew ye.

I finished the jog with a sprint down my street, arms pumping, as Ozzie scampered alongside. Both of us were panting as we came into the kitchen. I filled his water bowl with fresh water and filled his dinner bowl with dry dog food. I poured myself a tall glass of water and drank it leaning back against the counter as I watched Ozzie lap up his water.

"I'm going to shower," I said, placing my empty glass in the sink.

Ozzie turned to follow me up the stairs. "That's okay," I said, kneeling beside him and scratching behind his ear. "Stay here and eat. I'll be back in a few minutes."

I stripped down to my bra and undies and had just turned on the shower when the phone rang. I briefly debated letting the answering machine pick up, but I turned off the shower and dashed back into the bedroom to pick up the receiver.

"Hello?"

There was static on the other end.

"Hello?" I repeated.

"Did you have a good run?" The voice was scratchy and hollow, as if it were being electronically scrambled and reassembled.

"Who is this?"

"You are prying into matters that don't concern you."

"What are you talking about?" I was gripping the phone. "Who is this?"

"Your meddling has already caused one man to die."

"What?"

"Now you've endangered your loved ones."

"Who are you?"

"When this calls ends, go to your dresser and open the top drawer. Under your white panties, you'll find your black satin ones. Take a peek inside them, Miss Gold. And when you do, remember that this is your final warning."

Click.

I was seated on the edge of my bed. I stared at the receiver in my hand and slowly replaced it.

I turned toward my dresser.

Catching my breath, I spun around and scanned the room, looking for signs of an intruder.

Nothing.

I stared at the dresser. At the top drawer—at the drawer where I kept my bras and my underwear.

"Ozzie," I called in a hoarse voice. "Ozzie, come."

I waited, my eyes fixed on that top drawer.

Ozzie came padding into the bedroom, his tail wagging. He stopped when he saw me seated on the edge of the bed. He gave me a quizzical look, head tilted.

I stood, my legs wobbly.

I forced myself to step toward the dresser.

I stared down at the top drawer, at the brass handle. The handle was shiny. I leaned closer, looking for fingerprints, for smudges.

There was a folded bandanna on top of the dresser. I lifted it and used it to cover my hand. As I reached for the handle, my hand was trembling.

I took a deep breath and pulled the drawer open. The bras were on the left, the underwear on the right—just the way they always were. I stared at the pair of white undies on the far right. I tried to remember whether they were on top of the others this morning. I couldn't remember. I couldn't focus.

I reached out my hand. Wincing, I lifted up the underwear.

Beneath it were my black satin bikinis. I could tell from
the ridges in the fabric that there was a thin rectangular object inside.

I touched the fabric with the tips of my fingers, feeling
the outlines of what was beneath. Playing cards? Cardboard?

I reached inside and removed them.

Photographs.

Three Polaroid photographs.

I stared at the first one as I stepped backward toward the
bed. My calves bumped into the edge of the mattress and I
sat down on the bed.

I was looking at a picture of my sister Ann. She was in
the driver's seat of her Lincoln Navigator, gazing out her
side window, waiting in what appeared to be a carpool line.
Stamped in red in the center of the photo was a round cross-
hair pattern that resembled the view through a rifle scope.
Ann's face was in the center of the crosshairs.

The second photo was of my mother pushing a shopping
cart down the cereal aisle at the supermarket. Her cart was
half-full. She had paused to stare at the cereal boxes on the
shelf. Her face was in profile, right in the center of the red
crosshairs.

The third photo was of Ozzie. He was staring up at the
camera, wearing a leather muzzle over his jaws and some sort
of leather harness contraption around his neck. Like the others, his face was in the center of the crosshairs. Visible behind
him was the edge of a piece of furniture. I held the photo
closer. The furniture looked familiar. I glanced up at my
dresser and back down at the photograph and back at the
dresser.

"No," I gasped.

I sat there for I don't know how long—shuffling through

the photos and staring at the open dresser drawer and looking around the room. I glanced over at the phone and then
down at the photos again, trying to grasp what had happened. An intruder had been in my bedroom today. A
stranger had handled my underwear. A stranger had broken
into my house, forced poor Ozzie into that muzzle contraption, taken his picture, snooped around my bedroom, and
shoved those awful photos inside my underwear.

I looked at Ozzie, who was watching me with concern.

"What happened today, you poor thing?"

I studied his eyes, trying to find a trace of what must
have been a frightening few hours for him. I leaned over and
kissed his forehead.

"What are we going do, Oz?" I whispered.

I rested my forehead on his and scratched him behind
his ears, my eyes closed. "What are we going to do?"

I slid off the edge of the bed and sat on the floor next to
him. I hugged him against me and thought of my mother and
my sister.

"I won't let anyone hurt you," I said, rocking him gently.
"Any of you."

CHAPTER 32

I had trouble keeping my eyes open during Shabbat services Saturday morning. Afterward, I stopped at a coffeehouse in the Central West End for a latte with three shots of espresso, hoping that a jolt of caffeine would rev my engine. I was functioning on less than two hours of sleep.

My first thought last night had been to call Jonathan. He'd been a prosecutor for years and would know what to do and who to contact. He'd know what to make of that creepy call and those photos. Even more important, he could talk to me. I'd needed that badly. He'd know what to say.

Then I'd realized it was Friday night, which meant that I'd have no way to reach him. He'd be at his parents' home in New York with his daughters. His family was Orthodox. Not only wouldn't they answer the phone on a Friday night, they wouldn't even hear it, since they turned it off from sundown Friday to sundown Saturday. And he was on the East Coast anyway. What could he possibly do from there other than get distracted in the middle of his trial and worry himself sick?

I'd thought of calling Benny, but remembered his big plans for the night. Despite my fear, I'd almost smiled at the thought of Mister Built-for-Comfort-Not-for-Speed getting lucky.

Although I knew he'd be at my house in a flash, how could I do that to him on that night of all nights? Moreover, what could he do besides storm around the house and threaten to go postal on whoever was behind the break-in?

Seated on my bedroom floor and hugging Ozzie and rocking slowly, I'd gone through other possibilities, and as I did I gradually realized that the danger was not immediate—at least not immediate as in something bad happening that night. Not to my mother, not to my sister, and not to Ozzie. I'd been threatened. Placed on notice. What had the caller labeled it? *A final warning.* An attempt to scare me off. At the very least, the caller would wait to see how I responded. That meant that the next move was mine, not his.

I'd thought of calling the police but that presented other problems. First was the unknown risk of a squad car response. Whoever had made the threatening call had known that I'd been out jogging, had waited until I'd returned from the jog before calling, and had thus been watching me (or having me watched by one of his cohorts). Probably still watching me. The arrival of a squad car in response to my 911 call would let them know that I'd gone to the police. Would that make them think the warning had failed? If so, what would they do? I didn't want to trigger a hasty response from whoever made the threat.

The second problem was the jurisdictional gap. The University City police would answer my 911 call, since I lived in University City and was calling about a break-in and threatening call to my home. But I believed that the reasons for the threatening call were my efforts to uncover the connection between a real estate scam in the city of St. Louis and the death of Michael Green. Moreover, the caller had mentioned a dead man. That had to be Sebastian Curry, and he'd been killed inside the city limits. Would my hodgepodge of circumstantial evidence be enough to get the St. Louis police involved in an anonymous phone call in the suburbs? And if it did, how effectively would they coordinate with the University City police? And what if the mysterious City

Hall connection had influence with the St. Louis police—or just someone within the department who could tip him off? All of which made me realize that what I needed was an organization impervious to local politics. Fortunately, the caller's use of the phone wires gave them jurisdiction.

The FBI immediately grasped the situation, right down to the squad car problem. They even had a contingency plan for that. I put Ozzie on the front seat beside me and followed their directions to a nondescript house in Maplewood, where two special agents—a man and a woman—were waiting. They interviewed me until one in the morning, at which point the woman—a sturdy brunette named Holly Sarvis—called the assistant U.S. attorney on duty that night, Ben Harper—a stocky guy in his late twenties with a florid complexion and curly blond hair. Harper swung by the safe house about quarter after two with a pair of FBI tech guys. The five of us—Harper, the tech guys, Ozzie, and me—drove back to my house, where an FBI agent was already parked out front in a black government sedan. Harper assured me that there were agents parked in front of my mother's house and my sister's house.

As the tech guys moved from room to room, I sat in my kitchen with Ben Harper and answered his questions. He took careful notes as he walked me though every aspect of my investigation into the events surrounding Michael Green's death. The tech guys quickly found the point of entry—the dining room window. Someone had used a cutting tool to remove a small circle of glass above the window latch. Although the tech guys also found plenty of fingerprints in the house, the absence of any at the point of entry suggested that the other prints would likely prove to belong to my guests or me. They found nothing else incriminating in the house.

Harper made several official calls during those wee hours.

When he finished, he told me that Marsha McKenzie would want to meet with me when she returned from Washington, D.C., on Sunday. Marsha was the U.S. attorney for the Eastern District of Missouri, and she'd be the one to decide the next step in the investigation. Meanwhile, Harper assured me, FBI agents or U.S. Marshals would be on round-the-clock security details for my mother, my sister, and me. They would also coordinate with the U. City police to insure that a patrol car cruised by my house often enough to make someone think twice about harming Ozzie when I was out.

But I wasn't taking chances with Ozzie. I'd brought him with me to the synagogue. The rabbi welcomed him to services, and he actually behaved well. Better, in fact, than some of the kids.

I took a sip of my latte and started the engine. I looked over at Ozzie. He was on the passenger seat, watching me attentively.

"You hungry?"

His tail wagged.

I smiled. "I thought so."

I took another sip of the latte and placed it in the cupholder in the console between the two front seats. "I bought you a treat."

I reached into the take-out bag at my feet and pulled out a poppy-seed bagel. Tearing it in half, I handed him one of the pieces. "Bon appétit."

Ozzie scooted down on the seat, the bagel between his front paws, and started munching away. What a nice Jewish dog—went to the synagogue on Saturday, participated fully in the silent meditation portion of the service, and loved poppy-seed bagels.

I checked the traffic and pulled out of the parking space. I was still rattled—and still worried for my mother and sister—but my anxiety level had dropped several notches since

those awful first moments after last night's call. Glancing in
the rearview mirror, I watched the dark blue sedan pull into
traffic behind me. At the wheel was U.S. Marshal Tommy
Jenkins, all six feet four inches of him. There was certainly a
measure of comfort in that sight.

At a few minutes before one-thirty that afternoon, I turned
into the parking lot behind the Goodfellow Baptist
Church. It was an older brick structure located on a street corner in a neighborhood of two-flats along Goodfellow Avenue
on the north side of St. Louis. The U.S. Marshal pulled into
the space alongside me. I patted Ozzie on the head, closed the
car door, waved at Marshal Jenkins, and walked to the church
entrance. I glanced up at the marble slab over the entrance. If
you looked close, you could still make out the faint Hebrew
lettering. Many years ago, the Goodfellow Baptist Church
had been Temple Shalom.

Reverend Wells had given me directions to his study, and
I found it easily enough.

"Come in," a deep voice called when I knocked.

The reverend was seated behind his desk and writing in
a black notebook. He looked up as I entered, capped his pen
and stood to greet me. He was a tall, slightly stooped black
man in his fifties with a long, angular face and handsome
features. Bald on top, he had a fringe of salt-and-pepper hair
on the sides and a neatly trimmed mustache of the same mix
of gray and black. His dark skin, black suit, and clerical collar
only heightened his aura of solemnity.

"Thank you for meeting with me, Reverend."

"You are most welcome." We shook hands. His grip was
firm, the skin dry and rough. He gestured toward one of the
chairs facing his desk. "Please make yourself comfortable,
Miss Gold."

He took a seat behind his desk and steepled his hands

under his chin. He peered at me over tortoiseshell reading glasses. "You have come here today regarding Sebastian Curry?"

He had the voice of a preacher, or even of a god—a rich, orotund bass shaded with honey tones.

"I understand that you knew him, Reverend. That you were close to him."

He nodded pensively. "Sebastian was a troubled young man. He came to me seeking spiritual solace. I offered him what guidance I could." The perfectly enunciated words seemed to rumble down from the heavens.

"How did you meet him?"

A faint smile as he remembered. "My avocation is pottery, Miss Gold. I am decidedly an amateur, but a most fervent one. Occasionally over the past decade, I have exhibited some of my pieces at local art fairs. Through those events, I have met many gifted artists within the St. Louis community. Two years ago a group of African-American artists asked me to speak to their members one evening. My topic was the relationship between spirituality and art. Sebastian attended that event. He approached me after the meeting, and we went out for coffee. We spoke for what seemed hours—about his life and his dreams and his yearnings. Before long, the young man was attending our Sunday services here at the church. We continued our relationship."

His use of the term *relationship* made me glance at his left hand. There was a gold wedding band on the third finger. On the credenza behind his desk was a framed photograph of what I assumed to be his wife and three grown children posed in front of a fireplace.

"You said that he was troubled, Reverend."

"Sebastian was raised—or, rather, raised himself—in a broken home in East St. Louis. He never knew his father. His mother was an alcoholic and drug addict. He was tall for his age—decidedly a mixed blessing in his neighborhood, since he was only eleven when he was recruited by the Vice Lords, one of the dominant gangs on the east side. Eleven years old." He shook his head with sympathy. "Just a child. Those were dark, vicious, wicked years, but eventually he summoned the inner strength necessary to quit that life. Shortly after his twenty-first birthday, Sebastian moved across the river to St. Louis to pursue his dream of becoming an artist." Reverend Wells paused. "Alas, the plight of a young artist is a challenging one. Life remained a struggle."

"Are you aware that he worked for a few years in adult films?"

"That I am. He did it—or so he told me—to help finance his artistic career. Frankly, Miss Gold, that was another chapter of his life that caused much anguish for him in retrospect."

"Was he distressed by anything more recent?"

Reverend Wells studied me for a moment. "What is the nature of your interest in Sebastian, Miss Gold?"

"I think he was involved in some criminal activity several years ago—criminal activity that had a direct impact on my client. He may only have been a pawn, but I think he had guilty knowledge. That's why I'm here today, Reverend. I'm hoping that he shared some of that guilty knowledge with you."

Wells gazed at me pensively. "You are an attorney, Miss Gold. You understand that information disclosed to a minister in confidence is a privileged communication protected from disclosure."

"Perhaps, but he's dead now."

"That may be so, but the privilege was his to waive, not mine."

"Not if there is a strong justification to waive it, Reverend. I believe there is here. My client is alive. Sebastian Curry

is dead—murdered in his own bedroom. I believe that whoever killed him had something to do with the murder of my
client's ex-husband. My client was convicted of that murder.
She's been in prison for years, and she still has years to serve.
I am convinced she's innocent, but I can't prove it. At least
not yet. I'm getting closer, though. I think that someone that
Sebastian knew killed her ex-husband. Specifically, someone
he knew from his days in the adult film industry. If that's
so, then whatever Sebastian confided in you might help me
develop the evidence I need to free my client and bring to
justice whoever is responsible for Sebastian's death."

Something I said seemed to give Reverend Wells pause.
He was tugging absently at the side of his mustache. Finally,
he said, "What causes you to suspect that the killer was
someone Sebastian knew from his days in the film business?"

"My client's ex-husband was killed just before he remar-
ried. Sebastian knew the woman he was going to marry. He
also knew one of her former boyfriends. He knew him from
their days together in porno films. From what I've been able
to piece together, that ex-boyfriend was a disturbed and violent man. He was also still obsessed with his old girlfriend."

"What happened to him?"

"He's dead. Suicide."

"Did this man kill himself in front of her town house?"

I tried to mask my excitement. "So you knew about it?"

"Who is your client, Miss Gold?"

"Don't you know?"

He shook his head. "Sebastian never told me any of the
names."

"My client is Angela Green."

I watched him absorb that information. After a moment,
he leaned back in his chair and stared down at the carpet.
"Good Lord."

He turned toward the window. I said nothing as he

stared out at the small garden behind the church.

Finally, he turned to me. "Miss Gold, I am stunned by what you have told me. Sebastian never gave me names or dates. His tale corresponded with none of the public facts of your client's trial, which—as you know—occurred years before I met Sebastian. The version Sebastian told me did not include a trial." He shook his head, frowning. "I never put the two together." He paused and then sighed. "You are correct, Miss Gold."

"Correct?"

"Your client is innocent."

I caught my breath. "So Billy Woodward killed Michael Green?"

"I do not know any names, but if this Woodward fellow was once in adult films and was once the boyfriend of the victim's fiancée, then he is the killer." He had a pained expression. "Good heavens, Miss Gold, that poor woman."

"Did Sebastian tell you about the paintings he sold?"

"He did. He sold them at an art gallery operated by the fiancée, correct?"

I nodded. "Tell me what else he told you, Reverend. Tell me the whole story."

He leaned back in his chair and crossed his arms over his chest, his brow furrowed in thought. "Sebastian's remorse was obvious when we first met. His story came out in bits and pieces over the period of a year. It took months for the trust between us to build sufficiently for him to reveal some of the more appalling details."

He paused, organizing his recollections. "His paintings were his Achilles' heel. He had sacrificed so much over the years in the pursuit of his dream of becoming an artist. By the time of the events in question, the dream seemed to be receding. Then a new man came into his life. They became lovers. The man was apparently quite powerful."

"In government?"

"Perhaps. Or perhaps in business or law. Sebastian never told me. Several months into their relationship, this man told Sebastian that he could help him gain access to a far more lucrative market for his paintings. I don't recall the details, Miss Gold, except that a powerful talent agency placed Sebastian's paintings at a gallery that turned out to be owned by a woman he knew from his years in the adult film business. Purely a coincidence, apparently. Both had struggled to transform their lives, and now here they were, thrown together again by chance or by fate. In any event, his paintings began to sell, and at prices far in excess of any prior sales."

"Did he ever get suspicious?"

"Eventually he did, but he never asked questions. You must understand, Miss Gold, that after all those lean years his dream had come true. He was afraid to do anything that might burst that magic bubble."

"So what went wrong?"

"Someone began blackmailing his boyfriend."

"Over what?"

"It was never clear. But whatever it was, Sebastian's lover decided that the blackmailer had to die. Perhaps to motivate Sebastian, he told him that the blackmailer had threatened to destroy Sebastian's career as well."

"Did he tell Sebastian who this blackmailer was?"

"All Sebastian told me was that this blackmailer was engaged to marry the owner of the gallery that sold his paintings. Now, of course, I realize that the blackmailer was Michael Green."

"Assuming that there really was a blackmailer."

"You are correct. Sebastian relied solely upon what his lover told him. He never had any direct dealings with the alleged blackmailer."

"So what happened?"

Reverend Wells explained that Sebastian helped work out the details of the murder plot, including the choice of Billy Woodward as the actual killer. Sebastian's boyfriend insisted that someone else take the fall for the killing. He explained to Sebastian that neither one of them could afford the risk of having the police poke around in the victim's business affairs in search of a suspect. The evidence at the scene of the crime had to point conclusively away from Green's professional life. That meant that the killer needed to implicate the victim's wife, or at least that's what his boyfriend told him. Sebastian explained all of this to Billy, who readily agreed, apparently excited by the opportunity to finally, in his words, "hit the big time."

Billy threw himself into the planning phase, right down to preparing a "screenplay" in which he scripted out each of his various encounters with the victim's wife during the weeks leading up to the event. He rehearsed each scene, editing his lines, tightening the dialogue. Through it all, Sebastian served as his sole contact. Woodward never knew the identity of the man who was paying for the killing or the reason for the killing. He didn't seem to care. Woodward was operating in his own fantasy world where he was the knight in shining armor rescuing the fair maiden from the clutches of the evil lawyer Michael Green.

"What was the fee?" I asked.

"There were two, actually. There was a five-thousand-dollar fee for killing the man, and a two-thousand-dollar bonus if the killer was able to retrieve a certain videotape from the blackmailer's residence."

"What was on the videotape?"

Reverend Wells shook his head. "Sebastian never knew. Apparently, the killer didn't, either. He brought back all the videotapes he could find at the victim's residence. Sebastian told me that there were about two dozen videocassettes—

half were store-bought movies and the rest were home-taped."

"Did he watch any?"

"No."

"Were any of store-bought ones X-rated?"

"A few, but Sebastian didn't recognize the titles or the actors."

"So what did he do?"

"Sebastian turned them all over to his lover."

"And?"

"One of the tapes must have been the right one, because his lover gave him another two thousand dollars in cash to pass along to the killer."

"Did he learn which videotape it was?"

"I do not believe so."

I reviewed my notes. The factual chronology of Sebastian's story matched the sequence of events culminating in Michael Green's murder. Moreover, the blackmail twist made perfect sense. It was precisely the sort of spark that could detonate an unstable conspiracy. All of which made the two-thousand-dollar bonus maddening to contemplate. That videotape must have held the key to Michael Green's death. That was also the one videotape that had surely been destroyed.

What's gone is gone, I told myself, trying to quell my frustration. *Focus on what might still be left.*

"What happened after the killing?" I asked.

Reverend Wells sighed. "Things began to fall apart. Sebastian's artistic career came to an abrupt halt. He never sold another painting. A few weeks later his relationship with his lover ended. From there he descended into a period of depression during which he was unemployed and abusing drugs. It took him nearly three years to reassemble his life. By the time I met him he was painting again—working nights as a waiter and devoting his days to his art. Although he was drug-free and sober, he was a tormented soul, filled with remorse over his involvement in that murder." Reverend Wells paused. "The pathway to atonement is an onerous one for the wicked, Miss Gold. Over time, though, I sincerely believe that he began to find some measure of comfort in Jesus." He shook his head sadly. "I pray that Jesus is with him now."

"When did you last talk to him?"

"He came to church on the Sunday before he—before his death. We spoke briefly after the service. He seemed apprehensive. Unfortunately, there was a Sunday school picnic at Forest Park immediately following the service. I am afraid that all of us were a bit harried with the logistics." Wells made a helpless gesture. "I was unable to give him the time and comfort he needed."

I waited.

He looked down at the desk and sighed. "That was the last time I spoke to the young man."

I watched him sitting there, his head still down. In the growing silence I was beginning to feel like an intruder. I stood and gathered my things.

"Thank you, Reverend," I said quietly. "You've been extremely helpful."

He looked up at me. "I am so sorry."

"You have nothing to be sorry for. You helped him find some peace."

He shook his head. "When Sebastian told me of the killer's suicide, I thought in my weakness that perhaps the Lord had worked divine retribution—that Jesus had perhaps nudged the scales of justice a little more into balance. In my focus on Sebastian, I never thought to ask what happened to the former wife—to the innocent woman set up to take the blame for the murder. I never thought to ask if anyone had been arrested, much less prosecuted, for that heinous crime. I never thought to ask whether anyone else was suffering."

"We each do what we can, Reverend."

He waved his hand dismissively. "I could have done more. I *should* have done more. I have been derelict in my duties, and because of that an innocent woman has been unjustly incarcerated."

"She was already in prison when Sebastian confessed to you. You had no reason to know that she was the one."

"I had every reason to ask, Miss Gold. Instead, I compound the sins of others." He looked up at me, pain in his eyes. "Please tell your client how deeply sorry I am."

"No, Reverend. I'm going to tell her how much you have helped here."

He turned toward the window. I backed out of his study and softly closed the door.

CHAPTER 33

From Goodfellow Baptist Church, I drove east toward the Mississippi River. The address I'd scribbled into my appointment calendar turned out to be a storefront office in a dingy section of South Broadway near Soulard Market. I left Ozzie in the car with the windows vented and walked up to the office. As I did, the U.S. Marshal pulled in alongside my car. I looked back and he nodded at me. He left his engine idling, his windows up. I turned to the office door. The faded legend stenciled in black on the pebble-glass read:

THE BLITZ AGENCY
• Licensed Investigator •
• Divorce • Child Custody • Skip Tracing •
• Video Surveillance Our Specialty •

I knocked.
Silence.
I knocked louder.
"Hey," an angry voice called from somewhere inside, "I fucking heard you."
The muffled sound of approaching footsteps, the unclicking of a dead-bolt lock.
A man in his forties yanked the door open. His eyes slowly moved down my body and back up again. He stood about five nine and wore aviator glasses with lenses tinted a brownish yellow. His thinning brown hair was slicked

straight back, the comb lines still visible from whatever po-
made he used to lube it up.

"You Gold?" he asked.

"You Blitz?"

He grunted. "Nah, I'm the fucking tooth fairy."

He adjusted the wide collar on his gray polyester short-
sleeve shirt, which he wore with the top two buttons open.
He had on tight black slacks—probably tighter now than
when he bought them—and scuffed alligator shoes with
pointy toes. The edge of a tattoo peeked out from the sleeve
of his right arm. He wore a gold-link bracelet on one wrist
and a black watch with a leather strap on the other. No rings
or other jewelry.

He jerked his head toward the inside of his office. "Let's
go."

I followed him through a rundown reception area—four
metal chairs on a threadbare gray rug—and back into his
office. The smell hit me first—the sour reek of congealed
hamburger grease mixed with remnants of grilled onions,
fries, and ketchup. I spotted the crumpled White Castle take-
out bag and empty drink cup stuffed into the wastebasket
near his desk.

I glanced around the office. The wood paneling on the
walls was slightly warped and had peeled back in a few
places. A framed private investigator certificate was on one
wall and a mounted sailfish on another. The certificate had
faded to yellow and the sailfish looked as if he'd caught it
from the back of a pickup and drove off with it flopping and
dragging behind. Scotch-taped to the wall above his credenza
was a five-by-seven color shot of Blitz and a busty blonde
standing on the deck of a motorboat, each holding up a can
of Michelob. The shot was overexposed, as were both of
them—the blonde spilling out of her bikini top, Blitz striking

a jaunty pose, his hairy gut covering nowhere near enough of his tiny yellow Speedo.

"Grab a seat," he said as he moved around his desk. He paused to take a big unlit cigar from the ashtray and jammed the chewed end into his mouth as he settled in behind his desk.

I started to thank him for meeting with me but he cut me off, holding up his hands.

"First things first, lady. Let's see some dead presidents."

Dead presidents, I repeated to myself with a straight face. The guy was a piece of work. I reached for my purse and removed the envelope. He watched closely as I counted out the currency on the top of his desk. "Twenty—forty—sixty—seventy—seventy-five."

When I leaned back in my chair, he picked up the cash and recounted, just to be sure. Watching him count, I tried to imagine how Michael Green had hooked up with this sleazebag. Perhaps you could say that Ron Blitz had the look of a guy who got results for his clients—not a bad look for a private eye. He also had the look of a guy who got results with methods you were better off not knowing about—again, not a bad look for a certain type of case.

"Okay," he said, folding the money in half and stuffing the bills into his shirt pocket. He checked his watch. "Meter's running, lady. You got one hour."

"Let's talk about Michael Green."

"What about him?"

"You did some work for him. About six months before he died."

"Oh, yeah? Says who?"

"Says you."

"Me? What the hell you talking about?"

"Here." From my briefcase I removed the photocopy of

his billing statement to Green and slid it across his desktop. "This is your bill for services you sent him."

He snatched it up and studied it. He looked up with a grin. His uneven teeth were stained brown from the cigars. "Yeah?"

"What did he hire you to do?"

"Hey, lady, you ever hear about privileged communications?"

"The privilege is conditional. Did you work on a personal matter for Mr. Green or was it for one of his clients?"

"What's it matter?"

"If it's personal, there's no privilege."

"Why's that?"

"He's dead. The privilege died with him."

"Is that so? Maybe I should check that out with my own lawyer. Yeah, I think I will. I'll get back to you on it someday."

"Look, Mr. Blitz, I didn't come here to play games with you. I paid you for an hour of your time. I want what I paid for. I want you to tell me why Mr. Green hired you and what you did for him. We can do it the easy way or we can do it the hard way. Your choice."

He gave me an amused look. "What's the hard way, little lady? You gonna hit me with your purse?"

I gestured toward the front door. "I have a U.S. Marshal waiting in front of your office in a car."

He snorted. "Yeah, right. And I got J. Edgar Hoover waiting in my crapper in an evening gown."

I stood up. "Come on. I'll introduce you."

His grin faded. "The fuck you talking about?"

"Let's go, tough guy."

He stared at me a moment. You could almost hear the gears ratcheting inside his head. He got to his feet. "You shitting me, lady?"

"See for yourself."

He followed me through the reception area and out the front door. I'd suspected in advance that Blitz might try to jerk me around. I'd given U.S. Marshal Tommy Jenkins the heads-up before we left the Goodfellow Baptist Church.

As we came through the front door, Jenkins got out of his car. He had on a dark blue suit, white shirt, narrow tie, and reflecting sunglasses. He had the build of an NFL linebacker. He wore his thick blond hair in a crew cut.

"Marshal Jenkins, this is Ron Blitz."

Expressionless, Tommy Jenkins reached into his suit jacket pocket and pulled out a black leather holder. He flipped it open and showed Blitz his badge. Then he turned to me.

"Is this man obstructing your investigation, Miss Gold?"

"Frankly, he's not been real cooperative, Marshal."

"I'm disappointed to hear that." He turned to Blitz and stared down at him. "Do I need to take you downtown, sir? Do I need to ask two of my colleagues at the FBI to take charge of your interrogation while we thoroughly search your office?"

"Whoa, dude." Blitz had his hands up. "Time out, eh?" He was squinting into the distorted dual images of himself in Jenkins's reflecting sunglasses. "I'll answer the lady's questions, okay? I had some concerns about confidentiality, if you know what I mean. I deal in sensitive subjects. My clients are sensitive people. Real sensitive, if you catch my drift. Didn't want to breach any confidences. But the lady has allayed those concerns."

Jenkins stared at him, impassive. "Allayed?"

"Yeah. Like I'm okay with it now, okay?"

Jenkins turned to me. "Your choice, ma'am. You can give this man another chance or if you prefer I can haul him downtown and toss him in a holding cell."

I pretended to weigh the options as Blitz glanced back and forth between Jenkins and me. Like most men of his ilk, Blitz was entirely predictable, as if he wore the diagram to his hardwired brain stamped on his forehead. He was a bully and a schemer. Being in the presence of a woman seeking information triggered both of those qualities. The remedy was simple enough: set up a confrontation with an alpha male who'd growl and bare his teeth and make a symbolic display of a gigantic, engorged penis. Blitz responded as if he were hung like a hamster.

I said, "I'll give him one more chance, Marshal."

"I'll wait right here, ma'am."

"Thank you, Marshal."

He nodded. "Ma'am."

Although Blitz didn't quite slink back to his office, he certainly was more subdued when I resumed my questions.

"Why did Michael Green hire you?"

"He wanted me to tail this big nigger."

I flinched at the term *nigger*. Trying to ignore it, I asked, "Was that individual's name Sebastian Curry?"

"Yeah," he said, raising his eyebrows in surprise. "That's him. A waiter. Fucking guy thought he was an artist, too. Painted during the day. Bunch of abstract shit, if you ask me. Like a kindergartner with finger paints. Anyway, Green wanted to see if I could catch him in a compromising position, if you know what I mean."

"Did Green tell you why he wanted you to follow Curry?"

"Just told me to stick with the guy, night and day, film everything, find out who he was banging."

So, I thought, *did Michael Green decide that Sebastian Curry would lead him to the source? But that made no sense. Green already knew the source. In fact, the source had ap-*

parently given him Sebastian Curry's name. So what was the point of tailing Sebastian?

"Did Mr. Green tell you anything else about Curry?"

"No."

"Did he tell you who his client was?"

"Nope."

"Did you ask?"

"Nope."

"Had you ever done work for Green before?"

"Nope."

"How did he get to you?"

Blitz shrugged. "Probably a referral. I get a lot of lawyer business on referrals."

"So you followed Curry?"

"Sure did."

"And what did you observe?"

"I observed that he was a fag, which, frankly, was a shocker."

"Why?"

"Green never told me that part. I first thought he might be banging this broad who ran this art gallery. Hell, I'd do her in a heartbeat. Anyway, I tailed that spade maybe ten days, and he visited her at least three times."

"Don't use those words," I said.

"Huh?"

"Words like *nigger* and *spade*. I don't like them."

Blitz raised his eyebrows and chuckled. "Well, whoop-de-do. Excuuuuuse me, Miss Manners."

I ignored his moronic repartee. "Let's go back to the woman who ran the art gallery. Where did he visit her?"

"At her gallery. He'd bring her one of his shitty paintings each time and leave it there. I thought maybe he'd try to nail her, maybe in the back room, but no dice. He only saw her at the gallery, and only during the day."

"What else did you observe?"

"He had this waiter gig at night over at King Louie's on Chouteau. Couple of nights he went out to bars or clubs after hours with some of the other staff, but he'd end up going home alone."

"Eventually, you caught him."

"Oh, yeah." Blitz chuckled. "Big time, lady."

"Another man?"

"You got that right. Turns out he was queer as a three-dollar bill. But the faggot was also hung like a bull, I'll say that for him."

"Who was his boyfriend?"

"Don't know."

"Did he look familiar?"

"Not to me."

"Only one boyfriend?"

"Only saw one."

"Did you get it on camera?"

He grinned proudly. "It's what they pay me for. Better than a goddamn episode on the Discovery Channel."

"Did you show it to Green?"

"Sure did. Right here in the office." He jerked his thumb behind him. "Got me a TV and VCR in the back room."

"How did Green react?"

Blitz took the unlit cigar out of his mouth and grinned at it, nodding his head. "He fucking loved it. Slapping me on the back, shaking my hand. Guy must have had a real hard-on for the nig—the Negro." He jammed the cigar back in his mouth and leaned back in his chair, pleased with the memory.

"Did you give him the videotape?"

"Two copies. That's what he wanted. Not one but two."

"Did he tell you why he wanted two?"

Blitz gave me a look as if I was a naïve schoolgirl. "Hey,

I didn't fall off the fucking turnip truck, lady. I didn't need to ask. He wanted one for safekeeping and one to make that big nig—uh, that large Negro gentleman squirm."

"Did he tell you what happened?"

Blitz shook his head. "Like in the military: don't ask, don't tell. I sent him my bill, he paid by return mail, I closed the file."

"You knew he was killed a few months later."

"Sure. Goddamn ex-wife chopped off his johnson. Sounds a little like my ex, for chrissake. Man, talk about a ball-breaker."

"Any idea who else might have killed him?"

He gave me a puzzled look. "I'm not following you."

I switched subjects. "Did you get any other business from Michael Green?"

"Never heard from him again."

"I assume you kept the original of the videotape?"

"Jeez, do I look like a fucking moron?"

I chose to treat that as a rhetorical question.

"I'd like a copy," I said.

"Hey," he said, gesturing around his office, "does this look like Blockbuster Video?"

I stared at him. "Listen carefully, Ron. You have two options. Option one is you give me a copy. Right here, right now. Then I leave, and you probably never hear from me again. Option two is you refuse. Then the U.S. Marshal hauls you downtown, puts you in a holding cell, gets a search warrant, comes back here with three other federal officers, and they tear this place apart and maybe stumble onto some other incriminating evidence while they're dumping every one of your file drawers onto the floor." I folded my arms over my chest. "What's your choice, Ron? Door Number One or Door Number Two?"

I decided on a private screening. No Benny, no Jacki, and no U.S. Marshal Tommy Jenkins, who'd followed me home and parked his car along the curb in front of my house. I opened a bottle of Pete's Wicked Ale and carried it and the videotape into the den. I closed the shades, turned on the television and VCR, inserted the videotape, and sat back on the couch to watch.

The screen flickered, and then a familiar building came into view. Displayed at the bottom right corner of the picture were the time and date coordinates—9:47 A.M. on a winter Thursday about four months before Michael Green was killed. A gray, chilly morning. Old snow along the curbs, pedestrians in heavy coats, whitish puffs of vapor from the exhaust pipes of idling cars and trucks. The soundtrack, such as it was, consisted of ambient street noise—a car horn, a bus accelerating, a muffled conversation fading.

Ron Blitz spoke in a voice-over: "Surveillance team in position across the street from target's place of residence."

He announced the time, day of the week, and date, all of which matched up to the digital readout on the bottom of the screen. He concluded by stating the building's address, which made me realize why it looked familiar. I'd been there, upstairs and inside the loft where Sebastian Curry lived, and died.

The camera jerked toward the street corner and zoomed in on the street sign. Then it yanked back to the building and zoomed in on the address above the door, as if to corroborate Blitz's voice-over. The lens quickly pulled back, panning up to the level of Curry's loft, zooming in on a window that was opaque in the dull morning sun. The camera jumped back away and zipped diagonally down to street level. Blitz's camera technique made me nauseous.

I stared at the digital readout of the time and date as I thought back to what Reverend Wells had told me about the bonus Billy Woodward received for retrieving the video from Michael Green's condo. The person behind the killings probably assumed that the videotape retrieved from the condo wasn't the sole remaining copy, but unless he recognized Blitz's voice—not likely—there'd be no way to tell from the videotape itself who had filmed it. Blitz had confirmed that the two copies he gave Green were in their original Sony videotape containers with no external markings. As he explained while we waited for his video recorder to make my copy, he usually doesn't know what his clients do with the surveillance videotapes he creates for them, and thus he makes sure that there is nothing in or on the videotape that would identify him. The original master videotape—as with all of his originals—was stored in a safe-deposit box with instructions to turn it over to the police if something happened to him. The copy he made me came from his office copy.

On the videotape, we stayed in front of Curry's building, viewing it in twenty-second chunks throughout the day until 4:13 P.M., when Blitz zoomed in on the front door and announced, sotto voce, "Target apprehended."

Sebastian Curry came through the front door and turned left. He was wearing a dark green trench coat over black slacks and black boots. Although the cloudy winter sky was already darkening, he wore sunglasses. The camera panned along, jerkily following him until he reached his car, a black BMW sedan. The picture jiggled as Blitz mumbled something, then the screen went dark. Filming resumed with Curry walking into the entrance of King Louie's restaurant. The shot appeared to have been filmed through the front windshield of Blitz's car with the left wiper visible in the lower half of the screen. Almost twenty minutes had elapsed since the last shot, according to the on-screen clock.

And so it went—Curry leaving his apartment, Curry

shopping for groceries, Curry going into the restaurant where he worked, Curry leaving the restaurant. Three monotonous days in the life of Sebastian Curry, captured on nearly an hour's worth of videotape.

Blitz had warned me that my copy came from the original unedited videotape. He hadn't kept a copy of the version he'd given to Green, which he'd edited down to thirty minutes. Mine was almost three hours long.

"You got everything here you could want," Blitz had told me, "plus probably a little more than you might want."

An understatement.

I started fast-forwarding through the repetitive stuff, slowing at each scene change. I watched Sebastian's first visit to Samantha's art gallery—an event that, judging from Blitz's voice-over, intrigued the "surveillance team" as well. The scene had an eerie, melancholy quality—a moment of innocence before the fall. There was Sebastian Curry, alive and well and cheerful and vigorous. There was Samantha—a younger, prettier, and more vibrant version of the one I'd met at her lawyer's office last week. I watched her greet Sebastian in the front of her art gallery—a gallery that no longer existed and a man who no longer existed. When Blitz zoomed in for a close-up of Samantha, I paused the video and leaned forward. I could see the glitter of a diamond on her ring finger. A glance at the date in the lower right corner confirmed it. She was engaged to be married—no doubt delighted by the bright future that awaited her and her young son.

I hit the play button. Through the big picture window at the front of the gallery, you could see the painting that Sebastian had brought her that day. The two of them, their backs to the camera, were admiring it. Blitz was filming from across the street, the view interrupted occasionally by the blur of a passing car. Traffic sounds mixed with the other street noises. I looked closer at the painting. It was the same one Benny and I had seen at the Foleys' house. I paused the video again. There was Sebastian. There was Samantha. There was one of the twenty-three paintings. Only Michael Green was missing, lurking somewhere offstage, soon to be forever offstage.

I fast-forwarded through his next visit to Samantha's gallery and the rest of that day, slowing the video to normal as he emerged from a Washington Avenue nightclub with a pair of laughing women, one on each arm. The handheld camera followed the trio down the street, jiggling along behind them, until they disappeared into another nightclub. Almost two hours later, according to the on-screen clock, Sebastian came out of the nightclub alone. He staggered the two blocks back to his building where, at 3.28 A.M., he boarded his elevator. The screen briefly went dark. When the scene resumed, the camera angle had shifted to a new view, looking directly into the darkened windows of Sebastian's loft from the same level aboveground. Blitz must have found an empty office in the building across the street.

The lights inside Sebastian's loft across the street clicked on. He was locking his front door, his back to the camera. Then he hung his trench coat on the coat stand near the door. As he moved toward the bedroom area in the back, Blitz panned along from window to window. Sebastian was shedding clothing as he walked, piece by piece, until he was down to a pair of red bikini briefs. He stretched near a window, displaying a body that was absolutely gorgeous—tall and supple, with long athletic legs, high round buttocks, narrow torso. Over the next few minutes, I watched him smoke a joint, brush his teeth, take a pill, wash it down with a glass of water, and reach for the lights by his bed. The screen went dark and remained that way for nearly a minute. Blitz's voice-over announced that the "team will recommence stakeout of target tomorrow at zero-nine-hundred."

We were now almost two hours into the video and beginning the ninth day of surveillance. That day began like
days one through eight except that now we had a view directly into Sebastian's loft, where, at 2:24 P.M., he was standing in front of an easel and contemplating a painting in
progress. Today he was wearing a black T-shirt, snug black
jeans, and black boots. Over the next several minutes he
daubed at the canvas and spoke briefly on the phone. He
moved into the kitchen and took a beer out of the fridge and
a small jar off the shelf. Blitz kept the camera rolling as we
watched him do what appeared to be a line of cocaine on a
clear plastic cutting board. As the day progressed in two- or
three-minute scenes, he went to the grocery store, picked up
some dry cleaning, had a couple of beers at a corner bar,
grabbed dinner at a nearby Chinese restaurant, and returned
to his apartment around seven-thirty.

He was watching TV in the bedroom at ten minutes to
nine when apparently someone knocked at his door. He
stood, went to the front of the loft, opened the door and
admitted a male figure wearing a long overcoat, gloves, and
a snap-brim hat that hid his face. The man was carrying a
large briefcase.

"This is the first visitor to target's place of residence since
surveillance operation commenced," Blitz said in a dramatic
voice. He then stated the time and date "for the record."

The camera zoomed in as the male visitor first removed
his gloves and then his hat and coat.

I hit the pause button, leaning forward astounded. Standing in the entranceway to Sebastian Curry's loft was none
other than Nathaniel Turner, commissioner of redevelopment for the city of St. Louis. He was dressed in shiny blue
Nike warm-ups and sneakers.

I hit play and watched as the two of them shared a laugh

and then walked into the kitchen area, where Sebastian pulled an open bottle of white wine out of the refrigerator and poured them each a glass. They touched their glasses and toasted something, and then Turner drained his in two gulps while Sebastian took a sip and watched the other man with mild amusement. I hit the pause button as Turner refilled his glass.

Of course, I told myself, as several pieces fell into place. Nate the Great was the perfect City Hall connection—a powerful insider who could make sure that Michael Green's loan deals got approved without the requisite personal guarantees. Sebastian functioned essentially as Nate's money-laundering machine via the phony Millennium commissions that Green ran through the offshore bank account before funneling back to Nate.

But Sebastian was Nate's man, I thought, *not Green's.* Michael Green had known nothing about him—including even his name—before the scam began. That had to be a little unsettling for the guy running the scam. As I recalled from my interview with Samantha, Green had apparently grown troubled by some aspect of Sebastian. He'd starting asking her questions about him—but long after the scam had begun. Maybe the reason Green hired the Blitz Agency was to find out the nature of Sebastian's relationship with Nate. Or maybe he wanted to find out whether Sebastian had any tie to that creepy Herman Borghoff, who'd been so obsessed with my investigation into the real estate deals that he'd confronted me in my office and later snooped around the microfilm I'd been reviewing.

I hit the play button.

I watched as each of them did a line of cocaine on the cutting board, wondering to myself about their connection. A struggling artist and a City Hall wheeler-dealer. A true

odd couple—a nobody and a somebody. How had Nate selected Sebastian? And why?

I didn't have to wonder long.

Nate was wiping the powder remnants from his nose.
Sebastian stood watching him, his back against the kitchen
counter, arms crossed over his chest. Nate looked up. Sebastian towered over him, his powerful biceps swelling against
the sleeves of his black T-shirt.

Nate came around the table and sank to his knees in front
of Sebastian. Like a supplicant before a deity, he reached
forward and gently, almost reverentially, cupped his hands
over the bulging crotch of the black jeans. He gazed up at
Sebastian, who nodded once, unsmiling. Nate unzipped Sebastian's jeans and reached inside. Carefully, he pulled out
Sebastian's penis, cradling it in his hands. Already partially
tumescent, the uncircumcised phallus was enormous—
curved like a banana, thick and black, with a bulging vein
visible even on videotape. Worshipfully, Nate began kissing
and licking it.

"Oh, Jesus Christ," Blitz mumbled in voice-over. "Goddamn faggot cocksucker."

The picture jiggled for a few seconds until Blitz remembered his role and steadied the camera. Even so, he couldn't
help uttering an occasional grunt of disgust as the scene unfolded. I watched, astounded, as Nate, on his knees, used his
mouth and hands to bring Sebastian first to an erection and
then to an orgasm. At the moment of climax, Nate drew his
head back, fiercely pumping on Sebastian's penis with both
hands, and sprayed three big jets of semen onto his face.

"Oh, Christ Almighty," Blitz whispered hoarsely as
Nate wiped the semen off his face with his hands and then
licked them clean, "you fucking pervert loser."

I hit the pause button and leaned back.

I shook my head in wonder at the thought of what this

videotape must have meant to Michael Green. I could almost imagine him chuckling with surprised delight. The last two scenes made it the ultimate blackmail weapon against Nate the Great—and Green would have grasped that immediately. The blackmail threat was not one of general disclosure, of course. A public outing of Nate the Great, even with the added cocaine angle, might have generated a scandal with a half-life of a month in a country long inured to the sordid peccadilloes of its politicians. But Green would have had a special audience in mind—an audience of one. Green would have known that the mere sight of the commissioner doing a line of cocaine would have been enough to cause Congressman Orion Sampson to strip his nephew of office and power. But the prospect of Nate's uncle watching him give another man a blow job would have triggered abject panic in Nate. Possessing that videotape of Nate was the equivalent of holding a loaded gun to his head.

I hit the play button.

Sebastian and Nate had another round of drinks and did another line of coke. As Sebastian headed for the bedroom, Nate hurried back to the living room to fetch his briefcase. He carried it into the bedroom. Sebastian seemed reluctant when he arrived, gesturing toward the briefcase and shaking his head. Nate tried to convince him. He got down on his knees and begged.

Actually begged.

Nate the Great begging. I couldn't believe it.

When Sebastian finally nodded okay, Nate tried to embrace Sebastian around the knees, but Sebastian pushed him away and stood up. Nate quickly dumped the contents of his briefcase onto the bedroom rug. Leaning forward, I could make out a whip, a large tube of something, two lengths of rope, two pairs of handcuffs, and a pair of high heels. *Oh, brother.*

Nate slid off his warm-ups. I gave a startled giggle. He was wearing nothing but a frilly pink camisole and matching panties. Judging from the swelling in the front of those panties, Nate was ready for Act Two. He slipped on the high heels and sashayed in front of Sebastian, and as he did I recalled the story Angela Green told me from her baby-sitting days about slapping Nate after she caught him with her underwear and heels.

Nate snapped one handcuff from each pair around each wrist and—still wearing the heels—stretched out facedown on Sebastian's bed, spread-eagled. He looked back impatiently. Sebastian came around and fastened the other end of each pair of handcuffs to the bedposts. The ropes from the briefcase already had loops at each end. Sebastian used them to secure Nate's ankles to the frame posts at the foot of the bed. By this time, Nate was wiggling and grinding his hips in anticipation. Sebastian undressed and picked up the whip. He stood naked at the foot of the bed, his backside to the window, whip in hand.

The rest of the scene took about ten minutes. Sebastian began whipping Nate, halfheartedly at first, but eventually with some fervor. You could see the welts on Nate's back and buttocks. Eventually, Sebastian ripped open Nate's panties from behind, applied a big squeeze from the tube of lubricant, and mounted him.

Starting slowly at first, he began thrusting faster and faster to the accompaniment of Blitz's gagging noises and mumbled profanities. Eventually, Sebastian stiffened, his back arching, face toward the ceiling, eyes squeezed shut, arms rigid. Gradually, his body relaxed and he collapsed on top of Nate. A few moments later he rolled off, his eyes still closed.

He must have passed out, because he didn't stir until Nate started yelling and bouncing on the bed. Groggily, Sebastian unlocked the handcuffs, loosened the ropes, and collapsed on the bed, facedown. The scene ended with Nate slavishly kissing and snuggling against his sleeping companion.

CHAPTER 34

Sunday afternoon.

Inside a conference room at the offices of the United States Attorney for the Eastern District of Missouri.

There were four of us seated at the rectangular table. I was at the far end, facing the court reporter at the other end. Her name was Midge and she was a petite woman in her fifties with close-trimmed gray hair and a pair of half-moon reading glasses perched at the end of her ski-slope nose. Her chair was pushed back from the table to make room for the shorthand machine on the low metal stand between her knees. She was frowning as she checked the settings on the laptop computer and the small tape recorder resting near the edge of the table.

Seated to my right—Midge's left—was Marsha Mc-Kenzie, the United States attorney. She was dressed in a severe blue suit, white silk blouse, double-loop pearl necklace with matching earrings, and a hint of rouge and pale lipstick. Her straight brown hair was pageboy short and parted on the left, the bangs brushed to the right and falling across her high forehead. In her late forties, Marsha projected the aura of a stern elementary school teacher. She was slowly paging through the notes on a yellow legal pad, her narrow lips pressed together in concentration.

Seated alongside Marsha to her left was Ben Harper, the assistant U.S. attorney who'd met with me two nights ago after that awful threatening phone call. His complexion was even more florid today. Like his boss, he was studying a yellow legal pad filled with notes, many taken during the two hours that he and Marsha had interviewed me earlier that day.

The chair next to Ben—the one closest to me—was empty, as were the three chairs across the table. The door to the conference room was along the wall behind the three empty chairs.

There was a rap on the door.

Ben straightened and clicked the ballpoint pen in his right hand as if he were cocking a gun. He glanced at Marsha, who was studying her notes, and then he smoothed down the front of his blue suit jacket with his left hand.

"Come in," she said without looking up.

Special Agent Steven Whitley opened the door. He was in full FBI uniform this afternoon: black suit, white shirt, thin tie, shiny black shoes, grim expression. He nodded at Marsha and then glanced back.

"In here," he said, gesturing with his head.

Herman Borghoff lumbered through the door, his hands clasped over his stomach. He looked as if he'd been hauled out of bed—a white shirt flecked with food stains, wrinkled black trousers, scuffed shoes, mussed hair. He glanced around and took the seat directly across from Marsha McKenzie, his head down.

Following him into the conference room was a short, stocky man in his sixties who walked with a slight limp. This was Joe O'Brien, Borghoff's attorney. He wore a navy blazer, gray slacks, a blue dress shirt unbuttoned at the collar, and no tie. O'Brien took the seat next to his client, the smell of drugstore aftershave wafting in after him.

Special Agent Whitley stepped inside and closed the door behind him. He leaned against the door with his arms crossed over his chest as he surveyed the group around the table.

O'Brien squinted at me, his eyes magnified behind the thick lenses of his wire-rimmed glasses. He had a ruddy complexion, a completely bald head, an enormous flesh-colored mole on the right side of his upper lip, and lumpy protruding ears.

"What's *she* doing here?" he said. His squint tugged at the corner of his mouth, giving him an uncanny resemblance to an elderly version of Popeye the Sailor Man.

Marsha looked down the table at me and turned toward O'Brien. "I invited Ms. Gold."

He snorted. "Oh, yeah? What for?"

Marsha turned toward the court reporter. "Are you ready?"

The court reporter nodded.

"Hey," O'Brien snarled, "you going to answer my question?"

Marsha turned toward him. "No."

He grunted. "That's bull crap."

Marsha gazed at him for a moment. "Let me remind you of your client's predicament, Mr. O'Brien." She spoke calmly. "Within the next few days, I expect a grand jury to indict one or more persons for the first-degree murder of Michael Green and the first-degree murder of Sebastian Curry, along with enough felony counts of bribery, fraud, corruption, and malfeasance to guarantee permanent residence in a federal penitentiary for all those convicted, and a possible seat on death row for at least one, and maybe more, of the accused."

She glanced at Borghoff, whose head was down. The way he towered over his attorney made him resemble a glum circus bear seated next to a feisty trainer.

She turned back to O'Brien. "There are four conference rooms in this office, Mr. O'Brien. You and your client are in this one. Commissioner Turner and his attorney are in a second room. Donald Goddard and his attorney are in a third. Percy Trotter is alone in the fourth. You are all here today because I am looking for a cooperative witness. I am assuming that I can have a productive conversation on a variety of relevant topics with one or more of the other three gentlemen. In fact, I have already been assured that one of them is eager to cooperate. I am also assuming that each of the other three gentlemen has significant things to tell me about your client and his involvement in various criminal activities. And I am also assuming that your client has significant things to tell me about the other three gentlemen and their criminal activities. This room happens to be my first stop of the afternoon. I will stay in here as long as our conversation is productive. If our conversation proves to be extremely productive, Mr. O'Brien, I may have no reason to visit any of the other three rooms. If our conversation proves unproductive, however, I will terminate it, and then Midge and I will move on to one of the other three rooms to see if we have any better luck there."

She paused, her expression growing cold. "There is only one rule here today, Mr. O'Brien. If I leave this conference room, I will not return."

"Yeah, yeah, yeah." O'Brien shook his head, amused. "I'm shaking in my boots. So what are you offering?"

"An opportunity for your client to talk to me."

"What kind of offer is that?"

"The kind that I am prepared to make."

"We want immunity."

"I understand that, Mr. O'Brien. But as a wise man from England once said, you can't always get what you want."

"Maybe so, but today we get immunity."

"Actually, today you don't."

O'Brien squinted at her. "Then why should my client talk to you?"

She gazed at him calmly. "Because it's the smart thing to do. Because someone today is going to talk to me. That someone is going to tell me about the real estate scam and the fraudulent loans to Michael Green's clients and the fraudulent loans to Percy Trotter's clients. That someone is going to tell me why Michael Green died. That someone is going to tell me about Sebastian Curry's role and why, after all these years, he had to die." She paused for a moment. "And that someone will be in a far better position to bargain for immunity than the other three. However, at the moment, Mr. O'Brien, your client is not that someone. At the moment, your client has no bargaining power."

"What makes you think my client knows anything about these matters?"

Marsha turned toward me. "Ms. Gold has found evidence that your client has material knowledge of each of the crimes I've just mentioned. Unfortunately for your client, much of that evidence incriminates him as well."

"Oh, yeah. Like what?"

Marsha said, "I am here today to *ask* questions, Mr. O'Brien. I am not here today to answer them."

"Maybe so," O'Brien said, glancing over at Borghoff, who sat motionless, staring down, "but maybe my client doesn't want to answer them." O'Brien looked at Marsha, his lower jaw thrust forward. "And maybe I don't want my client answering any of your questions without first knowing the deal you're offering."

Marsha checked her watch and sighed. "I am afraid this conversation is not productive."

O'Brien chuckled. "That's because you're not giving it a chance."

Marsha stood and turned to the court reporter. "Let's go see Commissioner Turner, Midge. Maybe he has some information he'd like to share with us about Mr. Borghoff."

The court reporter nodded and began gathering up her stuff. Marsha moved around the conference table toward the door and I stood to follow her.

"Wait," Herman Borghoff said in a gruff voice.

She paused at the door, which Special Agent Whitley had opened for her. Turning back, she said, "Pardon?"

"I have things to tell you."

"Hey, Herm," O'Brien said, "you're not talking until I tell you to talk."

Borghoff stared down at O'Brien. "Shut up."

"Whoa, son," O'Brien said with an edgy laugh.

"I said shut up."

"Hey, I'm the lawyer."

"And I am the client." He spoke methodically. "You can sit here quietly and you can listen carefully and you can think about what I am saying, and when I am through you can work out a deal for me—or you can get up and leave right now."

O'Brien stared at Borghoff and tugged on an earlobe. Finally, he leaned back in his chair and shrugged. "You're the client, kiddo. You're calling the shots."

Borghoff turned to Marsha. She was still in the doorway, staring down at him.

"Please," he said, nodding toward her empty seat.

She returned to her chair and glanced at the court reporter, who had her fingers poised over the keys of the shorthand machine.

"Hold it," O'Brien said. "Let's start this off the record."

"Nothing is off the record," Marsha said. "Go ahead, Mr. Borghoff."

He had his hands on the table in front of him. Studying his thumbnails, he said, "I had nothing to do with the murders."

"Who did?" Marsha asked.

"The commissioner."

"You are referring to the killings of Michael Green and Sebastian Curry?"

Borghoff nodded. "He arranged them both. He had Michael Green killed by a whacko that Sebastian Curry found for him. But he had Curry killed by a pro."

"How do you know this?"

"I didn't know about the Green hit in advance, but I suspected the commissioner was behind it the moment I heard."

"Why?"

"Because he and Green had a major falling-out a few months earlier."

"Over what?"

"Money." Borghoff ran his fingers through his mussed hair. "The commissioner was angry when he found out how much more Green was making on each of those real estate deals—something like twenty-five grand, compared to six grand for the commissioner. He wanted the numbers reversed. Green refused. They had a big argument."

"How do you know that?"

"I was there. It was in the commissioner's office. He threatened to cut Green out completely. He said that crooked lawyers were a dime a dozen. He said he was going to find a new one to deal with. About two weeks later, Green approached us with another client wanting to do one of the deals. The commissioner had me tell Green we were no longer in business with him. Had me tell him it was all over."

"What happened?" Marsha asked.

Borghoff frowned. "That's the part I don't know. Something happened. A month or so later, the commissioner changed his mind about Green. He told me to arrange the paperwork for another deal. I did, but I knew something was wrong. The commissioner seemed rattled. The loan deal went through and all, but that was the last one. Green died two months later."

"What made you think the commissioner was involved in the murder?"

"Just suspicions back then—nothing specific, I guess. It seemed awfully convenient, of course, that they have this falling-out and then Green gets himself killed and all the evidence points toward the ex-wife. The ex-wife part was a good thing for the commissioner, because I knew if the cops started poking around in Green's affairs they might have found the connection to the commissioner." Borghoff gestured toward me, almost contemptuously. "Even she was able to do that. Anyway, the commissioner made some odd comments at the time. One night we were talking about the killing and he said that he thought blackmail was a worse crime than murder. I asked him what he meant—since the statement came out of the blue. All he said was that Green deserved what he got. Later, when that whacko killed himself in front of Green's girlfriend's place, the commissioner went nuts—had me use all kinds of pull to get a copy of the suicide note and keep him up to speed on the police investigation." He shook his head. "I should have figured it out then."

"Figured what out?" Marsha asked.

"Why he was so worried. There never was any question it was a suicide—I mean, talk about cut-and-dried. But when the cops officially ruled it a suicide and closed the file, you'd have thought the commissioner won the lottery. He told me the lesson with Woodward was that you never hire a boy to do a man's job. When he started doing the deals with Percy Trotter, he told me he'd never let Trotter get the drop on him. He told me we didn't need another dead lawyer on our hands." Borghoff paused, his eyes distant. "The commissioner kept Trotter on a real short leash, and when Trotter started hinting about getting a bigger slice, the commissioner cut him off cold."

"Why was Sebastian Curry killed?" Marsha asked.

"That was his own fault." He turned to glare at me. "Or yours."

I kept my face blank.

"Tell me what happened," Marsha said to him.

"Curry came to see me."

"When?"

"Few days before he died."

"You knew him?"

"Sure. They laundered the money through his paintings."

"What did Mr. Curry want?"

"He was freaking out. Tried to see the commissioner, but the commissioner wanted nothing to do with him, so he came down the hall to see me."

"About what?"

He nodded toward me. "Her."

"What about her?"

"About what she'd uncovered, about what she was working on."

"What did you do?"

"I made sure the commissioner saw him. And believe me, he was surprised, too."

"About what Rachel had found?"

"Sure, but he was really surprised about Curry. He hadn't seen the guy for years, I guess. He had no idea he'd become a born-again Christian asswipe."

"What do you mean?"

"He told the commissioner he couldn't live with the guilt anymore. Told him the time had come for both of them to step forward and admit what they'd done. *Both* of them. The commissioner told him he was talking crazy, but Curry held his ground. 'We have blood on our hands,' he kept saying.

'We must confess our sins.' Quoting Scripture and weeping and moaning and praying. The commissioner finally got him to go home and promise not talk to anyone until he got back to him."

Borghoff was silent. We all waited.

"And?" Marsha prodded.

Borghoff took a deep breath and exhaled slowly. "About ten minutes later, the commissioner called up a man named Maurice and told him he had a personnel problem he needed to discuss that day. They agreed to meet at a place called Sadie's."

Marsha looked up at Whitley. "Maurice? Maurice Patton?"

The FBI agent nodded. "Especially if the meet was at Sadie's."

"What is Sadie's?" I asked.

O'Brien snorted. "No place you'd want to be after dark, little lady. It's a bar in East St. Louis where thugs like Maurice Patton hang out."

"Two days later," Borghoff continued, "Curry was dead."

Marsha McKenzie studied him. "Nathaniel Turner is a careful man. I am surprised that he would let you witness those conversations."

"He didn't."

"So how do you know what happened?"

"I listened."

"Through the door?"

Borghoff smiled. "Through a transmitter."

O'Brien turned to his client. "What?"

Borghoff shrugged. "I didn't trust him. I'd handled dirty work for the commissioner over the years, and I'd seen what he could do when you crossed him. Michael Green was a good example of that." He glanced at me. "So was the condemnation of your shelter. He's done that to others, too. Never had anyone stop him, though." He chuckled. "He was pissed at you, lady. I decided I needed a way to level the playing field so if he ever turned on me I'd be able to defend myself. Right around the time he started in with Percy Trotter, I bought one of those bugging devices. Installed it in his office ceiling one night."

Marsha glanced at Whitley and then back at Borghoff. "He could deny that," she said. "He could claim that you made it up."

"I don't think so."

"Why not?"

He gazed at Marsha for a long time, and then his lips curled into a cold smile. "I might just have those conversations on tape."

Marsha studied him. "Might?"

Borghoff shrugged. "Depends."

"Depends on what?"

Borghoff gestured toward his lawyer.

O'Brien raised his eyebrows and leaned forward. "Sounds to me like it's time to play 'Let's Make a Deal.' "

We took a break after an hour. Borghoff was proving to be a treasure trove of incriminating information. More important for me, he had key exonerating evidence about Angela Green's case.

Delighted, I stepped out into the hallway to stretch. I walked down the hall to the drinking fountain, which was located near the rest rooms. Then I walked back to the large picture window in the reception area. I gazed out at the St. Louis skyline, the Arch and the Mississippi River visible in the distance.

I heard one of the rest room doors open behind me. I turned. Nate the Great was coming down the hall with his attorney, a tall white man in his fifties with short hair, small round glasses, and a long narrow face deeply etched with lines. Nate was his usual dapper self in black slacks, a silky gray turtleneck, and lots of gold. He touched his attorney at the elbow and said something to him under his breath. The attorney nodded and moved off to the side. I stiffened as Nate came toward me.

"Well, well, well. The lovely Rachel Gold."

"Nate."

There was a hint of a smile on his lips as he studied me. "I understand you've been trying to cause me some trouble."

"You deserve it."

He chuckled. "And you think Michael Green didn't?"

"I don't care about Michael Green."

"Really? So what's this all about?"

"Angela."

He frowned. "Angela? You lost me there, Rachel."

"How could you?"

"How could I what?"

"Do that to her?"

"Do what?"

"Don't act cute with me, Nate. She didn't kill Michael Green, and you know it. You set her up. That was your idea." I shook my head angrily. "To do that to an innocent woman—to steal her dignity and her reputation and her freedom. I hope they take ten years away from you for every one you took from her."

Off to the side, his lawyer cleared his throat. "Uh, Nate."

Nate turned and held up a hand. "Hold on, Charlie. Give me a minute here. I know what I'm doing."

He turned back to me, his eyes narrowing. "Don't get your hopes up, white girl." He leaned in close. "You ain't fucking with some nigger from the projects when you try fucking with me. Same goes for that lady U.S. attorney. Let

me explain something about the real world to you, girl—
something they don't teach at that fancy law school of yours.
The legal process is a long and winding road, and plenty of
surprising things can happen along that road, especially for
someone in my position."

"It doesn't matter what happens on that road, Nate.
You're toast."

He laughed. "Those are tough words, girl. Where I come
from, folks don't make threats like that unless they can deliver."

"Same where I come from."

He gave me an amused look. "Is that so? You telling me
you think you can deliver?"

"Yep. In fact, I plan to deliver tonight. To your uncle."

His smile faded. "What you talking about?"

"The videotape."

"What videotape?"

"The one you killed Michael Green for. Guess what,
Nate? I've got a copy of it. I think your uncle is going to
find it quite informative."

"How'd you get a copy?" he asked, clearly shaken.

"Nate," his lawyer warned, stepping forward.

"Answer me, goddammit," Nate demanded, eyes ablaze.

His lawyer was at least a head taller than him. He
wrapped his arm around Nate's chest and pulled him back.
"Come with me," he ordered.

"Hey," Nate shouted at me as he strained against his
lawyer.

I gazed at him. "What?"

"Fuck you, bitch."

"No," I said. "Fuck you, bitch."

CHAPTER 35

Monday morning's edition of the *Post-Dispatch* ran a sketchy account of Sunday's events on the first page of the Metro section under the headline CITY HALL ROCKED BY CRIMINAL CHARGES. Above the fold were side-by-side shots of a haggard Don Goddard and a distraught Percy Trotter leaving the federal courthouse after making bail.

Over the next forty-eight hours, the scandal metastasized. On Wednesday alone, a task force of FBI agents and U.S. Marshals booked more than forty defendants, including three additional City Hall employees, four assistant court clerks, Maurice "The General" Patton, and all of the clients of Michael Green and Percy Trotter who'd participated in the fraudulent loan deals. Given that City Hall and the Civil Courts Building sat catty-corner on Tucker Boulevard and had each contributed several defendants to the scandal, it was probably inevitable that by Thursday evening the media would tag the scandal "TuckerGate."

However, before the week was out, another story knocked TuckerGate off the front page. That story began its journey toward the public domain on Friday morning shortly after eleven. Seven minutes after, to be precise. That's when I got out of my car. I'd parked it on Webster Street across from the courthouse in Chillicothe. Briefcase in one hand, purse in the other, I stared at the courthouse and then checked my watch. It was 11:07 A.M.

Inside the office of the clerk of the Forty-third Judicial

Circuit, I handed the woman behind the counter an original and two copies of the court filing. Preoccupied, she time-stamped all three, placed the original in the file box, dropped one copy into the press bin, and glanced at the first page of my copy as she started to hand it back to me. She paused, staring at the caption: *State of Missouri* v. *Angela W. Green,* and then at the title of the document: Petition for a Writ of Habeas Corpus. She looked at me and raised her eyebrows as she handed me my copy.

"My, my," she said.

In many respects, my habeas petition was similar to the thousands filed each year on behalf of state and federal prisoners throughout the nation. As with many such petitions, mine recited that the defendant was being unjustly held, that the defendant was innocent, that hitherto unknown exculpatory evidence had recently come to light, and that the interests of justice would best be served by an expedited hearing on same.

All well and good—the usual statements one expects to find in that type of petition.

Except for paragraph seven.

I'd certainly never seen such a paragraph before. Neither, I'm sure, had the courthouse reporter, who must have strolled into the clerk's office after lunch that afternoon to flip through the morning's filings in the press bin. I wish I could have seen his reaction to paragraph seven and overheard his initial call, but by then I was on the highway heading toward St. Louis. I'd left the courthouse shortly before noon after obtaining a hearing date on my petition for the following Tuesday morning. From there I'd driven to the prison, spent an hour with Angela, and then stopped by a grocery store to pick up a Granny Smith apple, a Snickers bar, and a large bottle of iced tea for the long drive home.

Although I averaged better than seventy miles an hour

the whole way, the fax, phone, and Internet lines far out-
paced me. As I reached the outskirts of St. Louis around four
o'clock that afternoon and turned the radio to NPR for the
news, I heard my client's name in the top story of the hour.

"According to paragraph seven of the petition," the female reporter was saying, "the United States attorney herself
will attend the state court hearing on Tuesday. There she will
present evidence that will not only exonerate Ms. Green but
also reveal the identity of the real killer. Almost as extraordinary, the court filing states that the Missouri prosecuting
attorney will appear at the hearing and, quote, confess to the
writ. In plain English, that means that the state of Missouri
will support the defendant's claim of innocence."

By the time I reached my office, a phalanx of print, radio,
and TV reporters and cameramen stood waiting outside the
building. I stared through the windshield as they scrambled
into position, all cameras now aimed at me. One by one, the
camera lights clicked on. I took a deep breath and opened
the door.

"Miss Gold!"

"Rachel!"

"Over here!"

"Hey, Miss Gold!"

"Please! A question for our viewers."

"Yo! Got a question here."

Shading my eyes from the glare, I shoved past the thicket
of microphones and minicams and bodies up to the porch
and through the front door. Closing it quickly behind me, I
twisted the dead-bolt lock and turned toward Jacki. She was
slumped at her desk. Both phones were ringing. The fax machine in the corner was printing a page into the overflowing
tray. Jacki gave me a weary sigh and pointed at the tall stack
of pink message slips in front of her.

"I stopped taking them at fifty."

I gave her a smile. "Don't worry. We have phone mail."

"Not anymore we don't. It's totally full." She gestured toward the stack of message slips. "Check some of these out. You're not going to believe it."

I leafed through the first dozen or so. Calls from producers for NBC, CNN, ABC World News. From reporters for the *New York Times, Boston Globe, Chicago Tribune.* From Larry King's producer. From Rosie O'Donnell's producer. From Katie Couric.

I looked up at Jacki. "Katie Couric?"

"It was really her on the phone, too. We talked."

"Wow."

"Wow is right."

Angela Green's habeas petition was the lead story that evening on the national networks and merited a full episode of *Hardball* on MSNBC. The guests included the usual gaggle of legal pontificators plus Maria Fallaci from a studio in Chicago. She managed to hold up under Chris Matthews's grilling. I watched it at my mother's house, seated on the couch between her and Benny.

"Come on, Maria," Matthews said with a sardonic grin. "You're a big girl. Admit it. You blew it on this case. We're talking major screwup. You tried to sell battered wife at a trial, and now you're the one getting battered. You're the punch line to the latest bad-lawyer joke. You're sitting here tonight mortified."

"Not at all, Chris. I'm thrilled for Angela. This is not about me, or about any lawyer. This is all about a wonderful and inspiring woman who is about to be set free. This is all about Angela."

"I call bullshit!" Benny shouted, jumping to his feet. "This is all about Rachel, you bitch." He was jabbing his finger at her image on the screen. "You fucked up big time. Rachel Gold rules!"

"Hush," I said, pulling him back down on the couch.

Although the hearing on Tuesday was broadcast live on television, radio, and the Internet, it was not quite edge-of-the-seat theater. For starters, the viewers—like those of us in court that day—already knew the outcome and most of the details. The previous afternoon, the U.S. attorney and the prosecuting attorney had filed their prehearing submissions, which included affidavits, exhibits, forensic reports, and excerpts from the transcripts of Herman Borghoff's secret tape recordings of his boss's conversations. Within hours, a complete copy of all of the filings was available on dozens of Web sites, and most of the newspapers the following morning had front-page summaries with highlights. Thus many in the huge audience that tuned in for the hearing in Chillicothe on Tuesday already knew about the real estate scam and the blackmail videotape and Nate the Great's role and, most important of all, the identity of the real killer of Michael Green. Those who'd watched ABC's *Nightline* the night before got an added prehearing thrill, namely, censored excerpts of Sebastian Curry and Billy Woodward from their porno days, including scenes of each man with the woman destined to become Michael Green's fiancée. (Although I felt sorry for Samantha that night, by the end of the following week she'd landed a six-figure book deal and a role in one of those TV commercials for Naughty By Night jeans.)

I may have provided the only surprise of the day, which came near the end of the hearing—*after* the judge had granted the petition, decreed Angela's innocence, and signed the discharge order directing the warden to release her from prison.

"Your Honor," I announced, "my client requests that the court postpone her release date."

The buzz in the gallery behind me echoed his surprised expression.

He said, "I don't understand, counsel."

"For the past seven years," I said, "the Chillicothe Correctional Center has been my client's home. Her only home. That is where she lived, that is where she worked, and that is where she founded her rehabilitation programs. She needs a few days to complete the transition plans for those programs. More important, some of her dearest friends live there. She needs time to say goodbye."

The warden helped us devise a plan to evade the press stakeout in front of the prison. At two o'clock that Sunday, I parked my mother's Buick in the alley behind a pharmacy on the far side of town. I'd borrowed my mother's car for disguise, since most of the reporters and cameramen at the hearing last Tuesday—almost all of whom were still in town—had seen me arrive and depart in my red Jeep.

Seated behind the wheel, the engine idling, I waited. Twenty minutes later, the prison laundry truck turned into the other end of the alley. I watched as it approached and stopped in front of me. The driver—a skinny guy in his fifties with a green John Deere cap—was alone in the cab. I pushed the button to pop open the trunk and got out of the car as the driver was stepping down from the truck cab. He nodded at me and touched the brim of his cap before heading toward the back of the truck. I heard him unlatch the rear door.

A moment later, Angela Green came around from the back. I burst into a smile at the sight of her. She had on a navy blue cardigan sweater over a white turtleneck shirt, khaki slacks, and black flats. To help conceal her identity, she wore sunglasses and a floral chiffon scarf wrapped around her head. She was carrying a dark canvas suitcase and shoulder strap purse. She set down the suitcase and we hugged.

"You're an angel, Rachel," she said as we separated.

I couldn't find any words.

She turned toward the truck driver and shook his hand. "Thank you, Henry."

"Good luck to you, ma'am." He tipped his cap at her. "From me and the wife."

She waved as he backed his truck out of the alley. After he drove off, she gave a big sigh and looked up at the clouds. With her head tilted back, her arms outstretched, and her fingers spread wide, she turned slowly all the way around once. She let her arms drop to her sides.

"I feel like I'm in the middle of a dream," she said.

"But no longer a nightmare."

She lowered her sunglasses and smiled at me. "True."

"Shall we?" I said, lifting her suitcase.

"We shall."

Angela read me the warden's handwritten driving instructions as I pulled out of the alley onto the quiet street. The directions took us out of town along side streets and back to the highway about seven miles south of Chillicothe.

"Are we really going to an ostrich ranch?" Angela asked after we were on the highway.

I smiled. "That's where Sonya and I agreed to meet. I didn't want to drop you off at her apartment. The press has had it staked out night and day. This way you can have some privacy. Sonya told me she has airline tickets and hotel reservations."

"Oh? Where?"

"She wouldn't say. I'm sure it's somewhere special—

somewhere a mother and daughter can have some peace and quiet before the craziness resumes."

She leaned back in her seat and took in a deep, relaxed breath. "That does sound nice."

"Speaking of press craziness, famous lady, you're going to be on the cover of this week's *People* magazine."

She snorted. "Oh, wonderful. Actually, speaking of famous"—she turned to me with an impish grin—"I heard someone in this car was on the *Today* show last Wednesday."

I blushed. "I said no to everyone else, but how can you say no to Katie Couric?"

A few moments later, Angela asked, "Why an ostrich ranch?"

"The owners are clients of mine. They're having a big party tonight to celebrate a lawsuit we won."

"A lawsuit? Did it actually involve ostriches?"

I laughed. "I'll tell you all about it sometime. But for you, the party is perfectly timed. Originally, I'd planned to drive to it after dropping you off, but when Sonya and I talked yesterday, we realized that the ranch was a great place to meet. It's out in the country, which means you'll have some privacy. Moreover, it's a straight shot down Highway 70 from there to the airport."

The drive across Missouri gave us a chance to go over various matters, the most important of which was Angela's financial situation. With the assistance of the U.S. attorney's office and the State Department, I'd been able to get access to the offshore bank account established for Millennium Management Services, which had been opened in the name of Michael Green d/b/a Millennium Management Services. That was good news for Angela. Under the terms of her divorce decree, she was entitled to the assets of all bank accounts, whether owned jointly or individually at the time of the dissolution, except for Michael Green's office account at

Mercantile Bank. The other known bank accounts back then had held approximately $150,000 in total—an amount quickly consumed by Angela's legal fees in her murder trial. Under the terms of the divorce decree, the offshore account thus belonged to Angela Green since it had existed at the time of the divorce. Even with all of Green's payoffs to Nate the Great, the account balance stood at close to $300,000. Better yet, the feds were willing to cut a deal in which they would waive all tax and other claims to the money in exchange for unfettered access to the records related to the account to use in the TuckerGate prosecutions. When you added that offshore money to the publisher's advance Angela would soon receive for her book—money no longer threatened by the Son of Sam suit—financial security would not be among her postincarceration concerns.

Our conversation grew more sporadic as I drove on. We talked some about Sonya and about her sorrow over her estrangement from Michael junior. We talked some about the Oasis Shelter and how its future seemed more secure with Nate the Great out of the way. We talked some about what she would do with the rest of her life. But by the time we passed through Columbia, we were riding in silence. The Temptations' *Greatest Hits* was on the car stereo, our heads nodding in time to "My Girl," each of us lost in our own reverie.

I could feel the connection between us starting to slacken. No surprise there. I knew that it would. It always does. It's what's supposed to happen. We were, ultimately, just an attorney and a client—two people with little in common, brought together under extraordinary circumstances, sharing moments of intimacy along the way, drawn ever closer by the process, but ultimately just an attorney and her client—a relationship that, at its core, was not personal but professional. I knew that we would remain friendly, and no doubt she would call upon me to act as her attorney in some future matter, but the legal mess that brought us together was now resolved, and with that conclusion came a loosening of our bond. Angela's legal problems were behind her. Her new priority was to piece back together her life—and her family.

I had my own priorities as well, including other clients with needs and, frankly, a life of my own that could use some attention—especially dealing with the inevitable confrontation with Jonathan over Orthodox Judaism. My anxiety over that problem was beginning to ruin my sleep.

The thought of the ostrich ranch rendezvous ahead of us added a surreal touch to what was already a strange day. Presumably, the members of the press laying siege to the Chillicothe women's prison had learned by now that Elvis had left the building. I glanced in the rearview mirror. I don't know what I was expecting to see. Perhaps one of those bizarre vehicle cavalcades from a Mad Max movie—hot rods and pickups and jalopies and dune buggies careening down the highway crammed with rowdy tattooed journalists. But there was nothing back there except three tractor-trailers and a pair of minivans.

After the Temptations, we listened to a Bob Marley album and then Frank Sinatra's *A Swinging Affair.* I took the Warrenton exit just as Frank reached the end of one of my favorite songs, his version of Cole Porter's "You'd Be So Nice to Come Home To." The song reminded me of Jonathan Wolf. I gave a wistful sigh. I missed him like crazy. Although I had plenty of ambivalence over his religion, I had none over him. He'd definitely be nice to come home to.

Angela was checking her hair and makeup in the vanity mirror on the sun visor as we came off the exit ramp onto Highway 47. "Will your crazy professor friend be there?"

"Oh, definitely," I said with a smile. "He would have

been there anyway, since the ostrich case was originally his. Now that he knows I'm bringing you, he wouldn't miss it for the world. He wants to meet you."

"I want to meet him. I know how helpful he's been for you."

"He's an acquired taste," I warned. "But he's actually quite lovable in his own totally repulsive way."

She paused to reapply her lipstick. "What about your secretary? Jacki is so sweet whenever I call."

"She'll be there. She's dying to meet you."

"Jacki's a large woman, isn't she?"

"Actually, yes. How did you know?"

"From the sound of her voice when I talked to her that time—so deep and full. I picture one of those big earth mother types."

"Benny calls her a big mother, although not in quite the same sense." I decided to leave it at that. "You'll see when you meet her."

Dusk was falling as we approached the ranch. The flock of ostriches in the pasture to our left—the ones who'd jogged alongside my car my first time here—were standing motionless. One or two glanced our way, but the rest ignored us. No doubt they'd seen plenty of passing vehicles that day. We drove through the gated entrance to the ranch and onto the gravel road. As we approached the house, there were dozens of cars and pickups parked at various angles on either side of the road. About thirty yards from the front yard, I pulled into a spot between a Dodge minivan and a Ford Explorer.

We could hear the country music as we got out of the car. Angela watched with an amused smile as I tied a red bandanna around my neck. For this party I was determined to shed the lawyer image for the rancher look—or at least as close to the rancher look as a nice Jewish girl from the city could get. I had on my faded Levi's, a blue chambray shirt over a white tank top, a Western-style tooled leather belt, and my Doc Marten hiking boots. As we started our walk toward the house, I adjusted my Australian bush hat. It was the closest thing in my closet to a ten-gallon hat.

We followed the hand-lettered signs and arrows around to the back of the house, where the party was in full swing. There were dozens of people talking and laughing as the Dixie Chicks blared from two large speakers set up near the barn. Three white-hatted chefs at the barbecue pits were grilling steaks and slathering sauce on the hamburgers and sausages and turning ears of corn. The steel water trough was filled with iced bottles and cans of beer and soda. There were four picnic tables, each laden with bowls and platters of appetizers and side dishes.

"Hey, Tex!"

The voice was unmistakable. I turned to see Benny heading toward us through the crowd, a white cardboard bucket under one arm and a bottle of Budweiser in the other hand. He was wearing baggy cargo pants, a blue River Des Peres Yacht Club T-shirt, and a Portland Beavers baseball cap. For that final touch of sartorial elegance, he hadn't shaved since Friday.

"Hot damn, you looking mighty fine." He gave me an appraising look. "Saddle me up, cowgirl, and you can ride me all night."

I glanced over at Angela. "As you may have guessed, this is Benny Goldberg. Benny, this is Angela Green."

"Honored to meet you, Angela." He jammed the beer bottle under the arm holding the bucket and shook her hand.

"Same here, Benny. Rachel has told me wonderful things about you."

"They're all true."

"What's in your bucket?" I asked him.

"Ah," he said with a beatific smile, "a veritable slice of heaven, ordered especially for you, Rachel."

"I give up."

"Here's a hint." He cradled the bucket, his hand on the lid. "These come to you direct from C and K Restaurant in north St. Louis."

It took me a moment to make the connection. "Oh, no. Pig noses?"

"Snoots, you boorish lout. Hickory-smoked snoots, ready for your delectation. Tonight will be the culinary equivalent of your bat mitzvah, cowgirl. Tonight you will bid farewell to girlhood and become a woman." He removed the lid, closed his eyes, and breathed in deeply through his nostrils. "Indulge your senses."

I peered into the bucket warily. "I don't know about this."

From the distance, someone called, "Benny!"

A platinum-haired woman in what looked like a leather catwoman bodysuit was waving at him from over by the fence.

"Good grief," I said, "is that the one from the bar?"

"Ah, yes. The sassy yet understated Sabrina."

"So she's not too kinky for you, eh?"

"A woman too kinky for me? Not in this solar system." He waved to her across the crowd and then turned to me. "Actually, Sabrina's perversity has been greatly exaggerated. The two of us are almost quaint together. When you think of us, think of Ozzie and Harriet."

"Actually, I'm thinking of Mr. Ed and Catherine the Great."

He laughed. "Well, maybe them, too." He turned to Angela. "I have to get back to my date."

"Don't forget your noses," I told him.

He lifted the bucket. "You can't dodge these babies that

easily. By the way, have you seen the surprise guest?"

"No, we just got here. Who is it?"

He gave me a wink. "You'll see." Hefting the bucket, he gave a horse whinny, stamped his foot three times, and started to leave. "I'll be back," he called over his shoulder in a Mr. Ed voice, "so save some room for snoots, Wilbur."

We watched him move through the crowd toward Cat-woman, the bucket held over his head.

I turned to Angela. "Let's find your daughter."

We stopped at the iced trough—a diet Coke for Angela, a Corona for me—and then set off to look for Sonya. She wasn't in the back area. For that matter, neither were our hosts, Maggie Lane and Sara Freed. They were probably inside attending to party details. Angela and I walked around to the front of the house.

"There she is," I said, pointing down the driveway.

Sonya brightened when she saw us.

"Momma!"

She started running up the path toward Angela.

"Oh, baby," Angela called, moving toward her.

I hung back, watching as they embraced, both of them crying.

Eventually, all three of us started down the road toward my mother's Buick to get Angela's luggage.

"Where's your car, baby?" Angela asked Sonya as I opened the trunk.

"Just over there, Momma."

I lifted out the suitcase and set it on the ground by Angela's side. She was squinting toward Sonya's car.

"Is there someone in there?" she asked.

"Yes, Momma."

"Who is—?" She paused and then gasped. "Oh, Lord."

I followed her gaze. Sonya's late-model Toyota was parked farther down the road. Seated in the passenger side of her car was her brother Michael. He'd been watching the ostriches. Now he turned toward us.

"He's coming on the trip with us, Momma," Sonya said gently, putting her arm around her mother's shoulder. "We're going to make us a family again."

Michael opened the door and got out. He stood there facing his mother. After a moment, he smiled at her.

"Oh, dear Lord," Angela said, leaning against her daughter, her hand at her mouth.

Sonya reached down and lifted the suitcase. "Come on, Momma. Let's go join Michael."

I watched the two of them head toward her car. About halfway there, Angela turned toward me. "Rachel, honey," she stammered, "I never said—"

"Go," I told her with a smile, blinking back tears. "We'll talk when you get back to town."

She gazed at me a moment. "Thank you."

"Good luck."

I turned and started toward the house, not wanting to intrude any further on their family reunion. It was almost dark when I rejoined the party. Maggie Lane had just come out of the back door carrying a serving platter heaped with what looked like potato salad.

"Rachel!" she called, setting the platter down on the nearest table. "Oh, I'm so glad you made it."

We hugged.

"Where's Sara?" I asked.

"She'll be back any minute. She's giving a group a tour of the ranch." She paused. "Did you just get here?"

"About ten minutes ago."

I explained my arrival with Angela and our search for her daughter.

"Was Sara already on the tour?" Maggie asked.

"I guess so."

She gave me a kiss on the cheek. "Oh, Rachel, you're going to love this party more than you can imagine."

I gave her a curious look. "What do you mean?"

There was a twinkle in her eye. "You'll see."

Five minutes later, I was eating a quesadilla wedge and chatting with Martha Hogan when I spotted Sara Freed's tour group coming toward us from across the pasture. She was leading a group of seven. I watched as they approached the fence, the group gradually emerging from the darkness as each passed through the gate. There was Jacki, flirting with Bob the UPS guy, who was not only dressed in cowboy gear but looked the part. I smiled at the sight of the two of them.

Then I saw him.

"Oh, my God, I can't believe this, Martha. He's here."

"Who is?" she said, turning to look.

By then I'd put down the quesadilla and was racing toward the fence. I reached it just as Jonathan Wolf stepped through the gate. With a big grin, he caught me in his arms and lifted me off the ground.

"Hi, beautiful," he said softly.

"Oh, Jonathan."

He held me in his arms, my feet off the ground. I hugged him ferociously, eyes shut tight, my face buried against his neck, breathing in his scent. Finally, he lowered me to the ground.

Holding me gently around my waist, he stared into my eyes. "I missed you so much, Rachel."

As usually happens when I hadn't seen him in a while, his good looks made me catch my breath. Jonathan Wolf was my idea of tall, dark, and handsome. Standing just a shade over six feet, he still resembled the light heavyweight fighter he once was, right down to the nose that had been broken and never properly reset. Although that imperfection scratched him from the pretty boy category, to me it only

added to his allure. He had a close-trimmed black beard
flecked with gray, and intense green eyes. Tonight he wore
a black cotton turtleneck, khaki slacks, and leather hiking
boots. And, of course, a yarmulke.

The next hour passed in a blur as we caught up on our
lives. Occasionally, a party guest would interrupt—some to
meet Jonathan, others to say hi to me, a few to share a memory from the ostrich lawsuit. Between interruptions, I
learned that Jonathan's trial had ended Friday afternoon
when the jury returned a mixed set of verdicts that acquitted
his client on most but not all counts, did much the same with
the other defendants, and thus guaranteed a complicated appeal. He'd left the courthouse late in the afternoon and
reached his parents' home by the start of the Sabbath at sundown. When the Sabbath ended the following night, he
booked flights to St. Louis for the next morning and packed
up his daughters' things. By the time their plane touched
down at Lambert this morning, I'd already left for Chillicothe to pick up Angela. Jonathan called around, eventually
reaching my mother, who told him about tonight's party. He
called out to the ranch, and Maggie insisted that he come.

The two of us had moved away from the crowd and were
standing in the darkness near the fence that ran around the
main pasture. The party was still in full swing behind us.
Jonathan has his arm around my shoulder. I leaned against
his chest and gazed up at the clear moonless sky. A thousand
stars twinkled overhead. The trees on the far side were sil-
houetted against the night sky. In the pasture nearby stood
a pair of ostrich hens. They watched us silently, their small
heads towering over ours.

"I missed you so much, Jonathan."

"I missed you, Rachel."

"No, you have no idea. I couldn't stand it. We've got to
talk. I know this isn't the right time or the right place, but

we're going to have to sit down soon—tomorrow, maybe—
and figure this out. Enough is enough already."

He turned to me. "I agree."

"Jonathan, you know I love you. And you know I'm
crazy about your daughters."

"They adore you. We all do."

"Good." I paused, trying to find the right words, to organize my thoughts, but everything was jumbled. "The only
thing I don't love," I said, "is your religion. I'm a Reform
Jew, Jonathan. That's who I am. I can't help that. I've gone
to those sessions with your rabbi and his wife this summer.
They've been great. And I've tried. Good Lord, I've tried.
It's just not clicking. Maybe it will someday." I shrugged.
"Maybe it never will. Look, everything that's worth fighting
for involves a trade-off. You want something, you have to
give up something else. I know your religion is important to
you, Jonathan. You're going to have to understand that mine
is important to me. I love my congregation. I love my rabbi.
I love my services. But guess what? My religion isn't as important to me as you are. Or as important to me as your
daughters are. I'm willing to meet you halfway. I'll keep a
kosher home, and I'll observe the Sabbath more strictly than
I do now. In fact," I said with a half-smile, "the rabbi's wife
told me that it's a mitzvah to make love on the Sabbath."

He smiled. "It is."

"Then I'm counting on some special Shabbat mitzvahs
from you." I paused, my smile fading. "I can meet you halfway, Jonathan. I realize Orthodox Judaism isn't big on halfway, but that's all I can promise for now. And that may be all
that I'll ever be able to give you."

"Halfway is enough."

He said it so quickly and emphatically that it caught me
off guard. But not for long. I gave him a fierce kiss.

"I love you," I whispered.

"I love you."

After a moment, I started to smile.

"What?" he asked.

"You know that awful, horrible prayer you Orthodox Jewish men say?"

"Which one?"

"The morning prayer. The one where you thank God—"

"Now wait," he said. "There's a common misunderstanding there. That prayer is actually an expression of humility. Jewish men are assigned more religious tasks than women are. Rather than gripe about the extra work, we express our gratitude to God for giving us the extra tasks. We do that by thanking God for not making us a woman, but that's solely because women don't have as many religious obligations. It's not sexist. Jewish women have their own prayer where they acknowledge that God created them closer to God's ideal of perfection. They get to express their gratitude—"

"Shush," I said, pressing my fingers against his mouth. "I wasn't asking for a lesson, Rabbi." I put my arms around his waist and looked up into his eyes. "All I was trying to tell you is that I've come up with my own morning prayer."

"Oh?" he said with a puzzled smile, his face close to mine.

"Yes." I kissed him softly, lingering a moment to nibble on his lower lip. "In my prayer," I said, "I'm going to thank God for not making *you* a woman."